"[Cecy] Robson's O'Brien family has the hottest brothers ever! . . . It's impossible not to keep your fingers crossed for an HEA, but the author knows exactly what she's doing as readers hold their breath during this roller-coaster ride of passion."—**RT Book Reviews**

"Cecy Robson will once again play your emotions like a concert pianist in her latest novel in the O'Brien Family series." - **Heroes and Heartbreakers**

"This story [Let Me] is filled with hope and passion, a really great read. I strongly recommend this book to any romance reader." --**Night Owl Reviews (Top Pick)**

"I'm just going to come right out and say it: I love the O'Brien family!" -**Feeling Fictional**

"Robson proves once again that she can sweep us off our feet with a fun, romantic tale. . . . [Once Kissed] is another must-read. I thoroughly enjoyed this novel."—**Rainy Day Ramblings**

"Devastatingly beautiful, heartbreakingly romantic and emotional, Cecy Robson's third book in her O' Brien Family series just might be my favorite yet. - **My Guilty Obsession**

"Confession: I'm a little obsessed with the O'Brien Family. Addicted, you might say. And this book? Fed my addiction. In the best possible way. I FLOVED Let Me."- **Give Me Books**

"Make room on your list of book boyfriends for Curran O'Brien! This bad-boy cop is fiercely protective of the feisty Tess, and the sexual tension between these two is off the charts!"—*USA Today* **bestselling author Lauren Layne**

"OMG! Robson delivered all the FEELS in a one two punch...If you love loud families, you will fall in love with this crazy, loving family! Let Me...read it, own it, love it!" **-Caffeinated Book Reviewer**

Let Me by Cecy Robson was a fantastic read. It has equal parts humor, sexy, heartbreak, and romance with a very satisfying ending. Ms. Robson did not disappoint." **-Under the Covers Book Blog**

"I love second chance romances and when you toss in a huge, crazy Irish family with nothing but love for each other… no one stands a chance against the O'Briens. THAT is what made this romance [Once Kissed] a riotous hit with me." **-Addicted to Happily Ever After**

"WOW!! Just WOW!!! I have to say that Cecy Robson has completely blown me away with Let Me. I'm an avid reader, and I love all sorts of books, but this one has probably touched my heart in ways that no other book has." **-Devilishly Delicious Book Reviews**

BY CECY ROBSON

The Shattered Past Series

Once Perfect

Once Loved

Once Pure

The O'Brien Family Novels

Once Kissed

Let Me

Crave Me

Feel Me (coming soon)

The Carolina Beach Novels

Inseverable

Eternal (coming soon)

Infinite (coming soon)

The Weird Girls

A Curse Awakened (novella)

The Weird Girls (novella)

Sealed with a Curse

A Cursed Embrace

Of Flame and Promise

A Cursed Moon (novella)

Cursed by Destiny

A Cursed Bloodline

A Curse Unbroken

Of Flame and Light

Crave Me

An O'Brien Family Novel

Cecy Robson

DEDICATION

To the O'Briens. You came from my mind, but will remain in my heart.

ACKNOWLEDGMENTS

I met Killian, my first O'Brien, in Once Perfect. I knew he was special, and that I had to hang onto him. I just never knew how special he and his wonderfully loud and animated family would become. Characters have a funny way of making their way into an author's reality. This amazing Irish clan was no exception. So, Angus, Seamus, Declan, Curran, Killian, Wren, and Finn, thank you for being you and allowing my overactive imagination to run amuck.

To everyone who met these characters, and walked away from each story feeling like they knew them, and wanting to know them more, it was your enthusiasm that encouraged me to keep going.

To Jamie, who probably knows my characters almost as well as I do, *almost*. Thank you for laughing in all the right places and your endless belief that I'm telling the right story. I love you. Keep believing and I'll keep trying.

To Nic. Your patience and generous heart never fails to astound me. Thank you for being you, and for all the love.

To Amanda Flower, Kate SeRine, and Beth Vrabel, my friends, you have my heart . . . and endless amount of bad jokes and Kevin Hart videos.

To the members of my team: Kimberly Costa, Gaele Hince, and Kristin Clifton. You make me better. Thank you for your amazing ability to promote my work and make me shine!

Lastly, to those who may not have had the best lives, but made their lives the best they can be. May you be blessed with the family you have or the one that you make.

CHAPTER 1

Wren

I drop the keys in Mr. Esposito's hand and smile. He stares at them in his open palm like a precious gift, because to someone like him who's worked hard all his life, it very much is.

"Thank you, Wren," he says, meeting my smile. "I never thought I'd own a new car. Let alone be able to give one to my son as a gift."

"You deserve it, Mr. Esposito," I tell him, shaking his hand. "And so does your son for getting into Drexel. Tell Antonio, hi for me—Oh, and be sure to have someone take his picture when you hand him the keys." I motion to my office behind me. "I want to add it to my memory wall."

"I will." He presses his lips tight as if considering what to say. "Your father would be proud of you," he tells me. His soft brown eyes take in the massive dealership, fixing on the sales board displaying my current rank at number one. "Very proud."

I hold onto my smile as he walks toward the brand new candy apple red F-150 hugging the curb, ignoring the brutal January wind that sweeps in when the doors to the lot zip open. Mr. Esposito pauses when he opens the driver's side door. I had the boys in the back place a bow on the dash like I do for all my customers. I think it's a nice touch, and a way to thank them for their business. Mr. Esposito tosses me a grin over his shoulder. Maybe it's the wind slapping against his face, or maybe it's because he's just that touched, but I catch his eyes glistening with tears.

Slowly he slips inside and grips the wheel, his widening smile lifting his deeply worn features.

The moment he pulls away, my smile vanishes. "Your father would be proud of you," he'd said. He meant it as a compliment. Mr. Esposito has always been nice like that. But instead of giving me the warm fuzzies, that familiar pang tugs at my insides.

My heels click against the bleached white tile as I cross the showroom. The phones ringing off the hook have me turning toward the finance department. It's been a nasty winter with all the snow we've been hit with, but I can't say it's been bad for business. One of the secretaries waves to me as she hurries to answer the phone. I wave back, not that she seems to notice. She starts writing as she takes the first call. Yeah, it's going to be a busy week. But busy means work, and that's something I've always been good at.

My eyes narrow when they fix on Oscar looming over Penny. Penny is smart, and an overall good person. She's young, and hasn't been here long, but she's trying, and I know she has it in her to succeed. Too bad Oscar is stomping on her success, luring customers away from her every chance he gets.

"You snooze, you lose," he tells her, pegging her with one of his more sleazy grins.

Penny was making headway with the guy who walked in, until Oscar shoved his way between them and baited him away, making Penny look like she didn't know what she was talking about. If I hadn't been busy with Mr. Esposito, I would have stepped in. Nothing gets me more than men who target those they think are weak.

"Wren!" Suze calls from behind the counter. "You have a call."

"Okay. Send it through to my office," I yell. I rush across

the last few feet of the showroom, but not before I make sure Oscar steps far away from Penny.

The phone rings once, twice, before I slam the door behind me with my foot and reach across my desk and put the call on speaker. "Erin O'Brien," I say.

There's a brief pause before I hear, "Hi, Wren."

Shit. My stomach twists the way it always does when I hear his voice. "What do you want, Bryant?" I ask, digging out my cell phone from my desk drawer.

"I miss you," he says.

"Do you miss hitting me, too?" I fire back.

I'm talking tough. It's what I do. Too bad I don't feel so tough right now. Not when it comes to Bryant. A familiar sense of dread sends a chill down my spine, reminding me what happened the last time I pissed him off. I hit the record icon on my cell phone, hoping to catch him saying something I can use against him. But the damn thing beeps, and for all Bryant is an asshole, he's not stupid.

"Are you recording me, pretty girl?" He laughs when I don't answer. "Now, why would you do a thing like that?"

"Because I don't trust you, because you hit me—oh, and because you're an asshole."

"I don't know what you're talking about," he says, keeping his voice easy. "I'm just returning your call. You keep calling me so—"

"That's a lie," I say, my face heating with anger. He knows I'm recording him and trying to switch things around. "Don't call me again. I want nothing to do with you."

I hang up the phone. It's been months since I last saw him, months since he last put his hands on me. But just when I think I'm rid of him, he reminds me he's still there.

I could call the police. The problem is, he is the police . .

Evan

My Jaguar skids, again, again, and again, fighting to keep pace with the other drivers insane enough to travel the Blue Route in this weather. Chunks of wet snow smack against my windshield. My wipers squeak against the glass as they race to keep my line of sight clear when another vehicle cuts me off, pelting my windshield with more ice. My current struggle with life and death does not evidently discourage Ashleigh from barking messages over my Bluetooth.

"Yodel called again, Evan. They want you to reconsider."

"No," I reply, cutting my steering wheel toward the left when my car veers right. "We're representing Mellon, their biggest competitor. It's a conflict of interest to supply both companies with the same technology."

I mutter a curse when the minivan in front of me slams on their brakes and I narrowly miss ramming the bumper. And I suppose, because we're in Philadelphia, the City of Brotherly love, the woman rolls down the window, permitting snow into her vehicle just to wave an irate middle finger at me.

"Rich Bitch loser," she cries out.

I rub my face. Bloody hell, why am I here again? Before I can finish the thought, Ashleigh reminds me.

"Evan, we're at risk for financial collapse. The company needs the revenue."

"Not at the expense of our ethics," I counter.

True, my company is at risk. But it's due to poor business practices, such as the ones Ashleigh suggests I entertain. I understand she learned these tactics from my predecessor, but he was a conniving snake—which is why he's currently serving time for embezzlement and I had to leave London to rebuild my father's dying empire.

"What about your eleven a.m. with the V.P. of County General?"

"Have Anne and Clifton start straight away. I emailed them the presentation last night—"

"Do you really think they're qualified?" she interrupts.

I open my mouth to insist that they are and to remind her I'm her superior, not the other way around. But I'm not oblivious to what she tells me. Anne and Clifton are fairly new and not at the level I'd prefer them to be. Nevertheless, they're learning fast under my tutelage and the only ones from the original staff I trust.

"*Evan*," she presses.

"Ashleigh, Anne and Clifton will handle it. That's my final word." I disconnect, swearing as I take the ramp and practically slide down sideways.

Another proud Pennsylvanian sticks his head out the window. "Get a real car, fucker," he hollers.

I rub my face again, tired and frustrated. I didn't arrive home until three this morning. It wouldn't have taken as long had I been driving a vehicle capable of enduring this ungodly weather.

I glance up, releasing a tense breath when the sign for the Ford dealership I researched comes into view. Saving iCronos will take me time. Time I can't spare driving a Jaguar on roads better maneuvered via dogsled.

My car slows to a stop in front of the massive dealership. The combination of the vehicle I'm driving, along with the expensive suit and coat I'm wearing, command attention. The moment I step inside, a young woman with dark spiky hair hurries over. "Good morning, sir. I'm Penny," she says. "Welcome to Ford Nation. Are you interested in acquiring a new vehicle?"

She seems young, but eager, a respectable attribute. Yet no sooner does she finish speaking than a man about my age steps in front of her, adjusting the jacket of his gray suit. "I got this, P," he tells her. "Get us some coffee, will you?" He holds out his hand. "Hello. I'm Oscar Nelson. Welcome to Ford Nation."

My frown bounces from his hand to the young woman whose face is now bright red with humiliation and possibly more. "Are you his assistant?" I ask her.

"No," she answers. "I'm a car sales representative—"

Oscar speaks over her, but it's the sound of quickly approaching footsteps that causes me to turn. A woman with a pinstripe jacket and matching skirt hurries forward, the quick motions of her long legs causing the edge of her skirt to brush above her knees and swing her hips seductively. Long hair flutters like streams of ebony smoke, revealing a staggeringly beautiful face better suited for my wildest fantasies.

I spent the first five years following the completion of my doctorate in either a lab or boardroom packed with men in alternating stages of balding, and these last nine months trapped in a building working a minimum of eighteen hour days. I haven't had the opportunity or time to meet women. But if I'd known she was out here, I'd have spared a moment.

Good . . . *God*.

I don't realize I'm staring until she stops directly in front of us and juts out her chin. "Problem?" she asks Oscar.

Oscar straightens to his full height. "No. I was just showing Mr. . . ." He motions to me. "My apologies, what's your name, sir?"

"Jonah," I say, returning my attention to the stunning young woman. I offer her my hand. "Evan Jonah."

Full pink lips lift into a dazzling smile that resonates in her deep blue eyes and lights her creamy white skin.

"I'm Erin O'Brien, but I go by Wren," she says. She shakes my hand with a firm grip, releasing me to guide the smaller woman forward. "How can Penny and I help you today, sir?"

"I'm afraid my vehicle isn't equipped for this weather and I am seeking a better alternative, possibly a truck or SUV," I reply, doing all in my power to keep my focus on her face.

"Then you've come to the right place. Penny, will you show Mr. Jonah—"

"Evan," I interrupt, mentally kicking myself for morphing into a fourteen year old boy the moment my eyes locked on this woman.

"Okay, Evan," she says. "Penny, please show Evan the latest members of the Ford family."

"Of course, this way, sir," Penny answers with a grin.

I reluctantly follow behind Penny. But as we reach a black Explorer my gaze trails back to Wren. She and Oscar have moved away from the showroom and closer to the rear offices. Yet it does little to muffle their exchange.

"What the fuck was that?" Oscar snaps.

My spine stiffens. I storm forward, ready to demand he apologize for using such foul language in the presence of a lady.

"You being a raging asshole," Wren replies.

I'll admit, her response gives me pause. And she doesn't stop there. "Look, I know you have to compensate for your less than average-sized dick. But that doesn't give you the right to mistreat Penny or pounce on every client she approaches. That's bullshit and you know it."

"Um, perhaps a truck will be more to your needs," Penny says, motioning to the opposite side of the dealership and away from the heated conversation.

I don't typically involve myself in affairs that don't concern me or interact with women who speak in such a manner. But it's not simply Wren's colorful vocabulary that captivates me, it's her strength and desire to defend her small friend.

"Where the fuck did you hear that?" Oscar responds. "I don't have a small dick."

Of all his possible retorts, *this* is the one he chooses?

"Suze," Wren calls over her shoulder in the direction of the finance counter. "What was it you said about that night you went out with Oscar?"

The woman behind the counter scowls and holds up her pinky. Wren smirks. "Looks to me like you should have called her back." She pats his shoulder. "My condolences to your man parts."

She starts to walk away, stopping when she realizes I witnessed their encounter. Instead of making a quick escape or pretending I didn't hear them, she walks toward me with her head raised. "Sorry about that, Mr. Jonah—"

"Evan," I clarify as she reaches me.

Her smile stirs one of my own. "Evan," she repeats, lifting a hand toward her friend. "I see Penny is taking good care of you."

"Um, maybe you can take over," Penny says. She edges away, aware of how taken I am with Wren.

Wren tilts her head. "I don't want to step all over your

pitch," she says.

"You're not," she responds. "I'll take the next one. Honest."

Wren waits for Penny to leave before turning to face me. She considers me a moment, but then motions back to the Explorer. "This is the latest model in Ford luxury," she begins. "Comfortable, secure, capable of meeting all your commuting needs, and packed with plenty of toys."

I follow her as she leads me around the vehicle. The ease of her speech and relaxed posture demonstrate a confident woman who knows her job well. I question her about the vehicle's basics first: mileage, warranty, and safety features, before testing her intelligence further. She doesn't disappoint, explaining everything in detail down to the engine's construction, adding to my growing attraction.

"Would you like to take her for a ride?" she asks. She punches my arm affectionately, the motion only briefly luring my attention away from her delicate features. "This way you can see how smoothly she handles the road and ask, 'Wren, how did I ever survive without a Ford?'"

"I'd like that," I answer, my deep voice quieting. This woman who appears more elite model than sales representative knows exactly what she's doing. "Very much."

"Good," she says, pointing at me. "You'll wonder how you ever got along without her."

As I watch her walk away, I start to wonder that myself.

CHAPTER 2

Evan

I open the passenger door to the dark blue Explorer, ushering Wren through. She pauses before slipping inside. "Hey, check it out," she says. "Chivalry isn't dead after all."

I chuckle because I have nothing better to say. Even if witty comebacks were my forte, this woman would still have me at a loss for words. It didn't take her long to verify my credentials or acquire an impressive vehicle to test drive, her command and efficiency making the process smooth.

I take a quick look at the interior as I glide inside, adjusting the seat to accommodate my height.

"What made you decide on an Explorer?" I ask, concentrating on the vehicle's features so I don't openly stare at Wren.

She tilts her head. "You're a suit, a businessman, right?"

"That's right."

"For starters, you don't need a truck. Trucks are good for hauling equipment, wood, things like that." She laughs a little. "That's not something you need. But a big guy like you does need something comfortable, and seeing how you're taking the Blue Route to work, you also want a vehicle that's going to keep you safe. The maniacs on the highway will bowl over a smaller ride, but in this, even the crazies will think twice before messing with you."

"That's understandable, but why didn't you lead me to the Expedition? They're more expensive and will guarantee you a higher commission should I decide to purchase."

Her smile will be my undoing. Perhaps she's aware, and why she widens it further. "I'm not here to sell you something for the sake of filling my pockets. That's not what I'm about. My experience is the Explorer is easier to navigate in the city, not to mention slightly better on gas. If you lived in the mountains or commuted from a more rural environment, I might have considered an Expedition. But for a badass, city guy like you, the Explorer is perfect." Her stare flickers over my body. "You feel me?"

As taken as I am with her, I wish she would have chosen a better phrase. "I do."

She winks. "Then see? I'm giving you exactly what you need."

"It would seem so," I respond. This woman is honest and ethical, but it's her ability to charm that continues to captivate me. "Shall we?" I ask, motioning to the road.

"Prepare to be awed," she responds.

I shift into gear and pull away from the building. "You're given name is Erin," I say, wanting to know more about her.

"Yup," she replies.

"But you go by Wren."

"I kind of had to," she says. "My brothers apparently thought Erin was too long and nicknamed me Rin, which morphed into Wren. The name stuck." She shrugs. "I can only imagine what I would have been called if my Ma named me Ivory like my Grammie O'Malley—God rest her soul—wanted."

"Ivory is quite lovely. But Wren appears to suit you."

"Yeah? I don't know. I think I could have pulled off Ivory seeing how my skin only knows white and whiter with the occasional freckle."

"If you say so," I say, chuckling.

No sooner do I pull onto the main road than my phone rings.

"Alfred, answer," I say.

"Who's Alfred?" Wren asks.

Before I can explain that it's the technology that commands my phone, Ashleigh's voice belts through the speaker. "Evan, where are you?"

I grumble. Is there no escape from this woman? "Ashleigh, I'm in the middle of a meeting."

She sighs. "A meeting? Can you be more specific?"

"No," I practically growl, well aware Wren is watching me.

"I'm trying to help," she says. "Do you understand that? Anne and Clifton are beside themselves without you here."

"If that were the case, they'd contact me directly," I respond.

She pauses, then adds, "They need you, Evan."

"Ashleigh, they're more than capable of getting on without me. I won't discuss this any further."

"Will you at least tell me what time you'll be back so I can reassure them?"

Her voice is terse, which only adds to my aggravation. When I first transferred from London, I counted on Ashleigh tremendously and appreciated her insight. Now I find her vexing and rather intrusive.

"*Evan*," she presses. "When can we expect you?"

"When I'm finished with my current business," I snap. "Alfred, end call."

The line shuts off. I turn to offer Wren an apology only to find her laughing.

"Uh, uh, uh. The little woman isn't happy," she teases. "I'm thinking you earned yourself a trip to the nearest florist and dinner out to make it up to her."

Wren's comment causes me to chuckle, dissolving my lingering annoyance. "She's not my wife."

"Girlfriend?"

"No, she's my secretary," I respond, steeling a glance her way. "I'm single."

My hope is to spark her interest, but I can't be sure I succeeded.

"By the way she was nagging you, you could have fooled me." Her lips curve. "So then who are Anne and Clifton?"

"Not my children, if that's what you're thinking."

She wags her finger at me. "It's exactly what I was thinking seeing how Ashleigh doesn't feel they can tie their own shoes without you."

She shifts in her seat and crosses her legs. I was hoping to keep my attention on the road and off her body, but I don't stand a bloody chance. Her smile widens. "You may want to go the speed limit there, big guy. My brother's a cop, but he'll kill me if I ask him to fix a ticket."

I ease off the accelerator when I realize I'm well over the legal limit. "It's fast," I mutter, surprised by the ease of control.

"It's the 3.5L EcoBoost®. It combines all the advanced technologies of turbocharging and direct injection." She points ahead. "Make a right at the light. Then a right on the next block. The neighborhood there has a lot of hills and is always the last one in the area to get plowed. If this doesn't convince you that you need this baby, nothing will."

I follow her directions, appreciating how the vehicle handles the overabundance of dips and potholes we encounter in the neighborhood. Mostly though, I relish Wren's presence.

It's been too long since I've enjoyed the company of a woman, let alone one this lovely.

Again, she crosses her legs, and once more my eyes are upon her.

Her smooth dark eyebrows lift into an arch. "You like what you see?"

"I do," I respond, my voice lowering.

Her hand smooths across the console. "They come in cream and tan."

"What?" I ask, jerking my focus between her and the road.

"The interior," she says, tilting her chin. She laughs when my face heats. "What did you think I was talking about?"

I pretend to adjust the mirror. "I thought you were discussing the vehicle in general."

"I don't believe you," she says. She pauses as my body temperature rises several degrees. "Were you looking at my legs?"

"No."

"Yeah, you were. You were totally checking me out."

I pause with my fingers over the controls. I'm an educated man, the CEO of a robotics and technological empire. There are times when I'm challenging a roomful of brilliant engineers and questioning their designs, and moments where I'm discussing complex technological breakthroughs with potential buyers. I know how to present myself in a professional and articulate manner, always.

Except perhaps now. "I was admiring your muscle tone."

"Is that so?" she asks.

"Yes." Among other things.

I steel myself for a verbal tongue-lashing given my asinine response. Wren may arm herself with a tough exterior, but she's very much a lady and deserves to be treated as such.

Yet anger isn't what comes.

"Thanks," she says. "I love to eat so I work out a lot."

Her response appears genuine, but I imagine she already suspects I'm attracted her. Given my deportment, how could she not?

My foot lowers on the accelerator when we reach another hill. The Explorer easily climbs with a simple tap. I'm impressed with how easy it is to maneuver a vehicle this large, but not to the point that I forget this woman beside me, or my desire to know her.

"What do you do to stay in shape, aerobics?" I ask.

She purses her lips, appearing to think about it. "Sure, if it were the 80's and I was into headbands." She laughs when I do. "If you want to know the truth, I kick box, dabble in jujitsu, and teach women's self-defense."

"Because of your job?" My voice softens when she hesitates. "I imagine climbing into a car with a stranger is not without risks, despite the safety checks implemented by your employer."

Her voice softens. "No. A girl can't be too careful. A lot

of shit—sorry. There are a lot of bad things that can happen to a woman."

Wren's voice is unique, not simply because of her thick Philadelphia accent, but because of the confidence behind it . . . a confidence that was very much present until now.

"My apologies," I offer, glancing her way. "I don't mean to make you uncomfortable."

"You're not," she says, glancing away. "Oh, turn right. This leads up one of the steepest hills in the area. I want you to get a feel for how this ride handles through the slush and snow." She turns back, tossing me an impish grin. "Can't keep you away from the missus too long."

I smirk at her good-natured needling. "Ashleigh and I have a strictly professional relationship, I assure you."

"Oh, yeah?" she muses. "How old is Ashleigh?'

I give it some thought. "I believe she's younger than me by a few years, twenty-eight or so."

"Is she in a relationship?"

My mind plays with the idea. She's young and pretty so it's likely she could be. Yet, like me, Ashleigh is always at the office and has made no mention of a significant other. At least not that I recall. "I don't think so."

"Hmm," she says, fidgeting with the lapels of her black leather coat. "Then unless Ashleigh plays for the other team, I'm not so sure she wants a 'strictly professional relationship,' as you put it."

"What?" she asks, her face lighting up at the sight of my frown. "There're a few things I know, and know well. Cars and women. If Ashleigh hasn't put the moves on you, it's because she's waiting for the right moment to pounce."

"That's absurd," I say, laughing.

"Is it?"

I give some thought to what she says. Ashleigh is hardworking and intelligent . . . as well as mothering and overbearing. She's attractive, but there's certainly no attraction there. My gaze flickers to Wren. Not like there is here. "It's not what you think," I begin.

"Sure it is."

I chuckle. "Why are you so certain she'll pounce, as you put it?"

"Because you're good-looking, in shape, and apparently have a decent job." She taps her fingers against her knee. "She may not have hit on you *yet*, but trust me, she will."

"You think I'm good-looking?" I ask, smiling her way. "Or are charm and flattery part of your sales tactics?"

Her eyes fly open. "Look out!"

My foot slams on the brake as a dog runs out in front of me. I stop almost immediately, my grip on the steering wheel loosening only when the dog speeds away unharmed.

"*Woo!*" Wren yells. She points to the dash. "You see that? Best breaking system in its class!" She drops her hands, beaming at me. "So what do you think?

I shift the SUV into park in the middle of the road, stunned I didn't run over that poor creature and impressed how Wren incorporated the experience into her sales pitch. I should apologize for my carelessness. But I can't explain that my inability to focus was due to her presence.

"Come on," she says, giving me a playful nudge. "If you were driving anything else we'd be scraping Snoopy off the tires and telling some poor family we killed their dog."

"I'll take it," I say, my voice lowering as I continue to take her in. I'll take three if it means staying with her a moment longer.

Her mesmerizing stare holds me in place. "In that case, I'm taking you to lunch."

CHAPTER 3

Wren

"Get the hell out of here."

Evan lowers his plastic menu, laughing softly at my remark. When he first walked into the dealership, I couldn't figure this guy out. The sides of his cashmere coat parted when he moved, exposing what looks like a pricey suit. But while he's clean shaven, he's not exactly clean-cut.

His dark wavy hair curls around his ears, long enough that I can tell he's overdue for a trip to the barber, but not so long that he appears disheveled. I take another long look at his straight nose, broad shoulders, and perfect posture. No, he's not disheveled. He's cute. Damn cute if you like pretty boys with deep green eyes with specks of gold, and a jawline angels must have chiseled from granite. Oh, and don't get me started on that accent. He sounds like David Gandy, and dear *God*, looks a little like him, too.

"I'm serious," he tells me, the way he looks at me taking him from damn cute to sexy. "I've never had a cheesesteak."

I reach for the iPad tucked in the bag at my feet, not that I want to. But I need an excuse to break away from those gorgeous eyes and thick lashes that curl at the tips. "So when I asked you if you wanted to go out for steaks, you weren't picturing enough flat screens to fill a cruise ship and

Yuengling on tap."

"What's a Yuengling?" he asks.

I cringe, setting my iPad in front of me. "Oh, Evan, you have a lot to learn if you plan on staying in Philly for the long haul."

He chuckles, his attention trailing to the foosball and pool tables on the other side of the room before drifting to the bar, where Sal's Sports Bar sign lights up in red, almost directly where Sal himself stands. "I didn't picture anything close to this," he admits. "I imagined a traditional restaurant and found your desire to eat a steak this time of day odd."

I point at him. "But you still came."

"I did," he agrees, tilting his head slightly. "And I'm glad."

There he goes, looking at me that way again. Most guys leer at me. Having grown up in one of the worst parts of town, I'm used to it, not that I like it. But Evan's not leering. Not even close. It's more like he's genuinely interested in what I have to say, even with all the ball-busting I've done.

"What are you thinking?" he asks. His voice is soft yet so deep and profoundly clear I have no trouble hearing it over the clamor of dishes being slammed down on the table behind us. "Wren?" he asks, his hypnotic baritone making it hard to concentrate on the contract agreement taking up my iPad screen. "I asked what you were thinking."

That I should keep my eyes off you, I want to say. But that's not what I say or do. "Just wondering why you're so un-American," I offer instead.

The two dimples on the right side of his cheek deepen when he grins. It should be fucking illegal to pull off this cute-sexy vibe he has going on. "Not having had a cheesesteak makes me un-American?" he asks.

"Yup," I say lifting my glass of water. "And don't tell me you've never been to a Phils game, cause then I'll have to run you out of town." His smirk and another flash of those dimples gives him away. "*Evan*," I say, throwing out a hand. "You've seriously never seen the Phils?"

"No."

"The Eagles?" I ask.

"You don't mean the band, do you?"

My shoulders slump. I'd like to say it's a grossly exaggerated gesture, but this is Philadelphia and we're talking about our two major sports teams.

"Please tell me you don't root for another team," I ask, like it pains me, because it physically does.

"Do you mean the Giants and Yankees—?"

I throw out my hands, shushing him when the table full of meatheads behind us grows abruptly silent. "Are you trying to get us in a fight?"

"Ah—"

"Damn it, Evan," I say glancing over my shoulder. "I can't kick ass in these shoes and I just paid off this suit. Don't get us in a fight."

My eyes narrow at the idiot behind us scowling at Evan. "You a Yankees fan, asshole?" he yells.

"He's from England or some shit and doesn't know better," I fire back, cutting Evan off. "Turn around and mind your damn business."

"Someone like him doesn't belong in Sal's," he counters.

"And someone with an ass crack that matches the Liberty Bell shouldn't be so judgmental," I snap. "Pull your pants up and shut up."

His face turns as red as the lipstick I'm wearing when his friends bust out laughing. That doesn't stop him from tugging up his waistband and returning to his food, grumbling something he's damn lucky I don't hear. It's only when I'm sure he's not going to do anything that I turn back to Evan, leaning in close. "We can't be friends," I tell him truthfully.

He shifts his stunned expression from the men back to me. "Why?"

"You're New York. I'm Philly. It's a religious thing."

Fuckin' A. Here comes that grin again. "I'm not a fan of any New York team," he assures me. He pauses and adds, "I'm not a fan of sports at all."

I blink a few times. "You don't watch sports?" He shakes his head. "I suppose the races are out of the question."

"Horse races?"

Jesus God, help me. "NASCAR," I clarify. I should revoke his man card and rip it to tiny pieces in front of him. But he's hot and there's too much alpha lingering beneath that suit. It's subtle, but I can see and sense it under all those straight-laced layers.

I lean in a little closer, skimming my gaze over his polished exterior, but it's what I catch beyond the expensive suit and a blue silk tie that must have cost more than my shoes, that give me a peek of who he really is. There's an allure there, a playfulness buried deep beneath all that controlled discipline, it's repressed and sealed tight, but I see it, and maybe taste it, too.

A beast beneath the business. That's who he is. I lick my lips, knowing I shouldn't go there and wishing I didn't want to. Christ, I just met the guy.

Evan hones in on my mouth as I slide my tongue back into my mouth to keep it from lolling. I ignore it, or at least, try. "All right," I tell him. "I suppose no team is better than rooting for all the wrong ones." I sigh. "Anything else I should know before I decide to sell you my vehicle?"

"Before *you* decide?" he asks, amused.

"It may not look it, but I've got morals," I assure him.

"In that case, I suppose you should know I've spent the better part of my life in London."

"Just London?" I ask. I picked up on the British for sure, but there's something else there.

He laughs. "I was born here, Villanova to be exact. But I attended boarding schools in Switzerland and Scotland before ultimately graduating in England."

I frown, sure I misheard him. "You went to boarding school all over Europe?"

Traces of sadness reflect along his irises, but as quickly as the emotion appears, it fades away. "That's right."

"People still do that?"

"Study abroad?" he questions.

I meant send their kids so far away. And while that's not what I say, the underlying suggestion is there regardless of how I respond. "There are a lot of great schools here in the U.S." I wink, to lighten the mood. "But then again, you are un-American."

He returns my smile though it lacks the luster that was there before. I was right. There's a lot beneath those layers . . . like maybe his share of heartbreak.

"Tell me something about yourself," he says.

"What you see is what you get," I answer. "I like hot cars, I sell them, love sports and good food."

"Tell me something else."

"Why?" I ask, ignoring the fact that I already know.

He folds his arms. "I want to know more about you."

Yeah. That was it. My finger slides along my iPad screen. He seems like a nice guy and while I don't think it'd hurt to tell him a little more about me, I thought the same damn thing about Bryant. So I give him what I think is harmless enough. "I attended Saint Therese Catholic School for thirteen years where I learned valuable life lessons like the Apostle's Creed, how to hotwire a car from Valentina Sigliani, and that if I didn't go to confession I was going to hell."

"You attend confession?"

"No, which is why I'm going to hell."

Laughs aren't supposed to be erotic or even slightly stimulating. But on Evan, God damn it, everything is. Not a good thing, seeing as trash-talking and swearing aside, I pride myself on being professional. "So have you ever been to a ball game?" I ask as his humor dwindles. "Any ball game?" He shakes his head, his stare never leaving mine. "What the hell am I going to do with you?"

It's a rhetorical question. But I swear to God, his eyes smoke hot enough to sizzle my panties and singe his initials into the silk. I think he catches himself, lowering his gaze, his skin flushing slightly. His somewhat shy-like response should give me a giggle and slap away all the naughty, but very nice thoughts are dancing through my head. Except I don't laugh and I sure as anything don't tame those wicked visuals. Not when his stare lifts and all I see is a pent up beast waiting to smash through that cage of pinstripes he's trapped in.

The cuteness I first noticed about him is long gone. His sex appeal, on the other hand, remains front and center. In fact, one might say he's waving that sex appeal like a flag while standing naked on the Rock of Gibraltar.

"What are you thinking?" I ask. Stupid question. But it beats asking if he wants to head back to my place so I can eat that cheesesteak off his bare chest.

"That out of all the dealerships, I'm glad I walked into yours." He cocks his head to gauge my reaction, or maybe because he can hear my lady parts pounding like native drums following a long and lonely winter.

"I'm glad you did, too," I say before I can stop myself.

He doesn't respond, but it looks like he wants to. Sal beats him to it, yelling from the bar where he's wiping down a beer mug with a rag. "Hey, Wren!" he calls. "When you going to get married and start popping out some babies? What are you? Twenty-eight now? You're running out of time and eggs there, woman."

Fighters need to be saved by the bell. I needed to be saved by Sal before me and Evan did something we'd both regret.

Seeing how this isn't the first time Sal has busted on me and my ovaries, I barely blink. "When I'm good and ready, Sal. Be grateful Mina married your sorry ass before it started sagging and dragging across the floor."

"Only 'cause I lost a bet," Mina mutters, stopping to my right. "You ready to order, Wrennie?"

She and Ma are the only people who call me that. "I'll have the usual," I tell her, turning to face her when I hand her my menu.

Mina tucks it against her side. It's barely eleven and the lunch crowd is only now shuffling in, but already her curly blonde-ish hair is going in every direction. She wipes her hand on her black apron and motions to Evan. "How 'bout your date?"

"He's not my date," I correct, knowing she's fishing for details. "He's a client."

"Uh, huh," she says.

Mina is one of my mother's oldest friends, and because of it Ma's going to be getting a call down in Florida the second Mina gets her hands on a phone. She's well into her fifties like Ma, but not blind to a fine-looking man when she sees one.

You might say Evan is a fine-looking man.

You might even say he has a nice ass. 'Cause hell, I'm not blind either and yeah, I noticed when he shrugged out of his coat and jacket.

Evan doesn't notice the attention he's getting from Mina or me, too busy darting his eyes across the menu. "I apologize, but I'm afraid I haven't yet decided."

"Want me to order for you?" I offer, knowing there's only one Mina, and more people sure to walk in. He frowns slightly. His eyebrows are really dark like his hair, drawing my attention back to his eyes. "Come on, you trust me don't you?"

"Of course. How can I not?" He passes his menu to Mina. "Thank you, miss," he tells her politely.

"Miss?" she asks, adjusting the menus together as she turns to me, scowling. "Is he screwing with me?"

I shift away from Evan before she can pick up on how much he's affecting me, in all the ways his type should *not* be affecting me. As it is, I'm already going to hear an earful from Ma. "No. He's just not from around here, Mina."

"I can see that," she says, like maybe it's a good thing.

"Double my order please," I tell her, ignoring the way she seems to wait for me spill details that aren't coming.

She sighs. "Fine. But I betcha your ma's gonna tell me."

"I have no doubt, Mina." I keep my eyes on her as she makes her way to the bar, trying not to choke on my water when Sal smacks her in the ass when she passes. Mina returns his show of affection by slapping him upside the head with the menus. If I have any shot at a decent future with a man, that's what I want: a hard-working guy who can't keep his hands off me, no matter how big my ass gets.

"What's the usual?" Evan asks.

I unfold the paper napkin wrapped around the utensils

and place it on my lap, ignoring my growing desire to tug him forward by that expensive tie and stamp my mouth on his. "Cheesesteak with mushrooms, peppers, a side of chips, and an extra-large pineapple milkshake to wash it all down."

His eyebrows raise almost to his hairline. "Perhaps it's a good thing I didn't have breakfast."

"You'll thank me for it later," I offer, wishing I didn't want to nibble on those lips. He rests his forearms across the checkerboard red and white plastic tablecloth. I want to warn him that the sleeves of the crisp white shirt he's wearing might not stay so crispy white against this table. But right now, I'm so into him and his easy demeanor, it's hard to speak, and maybe hard to think straight, too.

"Is a pineapple milkshake another Philadelphia delicacy I've deprived myself of?" he asks.

"No, it's an O'Brien thing." I beat back another wide grin. Christ, I can't remember the last time I've shown a stranger this many teeth. "Sal's started out as a hole-in-the-wall diner a few blocks from where I grew up. We didn't have a lot back then. I think I can count on one hand all the times we went out to eat as a family. But one thing Ma always did at the end of the month, after making sure the bills were paid, was take us out for milkshakes at Sal's. Out of every flavor, the one we all could agree on was vanilla with chunks of pineapple. It became our thing, you know?"

"It sounds like a much cherished memory from your youth," he says, his features softening along with his voice.

"It is," I agree, forcing myself to look at my iPad. I tap the screen and hit my sales app. "Let's get some of this paperwork out of the way," I add, trying to keep my tone relaxed. "Don't want to keep you away from the little woman longer than necessary."

My fingers scroll down to the customizer and accessories tabs, since Evan made it clear he wants all the toys to go with his new ride. I don't have to glance up to know my sudden switch into business mode probably took him aback. I'm not trying to be a bitch, but it's too easy to be with him, maybe too easy to laugh with him, too.

Evan . . . hell, he's not what I need, and it's not just because of Bryant the Asshole's call earlier. Me and white collar men don't mix. They tend to be uptight and boring. Too PC for my mouth, attitude, and patience. And while I've dated some who come across nice like him, experience has taught me that niceness doesn't last and morphs to superiority real fast.

My guess is he senses that wall I shot up. He grows quiet, allowing me to run through the details so I can place the order. I tell myself it's a good thing I'm doing. Not that I feel good about doing it. He was trying to be nice. But I'm trying to be professional. And professionals ignore hot guys they want to straddle all the time.

It's only when Mina returns with our order and he takes his first bite that everything changes. His eyes lower, savoring all that salty, juicy goodness pouring into his mouth.

I finish off my bite and take a sip of my shake. "You like it?"

He takes his time, swallowing carefully before he answers. "It's incredible. Will they deliver?"

I wipe my mouth carefully, thinking Mina would probably make the exception for Evan. "No, but you can always ask."

We return to our food, but as soon as we both take the next bite, we're back to eyeing each other and smiling. I reach for my purse on the floor when Mina drops off the bill, but Evan takes it first.

"What are you doing?" I ask. "I told you this was my treat."

"I can't allow you to pay," he says. "You've already done enough."

"What do you mean? You're the one who dropped over seventy grand on a car."

He smiles, dimples and all. "I meant by spending time with me I didn't realize I needed."

I should argue, snag the bill, crack a joke, *something*. This was my idea and another thing I do to thank my clients for their business. But what he says hits home.

This time with Evan was different. Easy. So I let him pay, realizing maybe I needed this time, too.

We don't say much on the way back to the dealership, unless you count tying up the loose ends on his purchase. I walk him out to his Jag and offer him my hand. "It was a pleasure doing business with you. I'll call you as soon as your new toy is in."

He takes my hand, curving it along his fingers as he bends forward. "The pleasure was all mine," he whispers along my knuckles.

His lips graze my skin. It's barely a kiss. Barely anything, stopping before it can really begin. But it's enough. Oh, Jesus, is it ever enough.

Ripples of desire surge through me, making me shudder and widening my eyes.

He releases my hand, watching me as I lower it to my side. I think I'm safe, and that maybe I can walk away with nothing more than a good memory of an even better day, despite how my nipples are now pointing to heaven *and* my Great Aunt Chloe who—God rest her soul—is probably giving me the thumbs up.

"Have dinner with me," he tells me.

So much for that.

"I don't really do that," I say.

"Eat?" he offers. "You could have fooled me with how much we ate at your friend's restaurant."

His smile is small, but there, even while mine is notably absent. "I mean I don't date my clients," I explain. It's the truth. But for him, I'm almost willing to break that rule. Almost.

The thing is, I'm pretty screwed in the head right now. The shit with Bryant ended more than a year ago. Never mind. That's a lie. I dumped his ass more than a year ago. That didn't stop him from finding me in Atlantic City months later on my way to a club. He seemed to come out of nowhere, acting like he hadn't taken advantage of me, and pissed when he thought I was meeting another guy.

"You're nothing but a whore," he'd told me. "No one's

ever going to fucking love you."

Holy shit, and didn't that set me off after what he did to me. I was livid and fought back. It was brutal and ugly, and something I'll never forget. I thought I moved past it, and that he was finally out of my life. Then today came . . .

"Wren," Evan continues. "I don't mean to make you uncomfortable. But I enjoyed your company and would like to see you again."

"I know," I respond, knowing my feelings toward Bryant are reflecting in my behavior. "It's just not a good time for me to get to know someone on a personal level. And when it comes to my job, I never want to leave anyone with the wrong impression." The gunmetal sky is fizzing out in that way it does when snow isn't far behind. I tilt my head in the direction of the dealership, where the bright lights showcase the building. "I've worked hard for the rep that I have and I don't want anyone thinking my sales are due to providing clients with more than just test drives."

He nods. "I understand."

Maybe he does. That doesn't make telling him "no" any easier.

I dig my hands into to my black leather coat, expecting him to leave in huff, but he doesn't, reminding me how nice he really is. "Forgive me, but I have to go. Will you call me when my Explorer is in?"

"Yeah. Don't worry, I'll take care of you."

"Thank you," he says. When it's clear there's nothing else to say he smiles softly. "Goodbye, Wren."

"Take it easy, Evan." I punch his arm affectionately and walk back toward the building and through the automated doors. I don't bother to turn and watch him drive away.

No matter how much I want to.

CHAPTER 4

Evan

Clifton and Anne rush around the long conference table placed near the wall of windows. When I originally set up my office, I envisioned it as the perfect place to work. I could take in the busy streets forty-nine stories below, as well as watch the sun set between the neighboring buildings. But my days have allowed me to enjoy very little, and for too many days the sun has set without me noticing.

Maybe I should regret the days that have passed. But I've been so focused on saving my company, regrets are something I can't afford.

I stop pacing, my attention pausing halfway down the diagnostics report I'm reviewing. "Have Davies and Munro implemented the changes to the capacitor for the new Mechanicus prototype?"

"Yes, Evan," John replies.

"And?"

John smiles. "The control is far superior."

"Good." I make a note on the page. "What about the new micro-camera?"

It's Scott who answers. "We subbed out the lens as per your instructions. The picture quality is twenty percent better. Trials will begin in two weeks."

"One week," I correct, meeting him in the eye. "Make it happen."

He looks at John who nods. "All right, Evan. You've got it."

Scott and John rush out, their lab coats flapping behind them in their haste. Clifton and Anne stay put, speaking quietly as they iron out the final details of the presentation. My building is filled with robotics engineers and software specialists, but it's my marketing and sales team led by Clifton and Anne who will make the world aware of what iCronos has to offer. I'm proud of the progress my company has made in the short time since my arrival, but there's more to be done before we work our way out of debt.

With the advanced technological breakthroughs we've developed here and in London, iCronos will be the global juggernaut the world needs. The first step, and one of the most important, takes place today.

I adjust the glasses I'm wearing. "The CEO of Presbyterian Medical Center is confirmed for this morning, correct?"

Clifton glances up. "Yes, Evan. Originally, it was going to be the Vice President and a few of the chairs." He sighs, appearing hopeful. "But after your call, the CEO plans to attend. Oh, and the board and CEO of Saint Martin's will follow after lunch."

"Good," I say. I place the folder down and reach for my coffee, taking a sip. It's already cold. That doesn't stop my smile when I see the large spinning flakes and remember who I met the last time it snowed.

Wren. Dear God, I can't stop thinking about her.

She's not someone I expected to meet, much less interact with on a personal level. A strong, vibrant woman with an underlying softness and sensuality who continues to fascinate me. I'd like to convince her to give me a chance, not that I'm certain how.

"It's not a good time for me to get to know someone," she'd said. If I'm being honest, it's possibly the worst time for me as well. But I can't ignore what I feel, and I'm thoroughly gobsmacked by this woman.

I've wanted to call her and thank her again, but refrained. She's worked hard to build her stellar reputation (yet one more thing I admire about her) and I want to respect her request for space. Not that this means I'm done pursuing her.

She texted late yesterday to tell me my vehicle had arrived. I was in the middle of a production meeting. My response was brief, informing her that a car service would take me to the dealership in the morning. I'd planned to call her, but the meeting's conclusions had me working late, and instead of the service taking me to the dealership, I had it bring me to the office just before dawn, to prepare for a meeting with my nanotechnologists. I've only had time to text her that I'm busy and that I'll be by around six this evening. She assured me she'd wait for me. My hope is once we're finished with business, she'll agree to have dinner with me.

"I have a good feeling about this, Evan," Anne says, beaming. "A great feeling."

I nod, but don't respond, forcing my thoughts back to the task at hand.

Anne straightens from where she's stacking the presentation folders. Her hair is bleached so blond it's white, cut short around her skull except for the top which is long enough to fall to one side. Today she's in a dark purple suit and black shoes that match the large black frames of her glasses. She is a very intelligent woman, and supremely gifted when it comes to marketing and developing new sales strategies. I trust her and Clifton immensely. I only wish I could say that about more of my staff.

"I've barely slept," she adds. "I'm so excited and really want this to go well today."

"I do, too," Clifton agrees. "But I'll admit, we're taking a risk by targeting hospitals that are community and charity oriented."

"We have an ethical responsibility to take that risk," I reply. "But both facilities need the technology to compete with hospitals in the surrounding areas. It's the only way they can continue to run and care for their aging and economically challenged population."

"It's the right thing to do," Anne says. "And a great product we're offering. Adeptus will help thousands suffering from cancer and propel iCronos as a leader in nanorobotics."

She's right. Adeptus will potentially change the lives of millions world-wide.

Clifton scans the table, appearing to relive the last few weeks he and Anne have spent familiarizing themselves with the details surrounding Adeptus. Not an easy task with the amount of products in our nanorobotics line alone. "I hope we can pull this off," he says.

"We will," I assure him. "We'll make it happen."

Ashleigh stomps across the gold and white marble tile floor in her absurdly tall shoes. How she hasn't pitched forwarded and landed on her face continues to astound me. Her gaze shifts between Anne and Clifton as if they're beneath her, before fixing on my face. She doesn't regard me with the superior manner as she does them, but I wouldn't describe her demeanor as welcoming.

She drops a file in front of me with a note clipped to it. "You need to return Mr. Langley's call."

I frown. "Langley of Yodel?"

She nods curtly. "He's interested in Hound Mechanicus and how soon it will be ready."

"How does he know about Hound?" I ask, lowering my coffee.

She crosses her arms. "Mr. Sherman made him aware and offered—"

"Hound isn't ready," I say, cutting her off. "And Sherman is no longer in charge of this branch."

My anger fires hers. "May I speak to you privately?" she asks, lifting her chin.

"*No*," I respond. "If I'm hearing this, Anne and Clifton will hear it, too."

She purses her lips with obvious distaste. Clifton is in his mid-thirties and almost completely bald. His suits appear outdated and need to be tailored to accommodate his gangly form, but they're clean and neat. Five years ago, he left everything he knew in his small Wyoming town to work here. In those five years, he's gone above and beyond without a pay increase or promotion. That changed when I took over. I respect him. Clearly, Ashleigh doesn't share my sentiment.

"Mr. Sherman made an agreement with Mr. Langley," she begins.

"In *writing*?" I ask, my temper building.

"I'm not sure," she admits. "But Evan, we're talking tens of millions in revenue," she whispers urgently, as if I'm missing the point.

"Find out if there's something in writing, and then let him know I'll call him this afternoon at four o'clock."

"Evan," she interrupts. "He'll expect a call sooner."

I don't dismiss her lack of respect, nor her tone. "*I* am not available until four. *He* is not privy to this technology. *You* will not tell him anything more than he needs to know." My jaw hardens. "Call Leesa in contracts and find out if anything was put in writing. If it was, phone the head of our legal department and have her see me between appointments."

Once more, I seemed to have angered our version of Norman Bates' mother. "Anything else?" she asks, crossing her arms.

"Yes, send two dozen roses to Erin O'Brien at Ford Nation on Lincoln Avenue."

I have everyone's attention now.

"Roses?" Ashleigh repeats.

"Yes." My request seems absurd even to me. I turn toward Anne as an uncomfortable heat crawls up my neck.

"Oh, do fire and ice," she suggests, appearing to think I sought her advice. "Purple and silver tones if they have it. Women like that."

"Purple, of course." Ashleigh smirks, taking another look at Anne's suit before returning to me. "What would you like on the card?"

Her grossly exaggerated enthusiasm grinds my patience. "Keep it simple. Just 'thank you' followed by my first name."

"Anything else, *sir*?" she asks.

Ashleigh is walking a fine line with me. Initially she was

courteous and respectful. The more I expressed how invaluable I found her, and the more supervisory responsibility I gave her, the more intolerable she's become. If I didn't need an experienced secretary, and had the time train one I could trust, I'd personally show her the door.

"*No*," I respond.

"Fine." Her response is more subdued and she quickly walks away, shutting the heavy door behind her.

"Have your staff ready the conference room," I tell Clifton. "Make sure it's equipped with everything we need for the meeting, including food and beverages."

"You don't want Ashleigh to do it?" Clifton asks.

I glance up and catch his grin. Like me, he's had his fill of Ashleigh. I chuckle. "I think it's best to limit her responsibilities." In other words, I don't want to see her for the rest of the morning or give her any more power. As it is she'll probably spit venom into my lunch.

Anne lifts a stack of binders into her arms as I return to my desk. My cold coffee is in one hand and the diagnostic report is in the other. "Evan?" she asks.

I place my cup in front of me and lower myself into my chair. "Yes?"

"Who's Erin O'Brien?"

I turn the page of the report, despite not having finished reading the previous. "A sales representative at Ford Nation," I explain, flipping to the next page.

"Just a sales rep?"

I raise my head in time to see her exchanging glances with Clifton. "That's right."

"Then why is your face so red?"

The added surge of heat is response enough.

Clifton turns quickly away in a pathetic attempt to hide his grin. "We'll have everything ready, Evan. See you in a few."

Anne spares me by following, but it's what I hear when she opens the door that causes me to glance up from my work.

"Is he expecting you?" Ashleigh asks. I don't have to see her to know she's irate.

I frown and leave my seat, wondering who she's trying to intimidate this time. From the small opening where Anne is holding the door, I see Wren lean forward and press her hand on Ashleigh's desk. "Just tell him Wren O'Brien is here."

CHAPTER 5

Wren

The blonde's focus dips to my palm where it's resting on her desk then back to my face, her lips pressing into a thin line. I'll admit, I have a gift when it comes to pissing people off. But this broad had it in for me the minute she saw me. She pitches me with an even nastier scowl than the one she met me with, when I entered her glass bowl office and asked if Evan was available. I was friendly, polite, the whole nine yards. But I'm not feeling particularly friendly now. Now, I'm ready to go at it.

The guy who stepped out from Evan's office shoots past me, appearing annoyed. From the open floor plan behind me, the voices of those working from their cubicles quiet. But their reaction isn't because of anything I did. She's the one being loud. My guess: this isn't the first time she's tried to scare someone off.

She tilts forward, the motion widening the neck of her black button-down blouse and exposing the lace from her bra. It's not a blatant show of her goods, but it's enough to give someone a peek of what's lurking beneath. I'm thinking that "someone" is Evan, seeing as she's seconds from leaping across the desk and digging her fangs into my throat.

"I told you, he's busy," she snaps. "Unless you have an

appointment, Mr. Jonah cannot be disturbed."

"Erin? Erin O'Brien?"

I straighten slowly at the sound of my given name. Another blonde (this one actually capable of smiling) stands by the door clutching a stack of folders against the front of her dark purple suit. "That's right," I answer.

Her grin widens as she glances over her shoulder. "Evan, Erin's here."

She doesn't quite finish before Evan appears beside her. "It's Wren, actually," he tells her, although his attention is fully on me.

He's shocked to see me. I'm shocked this other woman seems to know who I am. But that doesn't stop my smile or his. "Hi," he says.

"Hey," I reply. He's wearing glasses. Black ones like Henry Cavill did when he played Clark Kent. But Henry has nothing on Evan. *Damn.* Evan is hotness in a suit.

I dig through my purse, trying to keep it classy, and pull out two key fobs. "I have something for you," I say, shaking the keys at him.

He steps forward, frowning slightly. "You brought my Explorer here?"

"Just had it delivered to your garage." I shrug and drop the keys in his hands. "I told you, I'd take care of you."

The blonde, the nice one, hurries by. "I'll see you in a few," she tells him.

Evan nods, but doesn't watch her leave. Uh-uh. His eyes are all on me. "Nice suit," I call after her, giving me an excuse to stop grinning at him.

"Thank you," she says, her toothy smile skipping from me to Evan.

"I meant to stop by the dealership later today," he says.

His voice pulls my attention back to his face, not that I mind. "I know, but you seemed swamped and I wanted to save you the trouble." I adjust the strap on my purse. "Don't worry, I know a guy and had him tow it here."

"I wasn't worried," he says. He motions to the office. "Would you like to come in?"

"Evan," the woman with the stick up her ass interrupts. "You have a meeting."

Evan strikes me as the laid-back type, one who doesn't easily lose it or look for any excuse to rip someone to shreds.

I don't expect anger, but that's exactly what I see. "I know what I have," he bites back.

"You must be Ashleigh," I say, smiling. Oh, and my new friend doesn't like me calling her out one bit.

She tucks the strand that escapes her loose bun behind her ear, her scowl deepening. She opens her mouth to say something, but then quickly shuts it when she catches Evan's smirk. I ignore her because it's easy, and I know it will piss her off. "So are you going to show me your office or would you rather let my imagination run wild?"

"As much as I think it would be entertaining to watch your imagination run wild, it would be my pleasure to show you my office," he says walking forward. "This way."

He's not wearing his jacket and (bonus!) I get a nice long look at the way his tailored black pants hug the kind of ass cheeks that will barely move if spanked—not that I've thought about it, like I mentioned, I'm classy.

He holds the door open, allowing me through. I come to a halt when he shuts the door behind us. Holy shit. His office is bigger than my entire house, and I'm not exaggerating. Gold veined and white marble tile cover the spacious floor while modern dark wood furniture with gold accents are placed strategically, giving each area its own separate space.

Dark brown leather couches with matching chairs make up what resembles a screening room where numerous flat-screens are mounted to a wall. To the right, an immense granite conference table with eighteen plush chairs waits in perfect view of both the flat-screens and floor to ceiling windows that give one hell of a view of the skyline.

This isn't an office, this is a monstrosity of a room.

At the end there's a desk, his desk, I assume. But I've never seen a desk this large or one surrounded by multiple computer screens appearing to branch out from *inside* the colossal stretch of wood.

I think he's going to sit there, and motion me to sit at one of the four seats positioned in front of it, but he moves toward the leather couch.

I should sit in one of the chairs, but lower myself beside him before I can give it enough thought. I cross my legs and glance toward the opposite end of the room where his desk and chairs wait abandoned.

"Are we going to watch a movie or something?"

He laughs. It's short, but keeps his smile in place. "I wish that was a luxury I could entertain."

"No time for movies?' He shakes his head. I point to the flat-screens. "Damn waste of time with these beauties."

"They have their purpose," he says. "Alfred, view progress."

"Viewing progress," the computer system repeats.

Each screen lights up with a different image. There are twenty-four, six across, four up. Some show high-tech labs, different points in the underground garage, and a couple of conference rooms where training and meetings are taking place. Still more show different levels of the building where rows and rows of cubicles are assembled like mini cities.

"Are these people aware Big Brother is watching?"

"In theory," he says. "They sign an agreement recognizing this is a necessity to protect the advanced technologies we develop. But as the cameras aren't in plain sight, it seems they tend to forget."

Each picture is clear and detailed. I can't even imagine the level of technology these cameras possess. "Alfred's pretty damn handy."

"He is, but he has his limits." He motions to the bottom screen where a tall woman with all legs and very little skirt is bent over a cubicle, laughing and flirting with a man in a suit. Behind them, an older woman is going Mach 1 on a keyboard, speaking fast to what appears to be a courier. She stops typing long enough to hand him a pile of packages. "If he was everything I needed him to be, he'd let go of the employees I don't need and elevate those who work hard."

The screens switch over like dominos, showing

completely different parts of the campus. I've driven past this building several times, but I never understood how massive it is until now.

"How often does Alfred give you the low-down?" I ask.

"Only when I want to see it. This is the one task I can leave to my security team, thankfully. Their cameras have access to all rooms, except this one." He shifts back to the screens. "If I have a call requiring the presence of multiple team members or a particular device we're working on with our London branch, the screens are very helpful." He smiles. "Alfred, show room."

"Showing room," Alfred repeats.

I almost jolt when the screens morph into one giant image of me and Evan on the couch. Evan turns to me in high-def. "If you ask me, this is the view I prefer."

"I don't," I admit. "I look like Goliath."

"I apologize, I didn't mean to startle you," he says chuckling. "Alfred, sleep room."

"Sleeping," Alfred announces.

The screens shut off at once. I tug down the skirt of my deep red suit so it rests closer to my knees, trying to find my words. "Evan, what exactly do you do?"

"I'm CEO of iCronos," he responds like it's not a big deal. Like he didn't just show me enough tech to make the Death Star resemble a ping-pong ball sprinkled with glitter.

I blink back at him. "I should've sold you the Expedition."

This time when he laughs, his chest shakes. "And I suppose I should have mentioned it during our time together." His deep voice softens. "But you didn't ask, and we had other business to discuss."

"Like Ashleigh?" I offer. Hey, now that I'm here, I might as well let the bitchy cat out of the bag. Christ, I'm surprised said bitchy cat didn't try to claw my eyes out.

His humor dissolves, replaced by a sweetness I've never quite seen in a man, and a whole lot of sizzle. "Ashleigh is the last person on my mind when I'm with you," he murmurs.

Hmm. He had to go there. In that voice, too. But I can't,

even though I really want to. I glance in the direction of the closed door. "Maybe. Except looks like I was right, wasn't I?"

"Right about what?"

I tilt my chin, wondering if he's fishing for compliments. But then I realize he doesn't get it and it's up to me to show him into the hot, yet humble, light. "That Ashleigh wants to have her way with you in some desolate yet eerily erotic jungle."

He pinches the bridge of his nose. "Has anyone ever mentioned you have a tendency to exaggerate?"

"Never," I say emphasizing the word and leaning forward. "I'm picturing parrots, lots and lots of parrots, circling you while she eases you down into a thick bed of palm leaves in her Tarzan and Jane fantasy. You don't mind leather loincloths do you, Evan? You strike me as the leather loincloth type." He throws back his head, laughing. "Or maybe something in fur, leopard, minx, zebra—okay, maybe not zebra. They're a little too kinky if you ask me. Anyway, the toucans—"

"What happened to the parrots?"

"Oh, they're still there, too. But you can't have an erotic jungle without some toucans. You hear what I'm saying?"

"Of course."

"Good, 'cause I'm picturing some kind of aerial show with the parrots, toucans, and maybe a flamingo tossed in for a little pizzazz."

"Pizzazz?" he asks, his humor casting a shimmer along his green eyes.

"I'm just watching out for you," I point out.

"By warning me about Ashleigh and what she has planned for me in this make-believe jungle?"

"No, by giving you nice birds to sing to you when she pounces on you in this *erotic* jungle. Aren't you paying attention? This fantasy is taking some work on my part."

His widening grin warms my insides. Kind of like hot chocolate. Sexy hot chocolate. Sexy and very naked hot chocolate.

"Are you suggesting I thank you for this rather

descriptive vision of Ashleigh's supposed fantasy?" he asks.

I smirk. "I am, and you're welcome."

His gaze melts into mine. "Perhaps now is a good time to remind you that I'm not attracted to Ashleigh, nor have I ever been."

"Never?" I ask. So much for not going there.

"No," he says. "But I can't say the same about you."

And cue the dimples.

I bend my arm against the back of the couch and lower my head to my palm. "She has it bad for you," I remind him, trying to keep the talk on her and not on us.

Because there is no us.

And there shouldn't be.

Right?

"I don't agree," he says, looking at me like I shouldn't want him to look at me. But he does, maybe because I'm doing the same. We fall into what should be a tension filled, angsty silence. Except there's no tension or angst. It's just Evan and this 'way too easy feel' I get around him.

Ashleigh said he was busy and didn't have time to see me. But he doesn't appear rushed, taking me in like he's not the CEO of this super-tech company and giving me one more reason to like him.

"So you own the company?" I ask, when he doesn't say more.

"I do. My father gave it to me when I was twelve."

"*Twelve*?" I ask.

He nods. "You can imagine I wasn't ready to run it. I took my time, learned everything I could about nanotechnology and business, and then learned even more when I took over our London branch. Initially, we had an outstanding leadership team here. But they were older. Each retirement brought in more of the wrong people until this branch suffered an exorbitant amount of loss, dwindling the profit I'd secured us in Europe."

He leans back and rubs his jaw. "Our advisors thought it best to shut down this branch and continue to build upon our success in Europe. But in doing so, thousands would lose their jobs, and everything my father developed here would be obliterated. I couldn't do that to him."

"I can't blame you," I tell him, looking around as if Alfred is going to magically teleport his father into the room. "Where's your dad now? He must be really proud of you for stepping up."

He quiets. "He died when I was twelve."

At first, I don't move. Evan could have said he inherited the company and I would have understood he'd passed away. But in saying his dad gave it to him and everything else that followed, it's like he didn't want to be reminded he was gone.

I reach for his forearm and give it a squeeze. "I'm sorry," I tell him, gently.

"I am, too," he says.

His attention drifts to where my fingers rest along his forearm. He doesn't have to say he's done discussing his dad, I already know. I give him another squeeze. "So, how's reestablishing an empire working out for you?"

He smiles. "It's a slow and arduous process, which is why my time is so limited. But failing isn't something I contemplate. In fact, the first step toward global domination starts today."

"Global domination?" I ask.

"I have my first major sales meeting." He winks. "But global domination sounds sexier."

Oh yes it does, big boy. "And what are you selling?" I ask, realizing too late I'm inching closer.

"Do you really want to know?"

I'm surprised how much I do. "Yeah. Let 'er rip."

"My sales team and I are pitching Adeptus Mechanicus to two local hospitals. It's nanotechnology in its most advanced form, capable of delivering chemotherapeutic agents directly to cancerous tumors and breaking down the remains into minute particles, so the body can easily excrete them."

I straighten. "Tiny robots that kill cancer and then eat what's left?" He nods. "Did you come up with this?"

Again, he nods. "I began to conceptualize it at a young

age. But it wasn't until I began my undergraduate studies that I realized it was viable. It took close to a decade for my robotics team and I to fully develop it. But in perfecting Adeptus, we created Chaos, Eldar, and Ork Mechanicus. Different forms from that one prototype capable of treating a large array of diseases and damaged tissues."

"Damn. I should've sold you the upgrade."

That grin. *Jesus*, and those dimples! Evan is brilliance and sweet in one steamy package. Can't say I blame Ashleigh for wanting to keep him all to herself.

Speak of the devil in high heels. "Evan?" she says, throwing the door open without bothering to knock. She whips her head away from the desk where she was expecting us, to the couch where she isn't, straightening her spine hard enough to support that granite conference table on her head. "Everyone is in the conference room waiting for you."

She treats him like some disobedient kid. If I was him, I'd flip out on her. But this time, he keeps his tone steady and his attention on me as he rises. "My apologies, but I must leave you."

When I stand, there's only a few inches separating us. It's the closest I've ever stood to him, but he doesn't seem to mind and neither do I. "Don't worry about it. Your new ride is parked in the V.P.'s spot where your security guard told me to leave it. If you have any problems or concerns, call me, I'll take care of it."

I start to leave, but his voice keeps me in place. "How about we finish our talk over dinner Saturday?"

I don't have to see Ashleigh's face to guess she's about two point five seconds away from leaping onto my back. "I thought we were done here," I say, not that I want to be.

"I don't think we are," he says. He cocks his head slightly, examining me in a way that shows he can see past the pretense of professionalism and all the way down to Philly girl with the loud mouth who's dying to kiss him. "And I think you feel the same. Say you'll have dinner with me this weekend."

There's no hesitation. "Okay."

We're both showing more teeth than should be humanly possible. He probably thought he'd have to work for it. But he doesn't have to work at all. It's *nice* being around him. And this talk reminded me just how nice.

"Evan," Ashleigh calls.

She's closer and pissy. And even though I shouldn't, I lift up on my toes and press a kiss against his cheek. I linger long enough to let him know it's not so innocent, but short enough to be respectful. "Good luck," I tell him. "I know you'll knock them dead."

His eyes widen briefly and he lifts his hand slowly to remove his glasses. "Don't," I say, offering him a wink. "They look good on you."

I reach for my purse and walk out without another glance. My mother once told me if I go looking for trouble, I'm sure to find it. Based on that loathsome glare from Ashleigh, I found more than my share.

CHAPTER 6

Wren

My sales job requires me to dress for success. I have a lot of nice clothes and usually drop a few grand every couple of seasons to keep up appearances and keep kicking ass. But while I like looking nice, I hate shopping. And everyone hates me when I have to.

My sister-in-law Sofia is the only one patient enough to put up with me. She would've earned a shot straight into heaven for all the times she's tolerated my bitching, if Saint Peter wasn't already saving her spot for being the nicest person on the planet.

I put her on speaker the moment she answers. "Hey, Sofe. How you doing?"

"Hi, Wren." She pauses. "Is something wrong, honey?"

Like I said, Sofia is all sorts of sweet, but she's also really smart and knows I'm not calling to shoot the shit. "Nope. Just trying to decide what to wear. You know that houndstooth sheath dress we picked up at Talbots?"

"You're going on a date?"

Yeah, Killian didn't marry some airhead. "Slow down there, Sofe. I'm just trying to decide what to wear to work."

"I thought you were off this weekend?"

Okay, now those smarts are backing me into a wall. "I'm helping out for a few hours."

Again, she pauses. I'm not one to lie, but I don't want to go there with Sofia. She knows I haven't dated anyone since Bryant, which has already led to too many questions. My brothers, being as protective as they are . . . yeah, I don't need this.

"All right," she says, slowly, clueing me in she doesn't believe me.

"I was going to go with the strappy stilettos from Nordstrom's you insisted I buy. But it looks like it's going to snow so I was thinking about the ankle length boots with the three-inch heels." I hold up both shoes and take another look at the nose-bleed heels. "By the way, are you trying to kill me?"

She laughs in that soft gentle way of hers. "I wouldn't dream of it."

"I don't know," I say, giving the spikey heels another look. "All it will take is one false step for you and Killian to collect the insurance money."

"You know that's not true," she says. I don't have to see her to know she's smiling. "I think either pair would look great with the dress. But my suggestion is to go with the thigh-high knotted boots."

"Which ones?"

"The black ones we bought on sale last spring. Oh, and the multi-colored bead bracelet. There's too much black and white in that ensemble. You need a splash of color."

"The interior designer thinks I need a 'splash of color'. Geez, how on earth did I guess you were going to go there?" I ask.

I walk to my closet and dig through it after I tuck the other shoes in their boxes. "Wren, may I ask you something?"

My phone is on the floor by my left knee, but I can still hear her loud and clear. "Sure."

I reach for what I think is the right box, a white one with red lettering. "What's his name?" she asks.

My head falls forward. I don't want to keep lying to her. She and my other brother's girlfriend are the best friends I have. "Evan," I say, thankful she can't see the stupid grin on my face.

"Okay," she says, quietly. "What did you have in mind for earrings?"

That's one of the cool things about Sofia, she only pushes enough to make sure I'm okay. But this past year, I haven't been okay much, and have avoided her and my brothers because of it.

My phone vibrates against the wood floor as I shove myself into my boots. I frown when I don't recognize the number, but keep talking to Sofia. It's not until I disconnect with her that I realize whoever called didn't leave a voicemail, but did leave a text.

Hello, pretty girl.

I curse, realizing who it is.

I haven't forgotten our time together. Have you?

My mouth fires off another round of curses at the texts that follow.

Remember, no one loves a whore.

I take a screen shot of the text, including the number, but not before I text back, *Go back to hell and stay there, Bryant. I want nothing to do with you.*

I block the number and place the phone on my dresser, leaning forward and cursing yet again. Growing up where I did, I've seen a lot of bad shit. It's toughened me up and taught me to throw down. But what happened with Bryant . . . God damn it. I should have known better, and I didn't. I stayed with that prick until he used every last bit of me.

Shit. Every last bit.

My neighbor's dog's deep bark makes me jump. I run to the window in time to see him running to the end of his property line, but not much else. I walk away from the window after another few seconds and pull open the jewelry drawer in my dresser. It's not until I pull out the dangly earrings Sofia suggested and glance in the mirror that I get a good look at my face. I'm fair-skinned, not that it shocks anyone, seeing how I'd bleed shamrocks if cut. But I'm not just fair right now.

Beneath the few freckles scattered along my nose and cheeks I'm deathly pale. I don't want to think about how bad I look, or about the odd chill poking at my spine. And I especially don't want to think about Bryant.

I never thought *anyone* could ever make me feel so dirty. But Bryant isn't just anyone. He's a sociopathic asshole who couldn't stand me leaving him.

I straighten, lifting my chin and setting each earring in place. After a few breaths, and a few more after that, I return to my bathroom and finish getting ready.

Evan will be here soon. I pause as I lift my minute makeup bag from my drawer. "Evan," I say aloud. Even his name lifts the corners of my mouth. He's, I don't know, *real*.

Yeah, that's a good word for him. A big shot CEO who'll munch on a cheesesteak like it's the greatest sandwich in the world ('cause it is), put up with my trash-talking, and still ask me out to dinner. Twice.

I reach for my mascara and give my lashes a few swipes as I think back to that kiss I gave him. Maybe I shouldn't have with Ashleigh there. Maybe I shouldn't have at all. But, I couldn't help myself. Just like I couldn't say no to seeing him again.

Except that was pre-Bryant, again.

I toss the mascara back in my bag. This is yet another moment when it doesn't pay to be Catholic, when it sucks to have an overly superstitious mother, and grandmother, and neighbors when you're growing up. "It's a sign that you shouldn't get involved with this man," they all would have said, before crossing themselves twenty times in a row.

I shake off the thought. "Settle down," I tell myself. "It's just one date, and Evan is different."

I make a face. "That's what I said about Bryant. And we all know how that went to hell."

I shake off that horrible unease and dig at the bottom of my drawer for a lipstick. As much as I hate shopping, I hate makeup more. I follow up the mascara with a hot pink lipstick (another must-have Sofe insisted I needed), and nothing more.

My eyebrows knit as I step back from the mirror and take a good look at myself. I've never been a fan of pink, and this shade shouldn't work with my skin tone, but somehow it does.

The sound of the doorbell ringing has me hurrying, but my steps slow when I make it halfway down the stairs and don't see anyone near the door. "Shit," I mutter, walking carefully. I have my phone out, ready to hit 9-1-1 when Evan's tall frame steps in front of the glass.

I open the door, smiling when I see him with two dozen lavender and silver roses in his hands. "Hi," he says, his eyes widening when he sees what I'm wearing.

"Hey." I stop smiling when I see who's behind him.

"Damn it, Wren. You're supposed to marry *me*," the little neighborhood kid says.

Okay. Maybe "little" isn't the best word to describe Sauron. At eleven, he weighs almost as much as me, and his mouth is almost as big. Almost. "Sauron, what are you doing here?"

He crosses his arms. "Keeping you safe from the likes of him." He motions to Evan who is doing everything he can not to laugh outright. My stare bounces to him before turning back to Sauron.

"Sauron, you're eleven. I'm twenty-eight. I know you don't want to hear this, but you and me, are never going to happen. By the time you're even old enough to drive, I'll already be two point five kids in, driving a minivan packed with diapers, binkies, and one of those bouncy chairs your little sister can't get enough of."

"Love knows no age limits, baby," he counters.

I hold out a hand. "I'm going to stop you right there. Go home, be nice to your sister, and vacuum the house for Gloria."

He sighs, defeated. "Will you help me with my science project if I do? I have to build a volcano or some shit."

"No, but I'll kick your ass if you don't stop swearing," I tell him.

"Wren," he whines.

"Okay, look. I was never good at science, but me and my brother have always been good with projects. Do what I tell you, and me and him, we'll try to help you."

"Yeah?" he asks.

"I promise."

He adjusts the beanie on his head and starts to turn. But then he narrows his stare at Evan. "Let me ask you this. What does he have that I don't?"

"A legal age limit," I offer.

Sauron huffs. "Okay, I'll give you that one."

Evan and I watch him hop down my wood porch steps and onto the freshly plowed sidewalk. He jumps onto his bike, but it's not until he pedals onto the sidewalk leading back to his house that Evan speaks. "It seems you have suitor."

"Oh, yeah," I tell him. "Grade schoolers can't seem to get enough of my sparkling wit."

He laughs, stepping through when I pull open the door. I shudder when the frigid air from outside rushes in, and quickly lock the door.

My house isn't huge, but it's a good size and almost three times as big as the row house I grew up in. There's a small sitting area that doubles as a library to my right and a cozy family room with a fireplace to my left. But it's not until I see Evan standing by the couch, small flurries melting into his dark hair, that I see it in a different way.

This is home to me, with all its dark wood, plaster walls, and charm. This is my happy place. Evan's home is his work. I can tell by how at ease he was in that environment, despite how sterile the marble tile and expensive modern furniture felt. I don't fault him for it. We're just different. Maybe too different.

"You look stunning," he tells me.

Okay. We're different. But he's still a fucking sweetheart.

He steps forward with the roses in his hands. Suddenly, I'm thirteen again and waiting on Connor McGillis to kiss me before my brothers catch us and stomp his ass. "These for me?" I ask, my face flushing.

He does a subtle one shoulder shrug. "I'd say they were for Sauron, but I don't typically reward children who ask me, 'What the hell are you doing here, asshole?'"

My jaw pops open as I reach for the flowers. "He said that?"

He nods, thoughtfully. "It would seem I sparked his protective nature."

"And his evil side." I groan. "I'm sorry about that. He and me, we're going to have a talk."

"It's all right. He was . . . charming."

"Charming?" I ask.

He frowns. "Perhaps that's not the best word. But I commend him for looking out for you."

"Most people would have kicked him to the curb. Just last week I had to pull one of the neighborhood girls off him who challenged him to a fight. But give them a few years, my guess is he'll take her to prom."

I take another look at the heavy coat he's wearing. God Almighty, he makes everything look yummy. "If you want, place your coat on the railing," I say backing away. "It's warm in here and I want to put these in water. We have time, right?"

"Take as much time as you need," he says.

My steps slow to a stop when he tugs off his coat. We're going to a nice place for dinner that much I know. I expected him in a suit, but I won't complain about what I see. As he slips the coat from his shoulders, I get my first real look at his body.

Not that I can help it, not with the dark green V-neck sweater clinging to his frame. There's definition in his arms and shoulders, something I didn't notice in his business clothes. But I notice it now. Maybe a little too much.

He smiles, tilting his head as my attention lingers. "I went with casual attire this evening."

"I can see that," I say, inching forward. I want to brush my fingers through his hair and feel the moisture leftover from the melting flakes. I also want to feel the fabric slide against my palms as I pass my hands along his chest.

Somehow, I refrain. Not that he makes it easy.

The deep green of his sweater borders on black, but I catch enough of the color despite the dim light from the family room. It's brings out the green in his eyes and fades the gold away, tempting me forward to see if I can find those flecks. It's a hell of a thing, considering how shaken I was before he arrived.

"I'll only be a minute," I say, turning in the direction of the kitchen. Hey, it beats drooling and by now I'm pretty damn close.

There's just enough space in the hall for him to walk beside me, and that's what he does. "You have a lovely home," he says when we step into the kitchen. He slides his hand across the white granite counter with silver swirls, noting the stained cabinets with interest.

"Thank you. My sister-in-law picked everything out. She has a gift for these things. I have a gift for telling her she's crazy." I retrieve an ice bucket from beneath the counter. "I should know better than to doubt her by now."

He watches me as I fill the bucket. "Sorry, it's all I have," I explain. "And I need something big to accommodate these flowers. Christ, Evan. I've never seen blooms this big."

"Do you like them?" he asks.

"I really do," I reply, realizing how much I mean it.

Men I've dated in the past have mostly bought me lingerie. Sometimes even on the first date. Those dates have ended before they started, and they sure as hell never had a second opportunity to make up for the insult. The last time someone gave me flowers was at my high school graduation, and they came from my mother. Yet another reminder of how different Evan is.

"Your sister-in-law, is she married to your brother who's a police officer?"

He remembered me mentioning my brother the cop. "No, Curran is married to Tess, an assistant D.A. My other brother Killian is married to Sofia, the interior decorator."

"You have two brothers?"

I laugh as I reach for the first rose. "No, I have six."

This gives Evan some serious pause. "*Six*?"

"I'm the only girl." I wink at him. "I guess that explains a lot, huh?"

He laughs. "I suppose I can see where your strength comes from."

"Strength?" I wonder why of all things, he honed in on that.

"It's one of the first things I noticed about you." He leans forward, appearing surprised that I'm so surprised. "You're a very strong woman, Wren, in personality and demeanor. I'm stunned no one has ever pointed that out to you."

No, they usually point out my ass, I don't bother mentioning. "It's not that I don't consider myself strong," I say, ignoring how scared I was before he arrived. "But it's different to hear someone say that's the first thing they noticed about you."

He smiles softly, his gaze holding me in place. "There are many compliments I can give you, and perhaps I should have shared them first. But your strength has captivated me from the start. I suppose it's why I remind you of it now."

He's not bull shitting and it absolutely floors me. "You're really not from around here, are you?"

"I suppose not," he answers.

I reach for another flower and a few more after that. It's better than reaching for him and kissing him the way I really want to kiss him. "What about you?" I ask, shoving a rose between the others I placed. "Any brothers or sisters?"

"No. It's always just been me."

"I take it mom and dad discounted the rhythm method as an adequate mean of birth control." I laugh. "Unlike my parents."

My hands drop away from my work when I realize he's not laughing with me.

That trace of sadness he carries is barely visible enough to notice. But I do. "I'm sorry. I didn't mean to insult you."

"You didn't. My parents simply had different ideas." His mind seems to wander, but it's brief. "It's the reason I hope to have a large family one day." He chuckles. "If the time is ever right."

"I would think you'd want maybe two kids at best, seeing how it's not something you're used to."

He examines me. "Does this mean you don't want any, because it's something you know too well?"

"No, I want a million of them," I tell him, grinning.

"Is that so?" he asks.

"Yeah, there's sort of this unspoken motto in my family. Keep having them until you burst, or until your uterus drops to your ankles." I shake my finger at him. "That shit should be on a bumper sticker."

He drops his head and shakes it, all the while laughing. "We should add it to a T-shirt as well. I'll be sure to bring it next time instead of flowers."

"Next time?" I ask, lifting my brows. "I don't know, Evan. We haven't even gone out yet. I might piss you off, make you curse the day you met me, or send you running out of the restaurant screaming."

The smile he gives me is just as genuine as the last, but a whole lot sexier than the first. "I'll be the first to admit I don't know much about you," he says, hooking a strand of my hair and letting it slide through his finger. "But what I see is lovely," he adds, his gaze never leaving mine. "You don't piss me off, I'm more than glad we met, and there shall be no running. You're a breathtakingly beautiful woman, Wren. I want to know everything about you."

CHAPTER 7

Evan

I proved to Wren how much I wanted to know her over a five course meal I never wanted to end. I can't remember the last time I spoke at length to a woman I barely knew. But everything she had to say made me crave more.

I roll to a stop in front of her garage, barely managing to park with how hard I'm laughing as she shares another story from her childhood.

She slaps at my arm as I set my Explorer in park. "I'm serious," she says. "I'm like fifteen, Finn's thirteen, and the rest of my brothers are practically grown-ass adults. But holy shit, my mother and Grammie—God rest her soul—walk into the house, see half the neighborhood kids in the living room, and Angus lifting Seamus up for a keg stand, and it's like the world stops spinning and we know we're all fucked."

I cup my hand over my face, barely able to catch my breath. "Evan, my mother is five feet nothing and Grammie's osteoporosis had kicked in so bad by then, we could have legally registered her as a midget in thirty-two states. But they might as well have been mutant lumberjacks swinging axes by the way everyone was jumping out the windows, trying to get away. 'You're supposed to be in Florida,' Finn says like a dumbass, half a second before my mother grabs him by the throat."

"And what were you doing?" I manage, my hand falling away.

"What do you mean what was I doing? I was running for my life like everyone else!" She grips my arm. "Picture this, hordes—I'm talking hordes of teens racing down the street like some kind of freak evacuation. I was knocking people out of the way, speeding ahead, and Grammie still caught me—*by the hair!*"

The visual alone is enough to make me laugh uncontrollably.

"That tiny woman snatched me off the street, two blocks away, and dragged me back home, yelling that I was going to hell and begging the God Almighty not to strike me dead and take her with me." She holds out her arms and throws her head back, her voice morphing to that of an elderly woman with a thick Irish accent. "It's not me time, God. It's not me time, Jesus. Oh, sacred Mother, keep me from killin' this child."

I fall forward, holding onto the dash for the support.

"Just so you know, her prayers weren't answered," she says. "She still knocked me on my ass, *and* I spent the rest of the summer teaching the Sacraments to kids who looked like rejects from *The Grudge*." She makes a face. "But it was either that or be sent straight to a convent, so I went with the creepy kids and prayed I wouldn't find one lurking under my bed. God, I think at least two of them grew up and joined the circus or some shit."

I'm no longer laughing. You need air to laugh and I ran out long before this. "You think it's funny," she says, wagging her finger at me. "But you've never had your ass kicked by an old woman with ninja-like reflexes capable of wielding Catholic guilt like a light saber."

I wipe my eyes. My God, I don't think I've ever laughed this hard.

Wren could be a comedian, but she could also be a model if she wasn't busy ruling the car sales empire. As our laughter fades, once more the silence encompasses us.

I return her soft smile. This is simply one of many quiet moments we've shared this evening, where we simply watch each other, our eyes doing most of the speaking.

It should appear ridiculous, two grown adults taking each other in as we do. But I enjoy this side of her and I find myself torn between which of the Wrens I like best, the one who quietly regards me now, or the one who allows me to laugh and mean it.

I remind myself she's one in the same, and I don't have to choose. Perhaps that's what widens my smile.

"What are you thinking?" she asks. Her head falls against the seat rest. "I can usually read people pretty well, but I'll admit, you have me stumped."

I lift her hand, kissing it. "That I can't imagine a more perfect evening with a more beautiful woman."

"Did you read that shit somewhere?"

"What?"

She leans forward as if she's finally figured me out. "What you said has to be from a book, movie, or some poem no one but nerds have read."

My thumb grazes over the delicate skin along her jawline. "Why?" I ask.

"Because men don't say things like that and mean it."

"I do, but only to you." I wink. "Even though you think it's shit and called me a nerd."

"I didn't mean it that way. I just . . ." She shakes her head slowly. "You're a lot different from the men I've dated." Her voice softens, erasing almost all traces of her thick Philly accent. "But that's a good thing."

"I'm glad," I reply.

Again, silence takes hold. It's different this time, as if we reached a standstill.

"It's cold out here," she tells me. "Do you want to go inside and warm up?"

"I would." I switch off the ignition, holding her in place with my voice when she reaches for the door. "Wait until I come around."

"Why?" she asks.

"I want to open the door for you." I chuckle at her quizzical look. "It's what all decent men should do in the presence of a lady."

"You still consider me a lady?" she teases. "Even after all the swearing I've done?"

"Wren, there's no denying your vocabulary took me by surprise when we first met. But you don't curse to shock or intimidate. You're simply being true to who you are, and I very much like who you are."

She stills in place, her expression softening. "Thanks, Evan."

I frown slightly. "I haven't done anything."

"Yeah, you have," she tells me gently.

She averts her gaze, alerting me that a lot went unsaid in those simple words.

I want to question to her about it, but choose to open my door instead. The last thing I want is to make her uncomfortable. "Alfred, watch," I say, slipping out.

"Watching," Alfred answers.

I walk around and open the door for Wren. She hooks her thumb behind her as I help her out. "Our security system wasn't good enough for you?"

The lights flash, signaling Alfred's technology has activated the security system. "You've seen where I work and what I do," I say, offering her my arm. "Would you expect anything less of me?"

She leans her head against my shoulder, causing her hair to bunch and sending a whiff of her perfume into my nose. "No. But tell me this. Why Alfred? Are you secretly Batman?"

I angle my head. Her aroma is delicate, like gardenias following a spring shower. It makes me want to pull her closer. I wait instead, allowing her comment to makes me laugh as she intends. "If I was Batman, I couldn't tell you. A superhero must guard his secret identity at all costs."

She pulls out her key from her purse and opens the front door. "At all costs?" she asks. "So nothing I'd say or do will make you spill the location of the Bat Cave or give me a peek inside your utility belt?"

I follow behind her when she steps inside, shrugging out of my coat as I consider her comment. I dismiss it as innocent flirting as she clicks the lock behind me. "No, for the sake of Gotham and the world, I must protect my super secrets."

"Hmm, so you are Batman."

I chuckle and place my coat over the rail. I don't expect her to close the distance between us or to drop her coat off her shoulders in one slow seductive move.

That doesn't mean I object to what follows.

"Hi," she says, linking her arms around my neck, her voice barely above a whisper.

I don't feel my arms circle her waist. They're just suddenly there. What I do feel is the relentless desire to kiss her, something I can no longer deny myself.

My body curls forward, welcoming her tightly against me. Her lips are soft and silky, melting like sweet chocolate over mine. I push my tongue inside for a deeper taste, causing her to moan.

"Damn, Batman," she says when we come up for air.

We started out slow, getting a sense of each other, but as my mouth returns to her, a primal need I've never experienced erupts. My hands travel along her back and through her hair in smooth, quick motions, the force of my weight arching her back.

I think I should edge away, slow down, and not overwhelm her. But I can't stop and she won't let me.

Wren lifts her chin, exposing her throat for me to glide my tongue against. She shudders, but it's the gasp that accompanies my nibbles behind her ear that make me crave more than her skin.

Need. That's what this is. My need to touch Wren.

My hands slide down and around her back, returning to her waist to grip her hips. I leave her mouth to catch my breath. "Is this what you meant about coming inside and warming up?" I rasp against her ear.

Her breath hitches when my teeth skim along her jaw. "It's a start."

"A start?" My breath is ragged and my heart is battering my ribcage. I want more. But that can't be what she said, because women like Wren—gorgeous, intelligent, *sexy* women like her don't exist. Not in my reality.

She pulls away, her eyes glazing with raw desire. She lifts my coat from the rail, walking backward and up the stairs, her focus trained on mine.

"Come on," she says, smiling with enough sin to set me ablaze.

She's almost to the landing and I'm merely standing there, dumbstruck. This isn't real. It's a miscommunication of words, thoughts, desires—

"Evan?" she calls, her grin widening. "Are you trying to tell me I should sleep alone?"

I don't walk up the stairs. I run.

Two at time, that's how many steps I take, my body colliding against hers. This kiss is frantic and desperate, but also teasing and lustful. I morph into a horny teenager, grinding against her when she hooks her leg around my back.

The quick surge of lust between us isn't one I'm familiar with. Her head lolls back, sliding against the wall, her eyes scrunching tight as she swivels her hips with each measured movement of my groin.

"This feels so good," she mutters. I start to agree, but she cuts me off with, "Let's get naked."

My heart is no longer pounding. It's brutalizing my chest.

She bites down on my bottom lip, tugging it before staggering away and dragging me into her room.

She slams the door shut and locks it, rushing back into my embrace. My hands explore her, smoothing around her curves as we resume our kiss. They disappear beneath her skirt, stopping over the miniscule strip of silk covering her ass.

I want to strip her bare, and I do, starting with her dress despite my desire to tear her panties off in one bite. I hold back, lowering her zipper slowly as I watch her, giving her every opportunity to stop me.

I want to be sure this is what she wants. That *I'm* who she wants.

The dress falls in a crumpled mess at her feet, leaving her in her sexy, thigh high boots, panties I could stuff into a tin of mints, and a black see-through bra barely able to contain her puncturing nipples.

"You like what you see?"

I yank her forward, the yearning in her husky voice demanding I ravage her breasts.

She whimpers, aroused when my teeth clamp through the delicate mesh of her bra and graze over her nipples.

She pulls away enough to reach into her bedside drawer and remove a condom, then yanks me free of my belt. I reach around her to unhook her bra, pausing when fear sparks across her stare. My hands leave her back to cup her face. "What is it?" I ask, sweeping my thumb across her bottom lip.

She freezes, but then abruptly looks away and resumes her movements, tugging down my zipper. "Wren . . . I'm not going to hurt you. We can stop if that's what you want."

"I don't want to stop," she says, appearing to fight the doubt that lingers.

I lift her face, kissing her in delicate passes, taking my time until that fire between us builds.

Our skin heats, boiling my blood with ardor, but I don't push her. "Are you sure?" I ask between flicks from my tongue, careful to avoid touching her intimate areas.

"Yes," she tells me. Her head falls briefly to my shoulder. "Evan, I swear, it'll kill me if I have to stop touching you."

She falls to her knees, tugging my pants down with her, her hand disappearing into my briefs to grip my growing erection. She starts at the base, travelling up my lengthening staff in a twisting motion. I mumble a curse, my muscles tensing with each pass.

She freezes in place after another few strokes, her eyes widening as I thicken and stretch several more inches. She gasps with apparent shock. I'm almost embarrassed. Almost. She knows I have what it takes to please her. It's up to her to decide whether to let me.

As much as I desire her, I'll walk away if she's not ready.

She slides the condom in place, lifting her chin and meeting my face when she reaches the base. Any semblance of doubt is long past. All that remains is an impish gaze and an unspoken promise to fulfill my deepest fantasies.

I pull off my sweater and toss it aside, not wanting to miss a single moment. "I'll . . . I'll respect you in the morning," I say like an imbecile.

A wide smile claims her features. "Good," she says. "But it's not morning yet."

She licks her lips and opens her mouth wide. I don't move. I simply watch her take me deep.

"*Fuck*," I grunt, curling forward when I feel the back of her throat.

She pops me free from her mouth, strengthening her pulls. "Soon," she promises, dipping her head down and driving in deeper.

Burning desire engulfs me in an inferno. Every nerve from where she sucks is electrified and shooting jolts of blinding euphoria out to my limbs. My thighs tremble with the desire to pump, the yearning to release turning painful as she intensifies her suction and increases her speed.

But I meant what I said, I won't hurt her. That doesn't mean I'm not ready to take her.

I lift her hair away from her face. Her expression is erotic, licentious, yet astoundingly beautiful in her motions. She digs her nails into my hips, encouraging me to thrust and match her speed.

I spit out a slew of swears, ready to come, my heart seconds from detonating. But my need to please and taste her overshadows anything I want for myself. Like a flash of lightning, something switches in me, turning me more savage than man.

My hands wrench her up, lifting her for a sultry kiss as I free her from the last of her clothes. She barely has time to shake her boots off and peel off her socks when my fingers slip between her legs.

"Shit," Wren says, her head snapping backward as I push

in and swirl. I guide her to her bed, attacking her neck with my lips as I explore her slickening core.

Her back bounces off the mattress when we land. I move fast, trailing kisses down her body as I work her.

"Evan," she moans, her hips tilting rhythmically with my increasing speed.

Fucking hell, never has my name carried so much blatant sex.

My mouth pulls in her straining nipple as I kick off what remains of my clothes. My stare lifts to her face as I nibble, watching her skin redden when what remains of her composure abandons her in a crazed eruption.

I can't take it when she surrenders to the orgasm that follows. She's barely finished when another builds.

"Don't stop," she whimpers, rocking against my palm. "*Please*. You're so fucking hot."

Her words and actions spiral my aggression. My tongue circles her nipple and my mouth sucks harder, inciting guttural moans. Her legs jerk when she releases, but it's not enough for me. I prolong her orgasm, easing away when the quivering of her thighs finally recedes.

I ease up slowly, every part of me stiff and hard for her. Despite what I've given her, it's not enough. I want more.

I flip her onto her chest, lifting her lower body onto her knees. She bows her spine backward as I hover over her, meeting me with a grateful and generous kiss. My lips seduce her, passing slowly over her mouth, cheek, and neck as I tease her folds with my thick, throbbing tip.

"Are you ready for me?" I ask.

She trembles as my dense head glides along her velvety core. "Yes," she whispers, her lids lowering as I make my way in.

It takes time to fill her completely. I stretch her slowly, needing and wanting to make love to her. We groan when I finish pushing through. I angle her chin to see her, kissing her gently as I withdraw and thrust, gradually at first until I find the perfect rhythm.

Her head falls forward, appearing too heavy for her to

lift. I pound faster, adjusting my legs on either side of her, alternating from leaning over her with my legs straight and behind her, to bending on one knee, maintaining my pace. But the tighter her body clenches mine, the louder she becomes, and the more she rakes her nails across the sheets, the more I change positions and drive deeper.

I've never taken a woman like this. But I've also never felt this degree of passion. I'm listening to her body, allowing it to guide me, to show me what she needs to draw out her pleasure and make her scream with bliss.

As hard and fast as I'm going, I can't stop touching her, kissing her, my mouth tasting every part of her skin I can reach.

My legs bend on either side of her, crouching low as I grip her hips, my pelvis ramming and the sounds of our lovemaking filling the room.

"Jesus, Evan," she cries out. "*Fuck*."

I'm not groaning, or swearing. The animalistic urges she awakens have me roaring. Pain mixes with pleasure in an escalating wave I'm fighting to suppress. But when her body bucks beneath mine and clamps down, I unravel, my release tearing out of me.

My palms smack down on either side of her, barely keeping me from falling on top of her. I can't catch my breath and neither can she, her shoulders rising and falling harshly. But like before, I don't want to stop kissing her.

I ease out, cursing and hating the separation as I lower myself to her side. I clasp the back of her neck, seeking her mouth.

"Damn," she whispers, smiling against my lips when I finally pull away.

"That's one way to put it," I murmur, nuzzling her neck. I slow the tease of my tongue to speak. "Are you all right with everything I did to you?"

"No," she admits.

"No?" I ask, stopping immediately.

She shakes her head slowly, her eyes feverishly glazed. "Uh-uh. I want more."

Wren scrambles on top of me into a straddle, fisting her hair out of her way so she can do our next kiss justice.

We kiss for what seems like forever, but I'm finding nothing between us is ever long enough.

"Evan," she says, pausing to lick the tip of my tongue. "You blew me away, baby." She scans my face in that way she does when she's trying to gauge my thoughts. "Any regrets?"

"None." I push away the hair she releases. Not because it's in the way, but because I enjoy the feel. Like me, her skin is soaked with sweat and equally heated. "Do you want to take our shower now?" I ask.

She tilts her head as if unsure what I'm asking. "A shower?" she repeats. She circles my chest with her nails, appearing to give it some thought. "I guess that can be hot. But why don't you make me a little more dirty first?"

Bloody hell, this woman can't possibly be real.

The sensuality in her gaze surges as she replaces the condom and glides her pelvis over my groin. My spine arches and that stabbing desire to enter her returns.

"You like that, don't you?" She laughs as she lowers her weight and repeats the motion. "Yeah, you do," she says, her lashes fluttering as I continue to harden.

All it takes is a few passes for me to become fully erect. She grips the headboard with one hand to keep her balance, reaching between us with her opposite hand. Her eyes ram shut as we merge. I hang onto her hips, steadying her as she falls to one knee, my hands shaking from the flow of adrenaline coursing through my cells.

But as her body lowers onto my lap, there's no hesitation. She moves quickly, alternating from bouncing to circling. I shove up into a sitting position, hooking her waist with my arm to help maintain her pace. She rewards me by pitching backward and offering a breast to suck. I draw it deep into my hot mouth while my fingers tug and roll her other nipple.

Wren cradles my head against her as our audible sounds take over the small confines of her bedroom. "That's it, baby," she whimpers, clutching me closer. "Show me how bad you want me."

CHAPTER 8

Evan

I turn my head slightly, my closed eyes scrunching when my neck kinks. All I want is to sleep, yet as I blink my eyes open and see strands of tousled black hair draped across my chest, I'm suddenly wide awake.

Last night was more of a dream. A perfect evening spent in the company of the most magnetic woman I've ever met. But what followed dinner . . . *Fuck*. I don't make swearing a habit, but no other word can describe what occurred more precisely.

My hand skims down her spine to rest against her lower back, a reminder to myself that she's as real as every kiss and touch we shared.

When I was young, the term "all night long" was referenced repeatedly by my peers, leaving me with the impression it was the sexual standard I should expect and look forward to. When I actually began having sex, "once a night" followed by a polite thank you was more realistic given the women I associated with.

Wren proved "all night long" is possible and ridiculously hot. I put her in positions I would have believed were improbable. She responded in turn, her motions sensual and encouraging, allowing me to lead her in an erotic escapade of sweating and swearing bodies and flailing limbs.

Everything about my time with her was different. We spoke and laughed at length, permitting me to know her on a personal level before she took me into her bedroom and allowed me to commit every aspect of her body to memory.

I stroke her hair when she stirs against me. Even the way she sleeps is different.

My last two lovers would be buried beneath the covers, the more recent one already dressed. Wren and I lie naked. What's left of the bedsheets spilled over the corner of the bed.

The strands of her hair slip through my fingers as she lifts off me, her eyes swollen from lack of sleep. But when she smiles her delicate features brighten, beckoning me closer.

"Hi," she says, tugging on my bottom lip with her teeth as I break our kiss.

"Good morning," I tell her, returning her smile.

She climbs on top of me, bending her knees on either side of me as she stretches and yawns. Her breasts lift, the tips pointing to the ceiling as she arches back. It's a sight that stills me in place, but that familiar ache surged the moment she straddled me.

Her hair falls forward as she looks down between us. She laughs, leaning in to kiss me. "Well, hello there," she says, wiggling her hips. "Looks like the big boss is up."

Perhaps I should be embarrassed how easily she arouses me, but like last night and very early this morning, my body simply responds to hers.

My hands skim past her small waist to cup her breasts and knead them. She covers them with hers and links our fingers, her grin sensually wicked. "Come on," she says, reaching for another condom and pulling me in the direction of her bathroom. "Let's get that shower you were talking about . . ."

We stumble out of her glass shower about an hour later. I barely keep my feet with her wrapped around me. Her bathroom is quite small, fortunately. I manage to grip the edge of the sink to keep us from falling.

We laugh as we straighten, her eyes shimmering as she fumbles through a drawer. She passes me a toothbrush and reaches for her own. I don't quite have the package open when she pinches my ass.

"I knew you had it in you."

Without thinking, my stare travels below my waist.

"I didn't mean that," she says, laughing. She shakes her toothbrush at me. "*That* was a very big and very nice surprise." She glances down, taking her time to look at me before adding toothpaste to her toothbrush. "What I meant was, I knew you were a beast beneath all that business."

I pause in the middle of squeezing the paste she hands me. "A beast?"

"Uh, *yeah*," she replies as if stating the obvious. "Last night was totally hot. Honest to God, I didn't know I was that flexible."

"Nor did I," I admit. I lean toward the sink, thinking back to everything we did and how our bodies reacted. She called me a beast. Perhaps I was, but it's her allure that set the beast free of his cage.

Wren is a woman comfortable with her sensuality. She's daring and fearless, allowing herself to enjoy sex without reservations. It's why I could respond with such fervor and the reason I couldn't do enough to please her. I thrived on each passionate scream and inviting tease of her hands, and most especially how she couldn't have enough of me.

"I'm excited you didn't drown." She points at the shower. "Considering what you did to me in there."

I chuckle, not bothering to explain that death by drowning would be worth everything I was doing to her. We consumed each other, but it's the way her eyes met mine as I lifted her against the tile that momentarily held me in place. She wanted me . . . and she trusted me.

We steal glances as we brush our teeth, our smiles never wavering. She gathers a few towels as I finish rinsing my mouth, passing me one as I straighten.

"Thank you," I tell her

"Evan," she says, watching me as I towel off. "About last night."

I don't like the shift in her tone, or how she gathers a robe around herself, appearing to shield her body from mine. She was so open, exposing herself freely until now.

"Yes?" I ask when she fails to speak.

"It's not something I do." She reaches for a comb and works it through her thick wet hair, growing abruptly silent.

The tension drifting between us isn't something I'm used to around her. I finish toweling off, waiting for her to speak.

She pauses with the comb in her hand, her thumb passing along the teeth. "I don't have one night stands. Ever," she says meeting my face. "And I sure as hell don't sleep with men I barely know." She sighs. "But you . . . you made it too easy."

I've seen enough horrific movies with dominant male leads who'd brush aside a comment like this, or perhaps use it to their advantage. But I'm not one of those men. I let the towel fall at my feet and step forward, my hands finding her hips and pulling her to me. "You made it easy for me, too," I admit.

"Because of the blow job?" she teases.

"No," I respond. "Because of you."

My comment draws her smile. "See, here you go again, making things easy."

"Good," I reply. "That's how I want things between us."

The kiss I give her is brief, allowing her the space I think she needs. I'm exhausted and sexually spent. Yet if she wanted, I'd carry her back to bed.

I imagine she guesses as much when she closes her eyes briefly and sighs. Rather than questioning my intent, she reaches for a bottle of lotion, warming it in her hands before passing it along my shoulders. "Do you do that a lot?" she asks.

"Sleep with a woman I just met?" I shake my head slowly when she nods. "My position in my company keeps me busy. The few women I've met work directly for me, and I assure you, none have sparked my interest."

"None?" she asks.

"Not like you have," I confess. I stroke her face. "It's been a long time since I enjoyed the company of a woman."

She tries to hide her smile as her slick hands massage the length of my arm, but I catch it nonetheless. "How long is long?"

I consider her question. "About ten months."

She stops as she reaches for my hand and glances up. "*You* haven't had sex in ten months?"

"Why do you find it so hard to believe?" I ask.

She reaches for the bottle of lotion. "Because you're cute," she says.

"Cute?"

"And smart, successful, and sexier than hell. I'm surprised you don't open up your office every morning to find a naked woman sprawled across your desk, wearing a smile and nothing else."

"I assure you that's never happened," I say chuckling. "The success of my company means everything to me. With the hours I keep and the work I do, it's a rarity to meet women like you."

"Loud women like me?" she offers.

"I mean mesmerizing," I tell her, because it's true. "And unique and kind."

She groans. "There you go again," she says. "Making it too easy to like you."

"I like you, too," I remind her.

I don't want that strain between us to return, but I want to know where I stand. "What about you? How long has it been since you spent the night with a man?"

She places the empty bottle aside and reaches for another one beneath the sink. It's a casual response, but I can't help thinking it's an excuse to turn away from me. "Over a year."

"You can't be serious."

She squeezes my arm playfully. "I'm not as easy as you think I am."

"That's not what I'm saying."

"Then what are you saying?" She turns around, applying lotion to my back in long, careful strokes.

"That you've had opportunities to meet men and that only a fool would ignore you."

In the quiet that follows, her thoughts appear to drift. Her hands move to my lower back, continuing her massage of my skin. "I'm going to give you a little TMI about me," she says, after a long moment. "Are you ready?"

"Go on."

Her fingers tense along my muscles. "The last relationship I had was bullshit," she says. "I wasn't exactly ready or willing to go through that again. I was asked out a few times, but it was by the same idiots I've been trying to avoid. I was tired of the attitudes and expectations, so instead of giving in, I've spent the last year alone." She presses a kiss between my shoulder blades. "What about you? When was your last relationship?"

I want to probe more about her last experience. But I'm not insensitive. It's clear she's still troubled by what occurred. "In London, I dated someone for three years," I confess. "And before her, a woman just slightly over two."

"Five years' worth of relationships before last night? Damn. I don't even keep shoes that long." She waits, then asks, "Were you engaged to either of them?"

I quiet, remembering. "No. The first was more casual. We were young, both of us looking more for someone to pass our free time with rather than commit to anything serious. The last woman, I thought marriage would eventually be our next step. But things never felt like they should."

"What do you mean?" she asks.

I reach for the towel and tie it around my waist. "It wasn't a relationship, exactly. At least not in the traditional sense. For all the years we shared, our moments together were brief. She travelled extensively, attending lavish parties while I worked and dedicated myself to my research. We'd see each other on occasion, but then return to our respective lives."

"Why didn't you travel with her?"

Wren isn't judging me. She's honestly confused by what I tell her. "I was committed to developing new technology and teaching myself to run an empire. I didn't have time to engage in that lifestyle. Initially I tried, in order to spend time with her, but the parties were too much."

"Why?"

"They weren't real." I'm surprised how quickly I answer and how much truth lies in those simple words. "They were events thrown solely to boast and display wealth."

"But that didn't seem to bother her."

Again, despite that we're discussing my former lover, she's not judging her. She's trying to understand the world I was born into, but never wanted to be a part of.

"No, it didn't," I admit. "This was how she was raised. She didn't work and didn't have to. Enjoying life was her job."

"I don't fault her," I clarify when a small wrinkle forms between her eyebrows. "It's simply who she is. The last time I saw her was several months ago."

"The last time you had sex, I take it?"

I nod. "I hadn't seen her in several weeks. But instead of feeling closer to her, I realized there was nothing there. At least, not enough to keep me."

"What was her name?"

"What?" I heard the question. It just seems odd for her to ask. Given how primal I become around Wren, I don't want her speaking a lover's name except my own.

"What was her name?" she asks again.

"Saundra," I reply.

"Did Saundra feel the same way…that it was time to move on?"

As much as I don't want to keep discussing my former relationship, I don't want to hide anything from Wren. "No. She was ready for the next step she presumed was coming."

She makes a face. "Oh. I guess that didn't end well then, did it?"

"Not at all." I gather her to me and kiss her forehead. "But it could have ended worse had I given into what her family and, I suppose society, expected from us. I'll admit, the termination of our relationship left me bitter. Not because of what I didn't get, but because of what never was." I stroke her chin. "Does that make sense?"

"You wasted your time," she concludes.

"We both did," I agree.

Her head falls against me, her wet hair soaking my shoulder. It should feel uncomfortable, but I like her close to me.

We laugh when our stomachs simultaneously growl. "Are you hungry?" I ask.

"Considering how many calories we burned last night and this morning? I could eat a damn cow."

"How about I make you breakfast?" I offer.

"Yeah?" At my nod she adds. "You're all sorts of hot, you know that?"

She clutches me when I bend and kiss her. Like all the kisses we've shared, it quickly turns heated.

She groans, pulling away. "Food now, dessert later, okay?"

"Later?" I ask, still struggling to grasp this woman is real.

"Oh, hell yeah. You think you're getting away from me that easy?" She turns toward the sink. "Help yourself downstairs. I'll be down as soon as I'm ready."

"All right," I say, stealing one last kiss.

I return to her bedroom and yank on my briefs and my trousers, not bothering with a sweater.

The wood floors and the kitchen tile feel cool against my bare soles despite how warm the house is.

I'm taken aback when I open the stainless steel refrigerator and find it packed with an outrageous amount of meat and vegetables. I dismiss it as a healthy appetite until I'm almost done frying the bacon and a shirtless young man with reddish blond hair wanders into the kitchen.

He takes a seat on the opposite side of the counter.

"Hey," he says. "Oh. *Bacon.*"

He reaches for two slices on top of the pile I placed on a plate. "I'm Finn," he says, ramming the bacon in his mouth and offering me a hand. "You a friend of Wren's?"

"Ah, yes. I'm Evan," I answer, shaking his hand.

I freeze when a young woman stepping into the doorway comes to an abrupt halt. She's in a T-shirt that appears too big on her and nothing else. Apparently, she's just as stunned to find me here as I am to see her.

"Hey, *Evan*," Finn says. "That's my woman you're looking at."

I turn abruptly as she races down the hall. "My apologies," I say. "I wasn't aware Wren had roommates."

"I'm not her roommate. I'm her brother." He frowns. "You don't sound like you're from around here. You visiting from Alaska or something?"

"I've spent the last few years in England," I reply slowly.

"Close enough," he says, reaching for another piece of bacon.

The young woman returns in sweatpants she appears to be swimming in. I'm assuming they are Finn's clothes, now that I'm aware she's his "woman".

She finger combs her blond highlights through her darker hair. "Hey, I'm Sol," she says, reaching for a stack of plates and bringing them to the counter.

"Evan," I say. "It's a pleasure to meet you."

"Nice to meet you, too," she says. She makes a face. "Sorry, we didn't know anyone was home."

"It's all right, and I apologize. I didn't realize anyone was here as well."

"Don't worry about it," she says. She fumbles through the drawer and removes several sets of utensils. "Do you need help getting brunch ready?"

"I'm fine, thank you." I turn and reach for the bagels I'm toasting. If I gave it some thought, I'll admit she's an attractive young woman, petite yet curvy. But I can't give it much thought, not when all my thoughts return to Wren. Shit. I never expected to meet her family like this.

I place the bagels where Sol laid out cream cheese, butter, and a pitcher of orange juice. "Looks yummy," she says, reaching for a bagel.

"Thank you." I keep busy, worried I left the wrong impression. However as Finn and Sol relax, the strain of our encounter lifts as quickly as it began.

There are six stools placed across the long counter. Instead of taking one of them, Sol walks to Finn's side. Without blinking or leaving his food, he pulls her onto his lap. Given the bulk in his muscles, I suppose it's not much of an effort. Yet it's the ease in which they demonstrate affection that impresses me.

In all the years Saundra and I were together, we were never this comfortable around each other, let alone in the presence of strangers. "How long have you been together?" I ask.

"Almost a year," Sol answers, glancing a Finn.

He squeezes her hip. "That long?" he asks.

He laughs when she nudges him playfully, stealing a kiss when she tries to close the lid to the cream cheese container.

A year and still going strong. Perhaps love isn't the impossibility I believe it to be.

"Hey, Evan? You gonna fry up some sausage to go with that bacon?" When he grins, I see the resemblance between he and Wren. "Can't have bacon and no sausage. You hear what I'm saying, man?"

I chuckle. "Of course."

The whole thing is bizarre. I'm standing here, shirtless, having spent the most incredible night of my life with a woman whose family I'm currently feeding. Yet there's no tension.

The front door crashes open and voices drift in from the foyer. "Finn, Wren, where the hell are you?" a deep baritone calls out.

"Stop cursin'. It's the Lord's day for fuck's sake," a shrill woman's voice responds.

Finn and Sol barely react. "In the kitchen," Finn yells through a mouthful of bacon.

Rumblings fill the hallway as bodies in varying sizes pile into the kitchen, every one of them abruptly silencing when they find me standing here.

There's that tension that was missing.

A large man with dark hair and big meaty hands scowls in my direction, but he's not alone. Every gigantic man on either side of him with shades of blue eyes, and wavy and straight dark hair, (the blond, buzzed cut male with a gun strapped to his hip the exception) is glaring at me.

"Who da fuck are you?" the first man says, dropping an aluminum foil tray on the counter beside him.

Finn rolls his eyes. "Relax, Angus," he tells him. "He's a friend of Wren's."

"A *friend*?" a younger and slimmer version of Angus growls. "What kind of *friend* takes his shirt off in front of our little sister?"

Echoes of agreement flow around the room, and suddenly the kitchen feels much smaller.

"I'm going to kick your ass," Angus says, storming forward.

A heavy set woman with ginger curls spilling down her back hurries forward, blocking him and the other man. "What the hell do you think you're doing?" she screams at Angus, her already shrill voice rising an octave. "Seamus, I swear to God you better stay put," she adds, pointing to the second man when he lunges.

Angus deepens his scowl, as does Seamus, but neither dare move. "Finn, da hell?" Seamus yells. "You going to put up with this asshole disrespecting Wren?"

Finn eases Sol to the floor. "Hold on a second, will you, babe?"

Sol tosses her bagel on the counter, scrambling in front of him and placing her palms against his broad chest. "Wait, what are you doing?"

"I'm gonna kick his ass," he says, as if it's the only obvious alternative.

"You're seriously going to kick his ass?" At his nod, her eyes widen and she points frantically to his abandoned plate. "But-but he made you bacon."

Finn glances at the plate and back at his brothers, appearing torn. "Yeah, but that's before I knew he disrespected Wren." He shrugs. "I kind of have to, now."

"I didn't disrespect her," I say. My words fall on deaf ears and I very well expect to die until a pregnant blonde woman hurries forward with a child perched on her hip.

"Take the baby," she says, shoving the tiny version of herself into my arms.

"Tess, what are you doing?" the man with the gun and the buzzed blond hair asks, stepping forward.

Tess adjusts her small black glasses. I'm not acquainted with her at all, but considering how the man stiffens at her response, she means business. "Curran," she begins. "As an officer of the law—"

"Here we go," Angus says, rolling his eyes and cutting her off.

"Did you say something, Angus?" Tess fires back. She's not yelling, yet her tone is as absolute as a headmistress wielding a ruler.

"Ah, no," he replies, finding someplace else to look.

"I didn't think so," Tess replies. She edges slightly away, allowing a very thin woman with long black curls to take point beside me and opposite Sol. "As I was saying, Curran, as an officer of the law and a member of the public sector, do you want to be privy to an angry mob, made up of *your brothers,* attacking an unarmed man who had consensual sex with your sister?"

"Oh." "Whoa!" "Yo!" the group of men collectively yell.

"That's our sister you're talking about," Curran reminds her.

"Your *adult* sister," Tess reminds *him.*

Curran clamps down on his jaw. But then his muscles relax as he appears to give in. "She's right," he says. My shoulders drop. "I can't watch this." I release a breath. "Give me the baby. I'll be outside."

"Wait, *what*?" Tess asks.

He shrugs. "Can't be privy if I'm not here to see it, babe."

Everyone lunges forward at once, except the women who hold their ground, and the baby in my arms cooing and appearing entertained by it all.

"What the fuck?" Wren yells, rushing in.

Her long hair is dripping wet and she's only wearing a towel, stopping everyone in place.

Everyone.

CHAPTER 9

Wren

I shove my way between the wall of muscle that is Killian and Finn, holding tight to my towel. Poor Evan is standing behind the counter with my niece in his arms and his jaw hanging open. Sol and Sofia ease away when I reach him and round on my brothers. "Seriously, I can't take a damn shower without you bozos picking a fight with my date."

"Date?" Angus bellows, motioning to my towel. "Since when do dates involve getting naked and taking showers?"

"Not my fault you haven't had sex in two non-fucking years," I answer just as sweetly.

Molly huffs. "Not my fault either," she says, rolling her eyes.

"Seriously, Wren?" Killian tells me.

As a retired professional fighter, and the biggest of the brood, he doesn't have to yell to be heard. Not with his deep voice. That doesn't make me any less pissed. "Seriously, what?" I ask. "I'm not doing anything you guys—except for Angus—don't do all the time. And what the hell are all of you even doing here? You're supposed to be in New York."

"The press conference got cancelled," Finn answers. He reaches for a piece of bacon, appearing to settle, with food so close to him. "Main card and their camps got into a fight.

Everyone got kicked out of the hotel and we came home." He cocks his head. "Didn't you get our texts?"

I shake out a hand. "Nah, I was too busy having sex."

I ignore the hollers, protests, and choruses of "what the fucks" and reach for my niece. "Hi, Fiona," I say lifting her from Evan's arms. She immediately starts to babble. "I know, I know, your daddy and uncles are out of control, but you still have Auntie Wren looking out for you. Oh, yes, you do."

"Hey," Curran snaps. "Don't talk to my kid like that. We're just trying to do the right thing."

I grin. "Says the man who knocked up his wife out of wedlock."

Tess reaches for Fiona when I turn. And even though she laughs, I can't tell whose face is redder, hers or Curran's. It doesn't matter, at least not now. I reach for Evan's hand. "Come on, let's get back upstairs."

More "what the fucks" followed by a couple of "you have to be shittin' mes". I lead Evan around the island, my chin jutting out when Killian cuts in front of me.

"Really?" I ask.

"Wren, this isn't like you," he counters.

"Which part?" I ask.

"Parading half naked guys in the kitchen in front of women and children," he responds, his deep voice more like thunder.

"Would you rather I parade him in the living room?" I offer.

"You're pissing me off," he says.

"Am I?" I have to crane my neck since like I said, he's the biggest, and as a former champion title holder, probably the baddest. But I don't crane it for long, stealing a glance over my shoulder. "Hey, Sofia," I call. "You going to put up with your man being all rude like this to his baby sister?"

Sofia's willowy frame appears as she glides around the dense crowd of bodies, her long mane of curls almost as wide as she is. I don't have to see Sol to know she's seconds from laughing her ass off. They may be cousins, but Sol always lets her presence be known. Sofia is more like an apparition, her motions as subtle as her reaction. She knits her brow in disapproval. It doesn't seem like much, but seeing how Kill's loved her since before he got pubes, it's enough.

"Killian," she says, keeping her voice soft. "Be nice."

His stare, which up until now could have sent a pack of pit bulls running, softens. He steps out of our way, allowing us through.

Of course, my brothers aren't going to let me go that easy. They file out behind us. We don't make it halfway up the stairs before Angus starts up again.

"This isn't over," he yells.

I point at him. "Just for that I'm going to straddle him when we get back to my room."

More hollers, more cursing, more threats. I shut my bedroom door behind me, doing little to muffle their loud and irate grumbling.

My back smacks against the door as I fall against it, covering my face. "God, I'm so sorry."

I drop my hands away to find Evan pinching the bridge of his nose. I want to kiss him and make it up to him, but mostly, I'm waiting for him to bolt. Given all the crazy waiting downstairs to have brunch, I would.

He lowers his hand when I reach him. "I was getting ready when I realized I still had shampoo in my hair." Like an ass, I motion to the bathroom, not that he's looking. "If I'd known they were coming, I never would have left you alone." My voice fades when I realize he's smiling. "You're smiling," I point out.

He chuckles. "I just met your entire family."

"Not really. There're still a few hundred more," I admit.

"It's not what I expected," he says.

I raise my head, feeling defensive. "They're good people," I tell him. "They're just not used to me having anyone here, let alone a naked someone here."

"That's not what I mean," he tells me gently. "It's clear that they love you and are only watching out for your best interests. I just expected to meet them over time."

"Over time?" I ask, barely believing it. "You're planning

to stick around? After all that?"

"I told you. I like you."

There he goes again, being sweet. This guy can't be real. But when he gathers me to him and kisses me, I remind myself that he totally is.

I stroke his five o'clock shadow, it's light but dark enough to give him an edge. If the angry mob downstairs weren't waiting to chow down on eggs and potatoes, I might hold off on replenishing my calories and burn a few more.

"We'll see how you feel after brunch."

"Brunch?" he asks.

"We have brunch as a family at least once a month. It was supposed to be next week, but I guess they moved it up when they were kicked out of the hotel—not that the news of my family getting kicked out of anywhere should shock you."

I laugh when he doesn't move. "Come on," I say. "You made it this far. Let's get dressed and see if we can survive the rest."

"All right," he agrees.

"Yeah?"

"Why not? Like you said, I made it this far," he adds with a wink.

The girls have my back, just like I have their's. By the time Evan and I are dressed and make it downstairs, they've set up the dining room and are laying out the food. Oh, and look at this, with the exception of Evan, all the men have been herded to one side. Like I said, my girls have my back.

None of my brothers are smiling, except for Finnie. But there's bacon and Sol sitting in front of him so that's all he needs. "Pass the potatoes, will ya, babe?" he tells her.

She lifts the dish filled with hash browns.

"The hell, Finnie," Angus snaps. "Is that all you've got to say?"

Finn thinks about it. "Oh, yeah. The ketchup, too." He looks at Molly. "You brought ketchup, right Mol? We're all out."

"It's to your right, Finnie," Molly says. She scowls when Angus glares. "You know, I'm sick of all youz being pissy. Wren here's done nothing wrong."

"Thanks, Molly," I say, knowing she's not going to stop there.

"So she had some stud bend her over," she continues.

"Dear God," Evan says, pausing with the fork halfway to his mouth when more swears erupt around the table.

I reach for my napkin, trying not to crack up when Molly goes full speed ahead like only she and her Edith Bunker voice can. "She's got needs. We all do," she glances around the table. "Am I right, ladies?"

"Please leave us out of this," Sofia says, her face as red as the ketchup she hands Finn.

Her reaction causes Killian to smirk her way. Not that she sees it, seeing how her face is buried in her hands.

"All's I'm saying is every now and then we could use a little hair pullin' and some spanking." She spoons an extra helping of eggs onto her plate. "I mean do you have *any* idea how long it's been since Angus bent me over?"

"No. And please don't tell us," Seamus says, looking a little green.

"I can see that," Finn says, digging into his food. "What?" he asks, meeting my brothers' reprimanding frowns. "Don't get me wrong, I don't need a visual of Angus' big ass driving it home-"

"Oh!" We all groan except for Angus, who's smiling for the first damn time since he got here.

"I'm just saying women need their share of us," Finn adds. He points at Sol with his fork. "Take Sol for instance."

Sol's jaw pops open, a strand of highlighted blond hair falling in front of her face with how fast she looks up. "What do you mean *take Sol*?"

"I'm just saying if you don't get some—"

"If *I* don't get some?" she shrieks. "Seriously, Finn?"

"Baby, it's okay," Finn offers apologetically. "We all know how bad you want me."

"Finn, last night on the drive home you're the one who-"

She shuts her mouth abruptly when she realizes we're all looking at her, except for Sofia, who's all but shrinking beneath the table.

Finn grins. "You're welcome," he adds with a wink.

"Been there," Curran says, nodding like he understands. "What?" he asks, looking up at Tess from where he's feeding Fiona. "Isn't that how I knocked you up last time?"

Tess smiles, but I wouldn't call it friendly. Hell, I wouldn't even call it human. "Can we all just eat? Please?" she asks.

"Only if you make it up to me later," Curran replies, not missing a beat.

Tess pretends to narrow her stare, but can't quite suppress her smile. "Is it a wonder I'm expecting an Irish twin?" she mumbles.

"Nope." "Nah." "No," my brothers and I reply at once.

"So, *Evan*," Killian says, his deep voice more challenging than cordial. "What do you do?"

Evan's stare travels around the table before answering, well aware all eyes are on him. "I'm CEO of iCronos."

And cue the deafening silence in three, two, one . . .

"Is that a real job?" Finn asks. At Sol's nod, Finn returns to his food, appearing satisfied. "Cool."

"It's a robotics and technology company," Evan begins.

"We know what it is," Killian says, glancing at Sofia. "We use the security system at our gym and the malware protection on our software."

"And we use the phone systems and computer technology at the District Attorney's office," Tess adds. Her attention latches onto Curran's. They don't seem worried, exactly, but it's like Evan just proved how different he is with one blow.

Thing is, I see it, too, and it's not just because of where he works.

I stand when my family finishes off the first casserole dish. Evan stands, too. I think it's safe to leave him and give him a wink. "I'll be right back," I tell him.

"Bring back some more orange juice, will ya, Wren?" Angus tells me.

He's going to town on the waffles, assuring me he's done provoking my brothers and targeting Evan, at least for the moment. "Sure, Angus."

I don't expect Sol to follow me into the kitchen. Scratch that, yes, I do. "*Wren*," she says, beaming. "He's cute."

I rinse out the aluminum dish at the sink, trying not to grin and doing a shitty job. "I know."

"And employed—with like, a *real* job," she says.

"Oh, come on, Sol," I say. "The losers I've dated have at least had jobs."

I open the door leading out to the porch and dump the tray into the recycling bin. I shut the door slowly when I catch the way she's looking at me. "Evan's not a loser," she points out, like I don't already know.

"No, he's not," I agree, quietly. I place my palms on the granite counter and bow my head. "Did you hear us last night?"

Her eyes widen as she hurries forward to whisper. "No, did you hear us?"

I grimace. "No, and don't go there. That's my little brother you're talking about."

She giggles. "I get it. And believe me, I'm not going to shake the visual of Angus and Molly any time soon."

"Neither will I," I say, making a face.

I wash my hands and fill another pitcher of orange juice. Evan and I had sex. Lots of it. Lots of *amazing* sex. He's decent with a great job and an even better personality. And he already met my brothers. Jesus God, how the fuck did all this happen? I've only known him a handful of days.

Sol comes around the island and leans her back against the counter. "What's wrong? He's nice."

"I just met him, Sol. We've been out twice and already spent the night doing it like the zombie apocalypse came and went and it's up to us to repopulate the human race or whatever the fuck. Things are moving way faster than I'm used to."

She gives me a one shoulder shrug. "So slow them down."

"Slow them down? Aren't you listening? We had enough sex to make up for the year I went without it, and right now he's in *my dining room* sitting down and eating a meal with *my family*. I think it's a little too late to shift into park."

"I'm not saying come to a full stop," she says slowly. "Not that either of you could swing it." She laughs when I frown. "In case you didn't notice, he can't keep his eyes off you. He likes you, Wren."

"I like him, too," I admit, wishing it didn't suck to say it. "But he's a corporate giant and I'm me."

"And I'm studying for my doctorate in psychology and Finn's a fighter." She holds out her hands. "Doesn't mean I don't love him."

"I didn't say anything about love," I remind her.

I tug the long sweater I'm wearing over my skinny jeans, ready to head back to Evan. But Sol's question keeps me in place.

"So it's been a year, huh?"

Shit. She had to go there.

"Since Bryant then?" When I quiet, she leans in, lowering her voice. "Wren, what did he do to you?"

"Nothing worth mentioning," I say. She doesn't believe me, not with the way her features shadow with disappointment. But as assertive and Philly as Sol can be, she's also kind and respectful. She knows I'm not ready to say more.

"Okay," she tells me cautiously.

I sigh when she continues to eye me. "Come on," I say. "I have to get back to Evan before he runs out of here screaming."

She smiles softly. "I hate to break it to you, Wren, but I don't think he's going anywhere."

I'm not sure if that's good or bad. Not with how screwed up this last year has been. But I can't admit as much to Sol. She's a professional counselor, but she's my friend and my brother's girlfriend first. She wouldn't hesitate to run to Finn or my family if she thought I was in trouble. And Bryant is definitely trouble.

"Maybe," I say, trying to play off what I'm feeling. "But only because he has manners, unlike the rest of us."

I walk back into the dining room with Sol trailing me. Evan stands when he sees me, and I'm sure he's ready to tell me he has to go. But then he smiles, and sits when I sit, staying for the remainder of the meal and quietly observing the rest of us lunatics mouthing off.

"Fuck you, Angus."

"For shit's sake, it was the best play of the night!"

"Get your head out of your hairy ass."

"Did you not see the fight? He came out swinging."

"God damn it. It's the Lord's Day, watch your mouths."

Believe it or not, this is typical mealtime conversation. At least at my house, with my family. I have to say, the "hairy ass" comment gives Evan pause. But even with that little tidbit, it's only when brunch and clean up are done that he tells me he needs to leave.

Even then, it's like he doesn't want to.

I walk him to his SUV, my fists balling into my heavy coat, wishing he didn't have to go. God, what's wrong with me? I *just* met the guy.

"You seem quiet," he tells me.

"Are you saying I'm incapable of shutting my mouth?"

"Yes," he says, making us both laugh.

We stop in front of his driver's side door. "When can I see you, again?" he asks, gathering me into a cozy embrace.

"You still want to see me? After all that?" I turn my head in the direction of the house. The TV is blasting and I can still hear my family yapping away, trying to out-yell each other.

"I do," he says.

He bends forward, kissing me sweetly. Well, it starts off sweet. But when it switches to something hotter and tastier, and my womanly parts tighten and tingle, I'm reminded why I'm so freaking tired and not exactly walking straight.

"You're a great kisser," I murmur when he pulls away.

"Mmm," he responds, giving my jawline equal attention.

"With damn fine lips," I add.

My breath catches when he reaches my ear. I did the

same thing last night when he climbed on top of me, thrusting hard as he showered me with sultry kisses.

"I can't have sex with you with my family inside," I add when those damn fine lips trail down my throat.

"I think your brothers made that perfectly clear," he mutters, nipping my chin.

He dips his mouth to the sweep of my neck, making me shudder. But when he straightens and tucks a strand of my hair behind my ear, I can't help my smile.

I adjust my hold around his neck. "Do you want to stop by tomorrow night? I can't cook, but we can order in."

His features respond apologetically. "I can't. I have a very busy week ahead, I'm afraid."

"Oh," I say, thinking I know where this is headed.

"But I'd like to see you if I can." His hands glide to my lower back. "I realize it's not ideal, but I have some free time around lunch. I can't leave the office, but we can order in, as you suggested."

He's trying, but I'm starting to doubt whether any of this can work. "I don't know if I can. I'm working all week and only have a small break for lunch." I shake my head. "I can't make it to your office and back in time, let alone eat."

"No?" I shake my head. "When you came by with my SUV, I assumed your schedule was more flexible," he tells me.

"It's not," I admit. "I switched shifts with another rep to get you your ride."

"Why?" he asks.

"Because I wanted to see you."

Instead of smiling, he seems disappointed, his attention darting briefly toward the house. "Wren, I realize things have moved fast, and that we're both busy. But if it's possible, I'd like to give us a chance." The air is cold enough to make our breaths visible, yet his hand is warm when it finds my cheek. "And I don't want to go too long without seeing your smile."

"Okay," I say. "I'll try."

"That's all I'm asking."

He meets me with a brief and steamy kiss. As he releases

me and slips inside his Explorer, I don't want to think about how cold I feel without him, but it's hard not to. The man has a set of lips capable of melting an icy glacier stuffed with penguins, and his heart . . . that's something altogether different.

I wait on the walkway as he pulls onto the street, halting in place when he rolls past Sauron.

The little bastard is on his bike with a stiff middle finger up in the air. "Sauron, what the hell are you doing?"

"Watching out for my woman," he tells me, like that excuses his behavior.

"Get back in the house before I tell Gloria and she beats your ass!" I yell.

Even with the doors shut and the windows rolled up, I can hear Evan laughing. The guy is too perfect to be real. But as my phone buzzes in my pocket, and I see the latest text, I'm reminded that my life is far from perfect.

CHAPTER 10

Wren

Colin is losing his mind, swearing by the entrance to dealership floor. "Sixteen cameras, and they caught nothing that can help!"

He's not asking, he's reiterating what the rep from his dumbass security company is telling him. "This is horseshit!"

The other sales reps who came in drift around the lot in pairs, keeping their distance from our boss and scared to get too close. I'm the only one he allowed anywhere near him, but even I am waiting several feet away, my boots leaving marks along the fresh inch of snow.

Char marks coat the shattered Ford Nation sign and the awful stench of burning oil and rubber lingers in the crisp air. The fire department supposedly extinguished the last of the flames a few hours ago. But the smell is there, reminding us how bad the damage is, as if the skeletal frame of that F-150 being hauled away and busted building weren't enough.

I sigh, taking in the battered building and shards of broken glass near Colin's feet. I'm worried he'll finally have the big one and hope Marianne, his wife, will be able to calm him. She is always the level-headed one between them, but not now. Not that I blame her.

"I'm really sorry about all this, Mair," I say.

"Sorry?" she asks. "The only ones who are going to be sorry are those little fuckers when I get my hands on them." She scowls when the security rep looks her way. "What the hell are you looking at?"

"Ma'am, I know you're upset—"

"Upset?" she demands. "I would have been upset if I lost one car, but to have that car set on fire and bust my place up, I'm beyond upset, ya prick. My business is wrecked to shit and your worthless device didn't do anything but set off an alarm!"

I lead her away when her eyes brim with tears. These are furious tears, the ones that come from a woman seconds from assaulting the next person who pisses her off. With all the cops here, I don't want her doing something that will get her in trouble.

Marianne sniffs when a tear falls down her cheek, followed closely by another. But that's all she allows herself. Like me, she's a city girl raised on the kind of streets where you never show your weakness, no matter that you're seconds away from erupting like a busted hydrant.

For a long time, all she does is stare at the ground. I want to take her out of here and at least buy her a cup of coffee: black with a splash of cream. It's how she told me she liked it that first day I walked through the dealership doors at eighteen, begging for a job.

But Mair won't leave. She won't even move, too busy feeling every emotion that comes when someone soils your life's work.

"They destroyed my place," she says.

She's not telling me anything I don't know. Whoever planned this was pissed. An angry "screw you" meant to hurt.

"You have any idea how much bullshit we're going to have to go through with our insurance?"

She's not really asking so I don't answer, giving her a hug instead.

Marianne and Colin are good people. They don't deserve this and need all the help they can get. "I'll help with the clean-up. The damage, my brothers can fix within a month tops. They'll take care of you, I promise."

She starts crying against my shoulder, unable to keep that eruption of emotion she usually buries deep. I let her cry and grieve for her business, and for all that blood and sweat she and Colin shed making this dealership what it became.

It's only when she lifts her head and wipes her eyes that I let her go. "Thanks, Wren," she says.

Curran steps forward. He changed out of his jeans and T-shirt and is now in uniform, a light blue shirt beneath his heavy black bomber jacket and dark pants.

He should be back at my place, watching the game. But when I told him what happened, he asked his captain for permission to come in.

"Can I talk to you a sec?" he asks.

I frown at the way he's looking at me. He has his cop face on, that one that doesn't give much away. I don't know what's going on, I just know something is.

"Yeah, sure." I leave Mair and follow him toward the building.

"Did you talk to Angus and Seamus about helping them out?" he asks me.

"No, but I will." I tilt my chin when I realize how pissed he seems. "What's wrong?"

"I need to show you something." He pauses by one of the smaller glass doors leading inside. There's a chink near the corner, but otherwise undamaged compared to the main entrance.

One of the firefighters steps forward and opens the door, his face dirty from the leftover smoke and sweaty from the heavy protective gear he's wearing. "Can I take her in?" Curran asks him.

He nods. "Keep to the left and watch out for the puddles."

"Thanks, Keegan," he tells him.

I shadow Curran, stepping where he steps, avoiding the dirty water and the waste strewn from the sprinkler system and hoses. There's enough light coming in from the wall of windows to show me this side of the building isn't too bad off, minus the water damage. Where it's bad is near my office.

Exactly where the truck came crashing through.

"You all right?" Curran asks when I freeze.

I don't answer. I can't. My office wasn't just some small enclosure—a place where I sealed my deals, answered questions, and worked my ass off all day. It's where drivers found their dream cars, a job became a career, and clients became friends.

My office was my second home. To see it now, and remember how it was . . . it shouldn't twist my insides the way it does, but like with Colin and Marianne, this was my blood, my sweat, my hard work. Glass made up the front. It had a nice desk and set of industrial chairs, and a picture of me and Colin posing in front of the first car I sold when I was twenty.

"Wait here," he says, walking toward the warped pieces of metal and shattered glass that's left.

A cop, waiting by where the door once stood, glances up when he sees Curran. He waits for Curran to don vinyl gloves before passing him something in a clear plastic bag. He says something to Curran I can't hear. Curran nods, not that he seems any happier, and walks back to where I'm standing.

"Is that your office?" he asks.

"You know it is," I say. Why is he asking me this? He's visited me here before.

He lifts the clear bag. "This yours?"

My eyes widen when I look at what he's holding. It's a picture from my memory wall, the one I made to commemorate my sales. The picture is torn, but I recognize enough to see it's the one of Amy, the young woman I sold an Escort to last year. "What the hell?" I ask.

Curran seems to be waiting for me to explain. "It's from a collage I made," I tell him. "My customers send me pictures of themselves posing next to the cars I sold them."

"I know what it is," he says.

And he should. As a joke, he and Killian took one next to the trucks I sold them with their middle fingers extended. They were daring me to hang it, and I did, with me posing with mine since I negotiated us such a sweet deal.

"Wren, what aren't you telling me?"

He's trying to pull me back into the moment, but my mind is already telling me more than I want to know. No, not . . . no.

"What aren't you telling me?" he asks again, this time louder.

"Someone was mad," I say, my voice oddly vacant.

"No shit," he says cutting me off. "Who was it?"

"I don't know," I say, even though I already know who it is.

"I don't believe you. Out of all the cars in here, whoever did this chose an F-150. The same damn truck *you* drive to plow through *your* office."

"It's the biggest one we have in stock and can do the most damage." I'm not trying to lie or come up with lame excuses. It's more like I don't want to believe what's happening.

"Bullshit," he says.

"Curran," I say, although nothing follows.

He doesn't give me time to respond, spouting everything he knows. "He poured gas over the same model truck you drive, crashed it into the building, and aimed it at your office. I could have chalked it up to an angry customer, someone unstable, *maybe*. But he didn't just torch the truck and walk out, he took an extra few seconds to rip up something personal of yours and write 'whore' across your desk."

Nausea burns my throat as I feel myself go white. He pauses, his voice quieting when he takes in my face. "Wren, who was it?"

I shake my head, not wanting to speak, but doing it anyway. "It must have been Bryant."

"Are you fucking kidding me right now?"

"No," I reply, an awful taste forming in my mouth. "He called me the other day."

Curran's face is unreadable. But I see enough in those hard features to know he's latched onto more than I want him to know. "And?"

"And I think he sent me a text after that, but it was from an unmarked number."

"*And*?" he presses.

"And nothing," I respond. "Both times I told him to fuck off."

"Why?" he asks. He leans back on his heels, watching me closely.

"What do you mean, 'why'? Things didn't end well," I remind him. "I told you this when we broke up."

Curran has this habit of scratching his buzzed blond hair when he's relaxed or trying to stay out of trouble. But he's not scratching, he's observing me closely. "But you never told me why you broke up. Did he hit you?"

I don't get a chance to answer. Just like I know them, my brothers know me. "Fuck, Wren," he says, his face reddening with anger. "Why didn't you tell me?"

"He's a cop, you're cop, I didn't want to stir up shit that might make someone think twice about watching your back." I'm not grasping at straws. Bryant hinted as much, not that the idiot had the balls to actually say it.

"He's not a cop," Curran grinds out.

My insides are already a mess, but it's like what's left of my stomach bottoms out.

"What?"

It's taking everything Curran has not to crumple the evidence in his hand. "He never made it past his probation period," he tells me.

Bryant, being the manipulative bastard he is, always had a way of making himself look like the hero, and me like a psycho slut. I did worry the men and women in blue would side with him instead of Curran, and that it would cause problems for Curran on the force. But the other reason I never told Curran how bad things were between me and Bryant was because of what happened long before he hit me.

"*Wren*," Curran says, his voice morphing to a growl. "What exactly did he say to you?"

"He told me—"

"What?" he presses, when I shut my mouth. "Look, you needed to tell me a lot more than you did long before this. So don't think you're keeping anything from me now."

He's right. But there are some things my family doesn't need to know about me, and this is one of them. So I tell him what I can, and hope it's enough. "He led me to believe you were going to be partners when yours retired."

"He's a Goddamn liar. His first training officer was a seasoned vet who picked up that something wasn't right, told me Bryant said too many of the right things. The captain thought it was maybe a personality conflict and paired him up with someone younger, but with a few solid years under his belt. Guess what? Both recommended against hiring him. The Captain ordered a psych eval, Bryant refused and was sent packing." He leans in close. "What else did he say?"

"Not much," I admit. "Just enough to convince me to stay with him a little longer." Too long, I should have jumped ship when I realized he was poison.

"And what else did he do?"

I half expect Curran to start yelling at me, but he keeps his voice quiet and gives me a moment. The thing is, I need more than a moment. "Remember when I came back from Atlantic City, when Kill and Finn were promoting that fighter who got busted for steroids?"

"Yeah . . ."

"I didn't get into a brawl at a club. I got into it with Bryant on the street."

Curran doesn't say anything, but the anger spilling from his pores says enough. "What were you still doing with him if he was hitting you?"

"He didn't hit me before that night. And I didn't invite him," I add quickly.

"He found you, all on his own?"

The way Curran asks makes it sound creepier than it was, and it's already an experience I'll never forget. The way he came at me was brutal, like he had to punish me for walking away. But after what he did, I wasn't holding back either. I nailed him as hard as I could, trying to make him pay for what he did to me.

"I was going to a party being thrown by Finn's sponsor," I say, forcing myself to speak. "Bryant came out of nowhere and told me that I needed to take him as my date to make it up to him."

"To make what up to him?" Curran asks.

"I don't know, for dumping him—for being the one to walk away when it should have been him."

Curran doesn't respond, but I can tell he wants me to keep going. "I told him to fuck off," I admit. "He grabbed my arm, but when I shoved him away we both went at it."

"Why the hell didn't you tell me, tell *us*? Kill and Finn were down there with you. They would have had your back. You had no right keeping this from us."

My face heats from my rising anger and humiliation. I've spent my life trying to prove to my six behemoth brothers that I don't need to be protected, that I'm strong and capable. For the most part, I've done all right, and looked after them like they've looked after me. But the one time I really needed them, was the one time I couldn't call them. Bryant struck a blow so lethal, it all but guaranteed I wouldn't run to my family. But I don't reference that moment. I *can't*, so I focus on what happened in Atlantic City.

"I had every right," I fire back, my pent up anger and shame rising to the surface. "Finn was breaking down. Do I have to remind you how bad he was getting?"

I don't mean to raise my voice, but I do. It's only when the cops and firefighters loitering nearby turn to look at me that I shut my mouth. Curran senses at much, quieting, but doing little to hide the rage building behind it. "Don't use what happened to Finnie as an excuse. Bottom line, you should've told us."

"It's not an excuse. Finn needed to come first. Under those circumstances, he needed us more." My voice is absolute. All the crap revolving around Bryant aside, our little brother was more important. I suppose the reminder of how bad Finn was quiets us, giving us a moment.

"I was also embarrassed," I add a few long seconds later, the weight of my stress pressing into my shoulders. "And I was the one who took the first swing."

"You swung first?" I nod. "Why?" he asks.

"I told you, he grabbed my arm and demanded I take him to the party."

"Uh, uh," he says, leaning in. "If you took a swing it's because you were afraid, angry, or both. So let me ask you this, why were you afraid?"

Yeah. There's a reason Curran is considered one of the best cops to ever wear the uniform. "Things didn't end well," I repeat.

"Because he was hitting you?"

"No," I reply.

"Wren," he warns.

"I'm not lying, Curran. I told you that was the first night he hit me. But we both messed each other up. You know how the law works. If there's evidence of domestic violence an arrest has to be made. So yeah, maybe he would have been arrested, but I would've been too."

His lips press tight. He's listening, not that he likes what he hears.

"We were in Jersey," I remind him. "Not here where you're a cop, and Declan and Tess are assistant D.A.s. It would have been messy, and loud—during a time when Declan was still being hailed for winning the trial of the century and in the process of starting the next." I take a breath, because as strong as my arguments are, I don't think he's convinced, and he needs to be. "Even with all that aside, think back to what happened to Finnie. Curran, he was spiraling down faster than any of us could have stopped him."

Everything I say is true, and valid, and shit that should stop him in place. But it doesn't.

"What did he do to you, Wren?"

It's the same question Sol asked me. But where she asked with a lot of heart, Curran's asking with barely controlled fury, cutting me off at the knees and making my excuses seem pathetic.

"He made me feel like I was less than I am," I reply, the quiver in my voice revealing the honesty behind each syllable. My gaze drops to the floor, but it's only brief. "Like I was nothing, and didn't matter."

"So it was emotional?"

He's trying to clarify what I mean, not that it lifts the tension straining his broad shoulders. Abuse is abuse. It doesn't hurt less because there's no physical evidence of what you've endured. Inner scars are a bitch to heal and can mar you forever.

I don't tell him as much. He knows all too well where I'm coming from. "Yeah. Harder to prove, right?" I ask, hoping he doesn't keep probing and find out how "emotional" it really was.

"Maybe, but that doesn't make it any less wrong. You should have told us."

"I know," I say, more because he wants to hear me say it. I rub my eyes, wishing this could go away, but recognizing it's far from over. "What are you going to do?"

"Knock on his door," he tells me, not even blinking.

It's probably what he'd planned to do long before I said anything.

"I figured as much." I glance back toward my office, where pieces of the Mustang Bryant hit on the way in are strewn. "I just didn't figure on all this."

"You should have," he tells me. He frowns when I look at him. "It's what these fucking stalkers do, Wren."

"He's not stalking me, Curran. He called, and maybe texted—"

"*And* found you in Atlantic City, *and* destroyed a fucking dealership the same night you happened to be out with another guy."

It's the last thing he says that almost has me hurling. "You think he knows about Evan?"

"Seeing everything he did in here, that's my guess." He works his jaw. "And if I'm right, he could be watching you."

"But why now? It's been months. God, everything he's done happened months apart."

"But they still happened, Wren. Sociopaths are all about control. Look at the women you've taught self-defense to. It's always the same story with these assholes. They latch onto their victims, get what they want from them, and don't let them walk away."

"I walked away," I say, and I did, but my voice is softer than it should be. I know where he's going with this.

"Yeah. Which put you more at risk." He holds out the evidence bag to the cop who wanders over. "Let's go back outside," he says, his way of telling me and his buddy we're not done talking.

The cold was tolerable when I was outside earlier. Now, it's like the temperature has dropped another twenty degrees. I should welcome the fresh air, but it doesn't make me breathe easier as I choke down Curran's words.

"You did the right thing leaving him," he tells me, slipping out of his vinyl gloves and replacing them with his leather ones. "But in doing so, you took away control he never intended you to have *and* put yourself at risk. Perps like Bryant, those angry, volatile ones, can't turn off the crazy. They don't go away and they don't give up," he says, the severity in his tone giving away what he's seen as a cop. "They may sub out their victims—"

"Stop calling me that," I say, my voice shaking from too much anger and all too real fear. I glance back at the dealership. Jesus, how the hell did things get this far?

I hope Curran thinks my quaking voice is due to the cold, but I know better. "My point is, even though one woman may replace another, they never forget the one they feel wronged them. You leaving him, he won't forget the insult, Wren. It's how these twisted assholes think. There's no rhyme or reason, just a sense of entitlement and what they think belongs to them."

Curran looks out to the highway when we reach my truck like he's expecting Bryant to be here, but also because he's trying to give me time to absorb what he's telling me. "I found out a few weeks back that my boys at another precinct responded to a D.V. call at Bryant's place in Ritten House Square. It's the third time they've been there within the past year, and like before, his live-in girlfriend called 9-1-1 scared out of her mind. She wouldn't tell them what he did, and wouldn't press charges, just like the one before her. From what I heard, he threw her out a couple days ago. My guess is, it's why he called you. He hasn't forgotten you."

The one who got away. He doesn't say it, but the meaning is there. I thought Bryant had moved on, but it's like Curran said, he only temporarily swapped me out for someone else.

"There's more," he says, his gaze sweeping over my sullen features. "Since the captain kicked him out, there's been info linking him back to an organized crime boss in South Jersey. It's enough to make us think he joined the force with other motives."

"Holy shit," I say.

"Yeah. You don't just go to work for the mob because you didn't make it as a cop. Something else was going on. Our problem is there's been nothing solid we can pin on him." He shoots me a look. "And I'm not sure we have enough now. In talking to the security reps, they didn't catch shit we can use— a shot of his face, the car he drove here, nothing. And think back to where he's living, fucking Ritten House Square."

"I know." He always had money, always. But it takes way over six figures to live there. I swallow down a few curses and maybe some anger, too. "Why didn't you tell me?" I ask.

"I couldn't tell you because I didn't know until a few weeks ago. I wasn't in on the investigation." He motions to the building. "But I sure as hell am in on it now. Except I should have known something, right? From you, from the start."

"I know," I mumble, wishing it wasn't so hard to meet him square in the face. "I'm sorry I didn't tell you, but Curran, it was shit I wanted to forget."

"Maybe. But he never did, Wren." He waits, then asks, "Anything else you need to tell me?"

"Need" and "want" tend to be two different things. "No," I respond.

He returns to watching me closely, expecting me to say more, but I don't. "Okay," he finally says. He gives me a one-armed hug. "You need anything, you call. He messes with you, you call. You don't keep shit from those who love you and can protect you."

It sounds good in theory, but sometimes to protect those you love, it's like you have to stay quiet, no matter how much it kills you to trap that shit inside.

"Curran," I say, halting him in place before he can turn away. "Look, if you're going to Bryant's house, stick to the damage. Don't make it about me, okay?"

I don't even get all the words out before he starts shaking his head in a way that shuts me up. "You don't get a choice, Wren. Not this time."

My stare falls to my feet. No, I don't have a choice. Bryant made sure of that long ago when he fucked me over in more ways than one.

CHAPTER 11

Evan

"No," I reply, not that I bother glancing up from my work. "Adeptus has been promised to the community hospitals where it can best serve the underprivileged."

"But Robert Harold has offered double," Remington counters.

As my Head of Finance, we habitually butt heads. Today is no exception. "Because they can," I snap, irritably flipping the page. "Their hospital and pharmaceutical company have made an exorbitant amount by overcharging for their medication and services, all the while paying pennies for their ingredients and rescinding on their promises to help underdeveloped countries."

"Maybe. But it's because of their success that they can give us more."

"You call it success," I reply, tossing my report across my desk to meet him in the eye. "I call it unethical and appalling. Tens of thousands of children in Uganda, Nairobi, and the Congo died because they weren't properly vaccinated with vaccines Robert Harold promised to deliver."

"They delivered them," Remington insists. "Due to paperwork, the shipment was delayed."

"The shipment was delayed," I agree, my tone razor

sharp. "But if they hadn't sent vaccines set to expire in three months' time, with proper packaging, it wouldn't have mattered."

I turn to Anne. "Where are we with production for the Adeptus commercial?"

"Shooting starts today, Evan."

"And the media campaign?"

It's Clifton who answers me. "Ready, when you give us the word."

I've moved on, Remington has not. "I ask you to reconsider," he says. "Partnering with Robert Harold will guarantee us millions over the next year, and possibly billions over time."

Remington is one of the men my predecessor hired. Like my predecessor, he believes in profit without a care to who it harms or who we deal with. The report I was reading outlined the millions in profit lost over the past three years, a reminder that iCronos is potentially months away from financial collapse. The report should work in his favor. Yet it's poor decisions and even worse business practices, encouraged by heads like him and former employees who illegally sold our trademarked technology to our competitors, that's almost ruined my company.

I won't stand for it. The employees who betrayed us are currently being prosecuted and we're suing our competitors for the violations and loss of revenue. Our legal team is certain we'll settle and be better for it, but that will take time. Time I'm wasting on employees like Remington.

"Evan, are you listening?" he asks.

There's so much steel behind my glare I can practically taste the metal slide along my tongue. "We're not selling to Robert Harold or any other company that practices like they do. You have a choice," I snap, interrupting him when he opens his mouth. "Work with us or leave."

I feel Clifton and Anne straighten as the tension between myself and Remington surges like a growing storm.

"Fine. I'm out," he quips, the presumptuous ass believing it's my loss.

I barely blink. "Anne, as of this moment Remington is banned from my building. Have security escort him back to his desk to collect his personal belongings and follow him off the premises, and tell HR to immediately revoke his access to our files."

"Yes, Evan," she responds, lifting my phone and speaking quickly.

Remington regards me as if slapped. "About my severance pay."

I rise slowly. "Severance is granted to deserving employees who have worked full-time for a minimum of five years. You're here barely four and are about as deserving as Robert Harold is of our technology and resources. *Get out*."

The first member of the security staff walks in. Remington's attention stays on me. "I thought you were smarter than this," he tells me.

"I am," I reply. "Which is why you no longer work here."

He turns abruptly, pausing when he sees three members of my security team now waiting. "This way, sir," the first one tells him.

The guards nod in my direction before leaving. Remington's departure should grant me a great deal of relief. It was necessary and we'll fare far better for it. But not one dismissal has been easy, each a reminder of how little loyalty exists in the pit greed that surrounds me. I'm desperate for the right people, yet can't be sure I'll find them.

"Do you want me to go with them?" Clifton asks.

"If you wish," I say, returning to my chair and the mountain of work waiting for me.

"I just received confirmation that access has been revoked," Anne says, returning the receiver to the base. "And Brenda from HR confiscated his laptop as Remington was brought back to the room."

"Thank you," I say.

I want to acknowledge Anne and Clifton better than this. But I'm so fucking tired of dealing with the Remingtons within my company the words don't come, only anger.

My fingers rub across my forehead. It's a wonder I can

find any trace of happiness these days, with my biggest source of happiness noticeably absent.

Wren . . . I can't begin to guess if there's anything between us. She didn't reply to my text until late Sunday, mentioning she was dealing with an issue at her job. Since then, her responses have been brief at best, and now, all but gone.

She assured me she'd try, as did I. But my long list of responsibilities have kept me from giving her the attention she deserves. It's been almost two weeks since I saw her smile and found mine because of it. That doesn't mean I've forgotten her.

"Do you need a moment?" Anne asks.

"Pardon?" I ask, glancing up.

She lets out a breath that flutters her long bangs away from her face, the tips lime green to match her suit. Like me, she's tired of all the wrong people at the right company. "I need to go over the presentation for Ork Mechanicus we're pitching to the burn center to be sure it's what you want."

"That's not necessary," I say, reaching for the pile of work that will take me well past midnight to read through. "You know what you're doing. I'd like you to spearhead the meeting, and Clifton to oversee and manage our deal with Adeptus."

"But," she begins.

"Make it happen," I tell her.

Excitement and fear war in her round features. This is a tremendous step, one she's earned. "Yes, Evan." She lifts the pile closest to my right and hurries out, pausing at the door. "Thank you," she says.

"For what?" I ask.

"For believing in this company."

Her kindness is refreshing. Unlike Ashleigh who enters the moment she leaves. "You fired Remington?" she asks.

"Yes," I reply, reaching for a pen.

"Do think that was wise?"

Today is not the day to question me. "Are you saying it's not? Because if you are, need I remind you that you are now questioning both my intelligence and my ability to lead?"

Her thin lips press into a ruler straight line. "That's not what I'm saying. Remington was trying to help you make money the company needs. Jesus, Evan, we're all trying to help *you*."

Her tone is accusatory, as if I've somehow betrayed her. "All you had to do was listen," she says. "Take this one opportunity to help iCronos before it's too late."

"By siding with a company and industry that for far too long has harmed many?" I ask. "iCronos is better than that."

"Not in the extreme direction you're taking it," she counters.

I'm ready to hurl my desk out the window.

Someone knocks on the door, loud enough to catch my attention, but not so loud that Ashleigh turns around.

Wren's long dark hair spills to the side when she pokes her head in. "Hi," she says.

"Hi," I reply. I'm stunned she's here, not that it keeps me from returning a smile I've fared too long without.

Her attention darts briefly to Ashleigh whose back is now to me. I'm can't be sure of the way Ashleigh regards her, but the amused shimmer in Wren's stare is telling enough. "How's it going there, Ash?"

"We're in a meeting," Ashleigh replies.

Her blatant dismissal of Wren has me reeling. "No, we're not," I respond over Wren's offer to wait. "Our conversation ends now."

I rise, removing my glasses and placing them on my desk as I walk around it. "What are you doing here?" I ask, my mood lightening with every step I take.

Had I known she was coming, I wouldn't have removed my jacket or tie, especially if I knew how she'd dress. She steps forward with a white paper bag clutched in her grip, the deep plum suit she's wearing accentuating her curves, while making her appear thinner than she is.

"I was passing by and thought I'd bring you lunch."

"It's lunchtime?" I ask.

She laughs a little. "Technically it's almost dinner."

Ashleigh stomps toward the door, shutting it with a sharp slam. I'm too busy eyeing Wren to care. "You look lovely," I tell her, reaching for her hand.

That's a lie. She looks positively breathtaking.

She watches me kiss her hand, but then glances down as I release her. "Your hair's getting long there, bossman."

"Unfortunately, I haven't the time for a cut," I reply.

"I wasn't complaining," she tells me quietly.

Her expression softens the longer I stare. My God, she is stunning. Yet as much as I can't stop looking at her, I notice she's doing her best not to look at me. "It's good to see you," I say, troubled by her unease.

Her demure smile does little to assure me. "Want to eat?" she asks when I take a step closer. She shakes the bag. "I don't want it to get cold."

"Very well," I reply.

She follows me to the conference table. I wish she'd lead so I wouldn't have to take my eyes off her. She's a reminder of what it is to feel like a man uninhibited by the burdens of an entire empire, one who can enjoy an evening with a woman without care or thought to the future.

I move another stack of work I have waiting for me and pull out her chair, my hand grazing her silky hair when she sits. She's wearing the perfume she wore when I first met her, the one that reminds me of warming honey. I want to meet her mouth with mine. But this isn't the morning following a very passionate night, it's early evening following far too many days without her.

She lifts her chin and offers another small smile. It's not wide like the one that lights her face when she laughs or shares a story from her childhood, but it's enough to ease the pressure gathering along my shoulders.

I sit across from her to give her space. "How long do you have to eat?" she asks.

"Not long," I admit.

"I guess I should have sent you a text." She shakes her head. "I wasn't sure I'd be allowed in, with the security you have in place. The first time, I had a truck on a flatbed and your signed paperwork to prove who I was and why I was here. This time, I just had me."

"That's all you need," I tell her. "I informed my staff you're permitted inside whenever you wish."

Her demeanor switches from almost shy to wickedly playful. She leans forward, pretending to whisper and doing a horrid job. "I don't think Ashleigh would agree."

"I don't care what she thinks," I respond in earnest.

"Don't get in trouble with the little woman because of me," she teases.

"There's a lot I would do for you," I confess. "Regardless of who it unsettled."

"Oh, yeah?" She adjusts the bag in front of her. "What have I done to deserve that?"

"You helped me find my smile."

My words halt her in place. She squeezes her eyes shut as if pained. "Evan, you can't say things like that." She opens her eyes, appearing miserable. "It's not what I need to hear."

"I don't tell you these things to win you over. I say them because I mean them," I reply, wishing she didn't feel so far away.

"That's the problem," she says. She sighs. "Did anyone ever tell you you're too good to be true?"

"No."

Whatever she catches in my expression appears to hurt her and her attention returns to the bag. She pulls out a long tube wrapped in foil and passes it to me. I don't realize how hungry I am until now, and the aroma of hot, thinly cut steak with melted cheese wafts into my nose. But all that is secondary compared with how she appears.

"Are you all right?" I ask.

"It's been a rough couple of weeks," she replies, reaching into the bag once more. She meets my face. "But I guess you've had it rough too, considering you're too busy to have lunch."

I don't respond with words. The muscles along my spine clench as I think through my business dealings these past ten days. I suppose my stiffening posture speaks loud enough.

"Let's eat, okay?" she says.

I reach for my sandwich, recognizing she doesn't want to talk about herself. Warmth fills my palm as my hand wraps over the foil. "Is this what I think it is?"

"Oh, yeah, it is." She slides a round tin container with a paper lid across the table. "And cheese fries." She winks. "You're welcome."

My eyes roll in my head when I take my first bite. "This is superb."

She reaches for a paper napkin, covering her mouth as she swallows. "Best damn steaks this side of Philly. Now, for wings, you'll have to hit Merve's."

"With you?" I ask.

She stops moving. "Maybe not with me."

"Why?" I ask.

Ashleigh opens the door, not bothering to knock. "Evan, you're needed at the lab."

I frown, turning my attention away from Wren. "For what, specifically?"

She huffs as if I'm bothering her. "John wants to discuss an issue with Eldar."

"Then put him through," I say, reaching for the napkin Wren passes me.

"He's requesting your presence," she repeats, as if I misheard her.

"I'm eating," I say, stating the obvious. "Put him through."

"Fine. But don't you think you should take this in private?" she asks, casting a pointed look in Wren's direction.

Heat burns through my face as my anger builds. "Do you have a problem responding to a simple request?" I snap.

"Don't worry about it," Wren says, pulling a cheese fry free off the tin plate. "I can step out."

I stand with her, ready to explode. The last thing I want is for Wren to think I mistreat women in any way. But I've had enough of Ashleigh's attitude and insubordination.

Wren, it seems, has had enough as well. The way she handles it however, is very different. She sashays past

Ashleigh, who is practically singeing a hole through Wren's face with her glare. "Don't worry about it, Evan," she replies sweetly, tossing me an impish grin. "You can whisper your secrets to me when I come back in."

She shuts the door behind her. I chuckle, my face reddening for far different reasons than anger.

"I see," Ashleigh replies. Her terse response takes me aback. "I've done everything for you. I've stayed late, worked weekends, and defended you every time anyone questioned your decisions."

"I don't need defending," I reply, my tone so sharp it could scrape along stone.

"Just like you don't need me," she says, her voice oddly cold.

I lean back on my heels, recognizing what Wren grasped the moment she heard Ashleigh's voice.

"I didn't know," I respond, not that it would have made a world of difference.

"No, you didn't," she agrees, crossing her arms. "Not that it matters. I wouldn't let you touch me now if you begged me."

"I wasn't offering," I assure her, causing the deep creases along her brow to multiply.

"Of course you weren't. Not with the caliber of woman you have waiting for you outside."

It's as if the room is drained of sound and the earth grinds to a halt. Ashleigh has mistreated my staff and those who work directly beside me. But to insult Wren is the final blow.

"How dare you talk about her that way?"

It's not simply the edge to my voice that causes her to straighten, it's the air of protectiveness I insert behind each word. She rights herself and starts to speak. I don't let her.

"I'm no longer in need of your services. The door is that way. Use it."

The angry tears pooling her eyes suggest she wants me to want her and beg her to stay. Doesn't she realize I could never desire someone so vicious and cold?

"You're going to be sorry," she says.

"The only thing I'm sorry about is letting this drag on longer than it should."

I'm not yelling, although I mean every word. Ashleigh storms out the door, I catch it before she slams it closed. I should have security escort her out, like I did Remington and every employee I've fired. But while Ashleigh has been far from professional, I can't ignore the pain lurking beneath all her fury.

Pain I caused by choosing another woman.

I watch her take her coat and purse from the cupboard behind her desk and stomp away.

The door leading out to the rows of cubicles and offices isn't spared from her wrath. It doesn't break, but the force she uses vibrates the glass enclosure, causing everyone to glance up. Given how unpopular Ashleigh is, I almost expect them to cheer at her departure. After witnessing Remington escorted out less than an hour ago, only tension follows.

Shocked looks skim my way, though they don't linger. Another person fired by me, another reminder that no job is secure.

My hands rest at my hips as I watch my employees return to their work. I want to assure them that they're safe. Yet no one is if I fail.

CHAPTER 12

Evan

Wren inches beside me as the office phone rings. Already there are two lines placed on hold. "So, you canned Ashleigh, huh?" she says, angling her chin in the direction of the elevators.

I drag my hand through my hair as Ashleigh disappears, the stress of too many long hours hitting me at once. "Yes."

"I'm sorry," she says.

I fixate on all the flashing buttons along the screen demanding attention. "She needed to go," I say, willing myself not to rip the phone off the desk and smash it against the wall.

"Oh, that's for damn sure," Wren says, walking toward the desk. "I'm only sorry for what it did to you."

I frown, my brow easing as I realize she understands far beyond what I told her. She motions to the phone. "You want me to get that?"

I start to tell her she doesn't have to when she picks up the receiver and taps the first line.

"Evan Jonah's office. This is Wren. How can I help you?" Her gaze shifts across the desk. "Uh, huh," she says. She picks up a pen, then scrambles through two drawers before she finds a pad of legal paper. "Right, okay. Well, let me ask you this, John," she adds, scribbling fast. "Is this something that he has to go to the lab for, or can you come up to see him?"

She reaches for the laptop on the desk. "What's the passcode?" she whispers.

"What?" I know what she's asking, I'm simply dumbfounded by how easily she took over. I take the pen and pad she offers and jot it down.

She sits, typing fast, her eyes darting across the screen until she taps the icon that opens my schedule. "Okay. If you come up now, he can see you until his next appointment at four-thirty. Does that work?" She smiles into the phone. "All right, see you in a few."

She disconnects. "What are you doing?" I ask like an idiot.

Her wink is her only reply. She hits the next button. "Evan Jonah's office, this is Wren," she says. "Hi, Alex. How can I help you?"

Again she returns to my schedule, but something she hears causes her to straighten. "Look, Alex, I'm not trying to tell you what to do, but if the boss says he wants to see you at nine in the morning, you need to be here at nine in the morning . . . No, no, that's his only available spot tomorrow . . . What's going on that you can't be here? According to the notes, you made this appointment a week ago . . . Oh, I see . . . Okay, hold on." She puts him on hold, answers the other two lines ringing, asks each politely to wait, and then places them back on hold.

"How late are you staying tonight?" she asks. "Your last appointment is at six, but I saw that stack of crap you have on your desk."

"Likely until midnight," I answer slowly, noting how nothing seems to escape her.

"Can you meet Alex at seven? His wife is expecting their first baby and they had to schedule an ultrasound." She holds out a hand. "It will keep you later, but I'll block out the time you were supposed to meet with him so you can sleep in." She gives me the once over. "You look like you could use some sleep—not that you're not hotter than Brock O'Hurn munching jalapenos in hell, I'm just saying, the rest will be good for you."

"All right," I say, trying to absorb what I'm seeing and what she said.

She returns to the call. "Hey, Alex. It's Wren. Evan can see you at seven. Does that work?" She waits for his answer then laughs. "No, problem. Oh, and good luck at the ultrasound tomorrow, you'll have to let Evan know how it goes."

She disconnects, doing a double-take when she sees me still standing there. "Go eat," she says. "John says he just needs the okay to switch Mechanicus Orcus—"

"Ork Mechanicus?" I interrupt.

"Sure," she says laughing. "Anyway, he wants to try to switch the body armor to a lighter steel." She shakes her finger at me. "That, I didn't have an answer for. That's all you." She pauses. "You know what to do, right?"

I smirk. "Yes. But we need the current weight to feed it into the system."

"Good. You can tell him that when he gets here, because he thinks it will work better on surface cells or something like that."

She looks up when John walks in. "Hey, you must be John. I spoke with you on the phone. I'm Wren," she says, offering her hand. "Evan can see you, but he'll have to talk to you while he eats."

John releases her hand slowly, glancing from Wren to me. "That's not a problem," he replies.

He starts for my office, pausing when I don't move. "Go," she says, waving me on as she reaches for yet another call. "I've got this."

"Who is that?" John asks as we I step into my office.

"Wren," I reply as if that explains everything.

He doesn't ask what happened to Ashleigh. "Oh, I like her," he says.

He hands me a report, but I barely see it. All I can think about is how much I like Wren, too.

My meeting is more complex than I anticipated. While I developed the concept for Ork, John and his team are helping me perfect it. John is a brilliant engineer, though often harried and unable to keep up with his thoughts. Today, that's a good thing. It gives me time to eat my sandwich while we bounce ideas off each other until we're satisfied.

John waves to Wren on his way back to the lab. She's busy typing and doesn't glance up when I approach. "How are you so familiar with this?" I ask.

"The software?" she asks, her fingers flying across the keyboard. "Believe it or not, we use it at the dealership. I just never realized it was yours." Her eyes round as her stare skips along the screen. "Although this is a better version than what I learned on. It's faster, and it looks like you worked out all the bugs."

"We try to address all complaints. There was one in particular that was especially heated and detailed."

"That might have been me. But in my defense, I didn't know you then and it was probably close to my monthly."

I can't help laughing. "There's no need to apologize. But what I'm asking is, how is it you know what to do? Clearly, you have experience in this line of work."

The ends of her hair brush along the top of the desk as she turns to regard me. "I graduated high school desperate for a job. Any job." She makes a face. "You wouldn't believe some of the things I've done for money."

"I can imagine," I say.

She shrugs, appearing embarrassed and equally anxious to forget. "Anyway, Colin, my boss at the dealership started me as a secretary. I worked my way up to rep while I attended college." She taps another icon. "I majored in Women's Studies. You can imagine how many doors that opened when I graduated."

She laughs when I do. It's the first time I see the Wren I adore, the one who doesn't hold back. "It wasn't the best idea I ever had," she confesses. "But I wanted a college degree and that's the only course of study that kept my interest. Either way, I turned out to be really good at selling cars so here I am." She quiets. "Or was."

As simply as that, the apprehension she demonstrated earlier returns. "What do you mean by that?"

She holds up a finger when the phone rings again. "Evan Jonah's office, this is Wren." She nods, listening closely. "One moment please while I check." She looks up. "It's Akira Brown from Finance."

"Tell her she's in charge and that I'll meet with her at nine to discuss her promotion."

"How can you meet her at nine? You're supposed to sleep in," she reminds me.

"I can't sleep in. There's too much to do." I shove a hand into my pocket. "Besides, I'll be in promptly at seven to meet my personal trainer."

"Personal trainer?" She drags her gaze along my form, turning away when she notices me watching her and switching back to the call. "Akira, Evan will meet you at nine at his office. Oh, and congratulations on the promotion, girl."

She hangs up, motioning to the office phone with a tilt of her head. "She seemed floored. Guess she wasn't expecting that one."

"Although many are qualified, it was rare for my predecessor to promote a woman to department head."

"Are you serious?" At my nod, she adds, "What an idiot." She stands and brushes off her skirt. "So why did you promote Akira?"

"She works hard and is committed to helping my company succeed."

"Then she sounds like the right choice," she says, her voice dropping to just above a whisper.

I reach for her hand, ignoring how the glass front exposes us to rows of cubicles that make up the floor, but she edges away. It's only when I see her lift her purse from the desk that I realize she's leaving.

"Wait, where are you going?"

Her smile seems forced. "I have a job interview to get to. Don't worry," she adds quickly, motioning out to the floor.

"Nicole over there says she'll transfer her calls here and cover you."

Nicole waves and stands, alerting us that she's ready to replace Wren.

"She already covers several managers," I explain.

"Oh," Wren replies. "She didn't mention that, and I didn't think to ask. I was more worried about leaving you hanging."

"Hello, Mr. Jonah," Nicole says, rushing to take a seat. "Is there anything pending I need to be aware of or something you'd like me to do?"

"No." I huff, holding out my hand. "I mean, yes. Wren, may I see you in my office?"

She digs through her purse, keeping her attention away. "I can't. I have fifteen minutes to get to my interview, and driving will take twenty."

I place my hand on her lower back and lead her into my office. "We're going to need longer than that."

The door shuts as my hands grasp her hips, my thumbs grazing along her curves. Her palms glide to my chest. For a moment, I think she'll return my embrace and allow me to kiss her. But she doesn't move, meeting my face with that same disheartened expression. "You have a job interview?" I ask.

"Yeah," she answers quietly. "At another Ford dealership a few miles outside the city."

"What happened to the one you had?" My arms drop as I feel her withdraw. I follow her across the room, recognizing something is very wrong.

She turns, her hands clasped in front of her. "It's gone."

"What?"

She sits back against the conference table, appearing lost in her thoughts. "Someone crashed a truck through the dealership and then set it on fire. Me and a few of the workers have spent the last few days cleaning up. My brothers came in to help repair all the structural damage, but the owners have called it quits."

Her attention falls to her feet. "My boss isn't the

healthiest guy you'll ever meet. He told us yesterday that it's better for him to get his money back from the insurance and sell the building." She sighs. "I can't blame him, you know? He'll end up with more than he had, lose the stress that comes from owning and running a business, and actually enjoy his retirement."

There are a million things I can say, like "I'm sorry" and "What a horrible situation to live through." Mostly, I want to tell her not to worry, that I'll take of her. I don't, of course. While I want to, and it's what I did for my previous lovers, Wren isn't a woman who wants to be cared for.

That doesn't mean I'm not willing to help. "Work for me."

She lifts her head. "What?"

I lose the space between us. "I need an assistant, one I can trust and don't have to train." I reach for her hands. "You know what you're doing, and I already trust you. Work for me."

Her stare falls to our hands. "Evan, if I wanted a secretary's pay, I wouldn't have worked my ass off to be a rep and make more."

"How much do you make?" I ask, smirking.

"You can't afford me," she tells me, keeping her focus on our hands.

"Try me."

She lifts her head. "It depends on what I sell, but I sell a lot."

"Ashleigh made two hundred thousand a year. You can have her salary. If it's not enough, I'll raise it."

I have her attention. "Your secretaries make two hundred thousand a year?"

"No. Ashleigh's case is unique because she worked as the administrative assistant for the CEO of iCronos, the position I'm offering you."

"Evan, I can't."

"Why?" I ask. "My company is facing a tremendous financial crisis. With the right people at my side, it has the potential to take the world by storm. But I don't have enough of the right people, and very few I trust. I trust you. Say you'll work for me."

I expect questions or possibly a negotiation of salary. I don't expect her sadness, yet it comes.

"You say you trust me?" I nod. "Evan, you don't even know me."

My thumb skims the back of her hand. "What I know is enough. You're brilliant and exactly who I need."

The manner in which she shakes her head alerts me to more of her sadness. "I want to help you," she replies. "I really do. But there are things you should know about me. None are good and will make you take back your offer." She huffs. "Not that I'll blame you."

"Is that what you think?" She doesn't reply. "Then you owe it to me to tell me. Allow me to decide for myself."

It takes her a moment to speak. "We think my ex-boyfriend is the one who set the car on fire and wrecked the dealership."

I'll admit, I'm not prepared to hear this and my expression evidently reveals as much.

Her cheeks flush with obvious embarrassment. "Bryant isn't a good guy and far from stable," she explains. "But he's worse than I thought and has ties to the mafia."

"I don't see how this connects him to you or what happened at the dealership."

"He used the same model truck I drive to crash through the building and into my office. He also destroyed that collage of pictures I showed you and wrote 'whore' across the desk." She averts her gaze. "Curran says Bryant still considers me his and is trying to prove he can still hurt me."

"What do you mean 'still'?"

Her blanching face causes my anger to return. "Like I told you, it wasn't a good relationship."

My feelings for her and desire to keep her safe tempt me to press for more details. But the fragility she demonstrates holds me in place. It's brief, but it's there. This is a man who clearly caused her pain. I won't cause her more. "Does Curran know Bryant's hurt you beyond this incident?"

"He does." She analyzes me closely. "And because of it, he's the one who knocked on his door along with a few other cops. Bryant was arrested, but was out in a few hours once his big-time lawyers, who he shouldn't be able to afford, arranged his release. I filed a report, but it's not enough, not when the security cameras didn't capture his face, and not when an airtight alibi popped out of nowhere. All charges were dropped as of last night." She eases away from me. "So when I told you this wasn't the best time, I wasn't exaggerating."

"Why?" I hold up a hand when she frowns. "This happened after we met. What was he doing to you before?"

Wren isn't happy that I picked up on what went unsaid. But as much as I don't want to force her to relive the experience with this imbecile, I need to know what's happened so I can help her.

"He called me the day you stopped in looking for a car. I probably pissed him off when I hung up on him. He also texted me, but we can't prove it was him," she explains. "Curran thinks he lashed out because he found out I went out with you."

"He doesn't want me with you," I say.

Again, she hesitates. Her worry as palpable as the strain between us. "That's what Curran thinks," she admits.

"Like I give a shit," I snap.

Her small brows knit. "Evan, I'm serious."

I scoff. "So am I." I mull over what she says. "How often does he contact you?"

Her brows knit as if bothered by my questions. But I think it's more than that. "Not often enough to press charges, but enough to remind me he's still there." She releases a small breath. "He's smart, Evan. But most sociopaths are."

"Sociopaths?" I ask, although by now it's obvious he is.

"That's right. My problem is I found out a little too late." She steps away and heads to the door. "Still want to hire me?"

"Yes."

My reply stops her dead. She glances over her shoulder. "Are 'must have a psycho ex-boyfriend' on your list of requirements for new hires, Evan?"

The reminder that he was her former lover irritates the hell out of me. Not because I'm threatened by him, not in the least. But because he clearly threatened her. "I'm not asking him to work for me. I'm asking you."

Her dark hair falls along her breasts as she covers her face with her hand. "Evan," she says. "I can't do this to you."

"Why did you come here?"

She drops her hand away as if unsure why I ask. "I wanted to see you."

"To tell me goodbye?"

The misery in her demeanor is telling enough, although she takes her time to explain. "I couldn't just blow you off, not after everything that happened between us. And I felt bad about not returning your texts." She sighs. "The least I could do was stop by and tell you I couldn't see you anymore."

"Because of him?" She doesn't reply, but I know it's the reason. She wants to protect me. But I already assumed that role for both of us.

I walk toward her slowly and wrap my arms carefully around her waist. "I don't want to say goodbye. Not to you."

Her hands clasp my arms. "I don't want to either. But you're a good man. You don't deserve all this crazy." She purses her lips. "Curran warned Bryant to stay away from me. So far he has, but that could change. I don't want anything to happen to you."

"It won't."

"You don't know that," she says.

"Wren, look around," I tell her. "My company is a virtual fortress. There's no safer place for you or us. Work for me."

For a long moment, she doesn't respond. Her gaze on mine as if waiting for me to reconsider. When I don't she finally says, "If I work here, he'll think we're together."

"Let him. It's what I want for us."

She regards me as if I'm mad. "But if I work here, we *can't* be together," she says slowly. "I can't have sex with you."

I freeze, my mind taking me back to the time I was six and I learned there was no Santa Claus. "You don't want me?"

Ardor warms her stare. "You know that's not true. But if I take this job, I can't have you, not like that." She groans. "Things are messy. You understand? I was part of a really bad relationship with a twisted and cruel man. And now this hot guy I can't have wants me working directly under him." She rolls her eyes. "You know what I mean."

"Why can't you have me?" I ask. "Hear me out," I add when she regards me as if I've lost my mind. "I would never ask or obligate you to anything you didn't want to do. But you're an exceptional woman who can help me with the challenges I'm facing. So why can't we have both? We'll see each other, and we'll help each other. To me, it's a win for both sides."

"Because I already screwed up once, pretty damn bad considering the type of man I dated. I don't want to screw up again, not with you. You and me, sleeping together *and* working together, that doesn't just have the potential to wreck things to hell, it has the ability to implode with like, flying monkeys flinging flaming chunks of zombie bits. You know, End of Days crap."

"Then we won't sleep together," I tell her, ignoring her reference and the shock riddling her features. I don't blame her for doubting me. I'd take her to bed now, if I could. But I don't want to ruin what we could have. Just as she's made mistakes with past lovers, I have as well.

Her silky strands glide through my fingers as I push her hair behind her shoulder. "You came here to tell me goodbye despite your desire for more." She bites down on her bottom lip, the motion confirming my thoughts. "If you take the other job, it will be goodbye given the schedule I keep. That's not what I want."

"I don't want that either," she admits. "Before all this, I wanted to get to know you."

"Then say you'll stay. Here, you'll know me at my best and worst." I smile softly. "And with time, I'll know you in the same manner." My lips pass over her cheek. "We don't have to touch or wake up next to each other, never mind that I want to."

She shudders when I whisper against her ear, "Very much want to."

"Evan," she says, her words releasing with a soft moan.

"The decision is yours," I say. I step away, although the last thing I want between us is distance.

She crosses her arms, appearing torn. "I don't know what's happening with Bryant," she says. "But my gut tells me he's not done with me."

"This is one of the most secure buildings in the city," I remind her. "He can't hurt you here. And if he tries, I'll make him regret the day he was born."

An emotion I don't recognize flashes across her face. She turns away, reaching for her phone as she walks out. I follow her, certain she's leaving until she opens the cupboard behind the desk and tosses her purse inside.

"Hey, Marcelo. It's Wren O'Brien," she says into the phone. "I'm sorry to call you at the last minute, but I won't be available to see you." She looks up, the corners of her full lips lifting into a hopeful smile. "I just accepted another job."

CHAPTER 13

Wren

Evan wasn't kidding when he said he was overwhelmed. It was almost one in the morning when he insisted I go home. He walked me to my truck and returned back to the office, but not before bending to kiss my cheek.

"Thank you," he'd said.

My fingertips circle the spot where his lips brushed over my skin last night, and every night for the past two weeks since I started working here. I can tell he wants to do more. And he's not alone.

Hotness and brilliance aside, Evan is a total sweetheart. But not everyone sees that side. His staff of engineers, techies, financial advisors, marketing and legal teams bustle in and out of his office all day long. He takes meeting after meeting, directing them so they can give him what he wants, or brainstorming with them when they can't. They see a professional man driven to succeed, but while he's polite, he keeps a professional distance. Except when it comes to me.

As much as I'm flattered, I want others to see the real Evan, the man who wants his company to succeed not just for him, but for them, and everyone who can benefit from his vision.

"Hi, Wren." The little intern grins when he sees me.

"Here's the coffee for Mr. Jonah." He waits, appearing nervous. "Do you want me to bring it into him?"

"No, he's in a meeting. I'll do it."

The kid's puny frame sags with relief. Like too many people who work here, he's worried about getting sacked.

The door to his office opens and everyone piles out. No one looks happy, which of course sends the intern bolting. I email the proposal I'm working on, making sure I smile at everyone leaving and reach for Evan's coffee.

"Come in," he calls when I knock.

I find him slumped forward with his head on his forearms and his sleeves rolled up. His glasses lay in front of him while the multiple screens in front of him create a strobe effect along his dark blue shirt.

This is another side of Evan most don't see either. But he knows I always ring his office when someone else is with me.

My hips swing a little too seductively in these heels. Not that he notices with his head laying on his arms the way it is. In a way, I wish he did and that I could spend the night tangled in the sheets with him. But I want to do right by Evan.

The more I know him, the more I realize how *human* he is.

When he first caught the business world's eye back in London, he graced the covers of all the money mags. Now, any references made about him are buried between larger columns applauding the next big business mogul. And instead of praising Evan, they only mention the "tremendous loss in revenue under his leadership" and the "empire on a bridge of collapse."

The latest column bashed him for all the people fired "amidst rumors of his inability to afford talent." The rumors (of course) were confirmed by Ashleigh Mitchum, former assistant and chief administrative lead, who was more than happy to rip Evan to shreds. Oh, but she was careful not to say anything that could be construed as libel.

That didn't mean I didn't want to punch her in the nose, especially when I saw her smug face featured in the middle of the article.

Christ. It's like no one cares about the millions of dollars and tech he's donated to hospitals and schools that serve the underprivileged globally.

But I do.

His kindness adds to his allure and gives me hope that a healthy relationship is something I can have. But it's like I did too much, too soon, and maybe sent us accelerating full-speed ahead instead of taking our time to enjoy the ride.

Don't get me wrong, the sex was mind-blowing. But damn it, I want more.

I want, I don't know, *love*.

I place the coffee in front of him and go around to massage his shoulders. "So, how did the finance meeting go?"

My sarcasm isn't lost on him and he chuckles. "About as well as you can imagine. What time is my next sales meeting?"

"Quarter to eleven."

"Quarter to eleven?" he asks, shifting his weight. "That's an odd time."

"I have a hairstylist coming in at ten-thirty to cut your hair. She's fast, good and promised to hook you up." My hands glide in wide smooth strokes. "I'll be in to supervise."

"I thought you said she's good."

"Oh, she's the best," I admit. "But she's also kind of slutty, and no way in hell am I leaving her alone with you."

His laughter turns to groaning real fast when I find a knot in his shoulder. "Geez, bossman. What the hell did you do to yourself?"

"I think it's the way I slept on the couch." He tenses beneath my touch. I don't have to look at him to know he's grimacing. "Yes. Right there."

His fingers press against the sleek mahogany when I go deeper. "Do you want me to hook you up with a chiropractor? I know a guy, but I don't think he makes house calls."

"No," he bites out, letting his head droop forward. "There are days I don't make it home. I don't have time to leave this office to go to another."

He doesn't have time to do a lot of things, including take

care of himself. But that's why he has me. It's funny, as much as we're not getting naked we are becoming more intimate, making me want him more.

I shake out my hands and move down his back. "Are you sure? It's like every inch of muscle along your back has been tied in knots. I can't even imagine the condition your spine is in."

He thinks about it. "Maybe you could schedule a masseuse. They often travel directly to their clients."

"You sayin' I don't give good massage?" I ask in my thickest Philly accent.

His shoulders tremble as he laughs, but as he settles, the strain in his muscles seems to double. "Not at all. I like you touching me." He waits and adds, "Perhaps a little too much."

I can't help the smile that comes. "Oh, yeah? Then why are you talking about me hiring some hot masseuse who can come here and give you a happy ending?"

"I never said she had to be hot," he says.

"But you wouldn't deny that happy ending if she offered, would you?" I tease.

I expect him to laugh, but he doesn't. "Like I mentioned, you're the one I want touching me."

"Good," I tell him, quietly.

I flex my fingers a few times and return to his shoulders, working them in longer gentler strokes. "You're very good to me," he says.

"I can say the same about you," I tell him.

"I don't agree." He eases himself up when I return to his shoulders. "If I were, I'd take you home and make you dinner, rather than keep you here working late."

"You'd make me dinner?" I ask.

He tilts his head so I can see him. "There are a lot of things I would do for you, Wren."

My hands glide down to his pecs. "There are a lot of things I would do for you, too, bossman," I whisper.

Like the rest of him, the muscles lining his chest strain beneath my fingers. I want to stay and play, I want to do a lot of things right now. But the hot union of sweating body parts doesn't a great relationship make. With Evan, it's safe to say I want it all, a good time in and out of bed.

"Can I talk you about something?" I ask.

The shift in my tone alerts him that at least for now, I'm done flirting. He leans his head forward, rubbing the spot on his shoulder I spent a lot of time on. "Does it involve me making more decisions?"

I adjust my position so I can reach his lower back. "Of course it does, but that's why they pay you the big bucks, and why you're going to launch this company into the cosmos."

He groans. I'm not sure if it's from his lingering doubts or because he's already fearing what I have to say. "Your administrative staff kind of sucks," I tell him truthfully.

His groans increase even though my kneading grows lighter. Well, at least I know where he's coming from.

"And your mid-level staff isn't that much better. But the good ones you have are awesome."

"Tell me something I'm not aware of," he says.

"Okay. I've assembled a team."

He stills beneath me, lifting his head. "What?"

"A team of specialists you might say." I cup his neck so my fingers and thumb work both sides.

"And who might these specialists be?"

"Most are car reps. Some worked in finance and even fewer worked desk jobs. But we need more support staff so I made a few calls."

"Car reps?" he repeats.

I'm not sure if he's fixated on those two words or if he thinks I'm screwing with him. "I'll show you what I mean." I scoot around him and pull up my proposal on his workstation, a mammoth piece of machinery with multiple screens that lifts up from the front of his desk with a verbal command.

The first picture that appears is Oscar's. Not the ray of sunshine he was expecting.

"Isn't this the man who was rude to your friend?"

"Oh, yeah, he's a total asshole, but he's smart and an animal when it comes to sales. It's the reason we're always neck and neck in revenue." I scroll down, showing him a picture of each rep, followed by their level of experience. It puts a face to a name and makes it more personal. Not that Evan seems blown away.

"Wren, there's over thirty people here. I can't hire thirty people."

He pushes away from the desk and rubs his face. It's something he does when he's close to his limit.

I plop onto his lap, shocking us both. But I hate seeing him like this and I want to feel close to him. A man so consumed with running an empire can become lost and isolate himself from the rest of the world. He needs reminding I'm on his side, and that he's not alone.

His hand slides along my hip and onto my ass. I smile. Maybe he needs to feel close to me, too. "Hear me out, okay?"

"All right," he answers.

I have a lot to say, but don't say it right away, taking a moment to play with the hair curling along the edges of his ears. He didn't shave today, and if it wasn't for the dress shirt, he'd resemble a sexy construction worker ready to pound nails. But he did wear the shirt, reminding me that this is business and not play. Damn, no matter how much I want to play. Hard to be a good girl when all I crave is time with him in bed.

"Your marketing team isn't hungry enough. Most are burnt out or just here for the paycheck. These guys," I say, jerking my head in the direction of the screen. "Are out of work. They're not just hungry, they're starving."

"I can't pay them," he says. "My recent dismissals have allowed me to save some money, but not enough to hire all these people. It's only enough to keep those I have."

"How bad is it?" I ask, seeing beyond the specks of gold in his irises to the worry lurking beneath.

"Bad enough that I've given up my salary to keep us afloat."

"Jesus, Evan," I say straightening. "All this work, and you're not even getting paid for it?"

"No."

His fingers skim along my backside. It's not sexual, at least that's not how I take it. He's taking comfort in my presence, just like I'm doing in his.

"I believe in this company," he says. "And I'll sacrifice whatever it takes to save it."

"But don't you have bills that extend past what you're shelling out here?"

"I do," he admits. "But I should have enough in savings and stocks to cover it."

"Should?" I ask.

He doesn't want to tell me. But I'm starting to think I'm the only one Evan confides in. "I may have to deplete my savings in the coming months if things don't change. It's either that or file for bankruptcy, and I refuse to go that route."

I kiss the spot between his ear and his cheek. Maybe I shouldn't, but I can't help myself around him most of the time, and even less now. "Then let me help you."

"Wren, I can't ask you to give up your salary."

"Good, cause I wasn't offering," I admit.

He laughs and nuzzles my neck. I wish he didn't feel so good there, he does. "How much did your marketing reps make? The ones you let go last week?"

"They were young, new, and inexperienced so only about a hundred thousand each."

I nod. "Okay. So how about we replace them with old and not so new, experienced people who won't need as much."

He shakes his head. "They were two people. You're talking about hiring what? Twenty reps alone?"

"You're not hiring," I tell him, grinning back at him when he cocks an eyebrow. "You're paying them by the sale, just like they would make at the dealership. Ten grand in their pockets for each sale they make. You teach them everything they need to know about Mechanicus Whatever-icus, pay them for their travel, lodging, and food, and you'll make close to ten times as much with the first good faith check the buyers drop." By now I'm really smiling. "A hundred times as much over the next few years, from that one sale."

His hand, the one that's been tracing invisible circles into my upper thigh stills. "Ten thousand dollars isn't a lot compared to what they'll bring the company."

He's not shooting me down, he's thinking out loud and coming to terms with the cost versus the revenue. That doesn't stop me from going full speed ahead. "I'm not talking salary. I'm talking sales bonus. A week to train. A week to sell. And you get ten grand. That's two-hundred and sixty thousand dollars a year, selling one product every two weeks—which is more than they would make selling cars, and a shit ton more for you."

"And I don't have to pay them insurance or benefits," he adds.

"Not unless you choose to hire them. And in a few months, you won't need to train them so intensively. They'll have all the basics down and still be selling like they're on fire." I smirk. "This company pays too many people who don't do squat a ridiculous amount of money, and doesn't reward those giving it their all."

"Wren, this sounds good in theory. But while they have extensive sales experience, they're unfamiliar with robotics, let alone nanotechnology of this caliber. Despite their strengths, a week isn't enough time to learn all the tech we've developed and need to sell."

"No, but it's enough for twenty people to learn one product each. Yeah, that one product is complex, but so are the car engines we've familiarized ourselves with. And they're not haggling on price or contracts like we had to. You have your legal team for that. Clifton, Anne and your senior staff can teach them what each product does and oversee their pitches via conference calls while my reps work their magic."

"All right, that's a solid plan for my sales department. What about the administrative staff?"

"I'll take care of the administrative staff. I can fire, hire, and reward. If you trust me, I can do that for you—"

His mouth crashes into mine and his fingers dig through my hair. That crisp shirt he's wearing doesn't stand a chance when I yank him closer, his sweet taste making me ache for more.

Jolts of heat burn their way through my core, adding an extra sizzle to our already burning kiss. "Bloody hell," he rasps, his voice tortured as he buries his mouth against my neck.

My nipples tighten to stiff points, straining and begging for his teeth to scrape along sensitive buds. But as ready as I am to continue, he doesn't appear ready to carry things through.

He pulls away slowly, his head falling against the headrest. "I'm sorry," he gasps. "I know I promised to behave like a gentleman."

Some kind of sound, maybe a squeak, escapes my throat before I manage any semblance of words. This is a man who knows how to curl my damn toes. "I'll let it go this time," I say, prying my fingers lose from his collar.

He laughs as I fall against his chest. "I like you here," he says, his hand returning to my ass.

"With your hand on my right butt cheek?"

"That, too," he says quieting. "But I meant having you close.

His lips feather over mine. "My favorite time of day is any time I get to see you."

"That's my favorite part, too," I admit, wishing I could say it better.

I close my eyes and rest against him, enjoying the feel of him.

We have a lot to do, but neither of us move for few long blissful minutes. "Are you sure you can do what you're taking on?" he finally asks. "It's not easy to let people go."

"It's not," I agree. What I don't say is that I'm willing to do a lot more for his company, and even more for him.

"All right," he says, switching back to big badass boss mode. "Cancel my next meeting, get the directors of HR, Sales, and Finance in here, and I'll make it happen. How soon can your former coworkers start?"

"They'll be here at eight-thirty tomorrow morning."

I don't have to look up to know he's smiling. "When did you phone them?"

"Two days ago," I admit. "After I worked out a plan, reserved the conference room downstairs, and had Clifton and Anne's secretaries free up their schedules."

He laughs. "How did you know I'd say yes?"

I ease away enough to see his face. "I didn't," I admit. "I only knew you'd listen."

His features split with surprise and what looks like the start of grin. Genuine feelings from a genuine man capable of stirring far too many good feels. I rise and walk out. I don't know what's happening between us.

All I know is that I'm ready for more.

CHAPTER 14

Evan

In the weeks that follow, the amount of work seems to increase, rather than lessen. Not that it slows me down. In fact, my drive to succeed surges, as does the need to hold Wren in my arms.

I step out of my office. There's no stack of folders I'm holding or documents I'm reviewing, there's simply a desire to see the woman I can't get enough of.

She glances up as she slips on her coat. "Hey," she says. "I was just on my way in to tell you I'm leaving and to thank you for my present." She tips her head to the side. "You're leaving soon too, right?"

"I have another hour of work before I can head out." I smile at the disbelief clouding her features. "This time, I mean it."

"I hope so," she adds, sounding worried. She lifts her new purse, showing it to me. Already it's stuffed with the contents of her old purse, and possibly the former purse itself by the looks of it. "This wasn't necessary. Pretty, pricey, and sweet, but not necessary."

"Yes, it was. I only wish I could do more."

"You already do enough," she says.

"Not for you," I admit.

I reach for her hand, wincing when pain shoots into my shoulder. A fine line forms across her forehead when she crinkles her brow. "Finnie worked you pretty hard this morning, didn't he?"

Yes, and I'm still feeling the effects. Not that I bother to mention it. "It's worth it," I say instead. "In the few weeks your brother has trained me, I've had better conditioning than in the months I worked out with that imbecile."

I don't bother to keep my annoyance from my voice. Wren, of course, notices. "Imbecile?" she asks. "Are you still pissed at your personal trainer for saying I have a nice ass?"

"No, I'm pissed at him for telling *me* you have a nice ass *and* admitting how he'd like to 'tap it'."

"All right," she says. "But in his defense, not that I'm nuts about what he had to say about me, he didn't know we were together."

"He does now," I remind her.

"Evan, everyone on the entire floor realized that when you went all caveman." She clears her throat, attempting to mimic my accent and doing wretched job. "Blimey, that'd be my woman you're talkin' about, ye bloody wanker. Bugger off before I shove your tiny bollocks up your steroid injected arse!"

"I never said that," I say, chuckling.

"Close enough."

"And you sound like Steve Irwin."

"The Crocodile Hunter?"

"That's right" I reply.

"Hmm," she says. "I was going for David Gandy."

I shake my head.

"Daniel Craig?"

"No."

"Hugh Jackman?"

"He's *Australian*."

"You sayin' I suck at accents?"

"Embarrassingly so," I admit."

She pretends to be offended when I throw my head back, laughing, but ends up laughing just as hard.

"Hey, I can do a lot of things, but English accents aren't one of them." She tugs my sleeve. "My point is you really lost it. I thought you were going to throw me over your shoulder or some shit."

"I wouldn't do that," I say, flashing what I hope is an innocent smile. "Unless you want me to."

She laughs. "I shouldn't say this, but it's nice to know that you care." Her tongue slides along her incisor. "About me and my assets."

"I do," I confess, reaching for her hand. "More than you realize."

Her playful demeanor leaves her, replaced with soft beauty that warms my chest. "You make it so easy to like you," she says.

"I can say the same about you," I tell her quietly. "And I like you more with each moment that passes."

She seems to think beyond what I say. My thumb carefully strokes the back of her hand as I realize how tired she seems. "It's late. Let me walk you out."

She knows I'm not asking. Every night I escort her to her vehicle, relishing any time we can spend alone. We see a great deal of each other now that we work together, and we often eat lunch and dinner in my office. But our intimate moments are limited and our conversations usually revolve around business or *"Evan Almighty Taking Over the World,"* as she describes it. With everything we're implementing, I'm hoping that will change and I can devote more time to our relationship.

Her fingers thread through mine, our steps as we walk down the hall of cubicles the only audible sound. I nod to the security guard stationed near the elevator. "Good evening, Mr. Jonah," he says.

"Good evening," I respond.

The corners of his mouth lift when he focuses on my lovely companion. "Night, Wren."

"See ya, Mikey," she calls. Unlike me, who can barely keep track of my immediate staff, she's already familiarized herself with the majority of my employees and made quite the impression.

"Oh, hey, Wren. Did you hear?" he asks. "The 76ers are up by ten."

"Of course they are, Mikey, because the Celtics suck and my boys are making sure they know it."

He laughs as I simply shake my head, wondering how she keeps up with it all. The elevator doors open, the tech in my watch in tune with the sensor fixed to the arch, summoning the elevator whenever I near.

"Alfred, parking level," I say, leading Wren inside.

"Parking level initiated," Alfred announces.

Wren leans her head against my shoulder when the doors close. I slip my arm around her waist. "By the way, California Medical emailed me a few moments ago."

She lifts her head. "And?"

"They don't want Eldar Mechanicus."

"For fuck's sake, why—"

"They want the entire line of Mechanicus," I tell her smiling.

Her initial frustration is quickly replaced by shock followed by elation. She throws her arms around me. "Evan!"

I pull her against me. "I believe the CEO's exact words were, 'your representative Penny killed it.' He was leaving for the day, but he's calling tomorrow to finalize the deal with me and my legal team."

"I knew that kid had it in her," she says, jabbing me in the chest. "Holy shit, that's sixty grand to her for a week's work—which means she just passed Oscar in sales!"

"And brought in six hundred thousand for the company in good faith deposits." Her eyes widen when she realizes what this means. That doesn't stop me from telling her. "We're looking at six hundred million over the next ten years with this hospital alone, more if they extend it to their network of clinics and doctors."

"You're doing it, Evan," she says. "You're saving the company."

I lean in for a celebratory kiss, but she steps away when the elevator door opens. Lionel, one of the key members of my legal and contracts team steps on, the exhaustion in his posture doing little to squelch his enthusiasm. "I just saw your email. Well done, Evan."

I shake his hand, smiling, then promptly return it to hold Wren's. She tries to keep a respectable distance in front of my staff, initially shying away from any show of affection. I don't want to pretend that there's nothing between us or deny what she means to me. I told her as much and prove it every time I walk her out.

Lionel's focus briefly drops to our entwined hands. Like many of my staff, he's likely had his suspicions, but I'm happy to confirm them all the same.

"What time do you want to meet?" he asks, turning to face the doors.

"I suggested noon since it will be nine their time." I look to Wren. "We'll notify you as soon as we know. Just make sure the team is available."

"Evan, the team will set up tents in your office to avoid missing that call," he says, causing us to chuckle.

We walk out of the elevators, through the enclosed glass lobby, and into the parking deck. "Good night, Evan. Wren," he adds, nodding.

"Good night," we reply.

He heads toward the right. My reserved parking space is just a few feet from elevator, as is the Assistant Vice-Chair spot where Wren's vehicle waits. "That's a good title for you," I say motioning to the letters painted into the concrete.

"No, that's a good spot for someone more qualified than me." She opens the door with the key fob and places her new purse on the seat.

"You may not hold the degree, but you have a gift for business." My gaze darts across her face as my arms find her waist. "You deserve a change in title and more money. But I'm too selfish to let you go."

"Then don't let me go," she tells me.

I suppose it's too soon to tell her I never want to, so I say something else instead. "Will you do something for me?"

Her smile is sweet while her tone suggests more. "Haven't you figured out that I would do anything for you?"

I close my eyes, relieved not only to hear her words, but how she says them. "I want us to go away next weekend. Pick the place, I don't care what it costs. My only wish is to be alone with you."

Since the day she fell onto my lap our kisses come more frequently, as well as our affection. We've also managed a few dinners out and some functions with her family. Just last Sunday, we went to see a movie that according to her had, "a lot of shit that will blow up and people shooting at each other, but you'll love it." She was right, but it was the time we shared that I most enjoyed.

As I ask her to plan our getaway, she knows I'm asking for more than a goodnight and a gentle touch. I want to wake up with her beside me.

"If I say yes, will you do a couple of things for me?" She grins at my nod. "There's a birthday party coming up that I've been invited to. I'd like you to go with me."

"Fair enough. What's the other thing?"

"I want you to go upstairs and finish your work." Her skin flushes as her smile widens. "Then I want you to come home to me."

I straighten. "You want me to spend the night with you?"

She meets my face, ardor erasing all doubt. "I've been trying to be good," she tells me. "But tonight, I want more than a little naughty. Tell me you want it, too, so I don't have to spend another night without you."

CHAPTER 15

Wren

Evan doesn't move. I supposed he's stunned stupid. But I mean what I say. Every night I leave, it's like I leave a part of me behind. At first, that nagging feeling made me think I forgot to send an email or prepare a document he might need. But when that nagging feeling continued without cause, I realized the one thing I was leaving without was him.

I wanted to bang my head against the steering wheel when it finally hit me. Not that this isn't a good thing. It's just, I don't know, *new*. I'm used to assholes like Bryant. But Evan isn't him. Every time we say goodbye, I have to fight the urge to run back to him.

"You're not saying anything," I tell him, smoothing the hair along his temple.

"Only because I have no intention of returning to my office."

"But you have to," I remind him.

"No, I don't," he says, leaning in to kiss me.

I press my hand against his chest, keeping him in place where his lips linger over mine. "I know what this company means to you, bossman, and I won't keep you from your work. Take your time, I promise to wait."

"Don't call me bossman." He winks. "Unless we're in

bed."

His mouth immediately seizes mine, his tongue pushing through in one rough stroke. This isn't our typical good night kiss. This kiss is more like the ones we sneak in his office when we're alone, in between meetings when our hands wander and the thrill of getting caught heightens our senses. He palms my ass, the motion possessive and filled with masculine power.

If I told him to stop, he would. But, just like the other day when I brought in his lunch and kissed him hello *and* he pulled me onto his lap, I don't want him to stop. That doesn't mean we shouldn't.

I pull away, my lips swelling from one hell of a kiss. I hold up my hand when he tries to follow. "Are you clean?"

"What?" He waits, realizing what I'm asking. "Yes, you don't have to worry about anything, beautiful."

"I'm clean, too," I tell him. "And I'm on birth control. I don't want to use a condom tonight unless you want to—"

I barely get the last word out before he's all over me again. "No condoms," he says, speaking low against my ear as he tugs the lobe with his teeth. "I want to feel you completely when I'm inside of you."

Between the flicks of his tongue, that accent, and his comment I seriously almost orgasm. Somehow, I ease away. "Give me time to get ready for you, and I promise I'll let you do anything you want to me."

The halogen lights of the parking deck bleach our faces, but don't quite suppress the blush claiming his gorgeous face. "Anything?" he asks.

I look at him dead in the eyes. "Anything," I promise.

I lean in for quick kiss. Well, at least I mean it to be quick. Evan deepens it, fusing our lips and pushing me against the side door. The hard bulge building in his pants rams me in the stomach, begging me to spread my legs.

Holy shit. Every minute Sister Marguerite spent during health class, proselytizing about the sins of the flesh and burning in hell if we surrender to it, is wasted. Fire and brimstone are looking pretty damn good seeing as I'm seconds from having sex, standing up, in a Goddamn parking deck.

He wrenches himself away when the double-doors leading toward the elevator fling open and a few staff members file out. My F-150 shields us, giving us time to compose ourselves, but just barely.

"Good evening, Mr. Johan, Miss O'Brien," they say at once.

Evan nods politely from where he's leaning over the hood of my ride with his hands clasped, appearing to pause in the middle of an intense conversation and *not* an intense moment.

I'm leaning against the door with my arms crossed, nodding like I'm agreeing and *not* thinking about the giant erection ready to bust through his pants.

He buries his hands in his hair as they step out of earshot. "You have no idea what you do to me," he tells me.

"You're right," I say, yanking open the door. "Why don't we hop inside and you can show me."

He groans, dragging his hand down his face. "You're forgetting the cameras," he says, motioning to the one perched on the closest pillar. "Not that I did a better job of remembering."

"Oh, the cameras. Yeah." I tug on his arm. "Why didn't you remember? You're supposed to be the reasonable one."

The dark and lustful look he pegs me with immediately erases my smile. "Any semblance of reason is lost the moment I touch you," he tells me.

"You've been reading that poetry shit again, haven't you?"

He laughs and pulls me to him, making me smile. Damn, I have it bad for him. "I'm not trying to seduce you." I think about it. "Never mind, I am. But I know you have a company to save. So if you have to go, go. Just promise to make it up to me later."

"I promise," he says, speaking as if he's gifting his soul in that simple statement.

My mouth is capable of three things: loud, louder, and

non-stop. But nothing I say will carry as much emotion as I sensed in those two words, except maybe three words I'm not ready to tell him.

I back away and slip into my truck. "Try not to be too long, okay?"

"I'll be with you soon," he assures me.

But it won't be soon enough.

It's not until I pull out and round the corner that he heads back into the building. I let out a sigh, wondering exactly when I fell as hard as I have.

The steering wheel slides along my fingers as I straighten my truck. With the exception of a few random cars, the three-level lot is almost completely empty.

I wave to the security guard as he opens the heavy metal gate to let me out. Every evening at six, all entrances are sealed tight. Access in and out is only permitted following a thorough clearance by armed guards. But I won't complain. I like feeling safe.

Yet when I pull onto the main road that sense of security immediately vanishes.

Last night, I left close to ten, something I do fairly frequently when I'm rushing to finish a project or brainstorming with Evan. Normally, it's no big deal. But from the moment I left the building, I couldn't shake the feeling I was being watched.

I didn't notice anyone tailing me and thought the lack of sleep was getting to me, until I turned onto my street. Finn jogged toward me when I pulled into our driveway and hopped out, having just completed his evening run. I started toward him when screeching tires had us looking up the block.

"What was that?" I asked.

"Some asshole in an old Jeep." It's what he claimed, but then he pressed his hand against my back, frowning as he led me inside.

He didn't have a good feeling, and neither did I. But when nothing else happened we brushed it aside.

I was so busy today, I didn't even bother mentioning it to

Evan. But now . . .

I switch on the radio when that awful sense returns. "Relax," I say aloud, forcing myself to take a few breaths.

The song finishes playing and the DJ announces more snow for the weekend when bright headlights flash across my rearview mirror, overtaking the expanse and closing in. I can't make out the car. I only know it's as big as my truck.

I push on the gas and he follows, staying close enough to blind me with his lights and keep me from getting a make on the vehicle. I try to convince myself I'm just being paranoid—that it's not Bryant. He doesn't know where I work and—

The car withdraws. It's only then I start to breathe again.

It's not him . . .

I shrug out of my coat when I realize how badly I'm sweating. What's wrong with me? It's only eight-thirty and this isn't the first time I've been out after dark.

I roll my shoulders, trying to shake the tension that remains when I just make the next light and think I've lost him. Two streets down, I make a right, but as I reach the next block those same damn headlights appear.

Paranoid or not, I'm done. "Alfred, call Evan."

"Calling Evan, Wren," Alfred announces.

I almost smile. Evan had his tech heads install Alfred's software in my ride shortly after I started working for him. They tailored it, and my new phone, to respond to my voice and needs.

But the smile that wants to come dissolves when I change lanes and the car follows.

The call goes to voicemail. "Evan is not available, Wren," Alfred's responds. "Leave message?"

I don't answer, too busy watching the car edge closer.

"Wren is trying to call you, Evan," Alfred answers, leaving a message for me.

"Alfred, call Curran," I say.

The line rings twice, the car inching closer with each long, dragged out ring. It's a black SUV, but that's as much as I see.

"Hey, Wren," Curran says. "What's going on?"

The tightening in my chest makes it hard to speak. "I'm on my way home," I manage.

"Why are you calling?" he asks, picking up that something's wrong.

I slam on the brakes when the car in front of me stops at a light. "Shit!" I yell, my tires screeching. The SUV zips around and past me, cutting a hard right.

"Wren?" Curran asks. "What the fuck's going on?"

I shake my head, pissed at myself for not being more careful. "I thought I was being followed."

"By Bryant?"

"I don't know," I admit.

"Did you get the make or a plate?"

"No, I almost hit the car in front of me and he sped past me before I had a good look."

"But it was definitely a guy?"

I stumble over my words. "I don't know," I say, wishing I'd been smarter. "All I saw were headlights closing in. But last night, I felt like I was being followed, too."

"By the same car?"

The truck behind me blasts his horn when traffic moves ahead without me. I mutter a curse and stomp on the gas.

"Wren?"

"No. That one was an old model Jeep, dark green maybe a 2004. Finnie saw it, too."

"Why didn't you call me?"

God, it feels like I'm losing my mind. "Because I didn't actually see it until I arrived home. But when I pulled out of work last night, just like tonight, it felt like I was being tailed."

"But you didn't see exactly who it was?"

"No."

"How long were followed?"

My pulse is pounding so hard in my ears, I can barely think. "Last night, it felt like the whole ride home. Tonight, not long. A few blocks." I glance at my mirrors. "Whoever he was is gone."

"You're sure?"

I take another look. "Yeah," I mutter. "Christ, I just want to get home."

"Finnie won't be there," he reminds me. "He left for the press tour this morning."

"I know. Sol, Kill, and Sofia are with him." Of course, they just happen to be the ones who live the closest and won't be home for another week.

When Curran doesn't say anything, I start hoping he'll tell me that it's probably nothing.

"I'm sorry I bothered you," I say as the silence stretches between us. "Give Fiona a kiss from me and—"

"Where are you?" he asks, his voice gruff.

"Curran, it's no big deal," I tell him, sensing his anger. "If anything I feel like a dumbass for calling you."

"You're not a dumbass," he says. "Look, I've been a cop long enough to know to follow my instincts. If something inside you is telling you something is wrong, then something probably is. Where are you?"

"On Walnut Street, approaching the Forest Theatre."

"Okay," he says, shuffling in the background. "Pull over and stop at Anthony's or Mulligan's. I'll meet you there and follow you home."

Almost at once, Fiona starts crying in the background, something she does every time she sees her daddy getting ready to leave. "Curran, don't. You're upsetting the baby over nothing."

"Shhh. It's okay," he says to her.

I can almost picture him gathering her little body into his arms. "Curran, Evan is meeting me at the house as soon as he's done at work."

"But he's not there now," he says, cutting me off as his daughter settles. "You still have at least another twenty before you're home and anything can happen between now and then."

I roll to a stop at a light. "But it's going to take you at least forty minutes to get to me and another two hours before you're back to your family—all because I'm seeing things that aren't there."

"Bryant's missing," he tells me.

"What?"

The car behind me blasts his horn when the light turns green and I don't immediately shoot forward. I flip him off and punch it, listening closely to what Curran says.

"We've been keeping an eye on him, but now we can't find him."

"Shit," I mutter.

"Wren, do you hear yourself? How upset you sound? Pull over and I'll leave now."

Fiona starts whimpering all over again. But even if she wasn't so upset, I'm not taking Curran away from his family.

"No," I say. "There's no one behind me." That's a lie. The same asshole who honked at me is still there, but he makes a left at the next block.

"Tess, can you take you take her a sec?" What sounds like heavy steps race forward. "At least let me send a badge who's close your location."

I mutter a curse, checking my mirrors again when I reach the next light. "What are you going to tell him? My little sister thinks she's being stalked?"

"Yup," he answers, the edge to his tone tightening the knot in my chest.

"But it's not true," I say, more because I need to believe it. "I haven't even heard from him."

"That doesn't mean you won't." He huffs when I quiet. "Look, just like your instincts warned you that something was wrong, mine are telling me Bryant is fucking with you. There's too many dots connecting him to you and I don't like it."

"I don't like it either," I admit.

A door swings open at the corner store. Two people stumble out, laughing and acting drunk. "Does Evan know about Bryant?"

"Yes, I—"

I jump when the high-tech Bluetooth rings and Alfred's techno voice streams through. "Evan is returning your call. Should I put Curran on hold?"

"Curran, hold on. Evan's calling. Yes, Alfred."

I start to correct myself and give the full command, "Yes, Alfred, hold Curran and answer Evan," but Alfred is already on it.

"Hi, are you home?" Evan asks, sounding confused.

He knows it's thirty-five minutes back to my place, and it hasn't been that long since I left him. "No," I say. "Are you on your way?"

"Soon, I have a few projects to sign off on and was delayed when the lab called with issues surrounding the new Mechanicus prototype."

"Sorry," I say. "I didn't mean to interrupt your work."

He pauses. "What's wrong?"

I tried keeping my tone even, but there's no hiding my frustration. "It's probably nothing."

"Then tell me," he says, his voice sharpening with concern.

I groan when traffic slows to a stop ahead of me. There's been an accident or something, delaying me even more. On the plus side, it gives me more than enough time to tell Evan everything I told Curran.

When I finish, he doesn't hesitate. "You're spending the night at my house," he says.

"Wait, I can't—"

"Yes, you can. Alfred, show Wren to my residence straight away."

"Initiating shortest route," Alfred says.

My navigation screen flashes, honing in on the surrounding area and spiraling out like some futuristic satellite. "Whoa, slow down there, Alfred."

"Shortest route initiated," Alfred answers, totally ignoring me and taking Evan's side. "At the next block, make a left on North 10th Street, travel three blocks, and make a left onto Vine Street toward the Vine Street Expressway."

I mumble a few swears, but make the left Alfred suggests.

"Alfred, shut down my office," Evan's voice booms.

"Shutting down office," Alfred repeats.

The sound of shuffling papers increases with Evan's words. "Alfred, protect Wren and see her inside my residence."

"Protecting, Wren," he repeats.

I stare blankly as an infrared netting flares out from the screen, onto the dash, and across the cabin. "Uh. What did you just do?" I ask.

"I'm protecting you," Evan says, like it's obvious.

A small light flashes on above my rearview mirror, extending the bright red, crisscrossing pattern of lights across the hood. "Evan, what the hell did your Geek Gang do to my truck?"

"Installed Alfred into your vehicle," he responds, his breathing increasing as if he's moving fast. "We discussed this. They applied our protection and intelligence to fit your needs."

"I'm not carrying the Hope diamond," I remind him. "You'll see for yourself when I strip down to my panties."

"I'm only assuring your safety so I can help you out of those panties."

"Wren secure," Alfred says, oblivious to the surge of blood now thumping my nether regions.

A 9-1-1 icon appears on the corner of the navigation screen, blinking as if readying to dial. "Is a bazooka going to pop out of my dash?" I ask.

"No, a machine gun," he responds, not missing a beat. "It carries more rounds and is easier to manipulate."

I only hope he's joking. "About your tech team," I begin.

"Yes?"

"They're all virgins aren't they?"

His tone drops an octave. "Perhaps, but I'm not."

"No, you're not, big boy." I glance around as the infrared lights dissolve into the vehicle. I think I read that if the software senses a crash, the police are alerted. "Okay," I say slowly. "All this Robo Cop tech is fascinating and all, but if Darth Vader pops up in my passenger seat and starts swinging his light saber, I'm going to freak out. This is a little much, don't you think?"

"No," he rumbles. The *ding* in the background alerts me Evan is at the elevator. "It took me years to find you and I'll be damned if I allow some manky bastard to harm you."

This is the part where the Wren who busts heads and kicks ass interrupts and tells Evan that she's fine, that she doesn't need protecting, and that *he's* coming to *her*. But that Wren is too busy laughing at the Wren melting into a pile of goo with sizzling lady parts. "You're all sorts of hot right now, you know that, bossman?"

His voice drips with sex. "I told you, there's only one place you can call me *bossman*."

"I know," I whisper, my body heating another notch.

"You'll be safe and in my arms soon. I swear it."

He releases a breath, appearing to fumble with something. "According to Alfred's message on my phone, you'll arrive at my house twenty minutes before I do. He'll allow you in and secure you inside. Make yourself at home. Should anything happen, Alfred will alert both me and the police."

"Okay," I say, well-aware of my quivering tone.

"Wren, don't be afraid. I'm with you."

"I'm not afraid," I tell him. *Not anymore.*

Again my voice trembles, but it has nothing to do with fear and everything to do with Evan.

Alfred chimes in, hauling me back to the moment. "Curran calling. Accept call?"

"Oh, no," I say, urgency replacing those warm feels. "Evan, I have to go. I left Curran on hold and now he's calling back."

"All right. I . . . I'll see you soon."

He seems to want to say more, and maybe I do, too.

"Accept call from Curran O'Brien?" Alfred presses when Evan disconnects.

"Yes, accept call, Alfred."

"What the hell, Wren?" Curran chimes in.

"I'm sorry, Evan called and didn't take what I had to tell him well."

"Is he pissed?" he asks.

"He is, but not at me. He wants me to spend the night at his place."

"Okay. Good," he says.

"*Okay*?" I smirk, the lingering tension in the pit of my stomach lifting. "When did you get all soft on Evan? Shouldn't you be telling me not to have sex with him or some crazy shit?"

"Damn it, Wren. I meant 'good' that you won't be alone. Did you have to go there?"

"Aw, come on. You and the others kept the key to my chastity belt too damn long. I would think you'd be happy Evan bit that lock free with his teeth."

"God, Wren. Shut it already." I don't have to see him to know he's making a face.

I laugh as I follow Alfred's directions onto the Blue Route.

"He's a decent guy," Curran admits, catching me off-guard. "Different from those asshats you wasted your time on."

"Yeah. He is," I say, losing my humor and probably too much of my heart.

"That's a good thing, Wren," he says. "There's no shame in finding love."

He said the "L" word, but I don't argue. "Like you did?" I offer.

"Yeah," he admits, his voice softening the way it does when Tess is near. "Hey, do me a solid and let me know when you get to Evan's. Unless you want to stay on with me until you get there."

"No, I'll text." There's a lot I want to say, but it's like the silence surrounding me muffles my thoughts. "Thanks, Curran."

"Anytime."

He hangs up, and again I'm alone. But as my attention drifts to the screen, I'm reminded of the man who put everything into motion to keep me safe. For once in my life, alone is the last thing I am.

CHAPTER 16

Wren

I'm not sure what to expect when I arrive at Evan's house. In Villanova, you can find anything from classic homes straight out of black and white 50s sitcoms to sprawling mansions with horse farms. Everything about Evan screams modern and high-tech, but the British-like accent and his personality are more Old World charm.

He's a blend of both, and his home reflects as much. Alfred allows me through the high metal gates, shutting them as soon as I pass. A blanket of snow from the late March blizzard covers what's probably a pretty garden, but the driveway is meticulously clean. It's not a long drive up compared to some of the homes I passed, but a thick line of pines and bushes swallow me whole, shielding me and the house from the rest of the world.

The house alternates between light and dark gray stone. Outdoor landscaping lights illuminate the path leading to the front door and the three car garage.

I start to park in front of the far left garage door, thinking Alfred will somehow magically let me in through the front entrance, but the center bay opens when I near.

Like the gates, it shuts when I pull in and cut the engine. My F-150 barely fits in my detached garage. But in Evan's garage, there's plenty of space on both sides.

I slip out, catching sight of his Jag as I wonder how the hell he keeps it so clean. Metal shelving lines the perimeter, appearing empty and surprisingly dust and streak free. The clicking sound of the door unlocking at the top of the stairs lures me toward it. I walk in through a laundry room and into a very chic black and white kitchen.

Dark hardwood floors extend out and into a great room roughly the size of Delaware. Floor to ceiling windows lead to a terrace, the exterior lights extending to reveal a privacy fence barely visible through the stand of trees.

"Wren is secure," Alfred's voice echoes around me.

I pause near the black marble-encased gas fireplace as the door to the garage clicks shut. "Thanks there, Alfred," I say. "That wasn't creepy or anything."

He doesn't respond this time, which is good, I'm already feeling out of place. My crimson coat is the only color in the very sterile field of black, white, and gray. Don't get me wrong, the house is gorgeous, spacious without being over the top. But it's as if Evan's playful side is absent, replaced solely by the serious and reserved side the world only sees.

"Well, I guess I'll have to change that."

"Change temperature of room, Wren?" Alfred offers.

"No, Alfred. I'll do that all on my own. And no offense, buddy, but can you tone it down some, you're freaking me out."

"Silence mode initiated per Wren's request," he answers.

Everything goes abruptly still. When Alfred doesn't appear with some high-tech sword to sever my head, I send a quick text to Curran and Evan, assuring them I'm safe. After another quick survey of my surroundings, I place my purse and coat on the white leather couch and strip completely out of my clothes. I leave on my knee-high boots because I'm a classy gal and find the closest bathroom to freshen up.

The garage door opens as I finish running a brush through my hair. Alfred announces, "Welcome home, Evan," as I hurry out and reach for my coat.

I manage to fasten the last button when Evan appears at

the doorway to the kitchen. He lets the heavy briefcase in his hand fall as he steps in, releasing a breath when he sees me.

"You're safe," he says, my presence appearing to settle him.

I shove my hands into the deep pockets as I leave the great room, shortening the space separating us. "I'm fine," I assure him, my cheeks warming as he pulls me against him.

I'm expecting a hot and heavy night. He is too, given the way he's clutching me. But the emotion written on his features isn't passion. It's relief. He's happy I'm okay.

He cups the nape of my neck, pressing a gentle kiss on my lips. "You were scared," he says.

I tense. It's not that what he says isn't true. But "scared" isn't a word I use when it comes to me. "Nervous" and "freaked out," sure, they're easier to say. They tone down the meaning and mask the vulnerability "scared" exposes.

Vulnerable . . . that's another word that freaks me out and something I can never be again.

"I didn't like it," he says, the gruffness in his tone revealing the anger that lingers.

"I didn't like it either." It's not something I'd tell anyone else. But just like Evan exposes himself to me, I know I can do the same.

I smooth my palms along the soft cashmere of his dark coat. "I don't want to talk about it anymore."

"All right, if that's what you wish." He cocks his head when it occurs to him I'm still wearing my coat. "My darling, are you cold?"

"No," I answer, tripping over the word. He called me his "darling." In that accent. No. That wasn't hot or anything. Nope not at all.

"If I help you out of your coat, will you help me out of mine?" I offer.

He watches me as I slip the heavy fabric over his shoulders and down his arms. He knows I'm up to something, but doesn't quite know what that something is. He unfastens my top button, allowing the thick material to pull away and expose the swell of my breasts as his lips seal over mine. It's not until his hand slips inside and my bare flesh meets his palm that he breaks our kiss.

His gaze smokes as he pops the last two buttons free and parts the sides. "Fuck. *Me*," he rasps, hauling me to him.

He frees me from the warm wool, greeting me with a searing kiss. My fingers work fast to tug off his jacket. I'm almost down to the last few buttons of his shirt when his fingers slip between my thighs. I clamp down, moaning when he goes deep.

Evan's mouth attacks my throat. "I need to be inside you," he grunts, his motions fast and demanding. "Every way I can."

I clutch his head, gasping when his tongue laves my nipple and biting back a curse when his teeth graze the pebbled point. His mouth feels good, *so good*. But it doesn't compare to the delicious pain below when his fingers curl and his palm bats against my tender flesh.

He bands his arm around my waist, easing me back toward the table. I unravel with the first orgasm that hits, barely keeping my feet. Evan holds tight, moving fast and propping me on the edge of the table. I'm no longer whimpering, I'm thrashing wildly, ecstasy blinding me to everything but him.

My reaction isn't enough for Evan. He falls to his knees, his mouth disappearing between my legs.

The heel of my boot slams into a chair as he parts my thighs, sucking hard. I push up on my elbows to watch, my breasts bouncing with how fast I'm breathing and my fingers digging through his hair to hold him in place. The hunger in his dark gaze assures me he won't let go, and I'm already begging for more.

My pelvis tilts to meet his mouth as he ravishes me. The first orgasm doesn't quite leave before another builds, tightening my core in agonizing bliss. It's almost too much, but I don't fight it, allowing his ardor to consume me and take me to the edge.

My legs kick out as I fall back. Evan holds tight, his deep, lustful moans vibrating against my pounding flesh and surging my pleasure. My vision swims with tears built from primal lust. I can't keep balanced. But when he stands, I force myself up, pulling off his belt with shaking hands, the trembles from my receding orgasm making me clumsy.

He rips off his shirt, not bothering to unfasten the last few buttons. They bounce off the floor as I reach for his zipper.

The thickness of his erection strains against the fabric and the glistening tip pokes above the waistband of his black boxer briefs. I lift my chin, my carnal stare meeting his.

Evan's breaths are ragged with desire. He's crazed for my body and how it will soon join with his. I can see it and feel it in his hardness when I reach in. But there's something more I need to do.

His breath releases in a pained hiss when I grip him. I don't tell him what I want, allowing my actions to speak for me. I pass my hand from the base to the tip, relishing the soft skin covering his dense and stiff length.

I adjust my body to lay across the table so that my head hangs over the edge and my throat lies exposed. "Come here," my husky voice calls, encouraging him forward with gentle pulls.

Evan's panting increases as he lowers his hands on either side of the table and grips the corners. He knows what's coming.

I open my mouth wide, watching his face scrunch as I take him deep before closing my eyes and going to work.

My arms stretch out, my nails digging into his ass, encouraging the steady pump of his hips as I force myself to relax and take him deeper.

But Evan is a generous and selfless lover, unwilling to take pleasure without giving it in return. His large hands return to my breasts, allowing their fullness to sweep through his palms before he pinches the tips and curls forward, his mouth returning to my core.

You could say we lose our damn minds.

It becomes a competition, who can make the other groan louder, tense harder, plead for more. He wins, finishing me off first, but just as I feel his release build, he pulls away, swearing as he pops free from my mouth.

With expert hands he flips me around to face him and props my leg on his shoulder. "What are you doing?" I ask. "I wanted to make you feel good."

I shudder when his thick tip rubs against my folds and he tries to make his way in. "You said I could have you, anyway I want you. This is how I want you."

My lids are so heavy I can barely see, but I see enough. He licks his thumb, returning it to my small bud and rubbing in slow gentle circles as he makes his way in.

My body clamps down around him. It's the sweetest torture, having him move this slowly. I whimper with need as my body accepts his. But once he's in as deep as he can go, he withdraws leisurely, as if we have all the time in the world.

When he's mere centimeters from pulling out, he rams forward, repeating the motion and throwing my other leg over his shoulder. His fingers fasten to my hips as he goes full speed ahead, the table slamming into the wall with each surge.

The steady beat fills my ears. Evan is more animal than man now, his hips lurching while his mouth devours me with kisses to my throat, breasts, chin, and mouth. It doesn't take long for that lovely pain to feather out, tantalizing every nerve cell I possess.

He clamps his jaw with his release, jerking forward and slamming his palms on the table. As he fills me, his motions slow, but not our breaths or the very grateful kiss I meet him with.

He tilts his head, smiling as he pulls me toward him. I stroke his sweat-soaked brow, laughing when he finally kicks off his pants and shoes and eases my legs off his shoulders.

I lock my ankles around his waist when he lifts me off the table and carries me away from kitchen. "What are you going to do to me now?" I ask, my voice a purr.

"You'll see," he says.

I almost expect him to take us upstairs. He surprises me by carrying me into the garage. I bite down on my bottom lip when he lowers me to my feet and pulls out. He angles me around to face the hood of my truck.

"Remember how you said you'd let me do anything?" he asks, flicking his tongue along the arch of my ear.

"Uh-huh," I respond, allowing him to bend me forward and spread my legs.

He glides his hardening tip along my slick center. "Here comes round two," he whispers.

CHAPTER 17

Evan

The sound of running water echoing from my bathroom stirs me awake. I glance up where trickles of light stream through the partially opened doorway. According to my digital clock teetering at the edge of my nightstand, I've only slept a few hours at best. That doesn't stop the smile that comes from knowing who waits behind that door.

I push up and onto my side, intent on going to her. I don't make it far. The light shuts off and the door opens. The moonlight streaming in from the window bathes her bare skin with light and tinges her long, fluttering hair a deep blue as she walks forward. She's beautiful, in heart and form. I can't tear my eyes from her.

She doesn't see me, her attention on her phone. I think she's scanning through the pictures she took of us when we finally made it to my suite. In some we're merely kissing, in others, we're doing a great deal more. All are erotic and deeply sensual, and while it's something I've never done, and only allowed to please her, the way she captured the intensity of our love-making is extraordinary, arousing me more.

"You need new screen-savers," she teased, holding the phone away from her as she took me deep.

The smile she had is noticeably absent, and as she nears, I realize she's upset. "What's wrong?" I ask.

Her head jerks up. "Oh, sorry," she says, bending forward to kiss me. "I didn't mean to wake you." Her lips are soft and her affection tender, yet as she places her phone on the nightstand and shoves the digital clock closer to the wall, she seems to withdraw. The defenses she wraps herself in are as tangible as the warmth radiating from her skin.

I gather her to me when she sits at the edge of the bed, pressing her back against my chest and kissing her shoulder. "You're upset," I tell her, waiting for her to explain why.

"Yeah, you could say that." She sighs, clearly troubled. "My brothers texted me while we were sleeping. Someone threw a brick though my front window."

"What the hell?" I say, straightening.

"There's more." She pushes her hair away from her face. "The word 'whore' was written across it."

Fury should have me lashing out and demanding more details. But the insult takes me well beyond fury.

"Hey," Wren says, turning to cup my face when she sees me. "It's okay."

"It's *not* okay," I snap.

"No, it's not," she agrees, her words trailing.

"And you are *not* a whore," I add, forcing my tone to soften.

"Thanks," she says, her fingers brushing along my jaw. "Believe it or not, I needed to hear you say that."

"Why?" I ask.

She releases a short humorless laugh. "Considering everything we did, just tonight?"

"Is that how I made you feel?"

She bows her head. "No, that's not what I'm saying."

I run my hand along her stomach, allowing her soft skin to brush along the thick pads of my fingertips. "You're beautiful," I tell her.

"Please don't give me compliments," she says. "It's not what I'm looking for."

"You didn't let me finish," I tell her, the way my tone drops causing her to glance up. "You're beautiful because you're bloody real. You don't pretend to be someone you're not. You're simply who you are, a stunning, confident woman who enjoys everything: life, food, laughter." I kiss her lips. "And pleasure, too."

"Pleasure?" she questions.

I can't be certain if guilt is what resides in her voice, but if it is, it's the last thing I want her to feel. "There's nothing wrong with enjoying sex or surrendering to what feels good when I touch you. Your passion fuels mine which is why I can't do enough to please you." I wrestle with whether to admit something I've kept from her. Ultimately I do.

"Remember the first time we made love?" I ask.

"Yeah." Her soft smile lights her face despite the darkness. "It was one of the best nights of my life."

"I feel the same," I admit, quieting. "Do you remember how I asked you if you wanted to take a shower?" She nods, appearing confused as to why I'm asking. "It's something that Saundra, the woman I was with for so long, insisted we do every time we were together."

"What do you mean?" she asks. Her hand stills over my shoulder. "Wait, you don't mean every time you had sex?"

I shrug. "She liked to be clean."

"Evan, there's a difference between clean and walking around with a stick rammed up your ass. It's a miracle you could bend her over."

"She could be intense," I agree. "But it's not my intent to disparage her. Sex with her, and with Aliyah—"

"Who's Aliyah?"

"She was the woman before Saundra." I smirk. "She liked to be clean, too, and would dress immediately after we finished.

"Holy shit. Are all English women like that?"

"Only the women I seemed to attract." I don't admit why I stayed with them as long as I did. They were safe. I didn't have to worry they'd find someone else to entertain them while I worked. Although that epiphany only appeared after I found Wren.

I gather the strands of hair dangling against her cheek, allowing them to glide between my fingers. "Before you, sex was something of a task, an attempt to be intimate for the sake of intimacy. That's not what I feel when I'm with you. When we make love, it's just one more thing that brings us closer."

"I think I know what you mean," she replies, her more serious demeanor returning. "But when we're together like this, it's extreme. I like it, don't get me wrong. I'm just tired of having sex and not much else. It's why I've held off being with you. I want us to be better than that."

"We are," I assure her. "You bring out the best in me, in and out of bed." I keep my eyes on hers to prove I mean what I say. "As much as I've lived, I wasn't alive until I met you."

She clutches my arms as they wind around her. "You really are too good to be true."

"I don't know about that," I admit, sweeping my jaw along the curve of her neck. "What I do know is you're the best thing that's ever happened to me."

A small gasp releases from her lips. I can't tell if she means to laugh or cry, but it's the latter that worries me. My arms tighten around her. "Tell me what happened at your house."

Her small fingernails pass along my forearms. "There's not much to tell. My neighbors called my brothers when they heard the crash and saw the damage. No one saw anything." She shakes her head. "But it's not like we don't know who did it. God, I guess that was him following me."

Her voice drifts as if picturing the damage. "Curran came over along with another cop who filed a report. Angus and Seamus boarded up the window and cleaned the mess. They're going to find a replacement when Home Depot opens. I'll have to leave work early tomorrow." She steals a glimpse at the clock, making a face. "I mean later today."

"You're not returning to your house without me."

"I won't be alone. My brothers will be there since Finnie's away."

"I don't care. Based on everything that's happened, you're not driving there alone." My tone is sharp and absolute.

Hers remains patient and as soft as her touch. "Evan, you have the biggest deal in your company's history taking place at noon."

"So have them meet us later."

"I don't want to keep you from your work," she says. "Especially when your competitors are going to be scrambling to steal potential clients and push their products at a cheaper rate. You have to be ready to strike and keep the momentum of this sale going."

"I will," I assure her. "But not at the expense of your safety. When we return to your house, I want you to gather your things and move in with me."

"I can't move in with you because some asshole's making trouble for me."

"It's not because of him. It's for us and what we're becoming." Her hesitation threads in the space between us, not that I'm surprised. While Wren has given a great deal of herself, she's never bared herself to me in the way I most want. The guard around her soul remains.

I nuzzle her close and give her a moment. It's something I often do. Many times, like now, it's all she needs. The corners of her mouth lift into a soft smile. "I wish I could tell you yes," she says.

"What's stopping you?" I ask, stroking her spine.

"I'm a good Catholic girl," she begins, only to grimace. "Scratch that. I suck at being Catholic. But me moving in with you, I'm not sure that's a good idea."

I prop the few pillows that remain on the bed and pull her up with me. She reaches for the sheet and tucks it around us, settling against my chest where she belongs.

"From the start, nothing has progressed the way either of us likely intended," I say, allowing each word to sink in. "But it has progressed and I love where it's taken us."

"Love?"

Her tone is barely audible and there's a great deal behind what she's asking. I don't back-peddle or dismiss the word. "That's right," I say, feeling her grow rigid. "We gave into our physical desires rather quickly, but it didn't ruin the friendship that had begun or the feelings that followed. You mean everything to me and I want you with me."

She shifts her position so she can see me. "It's only been a few months," she reminds me.

"Perhaps. But I know what I feel and I want us to grow closer." My lips brush against her hair. "Even more than we are."

She rests her chin on her hand, appearing to give what I tell her a great deal of thought. "At the very least, stay with me until your brother returns from his promotional tour," I whisper. "If you want to return home then, I'll let you."

"You'll let me, huh?"

I laugh when she does. "You know what I mean. If you need your space, I'll understand and respect your decision."

"You won't be mad and fire my ass?"

My humor fades although she means to make me laugh. "I only want you to be safe."

Traces of her worry return, dulling her features. "Me, too," she says.

As the quiet spreads, I'm almost certain we'll return to sleep. "Evan . . . tell me something about you."

"Like what? I'll tell whatever you want to know."

She tilts her head. "Why don't you ever talk about your parents? You seem to avoid mentioning them."

"Some things are too hard to speak of," I reply.

"I think I know what you mean," she says. "But I'll admit, I'm surprised to hear you say it."

"Why?"

"Because of who you are." She kisses my sternum, her lips barely grazing the skin. "Everything that makes you, you must've been shaped by someone special."

"And what am I?" I ask.

She lifts off me, smiling in a way I've not seen before. "You're the best man I know," she whispers.

I don't move. Despite hard work and my many accomplishments, nothing has ever meant more.

The edges of her hair trail against my chest as she climbs on top of me, our mouths immediately finding each other. We take our time, exploring each other and allowing our passion to build.

A soft moan vibrates in her throat as I harden beneath her. I should pour my heart out between kisses and confess everything I feel—for her and everything she does for me, and how I've only grown stronger with her at my side. Mostly, I want to tell her that I can't imagine life without her.

Instead, I flip her onto her back, slipping my arm beneath her waist and penetrating her deep. Her hands shoot up, her palms pressing against the headboard to keep her in place. She seems so delicate beneath my weight and large frame. But as always, her strength is never far from the surface.

"You're holding back, bossman," she tells me, nibbling on the soft spot behind my ear.

I groan when she bears down and her body fastens around me like a vice. "Would you prefer I try harder?" I ask, driving forward and giving her nipple a tug.

Her hands slip away from the headboard to grip the sheets, her grunts of passion urging me faster.

Every thrust and touch demonstrates what I fail to say.

I love you, Wren, and I want you to marry me.

CHAPTER 18

Evan

"You know what I think?"

My stare darts briefly in Wren's direction as I accelerate through the intersection. "Are we about to discuss business or pleasure?"

Her mouth twists into that smirk she uses when she's feeling exceptionally playful. "Both. But you're going to like what I have to say."

"All right," I say, turning as Alfred leads me into a residential neighborhood. "What is it?"

"I think we need to incorporate Naked Sundays."

I almost run off the road. "Excuse me?"

Her hand slips onto my lap. "You work too hard. Starting tomorrow we're starting Naked Sundays and implementing every rule implied therein. Everything you do, you have to be naked—unless you're frying food. Then I'll allow an apron." She dances her eyebrows. "Wouldn't want to burn your important bits, would you? Unless you want me to kiss them and make them feel better."

I make a hard U-turn. "Evan, what are you doing?"

"I think you're right. I work too hard. We should extend

Naked Sundays to include Saturdays, starting today."

She tugs on my arm, laughing. "Later, I promise. But let's go to the party first. Come on, you promised," she says when I continue ahead.

"Fine," I say. "Alfred, resume navigation."

"Resuming navigation," he calls.

I turn around at the next block. "Tell me more about Naked Sundays," I say.

"Oh, I don't think you'll find them as easy as they sound," she teases.

"No?"

"Nope. Because as a rule, you can't do anything that constitutes work." She counts off on her fingers. "No projects, no research, no business. That includes work around the house."

"And what happens if I do?" I ask.

"You'll be punished," she whispers in my ear.

I stop smiling. "Will I like this punishment?" I ask, all but begging her to tell me yes and fighting not to return us home and find out.

"Maybe, maybe not," she says. She extends her arms and folds them over her head, causing her breasts to strain against her blouse. "I can only guarantee you'll remember it."

"You have no idea what you're doing to me," I say over Alfred's command to turn right.

"Yeah, I do," she says. "Why else would I want you naked?"

I slow as I pull into a modest neighborhood packed with brick homes. "Are you trying to get back at me for the other day?"

"What do you mean?" She turns to glance out the window. "Oh, are you talking about when I walked into your private bathroom to give you a clean suit following your shower? And you pushed me up against the sink and slipped your hand up my skirt?"

"Ah," I say, thinking back to how her skin flushed and she whimpered.

"You think I'm mad about that? About you giving me a

screaming orgasm and then running off to take that call from the president of Mellon before I could return the favor?" She shrugs. "Nah, I've forgotten all about that."

I groan. "It was harder on me than it was on you, I assure you."

"I'll bet it was," she says laughing. She taps the navigation screen. "Looks like we're almost here."

"Destination three hundred feet ahead on right," Alfred agrees.

"You've never been here before?" I ask.

"Never," she admits. "Though I used to run a few blocks from here."

"This isn't a relative of yours?" I ask, trying to understand why she's unfamiliar with the residence.

She does a quick check of her phone as I park along the curb. "For once, no."

"A friend?" I press, shutting off the engine.

She reaches for the carefully wrapped gift at her feet. "I'm hoping he can be," she says, appearing to enjoy pulling that chain she's fastened around me.

I slip out of the SUV and walk around to open Wren's door. "Alfred, watch," I say, ordering the security system to activate as I reach for her hand to help her out.

"Watching," Alfred announces when the door slams shut.

We walk toward four large balloons fastened to a mailbox. They bounce as the warm spring breeze sweeps through them, and another car drives by. "My darling," I say. "What are you up to?"

"I'm not up to anything," she assures me. "Gavin Merrick is turning four and we're here to celebrate."

"Who's Gavin Merrick?" I ask.

"Clifton's son," she responds.

"He has as son?"

"And a wife he's been with since high school." She sweeps her fingers along my temple. "You have some really great people on your team. I think it's time you get to know them."

I rub my jaw. "It's hard to associate with employees on a

personal level, given the position I hold. I appreciate what you're doing, but should I fail—"

"You won't," she replies, glancing toward the freshly painted black door. "I know the last few deals have fallen through. But you're going to make it right."

"But if I somehow can't, how can I, in good conscience release someone who considers me his friend?"

She stops at the bottom of the brick steps darkened by time and the city's cruel winters. "Evan, you're the type of man who would feel bad about letting any employee you respect go. That won't change whether you share a few beers with them or continue to hold them at arm's length."

Her expression and voice soften when I start to argue, effectively cutting me off. "People like Clifton worship you. They see you as this god who walks the halls, emanating intelligence and success like air they need to breathe. Their last boss sucked balls. Big, hairy, wrinkled balls. Where he yelled, threatened, and obligated them to obedience, you guide them and give them something to believe in."

"You're giving me too much credit," I tell her.

"You're wrong." Her breasts graze my chest as she pushes up on her toes. I bend to meet her mouth, but instead of her open mouth sealing over mine and her tongue stroking lightly, soft lips press close to my ear. "You're a good man," she whispers. "Let the world see what I've known from the start."

Her words and the way she says them render me speechless. If it weren't for the front door opening, I wouldn't be able to turn away.

A woman with pale blonde hair pulled away from her face stands at the threshold, huddling into her thick brown sweater. "Hello," she says.

"Good afternoon," I reply, at the same time Wren says, "Hey, there."

The woman looks too young to appear so weary, the deep wrinkles and dark circles ringing her eyes suggesting the few decades she's lived have been challenging. Despite her troubles, she welcomes us with a warm smile, opening the door wider, so a small boy can inch through.

Wren steps closer when she sees the small boy cautiously edging forward. He leans heavily on a small metal walker, his skin blanched, but his gaze alert. And although he's at the top of the steps, Wren has to bend to meet his face, given his slight stature.

It's difficult to see someone so young and fragile. I force a smile, unlike Wren who beams at him. "Hey, handsome," she tells him.

"I'm Susanna," she says. "And this is Gavin." She laughs a little, appearing embarrassed. "I apologize. Are you a friend of Clifton's?"

"Evan?" Clifton calls. He appears at his wife's side, clearly stunned. "This is Evan Jonah," he tells her before I can reply. "My boss." He turns away from her gaping face. "I'm sorry, Evan. We weren't expecting you." He looks to Wren. "And this is Wren his . . ."

"Better half," I reply with a wink.

She glances over her shoulder just to smirk, the gleam in her eyes curving the corners of my mouth. I want to introduce her as my fiancée. But I haven't asked, and I won't until my company is secure and I can give her everything she deserves.

She turns her attention on the little boy. "Hi, Gavin. Is it your birthday today?"

Already he's enthralled by her, not that I blame him. But it's the way he seems surprised that anyone noticed him that troubles me.

"He's a little shy," his mother says, the admission adding an extra pitch of sadness to her tone.

"I can't blame him," Wren says, keeping her focus on Gavin. "You know, when I was your age I was really shy, too."

"Really?" Clifton asks.

"No. I came out of the womb mouthing off."

We laugh although it's the grin spreading across the little Gavin's face that makes me believe her comment was meant solely for him.

She told me I was kind. I try to be, though it's an

attribute that comes so easily to Wren.

"Oh. I'm so sorry. Here we are standing for no reason," Susanna says. "Please, come in."

Gavin stumbles back, the leg of his walker appearing to catch between the doorway and the steps. I hurry forward when Clifton has trouble pulling it lose.

"Careful, honey," Susanna says, placing her hand on Gavin's shoulder to steady him. "You don't want to bend the end."

"Want to come in with me, buddy?" Wren asks, extending her arms.

The boy briefly hesitates, lifting his hands and allowing Wren to gather him into her arms. "Ever hear of Jack and the Beanstalk?"

I don't hear the little boy respond, only Wren as she disappears into the house with him. "Well, let me tell you the O'Brien version, also known as 'Angus gets caught eating the pie for the church social by Ma, the not so big but scary giant.' I have to warn you, it doesn't end well for Angus.'"

Clifton and I laugh as we pull the walker free from the crack. I straighten to see Susanna smiling. "She's really great," she says, turning to me. "Do you have kids?"

"Not yet," I answer over Clifton's explanation that we're not married.

My reply gives Clifton pause, though it doesn't last. "I figured you guys were serious."

I'm mad about her, if I'm being honest. Not that I tell him.

"I'm glad you came, Evan," he says. "Do you want a beer?"

"Yes, thank you," I reply, reaching for the gift Wren left behind.

He leads me into a living room, decorated with paper streamers and a hand painted sign that says, "Happy Birthday, Gavin."

I follow him into a kitchen just large enough for a table and chairs and place the gift on the counter. The house is exceptionally small, one small room appearing to lead into another. Clifton is paid well. I question why he wouldn't purchase a larger home with an open floor plan to better fit his son's needs.

"Is something wrong?" he asks.

"Not at all," I reply. I take the beer he hands me, glancing around. "You have a lovely home."

"Thank you." He pops open the beer he takes for himself. "I'd like something bigger, but Gavin has a rare genetic condition. It affects his muscles and his lungs. He, uh, requires a lot of care that extends past what our insurance offers—not that you don't offer good insurance," he adds quickly. "It's one of the many reasons I work for iCronos."

I watch him take a pull of his beer. "Is your salary enough to cover his needs?"

"You pay me well, Evan," he replies, choosing his words carefully. "Gavin just has a lot of issues."

Which is why Clifton's suits are so outdated and his house is so small. Everything he makes goes to his son's care.

With the exception of Wren's voice in the background, and the laughter that comes from Susanna and Gavin as Wren finishes her story, there's no other sound.

"Is Gavin's condition treatable?"

I don't know why I ask. I suspect it's because neither Clifton nor Susanna have anyone to tell.

The shimmer in Clifton's eyes reflects his grief as well as his love. "No. Everything we do only prolongs his life a little longer." He laughs without humor. "The doctors originally told us he wouldn't make it to see his second birthday. But because of the treatment he's received here, he gets to turn four."

My vocal cords constrict as I force the words out. "How long do the doctors say he has?"

Clifton tips back his beer, taking several swallows before answering. "Not as long he deserves," he says, pain and bitterness shadowing his features. "I'm going to outlive my son by decades, Evan. But because of your company and everything it's allowed me to give him, maybe I'll get to see him attend his prom."

"I'm sorry," I say, never meaning those two words more. "Perhaps with medical knowledge and treatment advancing as it is, that will change."

"That's what we're counting on," he says, his resolve evident in his tone.

I lift the bottle to my lips when the quiet envelops us. In the next room, Wren asks Gavin what his favorite toy is. His mother answers for him when he appears to struggle to form his words. That doesn't stop Wren from asking him more questions, her animated voice absent of the sadness I suspect is there.

How can it not be?

Any other day or situation, I'd find comfort in hearing her voice, and in a way I still do, although this time the effect is muted. I want to gift that small amount of comfort to Clifton and assure him everything will work out. But I don't know that, and you can't comfort a man who knows that each day that passes is one day closer to losing his child.

"We should head into family room," he says. "Susanna bought crafts for kids to work on and I'm not sure if she put enough paint out."

"It's not much, a few birdhouses," he adds when I finally take my first sip of beer. "But the kids will like it and the therapist says painting helps Gavin's fine motor skills."

"I'm sure they'll enjoy it." It's all I manage to say. Because what the fuck else am I going to say? Life goes on, whether you want it to or not.

A few more people arrive, but not many children. The few who show glance around the living room as their parents urge them forward, evidently unfamiliar with their surroundings. Anne strolls in carrying a diaper bag behind a woman cuddling a small infant. She pauses when she sees me, waving madly.

The man who trails her almost runs into her when he sees me, as does the woman looking for a place to hang her coat. I recognize the man as Clifton's apprentice and the woman as his intern. It's safe to assume those who've gathered are the families from Clifton's department.

I nod in their direction as Wren takes a seat beside me on the couch. The woman smiles nervously. The man offers a rather awkward tilt of his chin.

"Hey, Roberto," Wren calls to him. "How'd you make out at the chiropractor?"

"Hey, Wren—I mean, Miss O'Brien," he adds quickly after another glance my way. "It was a great experience. Real great. The best."

He's an articulate man from what I've seen through my brief interactions with him, but he trips over his words and finds elsewhere to look when I place my arm around Wren. It's a natural response when she's near me, and one I imagined would help him to relax. Instead, he moves further away, appearing to find an excuse to speak to his wife.

Wren places her hand on my knee, unaffected. "Told you I knew a guy."

"What?" I ask.

She leans into me. "I referred Roberto to the chiropractor I've been bugging you to see. The poor bastard could barely turn his head before he saw Dr. Kapowski. Now, look at him. Good as the day he popped out of his mother's lady parts."

I chuckle, whispering in her ear. "Why didn't you tell me we were coming here?"

She lifts her chin, speaking so low I strain to hear. "Because you would have found some new technology to research, a report to read, or an email to write. You wouldn't have come, and you needed to."

The way she regards me demonstrates nothing but warmth. Her intent isn't to insult me. She's simply stating a fact I can't deny.

"Oh, by the way. We're going to Anne and Stefana's wedding in two weeks," she adds. "The Justice of the Peace is coming to their house, and the reception will be in their backyard. It should be pretty with the flowers and trees blooming like they are."

I smirk. "Anything else I should know?" I ask, watching

as Susanna explains the art project and Clifton lays out more newspaper.

"Yeah, you're giving Anne away."

"I beg your pardon?" I ask, certain I misheard.

"You were the only viable choice," she explains. "Her dad died a few years back and her brother doesn't approve." Her fingertips circle my knee. "You should have seen Anne's face when I told her you'd be thrilled to pieces to do it. I already ordered your tux—Oh, and guess what? I get to carry Ilona down the aisle." She motions to the baby Anne is holding. "Anne ordered the sweetest little flower girl's dress for her, but she's not walking yet, so I get to carry her. Don't worry, we're going to match."

"Heaven forbid we clash," I add, causing her to laugh.

Clifton kneels beside his son, helping him when he appears to struggle to hold the paintbrush. Susanna sits on the couch beside Wren, looking weary.

"Hey, Susanna, where does Gavin go to school?" Wren asks.

She smiles although it seems to take a lot out of her. "We home school. He has so many appointments, it's hard to find a preschool that will work with his schedule."

"Does he belong to a play group?" Wren asks, turning to face her.

She shakes her head. "Late afternoon and evenings are the only free time, but by then, most places are closed."

"So you and he don't get out at all?"

"We do. Every Friday I try to take him to the park," Susanna replies, her voice quieting.

She appears uncomfortable and is likely growing defensive. I only see the back of Wren's long dark hair, but I know she's smiling. "My Aunt Colleen started a play and parents group about twenty years ago after my cousin Marky was born," Wren tells her. "Marky's autistic, and back then services were limited and expensive, not something she and my Uncle Albus could afford since he worked at the docks and she stayed home to take care of Marky."

"A playgroup?" Susanna asks, slowly. "For autistic

children?"

"No, for kids with special needs," Wren explains. She crosses her legs, adjusting the cuff of her suede leather boots. "It was hard for her, being stuck at home with a kid no one wanted to play with. Marky didn't mind, my aunt and uncle were his world. But she did. She knew what he could have and wanted him to have it, too. She started it with some church funding and eventually got private grants. It became bigger than she intended, but it helped her connect with other parents going through what she and my uncle were experiencing. They have a mom's group that meets every Wednesday night with drop-in play care. Moms leave their kids and carpool to a local diner or catch a movie. In the summer they do miniature golf, things like that. Every other Friday is date night for parents with play care provided."

"Really? I've never heard of it."

"It's because it's private and out of her home. She never expected it to take off like it did, and didn't want it to become so big that she couldn't run it."

"Is there a waiting list?" Susanna asks.

"Oh, yeah, but I can get you in if you want," Wren offers.

"Are you sure?" Susanna asks.

"Of course. Not to brag, but I'm her favorite niece, I used to help out during the summers for free." She reaches for her purse and digs out her phone. Susanna simply blinks at her as she scrolls through her contact list, just as I do every time Wren does something I can hardly believe.

As always, she doesn't disappoint.

"Hey, Aunt Colleen," she says when the line picks up. "It's your favorite niece."

"Which one?" Aunt Colleen replies, her voice loud and clear.

"The one who helped your soda-bread-loving derriere three summers in a row instead of heading down to the shore with her friends."

The woman on the other end laughs with her whole heart, very much like her favorite niece. "Oh, that one. Well you can thank me later when you don't end up with skin cancer and moles with hairs shooting out of them like tentacles. What's up, Wren? And when are you coming for supper? Your Ma told me you're seeing some stud with a real job. 'Bout damn time you stopped dating losers."

She rolls her eyes, ignoring Susanna and I when we laugh. "Yeah, yeah, I'm sure Ma told you all about him. Listen, I have a friend with a four-year-old son who could really benefit from play care."

Aunt Colleen pauses. "You need him in?"

"I do," Wren replies, the shift in tone between the two women speaking volumes.

"You got it," Colleen says. "Just so you know, I'm expecting you for supper next Sunday. Bring your man."

"Okay, Aunt Colleen. Hold on, Susanna, his mom, is right here. I'll put her on."

Wren passes the phone to Susanna. "Hello?" she says, lifting it to her ear. "This is Susanna, Gavin's mother." She stands, hurrying into the kitchen when Aunt Colleen asks her if she has a paper and pen.

I turn to Wren, smiling. She shrugs. "I told you. I know people."

"The right people," I agree.

She settles against me, watching the children work on their projects. Snacks follow, along with cake, the afternoon slipping quickly by.

I take the time to speak to each of the people in attendance, and while I enjoy my time with them, it's the way Wren interacts with the children that stays with me. I've seen her around her young niece and cousins. Today is another indication of what a wonderful mother she'll make.

I open the door to my Explorer just as the sun begins to set, allowing Wren to enter. I walk around to the driver's side, taking my time to slip inside and start the engine.

"Alfred, home," I say.

"Directions initiated," Alfred responds.

The screen lights up, Alfred advising me to head west, although I can't bring myself to pull away from the curb.

"Did you know about Gavin's condition?" I ask.

"No," she replies, adjusting the strap to her seatbelt. "I'd seen pictures of Susanna and Gavin on Clifton's desk, and had an idea his son had issues, but I never knew it was this bad." She releases the strap and meets my eyes. "He doesn't have a lot of time, does he?"

"No."

We fall into a sad silence. I glance back at the house when the door opens and Roberto and his family step out. His daughter chatters away, carefully carrying the little birdhouse she painted.

"How much do you think it will cost to alter our insurance so it covers more, if not all of Gavin's care?"

The sadness Wren kept well hidden in Susanna's presence reflects in her gaze, yet it doesn't stop her small smile from forming. "A lot," she admits.

"Make it happen," I tell her. "Whatever it takes, make sure Clifton and my families have everything they need."

CHAPTER 19

Wren

The phone rings as I finish sending my email to the tech department, letting them know that Evan will be by at three. I reach for the receiver. "Evan Jonah's office. This is Wren."

There's no one on the other line, but it's not exactly dead. "Hello?" I ask.

Whoever called, disconnects. This is the third time this week this has happened, and from the digital display on the phone screen, it looks like it was transferred from the reception desk.

I house the receiver, my hand slowly slipping away from the slick plastic. Staying with Evan turned into living with him, although most of my things are still at the house I share with Finn. But since I moved in and we began commuting to work, Bryant seems to have disappeared. That doesn't mean I think he's done messing with me.

My gaze falls to the finance report I was reading. It's not even eight and I've already been kicking ass for two hours. I flip through it, trying to shove thoughts of Bryant away.

I read through the last page as I walk into Evan's office, not bothering to knock.

If I didn't know Evan's office was soundproofed before, I'd know it now, as the quiet from my office is replaced by my little brother's booming voice. "Jab, jab, hook, roundhouse, roundhouse, jab. Uppercut, uppercut. Dig deep, Evan. Dig deep."

"He's going to have to dig deep later, Finnie," I tell him, glancing from the report to the digital wall clock over the flat-screens. "He has a meeting in ten."

My voice cuts off as I see Evan nailing the heavy bag Finn set up. When Finn first took over as Evan's personal trainer, his objective was strength training and conditioning to help him power through the day and release some stress. But after attending Finn's last title defense, he asked Finn to train him in MMA.

I'll be honest, mixed martial arts is a brutal sport. I never expected Evan to love it. We've caught the last few pay-per-view fights on TV and we've already booked our hotel room for Finn's next fight in Vegas. Like me, Evan seems in it for the long haul.

I smile, watching his gloved hands connect in rapid fire, a fresh coat of sweat dripping lines down his bare chest. Oh, but my man doesn't stop with the sexy there. The skin-tight MMA shorts he's wearing show off the "V" at his waist and a very yummy and pronounced set of abs.

I close in, only because I need to talk to him and not just to take in the eye candy. But now that I'm here, it's my obligation to all the heterosexual women out there to take another visual lick.

His breath comes fast as he pummels the bag and wraps up the workout. Between the grunts and the way his chest rises and falls with each hard intake, I'm reminded of our very enthusiastic "good morning" sometime before dawn. With Finn here, I'll keep my hands to myself. Can't say I'll do the same once he leaves.

He gives me a wink as he rips off his gloves. "How was that?"

"Bad-ass, bossman," I tell him.

He laughs. "Thank you, but I was speaking to your brother."

"Your kicks need work," Finn tells him, nudging my

shoulder affectionately. "But I'll admit, you're a fucking natural when it comes to throwing a swing."

"My prior boxing experience helps. I took it for years as my physical education elective."

"Yeah?" Finn asks.

"That's right. It was that or ballroom dancing and cricket."

Horror finds its way into Finn's voice. "You poor bastard."

I reach for the towel placed on the chair and pass it to Evan as Finn carries the heavy bag to the large closet where he stores the training equipment.

Evan swipes his face and gives me a quick kiss. "How are we looking?" he asks, motioning to the report.

"Not bad," I say.

He straightens, knowing what I mean. The good faith deposits barely keep us afloat. Eventually, the existing sales will net billions, but for now we need revenue.

Out of respect for Evan, I don't mention anything in front of Finn. But for all Finn says things he shouldn't, he's not dumb. He lifts a hand as he heads out the door. "Later," he says.

Evan thanks him over my goodbye. The door shuts, the abrupt silence thickening along with the tension. I force a smile. "You have ten minutes before your meeting. I have a fresh suit hanging for you in your bathroom."

"Thank you." He swipes the towel over his chest. "I was expecting better news."

"Me, too," I agree, speaking softly. Neither of us move away. It's like magnets appear at once, keeping us locked together.

"I have to pick up the food for the meeting," I say, knowing we can't just stand there. "I'll be back in half an hour."

"Can't someone else do it?"

"With the new launch of Mechanicus?" I shake my head. "Everyone already has too much on their plates, babe, including the administrative staff." I push the extra mile for

Evan, so do his employees. But they're close to their breaking points and I'm not asking anyone for more than I have to.

Evan knows as much. "All right," he says, giving me another kiss. "Don't be long."

"I won't," I assure him.

My cell phone rings as I hurry down the hall. Given all the hang ups on my office line, I almost hesitate to answer. "Yeah?"

"Wren, it's Dee. I'm parked out front. You ready?"

"I'm coming," I say. I don't break my stride until I see Finn by the elevators, posing with fans for a picture.

"I didn't know Finn O'Brien was your brother," Alison squeaks as she walks by me.

"He is," I tell her. I don't think she hears me, too busy gawking at Finn.

He shakes the hands of the men he posed with. "Good to meet you," he tells them, rushing to catch the elevator with me.

He punches the button to the elevator, waving to a few more people across the sea of cubicles who also seem to recognize him. "So you and Evan are shacking up, living in sin and all that good stuff?" Finn asks, his big grin making him look younger than he is.

"I didn't move in," I remind him. "I'm just staying with him."

"You've been staying with him for a month, Wren. Just cause your shit's still at my place doesn't mean you aren't living with Evan."

"My shit is still in *our* place," I correct.

"Why?"

My stomach lurches as the elevator speeds down to the lobby. "Because Ma gave that house to us," I reply, although I know that's not what he's really asking me.

"You know what I mean." The echoing sound of chatter wafts into the elevator when the doors part. Swarms of iCronos employees march forward, ready to jump into their day.

I know many by name. But with Finn here, I don't stop to

say hello. I follow him off to the side, knowing he parked in the deck, but that he isn't done talking.

He leans against the black marble tile wall, beside a large palm stretching out toward the light streaming in through the glass atrium. "He's nuts about you," he tells me. "And it's obvious you're nuts about him right back. What's stopping you from committing?"

"You mean besides Ma driving up from Florida to beat my ass?"

"I don't think she would." He thinks about it. "Much."

"Much? Oh, yeah, that's comforting." I laugh, although for the most part, my brothers and I still know better than to piss her off.

"If you want the truth, I think Evan's given her hope that you'll give her another grandkid before your ovaries shrivel up and drop all their eggs, or whatever the fuck your womanly organs do."

"Is that why you and Sol are officially living together? To spare her organs?" I nod when a few of staff walk by me with their coffee cups.

"No, she's living with me 'cause I love her, and I'm asking her to marry me."

"Get the hell out of here," I say, throwing my arms around him.

He lifts me up, laughing. "Yeah, can you believe it? I actually found someone who'll put up with me, my dark past, and a clown car stuffed with crazy."

As much as he's joking, there's a lot of truth to Finn's dark past. Maybe that's why I squeeze my little brother tighter. "She's a good woman and you're great man, Finnie." I release him slowly. "I'm real happy for you."

"So does that mean you'll help me pick out a ring?"

"You want me to help you pick out a ring?" I ask, punching his arm affectionately. "I'd be honored."

"You helped pick out Tess's and Sofia's, it's kind of tradition now." He makes a face. "Besides it's either you or Angus. He and Molly have been engaged for twenty non-fucking years. You think I want that kind of Karma or whatever the hell that's called?"

"He loves her." He cocks a brow. "In his own non-fucking way," I add with a smirk.

He laughs again and gives me another hug. "Gotta run. I'll call you about the ring, okay?"

"See ya, Finnie," I say, watching him step into the elevator.

I start to walk away from the elevator when the doors close behind him, only to race across the lobby when I see Dee rushing toward the building. "God, I'm sorry," I say pushing through the doors.

"It's okay," she says, tossing her long braids over her shoulders. "Was that Finn?"

"Yeah, Evan hired him as his personal trainer. It gives Finn an extra workout."

She huffs. "It's working. He's huge. The last time I saw that boy, he was barely a man."

"Tell me about it. I still remember when I was taller than him."

Dee's a friend of my old friend Mateo. She's a single mom who just finished her college degree. I gave her a chance and holy shit she's been a Godsend. We chat away as we head down to the local diner that's been catering our breakfast meetings. I send a quick email to Anne, reminding her Evan wants to see her later today, so I don't immediately notice the car that parks next to us.

Dee and I slip out, she hits the key fob to lock her doors at the same time their doors shut behind them. "That's the great thing about whores," one of the guys say as they catch up to us. "You don't have to stop fucking with them. They can leave your bed, tell you they don't want you. But they know you have them and can do anything you want to them."

My gaze shifts toward Dee who rolls her eyes. Foul-mouthed assholes aren't uncommon in any city, but the way this guy talks, he's trying to make sure we hear him.

I throw open the door, letting Dee pass in front of me. But before I can follow, one of the guys shoots in front of me, the other guy at his heels, separating me from Dee and blocking my path.

They leer at me, dragging their stares down the length of my teal dress.

"Is there a problem?" I ask, jutting out my chin.

They exchange glances, laughing. "Hey, don't I know you?" the closest guy in a white-muscle T-shirt asks.

"No, and you don't want to," I fire back.

Dee shoves her way between them. "Get away from her," she says, clasping my wrist and dragging me forward.

I keep my attention on them as she pulls me into the diner. "Yeah. I do," the guy says. "I've seen you at Ragtown."

At first I don't know what the hell he's talking about. But when I realize what he means, it's all I can do to keep standing.

Ragtown. The bar where I met Bryant the night he screwed me over and showed me how toxic he really is.

"Hey!" The owner stomps over, his son directly behind him. "You giving these ladies a hard time?" he demands. The patrons at the counter gather toward us, their fists clenching as a few more leave their booths.

The owner doesn't wait for them to answer. "Get the fuck outta my place."

The guys don't argue, knowing they're outnumbered. They stomp back to their car and pull out, stopping long enough for the driver to roll down his window and yell my way. "By the way, 'B' says, hi."

Motherfucker.

I race down the ramp, Dee and a few of the patrons chasing after me so I'm not alone. I snap a few pics with my phone just as they speed away.

"You okay?" Dee asks, at the same time the owner offers to call the cops.

"My brother's a cop," I say.

I text the pics to Curran and call him, my hands shaking so damn hard I can barely keep from dropping the phone. I wrap up my call as Dee and the owner's son finish loading the car.

Dee locks the doors to her sedan when we slip inside, but

doesn't immediately pull out. "What did Curran say?"

"The pics are too blurry and I didn't get a plate. He's stopping by to take a formal report."

"Stupid pricks," she mutters. "I'm sorry, I should have taken their picture. But the way they were looking at you, I was more worried about them hitting you. Who were they?"

"Don't tell Evan," I say, not bothering to explain.

She frowns. "If you don't want to talk about it, that's fine. But you shouldn't keep things from your man."

"I'm not, and I won't. I'll tell him after work. He just has too much going on right now."

"All right."

Like the other employees, Dee knows the company is only barely hanging on. She cranks the engine and pulls onto the main road. We were talking up a storm all the way here, but the ride back is quiet. She's worried, and maybe scared, too. Me, I'm all rage.

It's taking all I can not to find Bryant and beat the unholy fuck out of him. But that's exactly what this manipulative asshole wants. He wants me to go to him. He's trying to turn the tables on me and make me out to be the whore he claims I am.

Son of bitch, he probably paid those two derelicts to mess with me. It's always been about power and control. I made it worse by walking away. How dare I reject him, right? How dare I say enough?

I'm ready to hit something. I'm ready to hit him, but the moment I see Evan's building come into view, I know I have to get it together.

Dee pulls onto the curb. I barely have time to slide out of the car when a security guard approaches me. "Miss O'Brien, can I see you? We have a situation."

Jesus. Like I need this. Dee walks toward me, her frown bouncing between me and building. "Go do what you have to do. I'll get one of the interns to help me. Don't worry," she adds when I hesitate. "I'll take care of everything."

She seems stressed, not that I'm exactly jumping for joy.

I expect another message from Bryant, instead the guard

leads me toward the lobby where a woman waits by the security desk. She's dressed in what might be a Chanel suit, with enough Botox to smooth out the forehead of every person moving through the lobby.

She smiles when she sees me. At least, I think she does, seeing how she can barely move her overly plumped lips. She pushes back her shoulder length blond hair, appearing to dismiss the guards standing behind her.

"That's Mrs. Hilliard," the guard mutters.

"Hilliard?" I ask, wondering how I know this name.

"She says she's Mr. Jonah's mother and is demanding to see him, claiming it's urgent," the guard tells me. "But their names are different and we can't reach Mr. Jonah. We figured you were the next best person to ask." He waits, staying out of earshot. "Do you want her out or are you going to speak to her?"

The security team takes their job seriously, and as a whole, they don't budge. But I can see why they'd hesitate to toss a woman claiming to be the boss's mother.

"I'll talk to her," I say, walking forward.

She seems young, too young to be injecting all that crap into her skin. Her body is bizarrely thin, her rack, not so much, and about as pricey as that diamond bracelet glinting beneath the atrium lights. She doesn't appear threatening, but there's enough superiority emanating from her form to taste.

Maybe it's the stress of working my ass off only to take minimal steps or the shitty experience at the diner. Whatever it is, I'm already on guard and feeling protective.

"You want me to try the boss again?" the guard asks, keeping pace with me.

"Not yet," I tell him. I stop just in front of Mommy Dearest.

"Miss O'Brien," the guard closest to him says. "This here is Mrs. Hilliard."

"Ah," she says, smiling with as much warmth as the diamond choker around neck. "You must be Evan's plaything. Not that I'm surprised."

I'll give her this, she's not much of a sweet talker. "What

do you want?" I ask, ignoring the jab and knowing it will bother her more.

"I'm here to see my son," she says, straightening. "Do your job and inform him I'm here."

I crinkle my nose. "Mmm, no."

"What?"

She's slightly taller than me, but she might as well be a cockroach by the way I stare her down. "I said, no."

"Polite" and "patient" left me the moment those two idiots messed with me, and they aren't traits that are coming back any time soon. Her half-frozen expression passes along my body, as if she's somehow in control.

"You have no idea who you're dealing with," she says.

"I know more than you think," I assure her, my voice and expression steady. "Evan is in a meeting and he is not to be disturbed." Maybe I should call him Mr. Jonah, but she's already assumed there's something between us, and I don't mind reminding her it's true.

"I'm sure someone as lovely as you can convince him to free his schedule," she fires back, her tone stiff. "That's why he keeps you, isn't it? To convince him in ways others can't."

Holy God, I'm ready to kick her in the face.

Two guards take point beside me. "I think you're under the impression I'm going take your shit," I say, not bothering to censor my remarks. "But this isn't your business. It's Evan's, and you don't get to call the shots."

"What are you doing here?"

I don't see Evan approach, but he's suddenly there, assuming a protective stance in front of me.

Mrs. Hilliard demonstrates as much warmth toward him, as she did toward me. "I came to see you."

"If so, you had your wish, and now you may go." He takes my hand, leading me away, but not before addressing the guards. "This woman is not permitted in the building. Please escort her from the premises."

A choruses of "Yes, sirs," ring out as Evan guides me toward the elevator. I jerk my head back, catching her blanched features as one of the guards motions her to the exit.

She's stunned by Evan's reaction, but it's the rage that overtakes her face that keeps me from feeling sorry for her. This isn't a woman who's hurt by the way her son treats her. She's pissed that she didn't get what she came for.

The people waiting for the elevator step aside as Evan leads me in. I don't know what they see in his face, but I feel enough tension within his grasp to understand why they don't follow us.

The moment the elevator shoots upward, Evan slams his fist into the metal wall, denting it. *"Fuck."*

I cover my mouth in shock. I've never seen him like this. But I recognize the hurt clouding his features, and all the resentment built from years of pain.

He seems close to the edge, but I don't say anything, trailing behind him when the elevators ding open and we arrive at the floor. We pass the conference room where Dee and the interns have set up breakfast, opening it up to the rest of the floor instead of the CEOs Evan was supposed to meet.

I wince, knowing this isn't a good sign. I shut and lock the door behind us when we reach his office.

Evan leans forward and presses his hands against the long marble table. Maybe I should give him space, but I can't. I come up behind him and wrap my arms around his waist, resting my cheek against his back. "What's wrong?" I ask, keeping my voice gentle.

"Too much," he admits, but for a long while, that's all he says.

I wait, giving him the time and patience he always gives me.

"I apologize for reacting as I did," he finally says, his voice quiet yet unbelievably rough. "But seeing her, after Clifton's news . . . She was the last thing I needed."

"It's okay," I tell him. "I was more worried about you than anything."

He stiffens further, deep-rooted rage clipping his tone. "Did she insult or threaten you?"

"She didn't say anything I couldn't handle," I assure him. I kiss his back. "What did Clifton tell you?"

I don't know why it takes him so long to respond until he finally shares just how bad things are. "You know the charity hospitals, the ones I tried to help instead of selling to their competitors, those who work solely for profit and don't give a bloody damn about the people who most need them?"

I try not to groan, but it's hard. "Yes?"

"Those same competitors bought them out today, and because they're now in charge, they'll be using *our* competitor's technology and releasing us from our contract."

If there was a wall close enough, I'd be taking a swing myself.

"The good faith money they gave us was used months ago," he reminds me. "We don't have to return it per the terms of our agreement. But the money we were depending on from this sale is gone." He sighs. "There's not enough coming in. Not for everything we need. I'm flying to London next week and connecting personally with the accounts we have pending throughout the U.K. It's strictly a business trip, and we won't have much time to ourselves, but I want you with me."

"All right," I say. God, he seems so far away even though I'm holding him.

My hands fall away as he turns to face me. It's only then I realize his knuckles are bleeding. I reach for a few tissues on the table and press them into his hand, almost at the same time I clutch his fist against my chest.

"Don't," he says, attempting to pull away. "I'll ruin your dress."

"I don't care about my dress, I care about you," I whisper. "Evan, we're in this together. No way am I letting you go."

The anger and worry deepening the faint lines around his eyes lessen at my words.

I want to mean what I say. But how can I help him when I can't even help myself?

CHAPTER 20

Wren

It takes a long time for our breath to settle after we finish, and even longer before we stop kissing. Evan smiles softly as he pulls away, his hand gliding from where it's on my face to my hip as we roll onto our sides. It's one of my favorite things he does: touch me like he needs to, like he needs *me*. That's a good thing, seeing how I need him, too.

Tonight is slightly different. Instead of the familiar warmth in his stare that follows our lovemaking: a seamless mix of fire and sweetness, the anger lingers.

I told him what happened at the diner. He hired a private investigator to track down Bryant. Curran took his side, and so did my brothers, but the resentment that remains isn't just about me.

"Can I ask you something?"

He nods, but he already knows where I'm headed. "Was that your mother who came by today?"

"It was." His hand pauses over where it's slid to my lower back, the motion is brief, but I notice anyway. "Hilliard is her fourth husband's name." He shrugs. "If she's still with him."

"She's been married four times?" He nods. "What makes me think she stopped being your mother long before that?"

"Probably because she never was," he admits.

"Do you want to talk about it?" I inch closer, causing my breast to tilt against his chest. "I'm not one to push." I smirk when he raises his brows. "Okay. I am. But only when it matters, and this seems to matter, even though you don't want it to."

I free my hand to stroke his face. Does he have any idea I would do anything for him? I want to tell him, but words, those that mean anything, have always been tough for me to share. I've told him as much, but I can't be sure how much he really understands.

"You haven't been the same since you saw her," I remind him.

"I don't mean to act differently," he says. "Especially around you, and I don't want my issues with her to affect us. But if I'm being honest, I'm more concerned about you."

"I know. That doesn't mean we should ignore everything else." I scan his features as my brain hooks onto something he said. "What makes you think she'll come between us?"

"Because as much as I've wanted to let go of my past, the bitterness I feel toward her remains."

"I think I know what you mean," I say. I smile softly, not that there's anything to smile about after such a shitty day. "I'll tell you what. You tell me about your mommy issues, and I'll tell you about my daddy ones. But if you don't want to, that's okay, too."

I'm trying to lighten the mood, but he sees right through me. "It was bad for you, wasn't it?"

"It was," I answer truthfully. "But I get the feeling it wasn't a good time for you either."

I shudder, but it's not from the cold. The thought of anyone hurting Evan makes me want to come out swinging and scares the daylights out of me. That doesn't stop me from wanting to know.

He reaches for the blanket at our feet and tucks it around us. That's what Evan does, seals me in with his warmth and his heart, even when I try and pretend I don't need it.

"I've never spoken to anyone about this," he says, almost like he's thinking out loud.

"Why?" I place my head on his chest when he rolls onto his back, seeking comfort from our closeness.

"There's been no one to tell," he explains. His voice fades. "Until now."

"Same here," I admit. He tilts his head as if unsure whether to believe me. He knows I have a minimum of ten people on speed dial I could pour my heart out to. But I wouldn't, because it's not something I do. But if I did, they'd be here.

Evan doesn't have a long list of people. He has me. And the way I feel, he always will.

"I didn't go to boarding school by choice," he begins. "My mother sent me away when my father fell ill."

It feels like someone just slapped me in the face. "Jesus, *why*?"

"Because she finally could, and he was too ill to stop her." He rests his temple over my head when I scoot up, his voice casual despite the pain.

"My father was twenty years my mother's senior and was never in optimal health," he says, keeping his voice quiet. "When he was eight, he was diagnosed with leukemia. The aggressive treatment left him weak and his body never fully recovered, as you can imagine."

"I can't even imagine," I answer him truthfully. "That must have been hell."

"I'm certain it was. He often joked about always being the last one picked on a team and how he was the smallest among his peers. But he was brilliant and used his strengths and talents to build an empire."

He's smiling fondly. There's not even a hint of anger or sadness. That doesn't mean I'm not feeling enough for the both of us. "You loved your father," I say.

"I still do," he admits.

"Then why would your mother send you away? You and your dad, needed each other."

"My mother never wanted children," he says. "A fact she kept from my father until several years into their marriage."

"Why?" I ask.

"Why didn't she want them, or why didn't she tell him sooner?"

This is all sorts of fucked up, but I'm trying not to show it. *FYI*, I'm doing a shitty job. "Both. That's not something you keep from someone you're marrying."

"My family comes from money. My father's side invested well and thrived for years, while my mother's family came close to losing everything." He takes a small breath. "Until she met my father. His family's fortune saved what remained of hers."

"I see," I say, my voice clipped.

"I didn't have a mother who demonstrated affection or one who was willing to spend time with me. But I had a father who committed to being the best father and role model he could be." The affection in his voice shows me what his father meant to him, but it doesn't last. "I knew from a very young age to keep my distance from her and to not ask for anything. That didn't stop me from wanting to be close to her."

"What would happen if you approached her?" I sit up slightly when he doesn't answer, my heartbeat slowing like it does when I know I'm going to hear something awful. "Was she abusive?"

"Not in the way you're thinking," he says, his voice dropping. "She'd ignore me, or leave. Often for days, claiming she needed to take a holiday. Children . . . they know when they're not wanted or loved. So they learn not to ask for or expect more than they're used to."

"Why did she send you away?" I ask. He frowns as if unsure what I mean. "If she'd up and leave, why didn't she stay away permanently? It didn't have to be you she sent packing."

"It did have to be me," he says. "You're forgetting, I wasn't necessary. My father's money was. It's the only reason she agreed to have me. He'd begun to pull away, and she wanted to hang onto him, or rather, hang onto his wealth."

I'm not naive. I know people like that exist. I just never expected one of them to be Evan's mom.

"Wealth is something she feels entitled to," he explains. "It's all she knows."

But what she needed to know was love. Not for herself. For Evan, who needed it most.

I embrace him. As strong as he is, I want to shield him, not because he can't handle anything that comes, but because he's already handled enough on his own.

His arms sweep along my back as he murmurs against my hair. "I knew my father was dying. No one had to tell me. I was furious God would take away the only person who loved me."

"Evan . . ." I say. It's the only word that comes. He'd told me it was too hard to talk about his parents. But I had no idea how bad things were.

"Dad had such a tremendous heart," he tells me, his features gathering that look people get when they're remembering the pain they've felt. "And more money than any one person could ever need, but neither was enough and it enraged me.

I began to act out. My mother used it as an excuse to send me away, insisting to those close to Dad that my presence would only kill him sooner." He huffs. "As it was, in my absence, his condition deteriorated quicker and she had plenty of space to do as she wished."

The resentment in his features morphs into an anger that seems almost foreign to a man as kind as Evan. I can already guess what happened, and he knows as much. He tells me anyway. By now, Pandora's Box is already open and the evil he's seen is flying out.

"My father admitted to a close friend that he never intended to marry someone so young. However, my mother pursued him, enticing him and convincing him she was the woman he'd dreamed of and would give him the children he feared he'd never have."

His demeanor steels and he quiets. "She used him," I finish for him.

"And many more following his death." The muscles along his broad chest tense. "My mother never had the drive to work, but she possessed the charm and beauty to seduce any man of her choosing. She took many lovers. Some married, some older. It didn't matter, they all gave her what she wanted. But that was then. Now that she's older, neither men nor money come as easily."

"Is that why she came to see you today? She wants more money?"

"It's the only reason she ever comes," he responds.

His voice isn't angry. In a way, I wish it was. It's better than the hurt.

I give him a moment to gather his thoughts. His attention lowers, as if analyzing the way our bare skin touches, and how close we are at this moment.

Except when he looks up, it's not to talk about us, it's to share another piece of himself. "My father realized, too late in life, that he'd been used. He knew he was dying. But what killed him was recognizing that he'd never have the love he'd sought, or the mother he knew I'd needed."

If his mother was here, I'd knock her lights out.

"But as sick as he was, he didn't fail me," he assures me. "Aside from a trust awarded to my mother, he left me everything. It enraged her when the lawyers disclosed the terms of his will. She lashed out, telling me everything she never dared to admit while he was alive."

I brace myself for the worst. "What did she say to you?"

"That she never wanted me or my father. But, although I already knew, I needed to hear her say it."

"*Why*? You were just a kid. It was such a shit thing to do to you."

He seems to still, but answers me anyway. "It helped me finally let go of the mother she never intended to be, the caregiver she never was, and the protector who only defended her own needs, wants, and desires." He looks at me. "Aside from watching my father's casket lowered into the ground, it was hardest thing I ever endured. In letting her go, I let go of the mother I longed for, the one I wished she could have been."

If my soul was made of glass, it would creak and crack down the middle. But it's what he says next that makes pieces fall.

"This was a woman who gave me life and ruined me, simultaneously."

"You're not ruined, Evan," I say, my fingertips skimming the soft hairs along his temple.

"I'm not," he agrees. "But for a long time, I believed that I was."

"And how do you feel now?"

Oh . . . I don't think I've ever been happier to see those two dimples. "Do you want the truth, something you may not be ready to hear? Or would you prefer I continue to hide what I feel?"

He's challenging me to step it up. And as much as I've tried to hold back, I don't. Not this time. "Let it rip," I say, meeting him square in the face.

"The truth is, despite the challenges I face, nothing can stop me." The beast within him flares, intensifying the specks of gold in his eyes. "And with you by side, my success will be that much sweeter."

I grin. "You're right. Because you're the baddest motherfucker in business, a god in bed, and an animal when it comes to getting what you want."

The joy he greets me with almost doesn't seem real. But it is. Everything about Evan is real.

"What about you?" he asks, his sudden seriousness suppressing the moment between us.

He's not asking how I feel. "You want to know about my father, don't you?"

"I told you a great deal, and while it wasn't easy, I'm glad that I did." He angles his chin, examining me closely. "But if you're not ready, I won't press."

"I know you won't." And it's because he doesn't, that I do.

"I was the sixth kid born, the girl my daddy and mommy wanted, and their little miracle and joy," I reply, not meaning a word of the latter. "My father, hmmm. I'd say he was about as good as your mother. He'd take his little princess around and parade her all over the neighborhood. At least that's what he let my mom think. The truth was, he'd take me to one neighbor's house in particular, the one he'd spent close to a decade cheating on my mother with."

"Shit," Evan says, sitting up.

"Yeah, it was," I admit. "I'm not sure how old I was when I figured it out. But I was old enough to know that he shouldn't be going into a bedroom with a woman who wasn't my mother and locking the door. I hated this woman for it." I quiet. "But I hated my father more."

He waits, listening and understanding in a way no one else can. "I'm the one who told my mother. I'm the one who made her cry. I think she suspected, but it took me telling her to believe it." My head falls forward as I bear the weight of my confession. "To this day, the people from my old neighborhood think I was my father's pride and joy. But I was just another female he used. He used my mom to give him a stable family, this woman to give him what he felt was missing in the bedroom, and me as a way to see her. Well, until he didn't need me anymore."

Disgust and anger tense the wall of muscle along Evan's chest. I recognize the emotions, because every time I think back to how my father treated my mother, I feel them, too.

"I'm sorry," he says.

"I am, too," I admit. "Mostly, I'm sorry for how mad I was at my mother. My *mother*, Evan—the woman who was tough enough to support and raise seven kids on her own, but too weak to let the man who treated her like she was nothing, go." I throw my hand up. "It pissed me off that she put up with what she did."

Until the same damn thing happened to me, and I realized how hard it is to let even the bad things in your life go.

I don't tell Evan this. I can't. Bryant doesn't belong here with us, especially not in bed.

"I can't imagine how much that hurt you," Evan says, his fingers threading along my scalp. "I would *never* betray you."

He thinks we're only talking about my father, so I take a breath and leave all traces of Bryant behind, focusing on the root of my pain. Daddy issues are real, and they can really screw a gal up. I'm living proof.

"It didn't hurt," I admit, causing him to frown. "At least not in the way that you think. I hurt *for* my mother, and brothers. Like with your mother, they needed him to be more than he was. God, they needed it so bad, it tore them apart when he died." I push up on my elbow. "But I knew who he was. So when he died, I didn't cry. That man who just left the earth had left us a long time ago, long before he had a heart attack in his mistress's bed."

"Jesus, Wren."

"Yeah. That's how he went. And everyone in the old neighborhood knew it." It didn't matter that my father left my mother his military and post office pensions, and every last dime he had in his will. No amount of money could erase the humiliation he caused her *and* us, which is why I say what I do. "I was glad he was gone. I could handle hearing my mother crying in her bedroom at night for the man she believed she loved. It sucked, but I could handle it. What I couldn't handle was her crying over the man she needed him to be, but who couldn't be bothered to try."

"I can relate," he says.

"I know you can," I tell him. It's such a shit topic. That doesn't stop me from smiling when I realize how much he understands, and how good it feels to have him beside me.

"My brothers never had a real father," I say, well aware how soft my voice becomes. "But I was lucky. As much as they make me crazy, I had six boys who grew into men I can count on. And because of my mother's love, they became better than anything my father ever was."

"They did," he agrees. "And better husbands because of it."

"Yeah," I say, realizing how true that is.

In the quiet that flows between us, I think we're done. But when something shifts in Evan's gaze, I know there's more he needs to share.

"My father, like your mother, always stood by me. Instead of teaching me to throw a ball, he taught me chess and helped me build my first robot. He'd play old movies in his den when he was too weak to take me to the cinema, and read to me every night." His voice trails as his mind appears to wander. "He was a gifted storyteller, captivating me with books like *The Adventures of Tom Sawyer* and *To Kill a Mockingbird.*" He adjusts his hold to better see me. "I didn't have siblings to lean on or guide me. And as you know, I didn't have a mother I could depend on. Yet my father looked after me and protected me. In spite of his ill health and age, he was always there for me."

"He sounds like a sweetie," I say, reaching out to stroke his face. "What was his name?"

A small smile lifts the corners of his mouth. "Alfred."

My hand hovers over his skin, the pure love in his tone freezing me in place. "Alfred," I whisper, a lump building in my throat.

I didn't cry when I told him about my father and how badly he hurt my mother and brothers. Crying . . . it's not something I let myself do. It takes too much out me, exposing every stitch of vulnerability I try to hide.

But I want to now. Around Evan, I *am* vulnerable. I'm that woman who lets everything out rather than tuck it away where it's safe. I'm the person who falls into his arms, worried he'll one day let go. And I'm that innocent little girl who once believed men can be loving, good, and honorable, regardless of all the wrong she sees them doing around her.

Evan could have been "ruined" like he claimed. He could have spent years fucking over women instead of creating technology that can save them. He could have sailed through life living off his inheritance, rather than depleting it to save his father's legacy. And he could have run for the hills when my family found him half-naked in my kitchen. But he didn't.

All because his father loved him like a real daddy should, and made him into the man beside me.

"I love you," I say before I can stop myself.

Evan doesn't move. Hell, neither do I. I've been naked with him more times than I can count, and have given him more than I thought that I could ever give, but I've never felt as naked as I do now.

"Wren . . ." he says, appearing at a loss.

"I'm not saying this because I feel sorry for you because of the way you were treated." I bite back a curse and momentarily avert my gaze, wishing this shit wasn't so hard to say—not to him. For once, I finally have what I've dreamed of, and I need him to know.

"I love you," I say again. "This thing between you and me, it's what I've looked for my whole life."

He smiles, his grin widening until I think he's ready to laugh at me. He doesn't. What he does do is lift me to him and kiss me, his tongue flicking generously over mine. I pull away, only for his head to dip against my neck and for him to nuzzle me with kisses.

I laugh because he's tickling me and being so damn sexy, even though—son of a *bitch*—

I'm actually saying something that means something, for once. He chuckles against my throat and finds that ticklish spot on my backside, making me jerk. He finds it again, this time making me jump and bust out laughing.

"Evan, for fuck's sake. I'm trying to be serious."

"I know," he says, pulling us into a sitting position.

My knees fall on either side of his hips. "Then what are you doing?" I ask, clasping his jaw and meeting his lips.

He grins against my mouth when I take nibble. "Trying to show you that I'm happy . . . and that I love you, too."

I release his jaw slowly as the truth behind his admission reflects in his eyes. He plays with my hair, allowing the strands to slip through his fingers. "I didn't believe in love at first sight until I saw you," he begins.

"*Stop*," I say, averting my gaze.

"I can't," he says, lugging me back into a straddle when I try to scramble away. "Your face, your heart, the way you spoke, *everything* about you ensnared me and refused to let go." His grin dwindles. "I can't sleep until I feel you beside me. And every time you leave, I'm empty and lost. It's only when I see your smile that I'm able to take my next breath."

"Quit reciting all that Shakespeare stuff."

"It's not Shakespeare," he says. "It's me, telling you how I feel."

I don't want to cry. And I won't. So I sit there with my hands covering my mouth like they can somehow hold in everything I'm feeling.

Just so you know, my hands are doing a shitty job.

"Never have the words 'raging asshole,' sounded as sweet as when they slipped from your mouth," he tells me. "Second only to 'mind your damn business.'"

"Oh, *gawd*."

He lowers my hands when I laugh, scanning my face. "I love you, Wren," he says again. "My heart and soul belong to you."

The force I use to throw my arms around him should have us toppling backward and onto the mattress. But Evan's strength holds, keeping us in place and making me whole.

CHAPTER 21

Evan

Bruce Langley steeples his fingertips as he blinks back at me from the monitor. It's what the CEO of Yodel does every time he believes he's winning and that I'm a blundering idiot. It's one of the many reason this pompous ass will have to pry Mechanicus products from my cold dead hands.

"You're in trouble, Evan," he says, shaking his head sympathetically, like someone who came across a dead fawn. "I'm offering millions, not just in good faith deposits, not in slow increments. I'm gifting you millions that you desperately need."

Ten million dollars appears appetizing on the surface. But as Wren would say, "That apple looked damn good to Adam, but he was a dumbass for taking a bite".

Like Adam, I'd be a fool to give into temptation. Langley currently has twenty-three lawsuits hanging over his head, two are for copyright infringement, and he's also currently under investigation for misappropriation of funds. And now, he's offering millions for a product that will earn over a billion dollars, in time.

I lean back in my chair, something I do when I'm frustrated in dealing with corporate fucks. The setup of my home office is almost identical to the one at iCronos, although instead of marble floors and sleek modern furniture, there are dark wood floors with rich mahogany panels lining the walls.

At the far end of the rectangular room, nine flat-screens are fixed to the wall instead of the twenty-four at my corporate office. And rather than several computer screens showing me multiple views of Langley's face, one large screen perched at the end of my desk shows enough. Maybe that's why my attention drifts…his face is not the one I want to see.

Wren worked close to seventy hours last week. I tipped the scales at ninety, often passing out in my office rather than coming home to her. I had hoped to spend the entire weekend together, but when I woke this morning she was gone. The note she left in our bathroom reminded me she had to meet Sol and Sofia at a boutique to try on dresses for Sol's wedding.

I'm very happy for Finn and Sol, but I'll admit I envy them. Every time I see Wren, I want to ask her to marry me. But when a new problem arises or I hear from greedy bastards like Langley, I'm reminded that I can't, yet.

I'm ready to end the call when Wren struts into my office. She's wearing the black pencil skirt that flaunts her figure, and possibly shoes, I think. I'm too fixated on her upper half to be certain or care.

Her small breasts and very alert nipples strain against the lace of her bra. The fuchsia lipstick glistens on her lips, drawing my attention to her face. *It's cold in here*, she mouths.

"Ah . . ." I'm ready to apologize for taking the call, to offer to warm her—*something*. She gives me her back and hurries to the end of the room. With a flick of her hand, she flips on the marble gas fireplace beneath the collage of flat-screens and walks to the plush suede couch, her hips swinging.

Without so much as a glance back at me, she dumps her large purse on the floor, bending over to give me a nice view, and shimmying out of her skirt for an infinitely better one.

A pair of panties that could fit into the fountain pen in my hand (with room to spare) barely contain the globes of her perfect ass.

"Jesus *God*," I say. Not that I'm complaining.

"All right, Evan," Langley says. "Twelve million, and that's my final offer."

She lifts the giant pad of paper I hadn't noticed was in here. It's the kind a grade school teacher would draw pictures on, and tucks it under her arm as she digs through the contents of her purse. She pauses, beaming when it appears she found what she's looking for.

I don't know what to expect, and am rather disappointed when she pulls out a thick black marker. That disappointment fades when she walks toward me and everything God gave her bounces with each step.

Seduction radiates from every part of her being, from the way she moves to the way she tosses her long mane of hair as she takes the seat in front of my desk.

"What are you trying to do?" I ask her.

"Help you," Langley answers. "All I'm trying to do is help you."

Wren ignores me. I ignore Langley.

She places a large pad of drawing paper on her lap and uncaps the marker with her teeth. She removes the cap from her mouth, gives the end a swirl with her tongue and throws it at me.

Maybe she means for me to catch it. Or perhaps not. I don't really care. The solution to end global warming could be shoved inside that cap and I could give a damn.

It bounces of the wood paneling behind me. Although she doesn't look up from where she's scrawling across the pad, her wicked smile indicates how much she's enjoying herself.

She lifts the pad, blocking the view of her breasts and making it clear I need to read what she wrote.

Last Sunday, you read an analytical report in bed.

"It's a generous offer," Langley says, "that will finally net you a profit."

I believe that's what he said. I'm too busy reading Wren's next few words.

Thereby violating the rules of Naked Sunday.

I swallow hard, though it does little to tame my desire when I read the words that follow.

You were naughty. Very naughty.

"Don't be afraid, Evan," Langley says. "We at Yodel are here to help you."

Now I have to be naughty and teach you a lesson.

She unsnaps her bra, using the large pad as a shield, she extends her arm and drops the transparent piece of scrap on the floor.

She hunkers down, scribbling fast and lifting the pad when she's done.

You can look, but you CAN'T touch.

With that, she places the marker on my desk and drops the pad to the floor.

She leans back, spreading her legs. I rise to get a better view, ramming my leg into the desk before I remember it's in the way.

Her hand pushes aside the silky fabric of her panties, permitting the fingers of her opposite hand to play.

Slowly.

Very slowly.

In careful, *lazy* circles.

Heat fires her stare punctuated with that wicked smile.

My lips part as my jaw unhinges, my breath increasing as her delicate skin plumps and glistens. As her motion increases, her smile fades, pleasure flushing her fair skin a deep red.

She's watching me, clearly aroused by what she's doing to herself and what it's doing to me.

Primal need to take her overtakes me, reducing me to a savage bent on taking her hard.

"Evan, are you listening?" Langley snaps. "Twenty million—"

"Perhaps you didn't hear me the first time," I snap. "You *can't* have her."

The screen goes blank as I end the call. Wren lowers her lashes, her lids heavy as her fingers move faster. "You said 'her,'" she rasps.

I tug open the buttons on my shirt as I prowl around the desk. "Did I?"

Her head falls back, exposing her throat. "Yes," she says, the word releasing in a gasp.

I fling my shirt off and whip off my belt, shoving the waistband of my pants and shorts down to relieve the growing strain of my thickening length. Wren's shoulders shake as she peaks, she's almost there.

But it's my job to please her.

I fall to my knees in front of her. Her motions slow, her words escape on tiny pants of breath. "You're not supposed to touch me."

It's what she says. Not what she means. The heels of her feet slide down my back and she keeps the crotch of her panties pulled away, exposing her to me.

I position my mouth in front of her slick center. "You said I couldn't touch you. You never said I couldn't taste you." She shudders when take my first lick. "And if you beg me, I promise I'll give you exactly what you want."

She bucks as I pull in her soft flesh, her hips swinging back and forth to meet me. "Evan," she moans.

Wren was already close, her skin so electrified it doesn't take her long to peak. I don't hold back. The way I devour her increases her whimpers and causes her to tremble.

Her ankles fasten behind me, her heels digging into my back as she unravels, spewing a mix of swears and half-formed words as she pleads for more.

"More?" I tease, lifting my gaze as I give her another flick from my tongue.

She struggles to speak as her legs fall away from my shoulders and I strip off my briefs. "Alfred, show room," she stammers.

"Showing room," Alfred announces.

The room reflects along the flat-screens. I peel off her panties and lift her to straddle me, her hair falling around us like a silk sheet. I clutch her face, kissing her between words. "You want to watch what I do to you?" I ask.

She whimpers when I graze her nipple with my teeth. I ease inside of her, her head falling back and her eyes squeezing shut with each press forward.

Once I'm in, she meets my gaze, hooking her ankles around my lower back. My arms shake with raw desire and the feel of her skin against my palms. I carry her to the couch. Each shift of my legs grinds me against her, taking me deeper inside.

"Alfred, show *us*," I say.

Wren gasps as the tech zooms in on our forms. She's captured our images on her phone, but to see our bodies joined as they are, our chests rising and falling in sync, and her warm skin pressed against mine is so unbearably erotic, for a moment, I don't move. I take in how perfect she is.

But then I do move.

And everything surges out of control.

I bend my knees, lifting her and bringing her down. My efforts are slow at first, watching her slide against me, the ends of her hair fluttering as she bounces. She adjusts her body around mine, tilting her head in the direction of the camera, fixated on the screen as we find our rhythm.

Our mouths meet for a lingering kiss, tasting and nipping our bare skin between stealing glances to watch our motions. Each rapid thrust and taste thunders my heart, perpetuating the ache in my groin. I'm close, the image of me taking her accelerating my release.

I curse, wanting and needing more of her. Wren whimpers, biting on her lower lip when I lower her on the couch and pull out. "Don't," she begs, reaching for me.

I tumble as she tugs in a twisting motion, her hands moving fast. My palm shoots forward, gripping the arm of the couch to keep me from toppling on top of her.

"*Fuck*," I say, my face scrunching from her eager strokes.

I groan, relishing each hard and possessive pass. She's demanding my release, I can see it in the way I watch her take me on screen. But I want to finish inside her, my need as a man demanding it.

With another curse, I tear my gaze from our image,

flipping her onto her knees and pushing back inside. Her head bows and her nails dig into the arm rest, the steady beat of my hips slamming against her. She lifts her face, her hair sticking to her skin from the beads of perspiration gleaming her skin.

"I'm so turned on," she whimpers, her attention returning to the screen as her hand disappears between her legs. "Fuck, I'm so turned on."

Her whimpering overtakes her words as do my increasing grunts. I rope her hair around my fist and away from her face, arching her back and enticing her hand to move faster. I'm so overcome with lust, the image of my body hammering into her blurs.

My foot slides off the couch, the heel striking the floor as my stomach muscles clench and I reach my breaking point.

Pain and euphoria detonates from deep in my pelvis, jetting out and constricting my lungs. I don't stop. The way her tight walls squeeze won't allow it, as my desire to prolong her orgasm drives me on.

My hand skims beneath her breasts as I reach to grasp her jaw, turning her for a kiss as I slide in and out. Every move is like torture, the head of my erection unbearably sensitive and aching with each pass. Not that I stop, seeking the wave of bliss that follows each moment of torment.

"You feel so good, baby," Wren says, moaning as I once more harden.

She pushes her back against me, alerting me she wants to play. I fasten my arm around her waist and lift her, edging to the opposite side and lowering my back at an angle.

My right foot stays on the floor, the other digs into the leather and keeps me in place as I reach to roll and pinch her nipples. She shudders, bending her legs on either side of me.

Her need and desire to please me, causes her to ride me hard. I can't tear my focus from the screens, entranced by the way our bodies move in a perfect meld of beauty and sin. She's not showing off for the camera, and neither am I. This is simply us and the way our bodies claim each other every time.

She quickens her speed, movements aggressive and how

I like her. It doesn't take her long to peak, her breasts bouncing in my hands as she trembles and cries out in ecstasy. I last longer, taking control and gripping her hips to lift and repeatedly thrust.

Watching everything I do and seeing how she reacts reignites a familiar strain and makes me lose my fucking mind.

Our labored breaths and slapping skin, amplified by the speakers are echoing around us, fuel our carnal desires. Wren collapses on top of me as I finish, my guttural moaning resonating in her ear as the rocking motions of my pelvis ease to a stop.

My hands slide up to knead her breasts. I nibble her ear. "If this is my punishment, I should break the rules more often," I murmur.

I expect her to laugh. Instead she slips off me, turning to lay her chest against mine. "Please don't," she says, her features riddled with sadness in spite of the soft smile she shares. "Evan, you work too hard. This, you and me," she adds, skimming my chest with her fingertips. "This is real life. As much as I want you to succeed, I don't want you to forget about me or what's most important."

"You *are* my life," I reply, frowning. "I could never forget you."

Her stare examines my face, as if she is unsure whether to believe me. "I don't want you to work this weekend." She silences me with a kiss before I can argue. "I want you to do anything but—read for pleasure, watch a movie, hell, take a bath. But no working, okay? I want you to make it just about you enjoying life."

"What do call this?" I challenge.

"You enjoying sex," she replies with one of her more impish smiles. "And me enjoying it right along with you."

She sits up and I think she's leaving, so I band my arms around her waist. "Where are you going? You have to keep punishing me for violating Naked Saturday."

"Sunday."

"Very well, both," I say, laughing along with her.

"You're so damn cute," she says, gathering her hair and leaning in to kiss me. As she pulls away, her dark strands fan around us. "I have to pick up the food I ordered for brunch tomorrow. Everyone is coming here, and then we're all going to the Phils' game."

"They're coming here, to our home?"

A smile forms, to match hers. This is a tremendous step for Wren. In inviting her family here, she's accepting my home as hers. It's been almost three months since she moved in. At first, she appeared out of sorts. I asked Sofia to help her decorate the house and make it more hers. Now, instead of décor primarily composed of gray, black, and white, the teal, deep orange, and gold accents compliment the new multi-colored rugs and window dressings, a reflection of Wren's vibrant spirit and Sofia's ability to bring it forward.

Yet what ultimately caused Wren to embrace the house is the security it represents. I've forced Bryant out of her life, blocking any calls to her desk with careful screening and assigning my car service to drive her home when I work late.

"Yup, they're all coming," she says. "Including Teo and his family, his sister Lety and her fiancée, Brody. Which is why I had to order so much food. I won't learn to cook anything decent between now and then, especially for all the mouths we have to feed."

"That is a large number of people," I agree, my hands gliding to her lower back and further yet. "Perhaps I should prepare something as well?"

"No, you already do enough. Besides, if my brothers find out you cooked, they're going to make you get a tattoo on your face, ride a bull, wrestle an alligator, or some other shit so they don't revoke your man card. This way, everyone eats, everyone is happy, and no one gets inked—unless you want 'Wren O'Brien is hot and rocks my world', scribbled on your ass. If so, I'm cool with that. I'll get one that matches."

"And what will yours say?" I ask.

"'Damn right' with an arrow pointing," she says. "What else would it say?"

I laugh, sweeping my lips along her neck. She groans and

pulls away. "Babe, I have to get to the caterer before they close."

"Very well," I grumble, causing her to giggle.

I loosen my hold, allowing her to stand as I rise slowly. She seems in a rush and is already dressed by the time I pull up my trousers.

"Where are you going?" she asks, pausing as she finishes applying her lipstick.

I slip my arms through my white dress shirt. "With you," I reply.

"No way. There's only one thing I want you to do while I'm gone and that's relax." She stops in front of me, her nymph's demeanor returning as her stare passes along my torso. "Okay, maybe one more thing."

She crouches in front of me, parting the sides of my shirt and swiping her lipstick across my skin. "Uh, uh, uh," she says when I try to see what she's doing. "No peeking until I'm done."

The muscles along my chest twitch as she passes the lipstick in slick, smooth motions. She falls to her knees, focusing hard on her task as she moves to my stomach.

I'm trying not to think about how she's inches from my groin, yet with her so close and in this position, it's a challenge.

I gather her hair, whispering low. "What are you up to?"

"Just letting you know what to do while I'm gone."

Her voice trails as I harden and she sighs with longing.

"What the hell," she says. "I have time."

She wrenches my trousers down, breaking the zipper and pulling me into her mouth. I stumble forward, clamping my teeth.

Her lips fasten around me and her hands aggressively play. With the camera fixed on us, I have a full view of Wren's profile and her skilled mouth, and how obsessed she is with pleasing me.

I don't last long, not with everything I see and feel, and with the audible pulls from her mouth and hands resonating in my ears. I double over, gripping the side of the couch.

Bloody hell. How does any man stand a chance against her?

She takes her time, her strokes decreasing in pace, her eyes never abandoning mine. It's only when she knows I'm satisfied that she stands, scanning my chest.

"Nice," she says, seemingly pleased with herself. "Later, bossman."

Her hips twitch as she tosses her purse over her shoulder and walks away.

"Wren, wait." I yank up my briefs and black trousers, swearing like madman when the fabric rubs against my throbbing tip. I pause when I finish fastening my belt and catch my image along the giant screens.

The corners of my lips tug into a smile as I spread the sides of my white dress shirt and read the two words written in hot pink across my torso. Two words that tell me exactly what she wants me to do while she's gone.

CRAVE ME

She wants me to miss her, to crave her touch and her smile. She didn't have to write it. It's something I do *every time* she leaves me.

CHAPTER 22

Evan

When Wren started working for me and our relationship developed, I knew it would be impossible not to touch her. And when she moved in, I knew it wouldn't be long before we began having sex in my office.

My office.

The place where brilliant minds gather, deals are made, and the sexiest woman alive spends the day swooping in and out, ensuring I have everything I need.

Everything.

After getting a taste of watching us make love, I was looking forward to seeing our images on the twenty-eight screens in my office. Apparently, so was she. "Adeptus is redefining the way all medicine is delivered," I tell her, my words releasing with each pound of my hips.

Wren's exposed breasts push through the opening in her blouse. I only managed to open the first two buttons and shove aside her bra before she hiked up her skirt and rubbed against me.

"Don't stop," she moans, whimpering as I tighten my grasp and thrust upward. "God, I love it when you speak nerd."

I chuckle and nibble her ear, watching our enhanced

images collide and discussing the engineering within the micro robots, all the while surrendering to the primal urges her body stirs.

She slumps against the conference table as she climaxes, sending the stack of reports in front of her flying across the marble surface. I steady her, hooking her waist and slowing my pace.

I lift my chin when we finish, meeting her grin reflecting back on me on the screen.

"I didn't like this thing when I first saw it," she reminds me. She wiggles. "But now, it's not so bad."

"It has its advantages," I gasp, struggling to slow my breaths.

I kiss her and separate us carefully, swearing when I catch sight of the digital clock. "I have a meeting in twenty-two minutes, don't I?"

She adjusts her thong and smooths out her skirt. "You do, but don't blame me if you haven't had time to prepare."

I pull up my pants and shove my shirt inside. "Do I have to remind you this was your idea, my love? Not that I'm complaining."

Her cheeks redden as they do every time I refer to her as "my love". She turns around, her fingers moving quickly to button her blouse. Aside from her flushed skin and a few misplaced strands of hair, no one would suspect what happened between us.

She brushes her hair in place with her fingers, reaching for the reports scattered across the table. In another few minutes her skin tone will return to that fair shade, erasing the lingering evidence, not that I'll forget as I look forward to the next.

I work on the buttons of my light blue shirt and straighten my tie as she stacks the folders into neat piles. "We didn't get to play last night or this morning," she reminds me. "My period is due in another three days and my fucking hormones are out of control." She reaches for my jacket and passes it to me, watching as I slip it in place. "You were stressed when I brought your coffee." She shrugs. "I was trying to help you relax. Besides, you know I don't stand a chance when you wear your glasses. Don't want me to straddle you, don't wear the glasses. It's a simple solution."

I pull her against me, her body melding against mine when I kiss her. Despite my urgency I give the kiss the attention it deserves. "I'll never deny you," I tell her, slowly pulling away and frowning as I take another look at the time. "But now, I have to prepare."

Her wavering smile reflects the extent of her emotions. These past few weeks, I've worked entirely too late, limiting our time.

She misses me. I miss us too, so consumed with the wheels I set in motion to fully enjoy the rare moments we've had alone.

"I know," she says. "Can we have dinner alone tonight? Sometime around nine? I can have them hold a table for us at that steakhouse you like."

"I can't, I'm reaching out to my contacts in Europe to give one last push for Ork and Adeptus." I press a gentle kiss against her lips, releasing her slowly and wishing I didn't have to.

There's a great deal I need to read through before my meeting if we're to implement the changes to our latest prototype. But I wait, watching Wren leave before returning to my desk.

As I lower myself into my chair, I realize how empty my office is without her. "Alfred, sleep room," I say.

"Sleeping," he calls, shutting off the multiple screens and blanketing that half of the room in darkness. I usually command Alfred to open the electronic shades the moment the sun rises. Wren's visit gave me a good excuse to keep them closed.

She thinks I'm pulling away, although that couldn't be further from the truth. Everything I'm doing, all the aggressive steps I'm taking are for her and our future. I want to commit to her without the added weight of my business troubles. The time to strike is now. I can't stop. Not if it risks my losing what I want for us.

I smile as I think how stunning she looks in that floral print blouse and skirt, and how her mere presence holds me in place.

With a sigh, I reach for the report I need to read before meeting with my engineers. I skim through it, frowning when something catches my attention on the second page. I cross out the microcontroller Keller chose, subbing it out with the newer model I've been researching, that is thinner, lightweight, and has stronger material.

Someone knocks on my door as I scribble a question in the margins. "Come in," I say, not bothering to glance up. The wiring the new lab intern suggests appears promising. I make a note to speak with John about hiring her upon the completion of her doctorate.

"Hello, Evan."

Ashleigh's voice stops my pen in place. I remove my glasses and set them on the desk, cocking my head when it occurs to me how much she's changed. If she hadn't spoken, I wouldn't have recognized her straight away.

Instead of her hair pulled up and away from her face, it hovers above her shoulders, held in place by the sunglasses perched on her head. The color is different too, dark yellow in tone rather than the white blonde I was accustomed to.

I only remember Ashleigh in suits, but today she's in a sundress, the thin straps appearing to dig into her slender shoulders. She's lost a fair amount of weight, though it's not her appearance that makes her look softer. It's her demeanor.

She's not scowling, and her posture, while straight, isn't as rigid as it once was, the familiar sense of superiority replaced by a quiet calm I would never expect from her.

"Still working hard, I see," she says, motioning to the pile of work in front of me.

I don't' reply, waiting for her to explain why she's here. "I, ah, thought I'd have trouble seeing you," she says. "And I changed my mind about coming here more than once." She looks around. "I expected you to revoke my clearance, which I assume you have, but you never banned my access into the building."

"No," I agree. My human resources and tech supervisors made sure Ashleigh was removed as an employee and that any attempts to take information would be blocked. But while she angered and insulted most of my staff, I never took that extra step to bar her from the premises. I couldn't ignore the fact that I'd unintentionally hurt her, or that my father had insisted I show women kindness, regardless of how my mother had used and mistreated him.

Not that I miss Ashleigh or welcome her presence. "What are you doing here?"

"Are you still seeing Wren?" She glances down when my features steel. "I thought you might be."

I stand, prepared to come to Wren's defense.

Ashleigh doesn't go on the attack. At least not as I expect. "I'm here for you, Evan. To caution you," she says, her palms opening. "She's not who you think she is."

"You're referring to the woman I plan to marry. I warn you, watch what you say."

Ashleigh's lips part in shock. She straightens, her voice quivering. "Evan, she's an amateur porn star—"

"*What*?" I storm around the desk. "Of all the lies you could spew and your attempts to disparage her, this is what you choose to tell me?"

"It's true," she says, angry tears forming in her eyes. She fumbles through her purse and removes a jump drive, holding it out at arms-length. "The link to the site is on here. Take it. You can see for yourself."

My glare lifts from the jump drive to her face. "For crying out loud, Evan," she says. "I'm not trying to hurt you. I'm trying to help. The firewall and all the protection you have will detect any virus before it can infect the system. There's nothing to lose by opening it, so look." Her voice softens as her tears spill from her eyes. "Please. Do this for yourself before you make a mistake that will cost you."

I'm ready to throw her out, this time the right way, with security escorting her off the premises. Yet everything about Ashleigh is different, reinforcing that at the very least, she believes what she says.

I take the jump drive, not because I trust her, but because I trust Wren. The moment I insert it into my computer, Alfred's program latches onto it, searching for anything that can harm.

"Alfred status," I say.

The system opens to a file titled "Evidence".

"Safe passage, no malware detected," Alfred says. "Open document and follow link?"

I frown in Ashleigh's direction. "It's the only thing on the drive," she says. "It will show you everything you need to see."

"Follow link in safe mode," I say, my annoyance surging and my patience running thin.

"Safe mode initiated, iCronos systems blocked, opening link."

My computer monitors light up one by one when Alfred reaches "Delicious Divas". The name alone has me rolling my eyes, my distaste growing as each projects women in multiple positions and locales, their images fuzzy from poorly lit rooms and antiquated lens quality.

My gaze skips over each one. I scoff, wondering why the hell I bothered to placate Ashleigh when my eyes fix on the bottom right corner.

"Come on," the lovely brunette with sparkling eyes teases. "Don't you want to fuck me?"

I lean in, my palm pressing against my desk when I realize that it's Wren. *My* Wren. She looks younger, thinner than she is now as she strips down. I click onto the image, certain I'm wrong, assuring myself it can't be her. But as more images of her scatter across each monitor, I know it's her face I see.

There is a GIF of her with her legs open, touching herself, the image repeating each time her head lolls back. In the upper corner, I watch her back slide against a wall as a man, who isn't me, rams his hips and lifts her body.

At the center she's sprawled naked across the bed, one leg bent, the other straightened, her preferred position when she sleeps. Comments as recent as a week ago are typed below: requests to meet her, remarks that she's their favorite to jerk off to, and detailed descriptions of what each commenter wants to do to her.

Another GIF flashes to my right. In this one, she's tugging on her nipples, mouthing, "Touch me, touch me, touch me," But it's the video at the center that shatters my world.

This image is more recent, her body more like it is now, thin, with definition to her arms and legs. Her face lights up as she licks her lips and smiles, those few and familiar freckles gathered along her nose and cheek lifting as she opens her mouth and . . .

"Alfred, sleep," I stammer, barely getting the words out as I straighten.

Nausea and fury roil for dominance in my stomach. The room becomes a vacant hole, devoid of sound and depleted of air. Inside me, a storm born of those vile images of gathers momentum.

"She goes by a different name," Ashleigh says. "Ivory O'Malley or something like that."

Ashleigh's words stab at my brain. Ivory . . . the name her Grandmother O'Malley wanted her to have.

My lungs are pained as I work through what I saw and heard. I want to break free of this mind-numbing fog I'm trapped in, find something to explain her actions away. But instead of finding a moment of clarity, of *fucking reason*, I remember her admitting how desperate she was for work when she graduated high school and how I wouldn't believe what she had to do to make money. I stare at the screen protector as it passes along each monitor. It's the one of me holding the Wren I know in my arms.

I don't move, I can't. Rage and humiliation prod me like blazing metal, branding me in agony.

I don't know how long I stand there before there's another knock on the door and John steps in. Behind him, the cluster of robotics engineers I am scheduled to meet halt in place, their enthusiasm and conversations dwindling when John blocks their passage.

John seems frozen by the ire chiseled into my features, his attention hopping to Ashleigh briefly before returning to me. "Evan?" he says.

"Get out," I respond, my voice unrecognizable.

He backs away. I barely register the sound of the closing door when Ashleigh edges closer. "I'm sorry, Evan," she says. "I wasn't trying to hurt you, that wasn't my intent."

I shake my head in disbelief that Wren could ever engage in something like this. But I can't deny the fact that it's her.

"I'm sorry," Ashleigh says again. "I didn't know—" She clears her throat. "I didn't know how hard you'd take this."

"Get out," I tell her, this time the words carrying all the weight of the devastation I feel.

"I don't want to leave you like this," she says.

I can't imagine what I must look like, my pain as real as the day my father was buried, and remembering all the lies my mother fed him.

"Get out," I repeat in that same dull tone.

I can't look at Ashleigh, the images of Wren blinding me to my surroundings. The way Wren acted in the most recent image wasn't the woman I recognize and love. Her motions were exaggerated and overtly vulgar, lacking the passion I've known so well.

I don't acknowledge Ashleigh until she reaches the door and calls to me. "Evan?" she says, her voice shaking. "Did I . . ." She releases a breath. "Did I ever have a chance with you?"

I meet her face, thinking back to how easily Wren captivated me with her beauty and ensnared me with her charms, exactly as my mother did to my father to get everything she wanted.

"No," I confess, despite it all.

She bows her head, carefully slipping through the door. It shuts with a small snap as my heart breaks away in pieces.

CHAPTER 23

Wren

The warm June breeze picks up, shifting my hair to the side. Behind me, someone barrels down on his horn, yelling at the garbage truck in front of him to hurry the hell up. I dig through the white paper bag stuffed with food. I have a proposal from the administrative staff to look through before ten, but when I remembered that Evan didn't eat breakfast, and it would be four more hours until his next break, I left it and the boatload of work I have littering my desk to buy him that egg white sandwich he likes, the one with blue cheese crumbles and fresh spinach. I also picked up another coffee and fresh fruit in case he needs a snack. I grin, wondering when the hell I turned so nurturing, only to swear like the guy in the garbage truck when I realize I forgot the damn fork.

Whatever. I'll pick one up in the downstairs coffee shop. Their coffee blows and the woman behind the counter keeps burning the bagels, which is why I walked two blocks to get Evan breakfast. God knows the guy deserves a decent meal.

I glance at the time on my phone. Evan is already meeting with John and the other engineers. Unless they hit a major hurdle, he'll have at least five minutes to eat before his meeting with Anne and Clifton.

I raise my head as I round the corner and the giant

metallic sign for iCronos comes into view. No matter how busy I am, or what I'm doing, I always look up at the sign, a sense of pride lifting my spirits when I think of the man behind the empire.

"Hey, pretty girl."

Bryant pushes off the side of the building, his red baseball cap shadowing his face. "What the hell are you doing here?" I ask, backing away.

There's ten feet separating me from the crosswalk leading to iCronos property, thirty feet from the nearest guard, and another fifty to the doors. But Bryant isn't moving.

He holds out his hands. "Take it easy. I'm just saying hello." He huffs. "Besides, I have a new woman and if you can believe it, she's exactly who I need."

Anger pushes aside my fear. "And what's that? Someone who won't leave your ass when you beat her and too naive to figure out what a manipulative prick you are?"

"Where's all this anger coming from?" He's smiling, but in a way that reminds me how twisted he can be. "We had some good times, you and me. Real good, remember?"

"No," I fire back. "All I remember is the shit you put me through, you fucking psycho."

A car rolls slowly past. The way the sunlight hits the windshield casts the light across his face, illuminating his seedy grin. The stubble on his jaw is thicker now, not quite a beard, but close to it. Strands of his straight blond hair poke through his cap. I suppose he's trying to return to that surfer look he had when I first met him. I also suppose I could give a rat's ass. But it's what's in his light blue eyes that I can't get past. They're unusually steely and absent of anything kind.

I take a step to my right, keeping the traffic to my back and distance from the small alleyway separating the bank from the insurance company beside it. Bryant can drag me behind there if I let him, but I'll be damned if I let him.

He's in jeans, the expensive kind with holes in all the right places and a tight rust-colored T-shirt that stretches across his brawny and tall frame. I don't know why the hell I was ever attracted to him. Everything about him is phony, except for the TAG Heuer watch on his wrist, reminding me his life of crime has been lucrative.

"So how you been?" he asks, chewing on his gum in that annoying way he does.

"Awesome," I say, taking another step and motioning to his watch. "How's life as the mob's little bitch going? I can see bending over for them is paying off big time for you. My brother, Curran the cop, and my other brother, Declan, you know, the District Attorney? They're just dying to know all about it."

He laughs, enjoying himself. "Don't know what you mean, pretty girl."

"Stop calling me that," I snap, keeping him in my line of sight as I edge toward the crosswalk.

"Shit, you're bitchy," he says. "What's the matter? Doesn't your new man know what you like to keep you happy? If you want, I can tell him exactly how hard and rough you like it"

"Fuck off, Bryant," I interrupt, my anger flaring. "You know nothing about us."

The street light flashes, signaling the all-clear to cross. I take off fast, spilling the coffee through the bag and singeing my hand. Bryant notices and I expect him to laugh. Instead, his smile dwindles.

"Hey, Wren," he calls. "Remember what I told you, no one can love a whore."

His haunting tone pricks at my skin. I keep my focus on him as I reach the walkway and step onto the iCronos campus. He keeps pace with me along the opposite side of the street, stopping where a woman with yellow blond hair in a sundress paces by a Maserati convertible. He stops in front her. I can't hear them, but the way her arms are crossed over her chest, I can tell she's pissed.

Bryant glances my way, then snatches the woman into his arms, kissing her like she's something he owns rather than someone he cares for. She shoves him away, slapping him hard across the face. He throws back his head, laughing. His reaction is weird, giving us both a peek at all that crazy he hides all too well. I don't think she sees it. She's too distracted by anger.

She storms away, furious, yanking the strap of her sundress back onto her shoulder. I can't see her well from where I'm standing, especially with the sunglasses she's wearing. She looks familiar, but she's too far away to place.

Bryant salutes me, like he doesn't care whether she comes back or not. He probably already has someone else lined up to take her place.

I dial Curran, speaking fast and reading off Bryant's plate when it goes to voicemail. God damn it. I wish I could shake this hold Bryant has over me. I thought I was free of him, but all he had to do was show his face to remind me that I'm not.

He hops into the convertible and speeds off as I reach the main doors to the lobby. I mutter a curse under my breath, and another one when I shove my phone back into my purse and reach into the bag. The sandwich is soaked and the bottom of the paper coffee cup is poking through the bottom.

I dump everything in the trashcan except for the container of fruit that was spared, using some old napkins I find in my purse to dry off my hands.

"Miss O'Brien, are you all right?"

The new marketing intern hurries over. "Hey, N'ivel."

"Looks like you lost your breakfast."

"I actually lost Evan's breakfast," I say, fumbling with my words and pulling a twenty from my wallet. "Do me a favor? Go down to Sorrentino's Coffee House and get me an egg white sandwich with blue cheese crumbles and spinach, and a large Americano with a splash of half and half."

He types away on his phone. "Got it. Anything else?"

"No. That's all, thank you."

I can't even pretend to smile, hurrying toward the elevator when I realize how bad my voice is shaking.

A few members of Evan's tech team pile out.

"Hey, Wren."

"Hi, Wren."

"How's it going?"

"Hey," I say, keeping my head down.

I fall against the wall when the doors shut, cursing out loud. Technically, Bryant didn't do or say anything I can use against him. *Again.* But the encounter shook me up all the same. He mentioned Evan. I'm not surprised he knows I'm with him. If he's still following me, he was bound to see us together.

Shit. As much as Evan can take care of himself, I want to spare him from all of this. "Top level, Wren?" Alfred asks, the device Evan gave me to keep in my purse alerting the system of my presence.

I sigh, realizing I never hit the button to the 50th floor and taking comfort in his techno voice. "Yes, Alfred."

The elevator zooms up without stopping. I push away from the wall when the doors part, wrestling with whether to call Curran again or speak to Evan first. My pace slows when I find John sitting at my desk, eating a bagel. He hurries to stand when he sees me, wiping the cream cheese caked on his fingers on his lab coat.

"Aren't you and your top guys supposed to be meeting with Evan?" I ask.

I snag a bottle of water from the mini fridge in the corner and pass it to him when he seems to struggle to swallow. He takes several gulps, and a few more before he speaks. "Thank you," he says, appearing more frantic than usual. "Something happened. To Evan."

"*What?*"

He grabs my hand when I launch forward. "Sorry," he says, pulling away as if afraid to touch me. "But, Wren, it's very bad I'm afraid. I've never seen him like this." He inches close, keeping his voice low. "I think it's the company."

"The company?" I repeat.

He nods, causing the strands of his disheveled hair to bounce in place. "Something horrible has happened." He shakes his head. "I've never seen him so defeated."

"*Defeated?*" I ask. His nod sends me into a panic. That word has no place being so close to Evan.

"I have to go," I tell him. I throw my purse across the desk and place the stupid container of fruit on the cabinet. I jet toward Evan's door, pausing when I realize John is watching me.

"Let me know if I can help," he says. "Whatever he needs, I'll do it—*we'll* do it. Let him know we're here for him."

"I will," I promise. I want to assure him that Evan is fine and not to worry, but I'm so out of my mind, I run into his office, stopping short when I find the room veiled in darkness.

"Evan?" I say, scanning the area as my eyes adjust.

One of the first things he does every morning is order Alfred to open the shades. This morning, for our privacy, he left them closed.

I glance in the direction of the conference table, walking toward the screening area as the door falls closed behind me. Considering what John said, I half-expect to find Evan sprawled across the long leather couch.

"I'm here," he says behind me.

His tone keeps me in place, the lack of inflection and emotion causing my worry to rocket out of control. I turn slowly, the heels of my shoes clicking as I cross the room toward his workstation.

I reach the desk where he sits and peer over the collection of monitors. His forearms are pressed against the slick wood and his hands are balled into tight fists. He's angry, that much I see. But it's the way the light from the computer monitors flash across his bleaching skin that scares the hell out of me.

"What's wrong?" He doesn't answer. "Evan, what happened?"

He rises slowly as if stiff from pain. I race around his desk, ready to throw my arms around him. But his rigid stance and the fury spilling from his tall form stops me in my tracks.

This isn't business. It's personal.

I scan his face, searching for any of trace of him that remains. All I find is barely controlled rage. "Baby . . ."

He rams his eyes closed. Torment replacing his anger, but it's brief. "Ashleigh came by today," he says.

"Ashleigh?" I ask, wondering what she could have possibly done to upset him this much.

"She showed me something I never expected." He swallows hard. "Much less wanted to see."

"What?"

I heard what he said, but it's like he's speaking in code. His glance toward his desk my only clue that there's something there I need to see.

I walk toward it, giving him ample space. Something bad is coming. I can sense it by how it's affecting him and how he doesn't want me anywhere near him. I'm expecting a tragic event, maybe the start of a war, or God forbid, children who were somehow harmed by his products.

I reach his desk, expecting to see a document or letter. When I don't find anything other than the familiar pile of reports, I look up. His screen bounces across each frame. It's a picture of me and him from Fiona's first birthday party. His arms are wrapped around me and we're smiling, happy. But I don't feel happy now.

All I have is the fear that something awful has happened to him.

I swipe my fingertips across his mouse pad, jarring the system awake. The image of us is replaced by multiple shots of a naked woman, one begging the man doing her against the wall to go faster, and yet another touching herself, her dark hair falling around her and veiling her face. Ads for the hardcore porn site flash beneath. On the bottom screen, the same woman is covered in sweat, shaking her ass as some guy takes her hard from behind.

It takes me a moment to realize the man is Bryant.

And that the woman he's fucking is me.

A chill, as fierce as any winter storm, carves its way into my bones. Every image is of me. Me moaning. Me writhing. Me begging for it.

My remaining breath leaves me in a painful rush. I cover my mouth as horror claims me, trying not to scream when I see how many thousands of ratings the feature has received—how many disgusting comments are posted, how many horny bastards are begging to screw me.

My hand slaps against the chair as I stumble backward,

trying to keep from falling. "What is this?" I ask, my voice shaking as hard as my hands. "What the *hell* is this?"

For all I think my world is ending, Evan is barely holding it together. His shoulders rise and fall with explosive rage. "You didn't know about this—any of it?"

"No!" I yell, backing away. "I would never do something like this!"

Bile beats my stomach in waves, burning into my throat when Bryant tilts his head back and comes. It's what he looked like when we were still together. His hair cut short to his scalp and his face clean-shaven. He groans, rubbing off when he pulls out and smiling in the direction of what must be the camera.

It's his final "fuck you" to me, and holy shit is it ever brutal.

My eyes burn as I bolt. I don't realize how fast I move until I'm almost halfway across the room. Footsteps stomp behind me as Evan clasps my elbow and whirls me around.

His voice is barely audible, but his rage is as evident as his grip on my arm. "There's an entire page filled with pictures, Wren, and videos. All of them of you with the name Ivory O'Malley."

I shake my head slowly, not because I don't believe him, but because I can't believe I was so fucking blind. "I didn't make those videos or pose for any pictures . . ." My voice trails when doubt plagues his face. "I know I've taken pictures of us—and-and we've watched ourselves, but that's different."

"*Why*?"

Sometimes the truth is more painful when it involves the person you most love. "Because you're the only one I've ever trusted."

He wrestles with what to say, and maybe what to believe, too. "You didn't consent to this—"

"*No*," I respond, cutting him off. "I wouldn't let him, even when he asked."

"Him?" he asks, his tone curt.

I'm barely able to speak, the ache in my throat twisting

into a knot. "That's Bryant in the videos with me," I admit. He has a different look in each one. Short hair. Long hair. In the one of me up against the wall he's wearing that stupid black cowboy hat he bought at that rodeo he'd dragged me to. I'm thin in the one where I'm touching myself. Real thin. Which means he started pulling this shit at the very start of our relationship.

God damn it.

God damn *him*.

Every muscle in my body threatens to give way as a floodgate of memories bust through my mind. I should have known he'd wreck me like this. But this isn't just cruel. It's sick. He took pleasure in exposing me at my most vulnerable to the world.

"He did it without me knowing. Evan . . . you have to believe me."

He doesn't respond. But how do you respond to something like this? Darkness claims him in a way I've never seen. I hate it. All of it—what I let Bryant do to me, but mostly what it's doing to Evan.

Bryant *made* Evan watch him fuck me, hand delivering everything to Ashleigh to make sure it would get back to him. That was her, waiting for him on the street. I glance around, working things through. It wouldn't take much for him to find her, not after those articles she was featured in, where she bashed Evan and his business practices.

She meant to make me look bad. But Bryant's sole intention was to cause us pain.

I bury my face in my hands, when Evan orders Alfred to turn on the lights. I don't want to think about what it was like for Evan to see me like that—me, the woman he loved, naked with another man on top of her.

"I'm sorry," I stammer, clinging to the last of my resolve.

He lets out a ragged breath as his hand falls to his side. I want to beg him not to let me go, but I'm so ill I don't manage.

"In the video, directly at the center," he begins, jerking his chin away and muttering a curse as he seems to recall it.

"You were different there than you are with me."

If he means to ask more questions, they don't come. Maybe that's better. As it is, my chest feels like it's caving in. "You can say I wasn't myself," I quietly answer.

He cocks his head as if he doesn't understand. But as anger replaces his confusion, I know that he knows, just like I realize I can no longer hold anything back. It's too late to spare him or myself. That doesn't make what I say any easier, or that I wouldn't give anything to take back that night.

"I told him I didn't want to see him anymore," I begin. "That I needed space. He kept calling, trying to get me back." I glance down to where Evan's hand rests at his side, wishing he hadn't let me go. "I finally agreed to meet him and talk."

My mind returns to that night. It was cold and I pulled on the sweater Ma had bought me for Christmas. A deep plum as soft as silk. He smiled when he saw me and told me I looked hot in the skinny jeans I wore. I don't bother sharing that much with Evan, because even then, Bryant didn't make me feel good. I just never imagined he'd make me feel worse.

"What happened?" Evan presses, when I suddenly stop.

"He bought me a drink, and another one after that."

"He got you drunk," he says, his comment more of a blunt statement than an actual question.

"Not exactly," I admit, my tone heavy with all the shit I tried to forget about that night.

Evan straightens while I shrink inward. "He drugged you," he says, his tone and expression so lethal, I can barely hold his gaze.

"I don't remember a lot about that night," I confess. "Just enough to know I participated." I glance at my entwined hands. "Very actively, as you probably saw."

He scrunches his eyes closed as if trying to erase the image of Bryant plowing into me. But it's fixed into his memory as much as it's fixed into mine.

With another wicked curse, he slowly opens his eyes. "It was not consensual," he states. "You were not in your right frame of mind."

It's one thing to know, but it's a whole different thing to

hear the man you adore say it. "No."

"*Christ*," he explodes. "Why didn't you tell me—why didn't you tell anyone?"

"Because this wasn't supposed to happen to *me*!" I fire back, my voice rising. "I got into my first fight before I lost my first baby tooth. When I was fifteen, I fought off a grown man trying to drag me into an alley. I have six monstrous brothers at my beck and call, ready to defend me and I teach women self-defense."

His breaths turn heavy and labored, but mine aren't any better. "This *wasn't* supposed to happen to me, Evan," I repeat, my strength crumbling. "But it did, because I trusted the wrong man to do the right thing."

"We have to go to the police."

"*No*," I snap, anger burning like lava through my veins. "It's been more than a year, and you saw the video. Did it look like I was fighting him off? No, I was begging him for it."

Repulsion paints his face a vicious red and I see the damage Bryant has caused flash across Evan's features. He doesn't answer me. He doesn't have to. "If I go to the police, everyone will know, and everyone will put a name to the face on that screen." I lift my arm, motioning toward his desk, but it feels so heavy. "Even if it goes to trial, the only thing a judge and jury will see is the slut he made me be."

Evan storms from my reach, his fingers digging through his hair as he nears the conference table. He doesn't take more than a few steps before he grips a chair and sends it flying.

"He can't get away with this," he hollers. "I won't fucking let him."

"He already did," I remind him, my voice barely registering. Evan turns to face me, fury spreading along his frame. "In the morning when I woke, he was lying next to me. I knew what happened, I'd remembered enough. But the worst part was remembering that I'd enjoyed it."

I sniff when those green eyes, the ones with specks of gold, mirror all the pain I feel. "He told me he knew I loved it by how I responded, and that it was the best fuck he ever had.

It made me sick. But as much as I hated him then, I hated myself more."

Evan shoots across the room, swooping me into his arms. In his strength, I lose what remains of mine. "I didn't even finish getting dressed before I ran out of there. I blocked his calls. I refused to see him. And when he showed up at my door with that sweater I wore that night, I threatened to go to the police. 'You know you liked it,' he told me, well aware it was exactly what he needed to say to shut me up and guarantee I'd never breathe a word to anyone." I force myself to speak. "And I never did."

I don't cry much. There are only a few times in my life I remember shedding more than a tear. Once was when we learned what happened to Sofia. The other times involved my brother Finn, and more recently when Evan told me he loved me. I didn't even cry when my own damn father died. I thought I should. You're supposed to, right, when you watch the man who gave you life lying in a casket? But I couldn't. Not when he caused too many of my mother's tears to fall.

Except I cry now. I cry for not leaving Bryant long before that moment—for believing he wasn't the bad guy that I knew deep down inside he always was. Mostly, I cry over how much it must have hurt Evan seeing me do what I did.

Deep-seated pain lingers in his strong features. *Strong.* That's who he is, yet unbelievably gentle when it comes to me. Even now as he raises his hand, it's not in anger. He gingerly strokes my cheek, like I'm the most important thing that's ever walked this earth, despite that it's far from how I feel.

"I'll take care of it," he whispers.

"I don't want anyone to know," I say, pushing the words out when they lodge in my throat.

"No one will know unless you disclose it. That doesn't mean I'm not going to make him fucking pay."

"What?" I ask, unable to understand.

His hands glide to my hips. "There are two things I won't stand for," he bites out, the rage resurfacing. "Someone else touching you, the way *I* touch you, and someone hurting you.

This piece of shit did both and I'm going to end him."

"Evan?" Clifton calls. He stills at the door when he realizes he interrupted more than a simple moment.

I give him my back, swiping my cheeks. "One moment," Evan tells him.

The door shuts quietly. I don't have to look to know we're alone.

Evan closes the small space separating us. He doesn't touch me. Not this time. But I feel his presence directly behind me. "I have to go," he tells me. "But you have my word, I'll take care of this and take care of you, *always*." He presses a kiss against the back of my head. "This . . . all of it, changes nothing between us."

The sound of his footsteps echo behind me until the door closes with a snap.

He says this changes nothing between us. That doesn't mean I believe him.

Nor does it stop my tears from running faster.

CHAPTER 24

Wren

I didn't see Evan for the rest of the day. He didn't text or call and he never reported back to his office.

He was supposed to meet with Anne and Clifton to follow up on an aggressive sales campaign he developed that could best be described as Guerilla marketing. Every rep we have was flown across the country, hitting over two hundred hospitals in ten days. We need close to fifty sales just to stay afloat. But Evan is expecting more. No, he's demanding it and he's inspired his reps to make it happen.

I thought he'd tell me how the meeting went. But when he didn't return, I couldn't shake the feeling he didn't want me anywhere near him. I know what he said, about nothing changing between us, but everything had.

My eyes dart across my computer screen, looking at everything and nothing at all. Between my office and his, this place is usually a beehive of activity, but although I can hear the buzz from the staff typing away on their keyboards, rushing to hand their reports to the courier stopping by their desks, and the constant ringing of phones, it's like everyone is keeping their distance from me.

Ever get so emotionally bitch-slapped that if feels like a part of you has died? That's how I feel, and when five o'clock hits. I'm done. It may sound like business as usual outside those clear glass doors, but inside my head and heart, it's been a nightmare.

Curran called me back. He didn't tell me anything I didn't already know: that I needed to file another report to create a paper trail, and that he and his partner planned to pay Bryant another visit, but that it's been too many months since I heard from him directly to substantiate harassment. The plate number I gave Curran wasn't anything the police didn't already have. They were looking for him for questioning, but they still don't have anything solid. Aside from everything Bryant's done to me, there's more tidbits linking him back to organized crime.

Curran is pissed. So is Declan. But they're not alone.

I gather my purse and jacket, lifting a progress report in my hands so it looks like I'm doing something and not wallowing in my anger.

"Going home, Wren?" Dee-Dee asks when I pass her cubicle, her comment causing those working closest to her to glance up.

I lift the folder. "I have a lot to read through."

My lie is believable enough and hides that awful dullness to my tone. Normally, Dee would be all over me, pressing me to tell her what's wrong. But like everyone else surrounding her, she's full speed ahead, working like she just arrived and raring to go.

She doesn't so much as look up, too busy sorting through the pile of work on her desk. "In that case, let me add to your to-do list," she says, passing me a folder shoved beneath at least six more. "It's a progress report on the new hires." She gives me a full smile. "You did good, Wren. The staff is kicking tail."

"Thanks, Dee," I reply, pretending to flip through the folder so I don't have to meet her face.

"No problem," she answers, returning to her computer. "See you tomorrow."

I place the file on top of my folder. Will she see me tomorrow? I wish I knew myself.

I walk as casually as I can to the elevators. In all the months I've worked here, I've never left so early. The exception was when Bryant (or whoever the hell he manipulated) tossed that brick through my front window and I had to return home to gather my things. But even then, I came back and stayed late to make up for it.

Like Dee said, the new hires, along with the workers we kept, are making a huge difference. I think I'm the first person to leave. It probably looks bad. But considering I've been torn between raging and crying since Evan left me this morning, I think I owe it to my sanity and his team to leave.

My stomach jerks into my throat as the elevator speeds down. I'm sure I'll get sick. I haven't eaten all day. Finding out your psycho ex turned you into an internet porn star tends to rob you of your appetite, along with your dignity and pride. I rummage through my purse and find a protein bar to munch on. My hands shake, not from lack of food, but from everything that comes with my life falling apart. I'm trying not to think about Evan and what he saw. But it's so damn hard.

I don't remember the drive back to our place. And I barely remember the progress report I started despite that I read the first paragraph about twelve times before setting it down. I don't even remember sleeping. All I remember is waking to an empty bed.

I showered and changed out of the dress I slept in then headed back to Philly with every intention of going to work. Instead, I drove back to my old place. I'm not sure why, maybe because I don't feel like I belong at iCronos anymore.

I accelerate as I go up the hill leading into my neighborhood, thinking about the text from Evan this morning.

Still working.

That was it. No, "I'll be with you soon", "I'm sorry I missed you", or "I love you". But then maybe the latter was too much to expect.

I'm not being overly dramatic. I needed to hear him say it. It's proof that nothing has changed between us.

I park in front of the house, not bothering to pull in because maybe I don't belong here either. For a fleeting moment, I want to run. Just leave. But as much as I think I should go in, all I manage is to stand on the walkway, staring at the way the shiny glass from the new picture window gleams in the sun.

The breeze picks up the longer I wait there. But I can't seem to move forward and it doesn't feel right to move back. Moving back means going to iCronos and facing Evan. I'm not ready to see him, scared out of my mind he's reconsidered me and us.

The thing is, the longer I stare at that window, the more that anger replaces my fear. Bryant violated my home in tossing that brick *and* my place of work when he drove that truck through the dealership. Before that, he violated *me* and shared it with the world, using the worst thing that's ever happened to me to ruin the best thing to come along.

I slip into my truck and pull onto the road.

The first call I make is to Curran. "What's wrong?" he asks, answering right away.

I hate the way my voice shakes, but I hate what I have to say even more. "I need to talk to you and Declan."

His pause lets me know he's already pissed. "What the fuck happened? Did Bryant—"

"I can't tell you on the phone," I tell him, muttering a curse when my voice trembles more. "Meet me at Declan's office, okay?"

"You sound like hell," he says. "Where's Evan?"

"He's not around," I answer quietly.

"What do you mean he's not around?"

"He didn't come last night."

My tone reflects everything I'm feeling: worry, exhaustion, and most likely my fear. It hurts to admit that Evan never came home.

"Wren," he says, his voice careful. "Tell me where you are and I'll come get you."

"I'm okay," I say, lying through my teeth. "I'll see you soon."

He doesn't believe I'm all right, but for once doesn't argue with me. "All right. I'll be there," he says.

I cut a hard left when he disconnects, stomping on the gas to make the next light. The D.A.'s office is only fifteen minutes away, but I can't seem to get there fast enough. It's like if I don't get there, and tell Curran and Declan what I need to say, I'll run out of courage.

"Alfred, call Evan," I say, my voice trembling so sporadically, I'm not sure he'll understand the command.

But then, Alfred's the best on the market for a reason. "Calling Evan, Wren."

The line rings. And rings. And rings. Each tone longer and more painful than the last. "Evan is unavailable, Wren. Leave message?"

In not answering, every worst case scenario plays out in my head: he's avoiding me, he's pushing me away, and he hates me. But it's the thought that he hates me that punctures my heart like a knife.

"Wren, Evan is unavailable. Leave message?" Alfred presses.

"Yes," I reply, my voice becoming eerily still as my truck rolls through the first city block.

"Recording," Alfred answers.

The beep that follows is like a death signal of sorts. That doesn't stop me from spilling my soul and letting death take me. "Hey. It's me," I begin, speaking each word carefully. "Look, I know what happened yesterday was two kinds of fucked up, and I'm sorry. I never knew that was out there. If I had I would've . . . I would've done something."

I want to mean what I say, but remembering how bad Bryant made me look . . . Christ. How did this happen to me?

"I'm on my way to the D.A.'s office to meet with Curran and Declan," I say, ignoring the humiliation wrapping around my throat like a noose. "As much as I don't want anyone to know what he did to me, I can't let him get away with it." I belt out a curse when I roll through an intersection and completely miss the stop sign. "I don't want anyone to know about me," I say again. "I don't want anyone to see me like that. But I want this to end and I don't know any other way."

My eyes burn when the courthouse come into view. "I love you," I say. "No matter what, I love you, Evan."

I hit the "send" icon on the screen before Alfred can ask and pull into the underground parking deck closest to the D.A.'s office. I cross the street, forcing my legs to keep moving.

I'm not sure what to expect when I arrive, and I've never visited Declan at work. I find the right floor and step into the reception area, ready to ask the woman with black hair and streaks of gray sitting behind the glass partition if I can see Declan.

Tess appears behind the receptionist before I can spit out a single word, her belly pressing against the light blue maternity dress she's wearing. Her blond hair is pulled up in a clip and her black framed glasses magnify her large eyes. But it's the concern behind them that keeps me in place. "Buzz her in please, Louise," Tess says, hurrying to the door.

The door clicks open and she's suddenly there. At least six people are waiting to get in, but she tucks the legal folder in her grasp under her arm and leads me forward. "Curran called to tell me you were coming."

She releases my hand as soon as we step inside the large office. "Is he here?" I ask, hurrying along beside her.

She knows I mean Curran and shakes her head. "No, but he's on his way in and asked me to meet you. Declan just finished a meeting." She grinds to a halt near a corner and shoots her hand out, keeping me in place. Two men in suits, along with four sheriff's officers surround a guy in county jail orange and shackles. I've seen felons on TV before. Hell, I grew up around plenty, but the crazy glazing this guy's eyes gives me pause. Maybe because I recognize the look from Bryant.

"Declan's new case," she whispers as they step out of earshot. "The Kensington Strangler."

The guy who murdered twelve young women over the

course of five years. "Nice," I say, not meaning a word of it.

The moment they round the corner, she leads me forward, shooting me a sideways glance. "Are you all right? You don't look good." I don't bother to answer, which I suppose is answer enough. "Wren…" she begins, her expression as miserable as I probably feel.

"Don't," I reply, letting her know I'm ready to lose it.

She nods like she understands, probably because she does. She had her share of bad before Curran came into her life. But just like he saved her, she saved him.

We stop in front of a corner office and she knocks, opening it before Declan finishes asking who it is.

He straightens from where he's leaning against his desk, the cuff links on his white shirt catching the light from his desk lamp. His short wavy blond hair is similar to Finn's minus the ginger tones, but unlike Finnie, his is neat and styled to perfection just like the rest of him.

He frowns when he sees me, causing the woman with chocolate brown hair sitting in front of him to turn. She's curvy, very curvy, and despite her chic and conservative dress, she resembles more of fifties pinup model than the Barbie dolls I'm used to seeing at Declan's side.

"What are you doing here?" he asks me.

I press my lips tight, trying to think of something to say without giving too much away. Tess beats me to the punch. "I apologize for interrupting, Declan. Your secretary informed me your meeting had finished."

"With opposing counsel, not with Melissa," he says, rising and walking around the desk. "Mel, this is my sister, Wren. Wren, this is Melissa, head of Victim Services for the State."

"Hello," Melissa says. She stands and offers me her hand. "Nice to meet you."

I shake it, noting her speech is slightly altered. "Hi," I say, my lack of conversation giving Declan signals that this isn't a friendly visit.

He looks at Tess. "Curran is on his way," she says as a way of an explanation.

I don't see the hearing aids Melissa is wearing, but based on the way she speaks, and how she focuses on the way Tess's lips move, I realize she's hearing impaired.

The door flies open and Curran steps through in full uniform, not bothering to knock. His face gives nothing away, but his presence does. Melissa frowns slightly and edges around me. "I'll leave you alone to talk," she says. "It was nice to meet you, Wren."

I smile politely as Curran positions himself between me and Tess.

"Mel, wait," Declan says.

Melissa doesn't seem to like the "Mel" reference. In fact, Melissa doesn't seem to like Declan at all, which is odd. Declan's looks and suave political persona have always made him popular, but it's his keen intelligence and killer rep in court that launched him into celebrity status at a young age.

Apparently, it takes a lot more to charm Melissa. Her posture is straight and guarded, unlike most women who fall all over Declan. She's wary of him, but I'm not sure why.

"You've worked hard on this case," Declan tells her.

She watches him carefully. "I don't mind. I'm happy to help."

Declan smiles, and it's genuine and warm, unlike the smile he usually flashes, the one that schmoozes and guarantees he'll get laid. "I know, but tonight, maybe you should go home and . . ." He takes a breath and motions with his hands, slapping his palms together and then pointing to her.

I have no idea what he said.

But Curran does.

And so does Melissa.

Her eyes fly open, scanning each of us as her fair skin burns bright pink. "You *asshole*," she tells Declan. She whips around, her steps quick and forceful, sending her hair sailing behind her as she storms away.

Curran rounds on Declan when the door slams shut, his expression split between stunned stupid and ripping him a new one. "What the hell, Deck?"

Declan's face flushes a furious red. "I told her, 'to go to bed.'" He repeats the motions. "Doesn't this mean go to bed?"

"No, dumbass," Curran fires back. "This means go to bed." He does something similar with his palms, but instead of smacking them together like Declan did he slides and joins them. "*You* told her to go fuck herself."

"Jesus *Christ*," he says. "How many fucking times can I screw up with her?"

Curran shakes his head. "I don't know. But I'm starting to keep score. Just so you know, it's the fourth quarter with ten seconds left in the game and the cheerleaders are lining up to punch you in the nuts."

It's just like Curran to bust some serious balls, and normally I'd slap Declan upside the head for being such a dumbass. But all I can do is gape. Holy shit. Declan likes Melissa—a real woman with real tits for once in his life. "Damn," I say.

He pauses, looking at me closer when he catches something in my expression. "What's going on?" His focus darts to Curran briefly before resting on me. "Wren, what happened?"

I came here to spill my guts, except it takes me way too long to speak. "I have to talk to you about Bryant."

"What about him?" Declan asks, his tone growing severe. "Did he approach you again since yesterday?"

"No."

Everyone falls perfectly still. Declan scowls, pointing at me when his office phone rings. "Hold that thought," he tells me. "O'Brien," he says, answering. His frown deepens, his face lifting to meet mine. "Evan's here."

"Evan is here?" I repeat, barely believing it.

He nods slowly. "He says it's urgent and he needs to see me."

Curran steps forward. "I thought you said he didn't come home last night," he reminds me.

If Declan wasn't already mad, he'll be furious now. "Am I showing him in, or tossing him out?" he asks.

"In," I say, swallowing back the shock mixed with relief I

feel.

"I'll go get him," Curran says, moving fast.

The carpet in Declan's office is that industrial gray. The kind that will take a beating for years to come and still say business. It's all I see, as I ignore the way Declan and Tess are staring at me. I don't know what they're going to think or say. But I know I can no longer stay silent.

My head swivels in the direction of the door when it opens. Curran walks in, tailed closely by Evan.

Evan's eyes immediately lock onto mine. I'm barely keeping it together, and while his presence gives me the comfort I lack, the reminder of everything he saw has me curling inward. Maybe he knows it. From one breath to the next, I'm in his arms.

"I'm sorry I didn't make it home," he whispers. This is coming from him, not anything Curran said. I know it by the way he holds me.

I nod, melting into him, the steady beat of his heart pounding against my ear. His warmth and presence, God help me, it's what I've both dreaded and needed. And now that he's here, it's like I can't breathe without him.

"What the fuck is going on?" Curran say, his voice mirroring the building anger in his features.

"Are you ready?" Evan asks me gently.

I ease away and look up at him. Thick stubble peppers his jaw and he's wearing the same suit he wore yesterday. My guess is that he barely slept, if he slept at all.

He leads me to the small leather couch while Curran gathers two chairs for him and Tess and places them in front of us. Declan leans against the edge of his desk, watching with, what to most, might appear as interest. I know better. Charismatic, future politician aside, my brother is a street kid at heart and he's ready to come out swinging. "I'm waiting," he says.

"Bryant sent Evan a message yesterday through Evan's former secretary," I begin.

"What kind of message?" Declan asks when I suddenly stop speaking.

"A link to a website," Evan answers for me, his tone more terse than Declan's.

He doesn't say anything more, leaving the rest up to me. As hard as it is, I tell them everything that's on the site, and everything that happened the night I met up with him.

I don't look up until I'm done. Tess has her hand clasped over her mouth, horrified on my behalf. Like Evan, my brothers are raging.

"I'll fucking kill him," Curran says.

"Curran," Tess warns, her voice soft, but heavy with worry.

He rises. "It's not a threat. I'm going to fucking kill him."

Declan doesn't say anything, but in a way that's worse.

Tess reaches out and clasps Curran's hand, trying to soothe him and maybe herself.

"You should have told us," Declan says, the anger he's feeling gathering close to the surface.

"I didn't want anyone to know," I bite out. "I still don't. But I don't want him to get away with this, either."

Curran leaves Tess cautiously. "If there's video, we have enough for a warrant to search his place. Maybe we'll find something there to peg him for some of the mob shit he's into." His gaze glides my way. "In addition to anything else he has on you."

"You won't find anything on Wren," Evan says, his stone-cold demeanor snagging our attention.

"Why wouldn't we?" Declan challenges.

Evan's gaze remains steady, as does his voice. "I told Wren I'd take care of things, and I have. But what I did may or may not fall within the confines of the law, regardless of what my legal counsel advised."

My chest constricts as panic sets in. "Evan, what did you do?"

He doesn't respond, meeting Declan square in the face, an unspoken request falling between them.

There's a reason Declan sailed through law school and graduated at the top of his class. He's smarter than hell and just as slick. "Tess, will you excuse us," he says.

Her attention shoots my way. "No."

"I'm not asking," he says, his tone respectful yet absolute.

"*No*," she fires back.

Curran doesn't miss a beat, siding with Declan to protect his wife. "You can't get into trouble if you don't what's happening," he tells her. "Wait for me in your office. I'll stop in when I'm done."

Tess seems torn, tossing me a glance. She's scared. Not just for me, but for everyone. "I'll be okay," I assure her, even though I sure as shit don't look the part.

Curran kisses her forehead when she stands, the tenderness behind the show of affection making her appear close to tears. "Don't do anything stupid, cop," she tells him.

"I'll see you soon," is his only response.

The moment the door shuts, Declan speaks. "Tell us," he says. When Evan pauses, Declan's attention darts briefly my way. "You protected my sister. You have my word I'll protect you if I can."

"*If?*" I ask. "You're kidding me, right?"

"We're still sworn to uphold the law," he reminds me.

Curran shrugs. "Doesn't mean we can't bend it a little."

Evan shifts his weight and pulls out a jump drive wrapped in a plastic bag from his suit pocket. "This is the drive Ashleigh, my former administrative assistant, brought me."

Declan lifts it out of his hand. "The one with the link to those images of Wren?"

He looks about as sick as I feel until Evan says what he does. "No. Links to every account Bryant is connected to, including those with the aliases he's used, as well as full access to his personal information and passwords."

"The fuck?" Curran says, stepping closer.

Evan barely blinks. "Years ago, I developed a program called Hound to track illegal downloads of digital books and music. I never released it to the public because there are imperfections in Hound that I haven't had the opportunity to fix. Imperfections that early this morning worked in my favor."

"Like what?" Declan asks, his expression darkening when Evan pauses. "What does Hound do once he finds the download?"

"He destroys it," Evan responds. "The moment I specify what I want him to hunt, he goes after it. Last night, I set the program to target not only the link to the website, but all the images and graphics contained within."

"You're serious," Declan says.

"I am," Evan replies. "But there's more. Once Hound latches onto the scent, he doesn't stop. He tracks it back to the original source." He looks at me. "In this case, it was Bryant's computer and his electronic devices."

I don't move and can barely breathe. "What are you saying?"

"That every image Bryant had of you, including video is destroyed. Hound broke apart the algorithms, downloads, and screenshots on every device connected to, or even remotely associated with the link and graphics. If there's so much as a trace, Hound sinks his fangs into it and it's gone."

"What about everyone else?" Curran asks, shifting his weight forward. "Visitors to the site? Hell, what about another site this asshole could have dumped these pictures on?"

"Any website containing the material and anyone who downloaded any part of the file, Hound found it and devoured it—"

I slap my hands over my face and curl forward, fighting tooth and nail to keep my composure. Evan's arms wrap around my shoulders as he kisses my temple. "It's okay," he whispers.

It's what he says, but I need to be sure. "So no one . . ."

I don't finish my question. Evan already knows what I'm asking. "Unless they recorded the image on a separate device by placing a camera in front of the monitor, which is unlikely, it's gone. Nothing of you remains."

My breathing is harsh, all the emotions I buried deep surging forward at once.

"Why haven't you released it?" Declan presses, trying to

give me a moment to calm. "Publishing companies and recording studios will pay tens of millions for tech this good."

Evan's weight lifts off me slightly, all the while keeping me cradled against him. "Because in addition to destroying the file, Hound attacks and corrupts the offenders' entire network, crashing their computers and infecting their databases."

"So anyone who did download images of Wren," Curran begins.

"Lost everything on their computer or device when it crashed," Evan responds without remorse.

I force myself to look up in time to see Curran's attention shoot toward Declan's. "He didn't break the law," he tells Declan. "Not technically. I mean, it's malware, yeah, but he didn't release it with intent to harm, only to protect." He motions my way. "Those who had their shit destroyed are the same assholes who illegally downloaded the file or stole the images, seeing how Wren didn't provide consent."

Declan sits in Tess's abandoned chair, rubbing his jaw as he thinks things through. "No, at best he's walking a fine line. The tech he created is too advanced for the current laws surrounding cybercrimes."

"My legal team concurred as much," Evan responds.

I almost expect him to smile. Except, while this is the best news I could have learned, the revulsion and shock surrounding the incident remains.

"And this?" Declan asks, shaking the baggie in his hand. "How are Bryant's files and links in here if his devices crashed?"

"In addition to hunting, Hound also retrieves. He brought back all of Bryant's information prior to dismantling his devices."

"Why only Bryant's? Because he was the source?" Curran asks.

Evan nods. "Exactly," he says. "It's another reason I haven't marketed Hound. In addition to crashing devices, anyone who used him would have access to countless amounts of private information."

The room falls quiet. "Did you touch the jump drive?" Declan asks Evan, as if it's the most important question left.

"No."

Declan turns to Curran. "If what's in here is what I think is in here, we have him—his distributors, his contacts, everything." He looks at Evan. "Am I right?"

"Yes," Evan answers.

"Holy shit," Curran says.

"I don't want this going back to Evan," I say, cutting Curran off.

"Why would it?" Declan asks casually. "Ashleigh gave him access to a potentially dangerous link with a file created by a person of interest we've been watching closely. His tech searched for malware on the device and this is what he found." He smirks. "As an outstanding member of the community and law-abiding citizen, he brought it directly to me, the D.A., and to Curran, a police officer. As far as I'm concerned, he's a witness and under our protection."

"You won't let anything happen to him?" I ask, my voice quaking over what legal ramifications Evan could face.

"No, and neither will my legal team," Evan answers for him. "Just as I'll never let anything happen to you."

CHAPTER 25

Evan

I rub my face, trying to relieve my exhaustion. Declan used the information Hound gathered to secure search warrants for the multiple properties Bryant owns. There are several in the area and in the surrounding counties, all of which he shouldn't possess the resources to afford. Evidence found within the fraudulent accounts connect him directly to crime lords in South Jersey, New York, and Boston. Currently, he's at large, and if he's smart, he's far away from the city and me. As much as I'm relieved for Wren, I'm not any less furious.

The gentle knock at the door has me lowering my hands. "Come in."

Wren steps in, pausing briefly before walking toward me. She's not in one of her stylish suits or a skirt and blouse that embrace both business and sensuality. She's in a simple dark pink dress and sandals.

The color is my favorite she wears. When I told her, she began adding more pieces to her wardrobe containing that shade. I think she intentionally wore it.

That doesn't make her any less beautiful.

She doesn't take a seat, choosing instead to stand in front of my desk. "Hi," she says.

"What are you doing here?" I ask.

She briefly drops her gaze. "You don't want me here?"

"That's not what I mean," I say, realizing how I must have sounded. "It's late. You should be home."

Our encounter with Declan the other day was a solid step toward alleviating the damage Bryant caused. At least it should have been. While I erased all evidence of Wren at her most vulnerable, I couldn't erase her memories, let alone mine.

Instead of returning to the office, Wren followed me home. We didn't talk through our feelings nor did we make love. We simply surrendered to our fatigue, and she slept wrapped in my arms.

I left her sleeping and returned to work early the next day, attempting to make up for the work I pushed aside to help her. When she called later that morning, I told her not to come in and to take a few days to recuperate. I assured her I would return. But the endless amount of projects kept me working, and I ultimately spent the night.

Although we've spoken briefly, this is the first time I've seen her since I left our bed yesterday around dawn.

"It's almost midnight," she tells me quietly. "I didn't want to go another day without seeing you."

I don't reply, too fixated on her words and how much I fucking miss her. Regardless, of my commitment to her and our relationship, the strain Bryant caused remains.

I never expected the tension between us to vanish all at once, nor did I count on it to surge. Yet there it is, worsening with each breath that passes between us.

Wren moves with a confidence most women lack and can only dream of. As I watch, it's noticeably absent, understandable considering—

Fuck.

I pinch the bridge of my nose, wanting to forget everything I saw. Even as my heart shattered, I wanted to believe her love was real and that she hadn't used me, and what she did was a mistake committed in her youth out of desperation. But in learning she knew nothing about it and *exactly what he did to her,* I can't forget.

My hands slap against the edges of my desk as I push away from it. I want to rise and meet her, but the weight of my anger keeps me in place.

I love Wren, her honest and outrageous way of speaking, her endearing demeanor with others, and how I knew the first time she smiled, no other woman would ever compare.

It's this love that fuels my rage and keeps me from sharing my news.

I'm not a particularly violent man. While I've had my share of fights and outbursts in school, I've learned to rely on my intelligence to win my battles and dismantle my adversaries. Yet when Wren told me what this bastard did to her, my first instinct was to find Bryant and kill him.

Death is something I've never wished on anyone, let alone by my hands. The thought should terrify an educated man like me. But the one and only thing that scares me is any harm coming to Wren.

"What are you thinking?" she asks.

I barely registered her edging forward. Yet here she is.

I meet the face that mesmerizes me and soothes my soul as effortlessly as my heart beats. "That the world can take my company, my money, and my health, but you're the one thing I can't live without."

I pull her onto my lap when her expression crumbles, wishing I can stop the pain she feels.

She links her arms around my neck, whispering against my cheek. "I really needed to hear you say that."

My tone is heavy, the residual anger tainting it regardless of how good it feels to have her close. "I can't forget what happened," I confess, wishing I could tell her otherwise.

"I know," she says, glancing in the direction of the wall of windows where only darkness waits. "I'd give anything to erase what you saw."

"That's not what I mean," I interrupt. My palm falls to her hip. "I can't forget how he exploited your innocence and how badly he hurt you."

"You think I'm innocent?" Her gaze skims to my chest. "After everything we've done?"

I lift her chin with my thumb and kiss her gently. "Your kindness and dedication to those around you, and the way you care for me and them comes from a pure place. If that doesn't make you innocent from harm or malicious intent, I can't imagine what does."

"You're all sorts of sweet," she tells me quietly.

"I mean it. But there's something I need to remind you of so we can move on."

She stills, waiting it seems for my final judgment to pass. Perhaps it's what she's used to. But an unkind word or thought will never come from me again.

"I love you," I rasp.

Her eyes shut as if in pain. My lips skim hers from side to side, the depth of my love trickling with each pass.

"I love you," I say again, pulling her closer, speaking low into her ear. "Just as I know you love me."

Her head falls forward and onto my shoulder, heavy from the burden she carried for too long. She's fighting not to cry. I can tell by how harsh her breaths come.

I hold her, refusing to let her go.

I *never* want to let her go.

Time slips by, in seconds, then minutes, then more. We let it, allowing this moment to heal as much as it can.

She lifts her head when I trail my fingers along the curve of her side. If she cried, I don't see any trace of her tears. What I see is a grateful smile. "Thank you," she says.

"Always," I reply.

"Can we go home? Please? I don't want to be there without you."

"Very well," I stroke her chin. "But there's one more thing I need to tell you."

Worry puckers her brow. "What's wrong?"

I sigh. "We needed a minimum of fifty hospitals to commit to one of our products from the Mechanicus line. It's the only way to keep the company running these next few months."

"Right," she says, remembering the aggressive sales tactics I implemented, and how I sent our entire team of reps to pitch to over two hundred hospitals across the country.

"As of today, we have one hundred and eighty-seven," I reply, doing my best to tame my smile so I may finish. "Each committing to a minimum of two products in addition to the thirty-four I sold to my contacts in Europe."

I expect her to throw her arms around me, or perhaps leap up screaming. Instead, her eyes warm and she smiles softly. "You saved your company."

No. I launched it into the cosmos as she predicted. I don't remind her; she already realizes. "You don't seem surprised," I point out.

"Because I'm not." Her fingers gingerly stroke my temple. "I knew you'd make it right."

"Regardless of what we were up against?"

"Yes." Her eyes glisten. "Evan. . . . You *always* make everything right."

My hand glides through her hair, palming the base of her skull and drawing her to me.

Her lips part, immediately welcoming me. The kiss is tender, built on longing, but as it deepens, everything we've felt: pain, anger, joy, and even hate turns it into something we both need.

Our hands reflect our desire to feel our bare skin connect, surging our passion with each caress. I slip off the straps of her dress, nibbling the spot separating her breasts as I toss her bra aside.

She hauls up her skirt, permitting me to tug her panties aside while she frees my erection.

A deep groan clenches her throat as I grip my staff and lead her down slowly. Our combined weight reclines the chair, keeping us at an angle and allowing me to fill her. She trembles, falling to my lap.

We begin to move, our rhythm increasing with each glide of her hips and lift of my legs.

It's not about lust, or how incredible she feels as I stroke in and out of her, nor how sweet she tastes or the way her body reacts to my touch.

It's not even a way to prove our connection.

It's about *us* and the love no one can take from us.

CHAPTER 26

Wren

The rumbling of voices slap like the splatter of heavy rain against the steel door. As per the mass company email I sent, everyone is filing into the auditorium we typically reserve to introduce new product lines. Not this time. This time, it's all about the overwhelming success iCronos is experiencing and the man who made it happen.

I'm wearing a blue dress with silvery tones to match his tie. He smiled when he saw me, knowing why I chose it. After everything he's done for me and for us, it's the least I can do.

He paces the conference room where we wait, his excitement building. I'm so proud of him and wish I could explain just how much. Except nothing I can think to say seems like enough. So I tell him a story, 'cause it's the one thing I'm pretty damn good at.

"Did I ever tell you about what happened between me and Carolina Delgado?"

He stops pacing. "Is she the one you punched in the face for seducing your brother?"

"No, that was Josefina Miller. I punched Carolina in the face for something entirely different."

He crosses his arms and leans into the conference table. "Was Josefina the one who taught you to ride a motorcycle?"

"No, that was Juanita Delaverde." I stop swiveling in my seat. "Besides, that was sixth grade and I'm talking about fifth."

He smirks. "No, I don't believe you've acquainted me with Carolina Delgado."

"In that case, listen up. It's going to help you out there."

"I have no doubt," he says, chuckling.

I clear my throat, my way of telling him it's going to be a doozey, because it sure as hell is. "When I was eleven years old, I had to stand in front of the entire student body at Saint Therese Catholic School, the staff, and worse yet Sister Hildegard and my arch nemesis, Carolina. By some miracle of God, I'd scored among the top ten students in our spelling bee and it was down to me, Carolina, and Yvette McGillicudy to represent Saint Therese at the state level."

"What was so bad about Sister Hildegard?"

It's so like Evan to guess she plays a big part of the story. "Oh, nothing, she just hated me since the time she caught me, Killian, and Curran lugging the holy water tank out of church. Long story," I add when he blinks back at me. "Let's just say Finnie had hit the terrible two's, the angry three's, and the fucking fours all at once. We were convinced he was possessed and were trying to save him." I hold out a hand. "Our hearts were in the right place. But in case you were wondering, he wasn't possessed."

"I wasn't wondering, actually," he responds.

"Good, but he was still a little bastard and we all have the bite marks to prove it."

I cross my legs when he laughs. "Anyway, Carolina's word was 'irrefutable'. The bat-shit crazy peroxide blonde nailed it. Yvette's word was, 'camouflage'. She was always smart so she spelled it out in one breath. Mine was 'silhouette'. Sil-hou-fucking-ette. The moment I heard it, I couldn't remember which came first, the "l" or the "h."

"How did it go?"

"About as bad as you can imagine and then a little worse," I admit. "I step up to the podium, pretty much knowing I'm screwed and wishing I didn't have to be. The bright lights from the stage added about ten degrees to the already scorching auditorium that subbed as our gymnasium, sending heat tearing across my chest. It was bad, Evan. Real bad. I was sweating so much I looked like I'd showered in my uniform. The polyester stuck against my skinny body and it was like I couldn't breathe."

"Darling," he says.

He sounds worried about me, even after all the years that have passed. I want to hug him for it. But I keep going. He needs to hear what I have to say.

"'Erin O'Brien?' Sister Hildegard said, her voice as sweet as vinegar poured over gasoline. 'Spell *silhouette*,' she repeated."

"Um," I said.

He adjusts his position, listening closely. "A flash went off in the audience," I tell him. "Followed by another. Ma and Angus were snapping away on the disposable cameras they'd picked up at the drugstore like this was the O'Briens' finest moment. In a way, it was, seeing it was the first good thing to happen since my father had died. Declan sat between them. Grammie was there, too, praying the rosary. I couldn't let them down, you know? But I did. I spelled, 'Silhouette. S-i-h-l-o-u-e-t-t-e.'"

"Oh," Evan says, grimacing.

"I know," I mumble. "Angus jumps up. Applauding and cheering, thinking I spelled it right. It sucked. Not only because I hadn't, but because at least half the audience laughed at him. Some of the snobbier kids even pointed. Declan turned around, told them to shut up. He, Ma, and Angus started arguing with the people directly behind them. They didn't hear Carolina tell me, 'Your brother's as stupid as you are'. But I did.'"

"My God," Evan says.

"She didn't know Angus took his GED at sixteen and started working full time to help support us after my father died." I shrug. "Or maybe she did. Carolina was always mean. So instead of taking a seat because my moment was over, I took a swing and knocked her on her ass."

He raises his brows slightly. "I can't say that I blame you."

I smile a little. "Neither did Sister Hildegard. She took me aside. Well, after she hauled me off Carolina and cleaned up my bloody nose."

"Carolina gave you a bloody nose?"

"Oh, yeah. That bleached broad had a mean right cross. Anyway, Sister Hildegard told me that while she didn't approve of me punching Carolina, she said I was right for sticking up for my family."

He pulls me to him. "I take it there's a point to your story."

"There is," I agree, wrapping my arms around his neck. "I wanted to tell you that no matter the pitfalls you've endured, and any that follow, I'm going to stand by you like my family has always stood by me—that I believe in you, like Angus did, even if things don't always go exactly as planned. And despite what tomorrow brings, you've earned your spot on that podium and all the success that's coming."

I expect him to laugh. Then again, maybe I don't. He looks at me, those specks of gold in his deep green eyes warming the same way they did the first time he told me he loved me. "Thank you," he says.

"Always," I say, meaning it.

He kisses my lips and gathers me close. "Just one thing, don't punch anyone in the face out there."

"I'm not making any promises, bossman," I say, inching away when someone knocks on the door. "I've seen the way Giselle from Accounting looks at your ass."

"Evan?" Anne smiles when she finds us laughing. "We're ready for you."

He nods, leading me forward. Together, we walk out into the hall and into the audience, my hand in his until he releases it to take his place on the podium.

I've always loved the feel of the Explorer as it takes the road. The cabin envelops us, stowing us away from the rest of the world and encasing us in its protection. I can't even hear the engine as we barrel off the highway and onto the exit leading to Villanova. But then, I don't hear much except for Evan's easy breathing.

He hasn't stopped smiling since we left iCronos, the pure excitement of his employees leaving him speechless. They leapt to their feet, cheering, but it was the ones who cried tears of joy who really touched his heart.

"You did it, Evan," Clifton told him.

"No, *we* did it," Evan countered, shaking his hand and clasping his shoulder.

"I didn't expect Anne to react the way she did," Evan says, verbalizing exactly what I was thinking.

"I know," I say, smoothing my palm against his thigh.

"She was close to hysterics."

"She was just happy." I grin. "She's always believed in her daddykins."

"Somehow I doubt that's how she thinks of me," he says, laughing.

"Of course she does. It meant everything to her when you gave her away at her wedding."

Evan's humor fades, likely remembering all the people who waited for a chance to offer their congratulations. Most he only knew by face, but they didn't seem to mind. Like me, they saw something special in the products he and his engineers created, and more importantly, they recognized the brilliant leader he was from the start.

He shook their hands. He smiled kindly. He was simply Evan.

The gates to his house part and he pulls into the long driveway. The bushes and trees are freshly trimmed, but hide the house away from the road. I love it here and love how it feels like home even more.

"That was pretty awesome," I say, my mind remembering how happy and excited everyone seemed.

"It was," he agrees.

"Like Jimmy Stewart in *It's a Wonderful Life*." I hit my seatbelt release and reach for my purse. "Except not as depressing and no angels in long underwear."

"I'll give you that," he says, flinging open his door.

He winks at me as he walks around to open my door.

But Bryant gets to me first.

"*Wren!*"

Evan lurches forward when Bryant grabs me in a headlock and hauls me out.

I kick back hard, nailing him in the shin.

The contents of my purse spill across the concrete floor.

And the cold barrel of a gun slams into my head.

CHAPTER 27

Evan

"Fucking, *bitch*," Bryant snaps.

His face is partially hidden by the red baseball cap he's wearing, but I know it's him. He must have shadowed us in as we drove through the gate.

Wren struck him hard in the leg, but he hangs on tight, limping backward and dragging her with him.

"Let her go," I bite out through my teeth. I follow them as he reaches the edge of the garage. "I swear, if you hurt her—"

"What?" he scoffs. "You think I care about this whore?" An inhuman smile crawls along his narrow face. "But you do, don't you?" He laughs, taking in my hardening breaths. "Yeah . . . you do."

"Evan, don't move," Wren cries out, wincing when Bryant digs the barrel of his Sig deep against her scalp. "*Please*. Just stay where you are."

"What do you want?" My voice shakes from the force of my accelerating rage. I should raise my hands and assure him I won't hurt him, if he doesn't hurt her. But that's a damn lie. I'm ready to tear this fucking tosser apart.

He edges back along the driveway where the exterior lighting ends and total darkness awaits. I trail them carefully, my focus trained on his movements. He tightens his stranglehold, making her cough. She can still breathe, but he's making it hard for her, pressing her tight against him and using her as his shield.

"I asked you what you wanted," I growl, taking another step forward.

My body stills when Bryant makes a twisting motion with his wrist, drilling the tip of the gun against Wren's temple. She spits out a curse, her soft features scrunching in pain. He's having fun with us. I feel his instability and menace as clearly as he senses my rage.

"I want my *fucking money,*" he grinds out. "I know you took it. The phony accounts, the passwords, I want everything back."

"You'll have to see the district attorney about that. He has everything you're looking for." I swallow hard. "I warn you, he won't take kindly to you harming his sister, and neither will I."

Wren's chest rises and falls in furious bursts, her terror keeping me from acting.

"Didn't you hear me the first time, dick?" Bryant counters. "I don't care what happens to her. But I guess you saw it for yourself in that video I sent you."

Fury roils my stomach. "Fuck you, Bryant," Wren tells him.

"I already did, pretty girl," he mutters against her ear. "And your boyfriend here saw just how hard."

I take another step forward. "I am going to destroy you," I reply, the edge to my tone sharpening. "Whatever mangy bits are left will rot in prison."

My voice is eerily calm, lethal. It's not a threat. It's what I'm prepared to do.

Bryant doesn't care. "The money," he repeats, emphasizing each word. "Just like you gave the D.A. access, you can give me that same access back. No trace, no bullshit." He inches away. "Wire it to the account Wren here will text you and you may or may not get her back in one piece."

"You *raped her*," I snap. "Now you're taking her hostage and willing to kill her?"

"I did, I am, and I will," he answers, without blinking. "I'm having it all. Including the twenty mil you fucking took from me. She stays with me until you give me what I want. You hear me? *I* get to have her all to myself."

He takes his final step out of the light and into the darkness, his form and Wren's becoming one with the night. "Later, pussy," he spits out.

My hands ball into fists. "Alfred," I say. "*Protect*."

Every security light flares on, bathing the driveway and front yard in an explosion of bright white.

"Protecting," Alfred's voice booms.

Bryant's head jerks back and forth. From the hidden cameras in the trees, infrared beams shoot out, linking with the beams from the concealed cameras above the garage and along the roof. I stalk forward as they crisscross over Wren's chest, forming a net and zooming up to zero in on Bryant's face.

"Surveillance video sent to Villanova and Philadelphia police departments," Alfred calls out. "Bryant Caribe, twenty-six year old Caucasian male, 76 Maple Avenue, Philadelphia, Pennsylvania, identified. Police are on their way. Digital recording remains in process."

The shock in Bryant's features is replaced with undeniable savagery. "You mother*fucker*—"

I launch forward. He points his gun and fires, the blast echoing as I haul Wren into my arms.

I wrench her behind me, catching her when she can't keep her feet. I'm unsure why, until warm fluid spreads across my palm.

"*No!*" I yell, my heart sinking when she collapses.

I ease her down, her body quaking in agony and her breath mere gasps.

As I watch, the light that shimmers her deep blue eyes fades.

Wren

My vision blurs as Evan sets me on the ground. Pain like I've never felt sears through my back, setting the surrounding muscles and bones on fire. I want to claw at the ground, it hurts so damn much. But I can't move my arms.

I can't move at all.

Evan's saying something, but his words sound muffled and far away.

"Help is coming."

"Don't leave me."

"You *can't* leave me."

Bryant was going to kill him. I realized it the moment he learned his actions and confession were captured on video. He knew he was screwed. Just like he knew he had nothing to lose. I could tell by the way he loosened his hold. He was done with me and going after Evan.

I didn't think about me or what could happen when the pressure eased off my throat. My full focus was on Evan as I threw myself forward.

It's too late for me, anyway. I know it, and I think Evan does, too.

Blood seeps through my skin, cooling as it spreads along my back and pours across the concrete in tiny rivers.

I don't want to die . . . I want to stay with Evan and travel the world with him. I want him to take me to all those places he's told me about, like that castle in Scotland that overlooks a valley covered with lilacs, and that trattoria in Milan with the best risotto he's ever tasted.

I want to be with him the day he decides to expand his company, and celebrate with him when it becomes the global giant we always believed it could be. I want to tell him that I'm proud of the man and leader he is, and how I never knew how great I could be until he showed me.

Mostly though, I want to tell him that I love him, that I want to make babies with him and watch them grow up as we grow old together.

But as my vision clouds and grows dark, and that pain morphs into an uncomfortable numbness, I'm not sure I'll be able tell him anything.

Another gun blast has me whipping my eyes open. But it's the one right after, and the pained grunt that follows, that forces me to loll my head in that direction.

Evan and Bryant are rolling on the ground, their fists pounding so hard that each strike reverberates across my skull.

The gun lays a few feet from me and even closer to Bryant.

I try and tilt, but it's like everything hurts and nothing is working right. The need to close my eyes returns. I fight it, trying to stay awake.

A spurting sound follows the solid crunch of bone. I can't tell who's winning. All I know is I have to move and get that gun.

My head spins as I pitch onto my side. Pain radiates from the hotspot in my shoulder, streaming out to my limbs. I fall onto my stomach, grunting as another wave of agony radiates down my spine and causes my feet to spasm.

I crawl forward, each movement making me want to puke from the way my vision fades in and out.

I reach for the gun, my fingers slipping over the handle several times before I'm finally able to grab it. I pull it to me, knowing I don't have the strength to fire, but scared shitless Bryant will turn it on Evan.

But Evan and Bryant are gone.

Angry shouts ricochet from the bottom of the driveway and what sounds like hard bodies collide against the asphalt. I crawl away from them and toward the garage. I think I see my phone lying on the floor. It's hard to tell, my world taking another revolting spin.

I push my legs out, hoping I'm going in the right direction. I spit out what might be blood halfway through, almost crying with relief when my hand touches a tire.

"Alfred, call Curran."

My head falls against my arm as sirens blare in the distance. I don't hear the phone ring, I only hear Curran yelling. "Where the fuck are you? We got a call about shots fired at Evan's place."

I don't answer. I can't.

"Wren? . . . *Wren*. Talk to me . . . Are you there? Me and Deck, we're coming."

My lips move. The words don't come out.

"Wren, God damn it—"

"I . . . hurt."

"*What?*"

My words are slurred and my head throbs with each breath. My back is drenched. I shudder, feeling my body temperature drop.

The sirens are closer. Just up the road. "I'm hurt," I manage, my words barely audible. "Bryant . . . shot me."

Curran doesn't hear me. Declan does. "Wren, you stay with us! You hear me? Don't you fucking leave us, Wren."

"Da hell?" Curran asks.

"She's in trouble," Declan bites out his voice cold and controlled. "Bryant shot her."

A clicking sound follows. "This is Officer Curran O'Brien, Philadelphia PD en route to 1239 Mount Pleasant Road, Villanova. Armed gunman in vicinity. At least one person shot and in need of immediate medical attention. Victim is my sister, repeat, victim is my sister."

"You stay alive—You hear me?" Declan says. "You and Evan both—God damn it, don't you leave us."

I want to tell them that Evan is fighting Bryant. That they need to help him. I don't get the chance.

More fluid leaks from my mouth and Evan is suddenly with me, cradling me in his arms.

His image is blurry, but I know it's him. I recognize the way he tucks me against him and how my body conforms so perfectly to his.

"Wren," he says, stroking my hair away from my face. "Baby, can you hear me?"

My lips part as I grip the front of his shirt. I want to sleep. God, I'm so tired. "Stay awake," he tells me, passing his hand down my throat to my sternum. "Don't close your eyes. I know it hurts, but you have to fight. For me. For *us*." He spits out a curse. "I don't want to live without your smile."

He thinks I'm dying. But I'm not the only one. I release his shirt when I feel how wet it is, the leaking fluid drenching my hand. "Evan, this isn't my blood . . ."

My eyes close. The last thing I feel is the partial weight of his chest pressing against mine as he lowers us to the ground.

That, and how much I love him.

CHAPTER 28

Evan

"He's waking up," a familiar voice calls. It's Clifton, I think. Anne follows, albeit more stunned, her tone bordering on hysterical.

"He can't be—Oh, my God. Oh, my God. Oh, my *God*."

"Fuck, he looks like shit."

Oh, and look, Finn's here as well.

I blink my heavy eyes open, though they fall closed more than once.

Clifton is at my side with Anne directly behind him, her hands clapped over her mouth.

Finn stands at the foot of the bed, eating what I imagine is hospital food. "Hey, Evan. How you feeling?" he asks through a large mouthful. He glances down at the spaghetti rolled up on his fork. "You don't mind me eating this, do you? You've been sleeping a lot lately and it's a sin to waste food, you feel me?"

I open my mouth, my throat feeling absurdly dry. I try to force myself up, only for a wretched burn to rip through my chest and threaten to tear it open. The plate smashes against the roll up table when Finn drops it and hurries to my side, opposite Clifton, each taking an arm and keeping me from falling back.

"Anne, get the nurse," Clifton urges.

"Where's Wren?" I manage.

I glance up at Finn when no one answers. "Where *is* she?" I ask, my stomach plunging.

"She's in ICU," Finn replies. "She's okay. Stable, but she lost a lot of blood. Even more than you." He huffs. "And you got shot in the chest."

"I was shot," I reply, slowly, the pieces of the night beginning to take form.

Wren put herself in harm's way to shield me. She felt lifeless as I lowered her to the ground. Initially, I was stunned, unable to move, as was Bryant who meant the bullet for me.

I recovered first, springing to my feet and charging. Adrenaline is a gift. I never knew until the sting of the bullet struck my chest and I kept going, tackling him.

The impact caused him to lose the gun. I tried to kick it away, but my rage demanded his pain. My fists became weapons, only he was armed with them, too. We fought until he stopped moving from the blows I inflicted to his face and skull.

"You fucked up Bryant pretty damn bad," Finn says. "He's at the ICU across town." His features morph to granite. "My only gripe is he's still alive."

Perhaps I should care one way or the other. I don't. "I want to see Wren."

"Mr. Jonah, you're awake." A nurse well into her prime hurries in, trailed by Anne and what seems to be an assistant. "I'm Amy, this is Traci. We're taking care of you today. Get water for him, will you, Traci?"

"I need to check you," Amy says, reaching for the buttons on the rails. "Let's have your friends step out."

"They may stay," I mumble, coughing from how dry my throat feels. "Speak freely, I trust them."

"If it's okay with you, it's okay with us."

The assistant pours water as the nurse raises the back of the bed so I may sit upright. Finn and Clifton edge away, allowing the medical staff to perform their duties. I down the water, passing Anne the empty cup. She clutches it against her, her gaze shifting from side to side, appearing to want to help.

The assistant takes my blood pressure while the nurse listens to my chest. I motion to the IV in my hand. "May I get this out? I'd like to see my wife."

"One thing at a time, Mr. Jonah," the nurse responds, her full attention on the bandages on my chest. "Your labs look good, but I need to make sure the rest of you is just as healthy."

I don't hear what follows, too fixated on the way Finn arches his brow. "Wife?" he asks.

I didn't realize what I said until he reminds me. "It's who she is to me," I answer truthfully.

A small smile creeps across his face. "Then maybe you should ask her." He chuckles. "You've had my blessing since you made me bacon."

I laugh, only to wince when pain stabs my chest. "Everything looks good, Mr. Jonah."

"It's Evan," I tell her. "And if so, I'd like to see her."

"Let's see how you do when we get you up to the bathroom," she says.

Wren

Ma brushes my hair with her old wooden brush, the one with the boars' hair bristles. It always left my hair smooth and silky. I think the last time she used it on me was to braid my hair all those years ago, back when she'd weave in those satiny ribbons.

How old was I then? Nine, maybe ten? I remember the girls at school making fun of me, telling me I was too old for them. I didn't care, knowing my mother carved out that pocket of time just to spend it with me.

"You always had the prettiest hair," she says, her accent likely as thick as the day she left Ireland. "Every little girl in the neighborhood used to admire it, wanting to touch it. But I knew we were in trouble when the boys began to notice it, too." She cocks her head, looking a little bit older, and a little more grey, but it's the sadness dulling her stare that worries me more. "I wish I would have spent more time braiding that pretty hair."

Her eyes well. I recognize that it's not due to my lost childhood, but because she almost lost that little girl whose hair she loved to brush.

"Ma, I'm fine," I tell her, forcing a smile even though smiling is the last thing I feel like doing.

Christ. Evan was shot. I was, too. But as much as I hurt, it hurt more knowing he'd almost died because of a man I'd forced into his life.

"How's Evan?" I ask, meeting Seamus's face because it's too hard to meet Ma's.

"He's all right," Seamus insists. "He was discharged late last night. Every time he came in you were out cold." He frowns. "You weren't doing that shit on purpose. Were ya?"

"No, Seamus," I reply. "Let's just say I've been really tired."

I don't want to remind them why I've been so tired, weak, and barely able to lift my head. It must have been something, getting that call that I'd been shot. I think one of us dying has always been our deepest fear, even though we've never talked about it. The seven of us, we're tight. Loud, obnoxious, borderline crazy, but tight as God and this tiny woman brushing the length of my hair intended. One of us going, especially so young, is not an option, even though it's part of life. And now that some of my brothers are married and have their own families, that fear has extended. That's a good thing in a way. It means there are more people to love and be scared for.

Curran and Declan poke their heads in, motioning to Ma and Seamus. "Your turn," I see Curran mouth to Seamus.

It was the same thing Killian said to them. Ma and Angus were the first. The only difference being that it was Finnie who lured them out. At first, I thought they just wanted their chance to see me since they limit visitors. Now, I'm not so sure. Not with the way Ma reacts.

A single tear drips down her cheek. But then she smiles, like *really* smiles in a way I've rarely seen. She doesn't show any teeth, but . . .

She presses a kiss to my forehead like she used to do when she'd kiss us all good night. There's so much—I don't know, *love*— behind that motion, I almost well up my damn self. But then she says what she says and it's like my body sucks the tears back up.

"Don't fuck it up, Wrennie," she tells me.

Her accent remains light and pretty, despite the F-bomb she just dropped.

"Ma said, 'fuck'," Curran mutters to Declan when she and Seamus step out.

Yeah, she did. I blink back to where she disappeared through the door. "What the hell?"

"She's been worried," Declan says. "We all have." He keeps his gaze rock steady. "How are you?"

"Tired of being here," I admit. My stare drills a hole into the far wall where there's a small cabinet stuffed with medical crap to keep saps like me alive. "What's going to happen to Bryant?" I ask. I haven't wanted to say his name. It makes what happened more real, I guess. I wish it didn't. But it does.

"With two attempted murder charges and all the money laundering he's done for the mob, he's not getting out, ever. I'll make sure of that."

"Except in a body bag," Curran adds. He shrugs, staring right at Declan. "He was technically a cop. I guess we'll have to let his new friends at the State pen know as much."

"I just want him out of my life." I stroke my hair, feeling how soft it is from Ma's care and wishing it wasn't such an effort to lift my arm. "I hate what he did to me, but mostly what he did to Evan." I shake my head, my misery burning way worse than the residual pain in my shoulder. "I almost lost him."

"I think he was more afraid of losing you," Declan says. He crosses his arms. "When we arrived, the paramedics were all over you. They told us they had to pull Evan off you. He was barely conscious, but they found him covering your body, trying to keep you warm and afraid to let you go. It looked bad, Wren. But it was worse on the surveillance video."

"It *was* bad," I agree quietly, remembering exactly how much. All the pain I felt was nothing compared to the fear. When I saw he was bleeding, I didn't care about me dying anymore. I just wanted him to live. I *needed* him to.

"I want to see him," I say, a lump building in my throat. "I have to tell him I'm sorry."

My voice trails as Evan appears at the door in a tux, with what has to be six dozen lavender and silver roses in his arms. My hands smack over my mouth, causing what feels like a set of daggers to rip across my shoulder.

But I don't care.

I think I know what he's doing, but when I look to my left to find all my brothers, Sol, Sofia, Tess, Molly, and Ma, too, pressed against the giant glass divider, the girls all crying, and Angus swiping his big cherub face, I know. Jesus, I already know.

Curran sniffs, his face turning red. Declan sets his jaw tight, burying whatever he's feeling deep inside of him. But it's the brief look he gives me, the one that tells me it's my time, and that maybe he wishes it was his time, too, that has me falling apart.

Evan sets the roses down at my feet, lowering himself to sit beside me. "Hello, beautiful," he whispers.

I don't answer, crying into my hands.

"I took Sol and Sofia out with me this morning. I hope you don't mind, but I needed their expertise in selecting something special."

"No," I respond.

"I also took your family aside and asked them for their blessing to give it to you."

"No," I say again, batting my hands like some kind of nutcase.

He keeps his grin, despite my eyes burning the way they are. "Before I ask, I think you should know it's something I've wanted to do for quite some time now."

"*No*," I insist. "You can't."

He takes my hand, falling to his knee.

"Evan," I plead. "You're not supposed to do this—not after everything that happened to you because of me."

His gaze softens as does his smile—as if I didn't tell him no—as if he wasn't shot in the chest. As if some psycho didn't come after him in his own home!

"All the good in my life has come because I know you," he begins. "And because you chose to love me."

My cheeks are already soaked, but then another sob cuts through my throat, spilling more tears.

"I never laughed with my whole heart until you filled it with humor."

"Oh, God," I gasp.

"I never knew how alone I was, until I discovered how much I needed you with me."

"*Evan.*"

"And I never understood love until you made me feel it and gave me a reason to share it." He pulls out a ring, a square pink diamond surrounded by smaller clear ones.

My hand shakes as he slides it on my finger. "The words are 'for better or worse,'" he reminds me. "We've had our worst. It's time for the better. My darling Wren, will you marry me?"

I never had the father I wanted or needed. But it's like I told Evan, I had brothers who became more than my father ever was. So I look to each one before I answer, gathering the strength they've always given me and all the heart they've never lacked.

"*Yes.*"

This book contains excerpts from *Let Me* and *Feel Me* from the O'Brien Family novels, in addition to *Inseverable* from the Carolina Beach series by Cecy Robson. The excerpts have been set for this edition only and may not reflect the final content of the final novels.

Let Me

An O'Brien Family Novel

by Cecy Robson

CHAPTER 1

Finn

I see the strike coming at me a split second before it connects with my skull. My head snaps back from the force, the crowds' hollers resonating like a muffled cry in the distance. It was a good punch—lightning quick with enough impact to knock most guys on their asses. But I'm not most guys.

You hit me, I'm only going to hit you harder.

My right hand shoots up, blocking and smacking away the kick gunning for my ribs. I pivot out of the way, again, and again, and again, avoiding Easton's arms and legs as they come at me. He's fast, strong, with a six inch reach advantage. But he's too eager to take me out and not pacing himself like he should. Already he's breathing hard and it's just the start of the second round.

I take my time to figure him out, planning each move, searching for that opening I need. Do I take a few bashes because of it? Sure. It's part of the job. But believe it or not, it's part of the job I look forward to.

Those punches and kicks remind me that I still *feel*, that I'm still human. And that for now, I'm still alive.

"Oh!" some drunk behind me yells when my uppercut finds Easton's chin.

He staggers back, swiping the blood oozing from his lip, yet he keeps his grin. He's trying to make like it was a lucky shot. That it won't happen again.

Like me, Easton needs to win this match. And if he does, he'll move up to the top ten, making him a contender for the UFC Lightweight title.

Talent aside, the guy's a raging asshole, and so are the idiots in his training camp. They've been trash-talking since the moment I agreed to this match. I didn't really care and laughed most of it off until they got personal and took it a step too far.

Again he nails me in the head. It's not as hard as it was last time which tells me he's getting tired. Does it hurt? I guess.

But let's say I'm a guy who's used to pain.

Easton grins. He thinks I'm afraid of him. He thinks he has me where he wants me. But fear is an emotion I don't allow myself to entertain. Fear gets you hurt and rips you apart till you think there's nothing left.

I dodge out of reach. He scowls and takes another swing. This one gets close enough to my jaw to create a breeze that whips across my skin.

"Finn," my brother Killian barks from the side. "Take him out *now*."

He's worried about me. So is my family. But now's not the time to think about them. I keep my hands up as I edge away, letting Easton think I'm backing down, that I'm tired and need to catch my breath.

I sidestep when he lunges forward, avoiding his next swing and use the momentum to drop my head and nail him in the temple with a roundhouse kick.

Like I said, Easton's fast.

Too bad for him I'm a little bit faster.

The kick is my signature move, as natural for me as the next breath. He goes down like I planned. But in the Octagon you don't stop just because your opponent collapses like timber. You charge forward. You show him what you're made of. And you prove just how tough you really are.

That muffled screaming, isn't so muffled anymore. The crowd loses their shit as I pounce, my blows nailing Easton in the face until the ref's arms hook beneath mine as he hauls me off. I back away, my fists up because I already know I won.

I should do a back flip or some crazy shit to incite the crowd. This is it. My time has come to own it. But the good things aren't as great as they can be. Not with the memories that haunt me. And not with the anger they stir.

Killian rushes in as the medic wipes down my face. I'm bleeding from the punch Easton caught me with at the beginning of the round. I didn't think it was that bad, but the way the ringside medic is pressing the towel against my head clues me in the gash isn't closing like it should.

"I'm going to have to stitch you up, Fury," he mumbles.

"I figured," I tell him.

Kill pats my back. "Good job," he says.

Maybe he believes it, but I don't miss the concern in his voice. He thinks I took too many unnecessary hits. I can't really argue, seeing how it's true.

He doesn't understand that I don't feel those strikes the way I should. Hell, I don't think I've felt anything the way I should in a long time. Not like I used to. I try to tell myself that maybe that' a good thing. That numbness is better than pain. But I'm not so convinced anymore, and neither is my family. I try to shrug it off like I'm fine. Except given the way they've been eyeing me, I'm not fooling anyone.

I'm scaring everyone around me. And it sucks. Not only because I don't want them scared, but mostly because I don't know how to stop it.

"The referee has called a stop to this match at two-minutes and forty-nine seconds into the second round," the announcer begins. "The winner by TKO, Finn 'The Fury' O'Brien."

The crowd screams and pumps their fists in the air when my hand is raised. I take the few seconds I need to thank my sponsors, my camp, and my brother, because that's what I'm supposed to do despite the fog clouding my senses. I wish that disconnect had something to do with all the hits I took, but deep down I know that it doesn't.

I'm back in the locker room before I know it getting stitched up, too many people talking at once. God, I barely hear their questions or my responses. But they're there and somehow I make it through.

"I'm worried about you, Finnie," Kill says when everyone piles out.

"Don't. I'm not drinking tonight. I'm headed home," I assure him.

"That's not what I mean," he says. He's sitting in a fold out chair, his arms resting against his muscular legs. "I think you need to talk to someone."

I stretch out my arms. By now they're so tight, they pull against the bones. "I am. I'm talking to you."

I don't have to see him to know he's shaking his head, or that he's looking sad, disappointed, and maybe something else, too. "I'm not who you should be speaking to," he says. "Not for what's going on in your head."

"You're enough," I say, even though I know it's no longer true.

"Finn," he begins.

I don't wait for him to finish, leaving the changing area and heading toward the showers. "Go find Sofia and Wren," I call over my shoulder as I strip out my shirt. "See if they're up for some dinner."

I don't remember peeling the rest of my clothes off. That numbness I've been feeling too much lately claiming me like a mist until it fully engulfs me. Fuck. It's like I've stopped living even though for the most part I think I'm still alive.

I lean against the tile with my arms spread, allowing the water to beat against my back. It's too hot. I should turn it down, but I don't bother. Eventually, like everything else, the sensation fades.

I'm not sure how long I'm in that position. A few seconds? A few minutes? But then Easton and his trainer Yefim are suddenly there. "You got lucky, O'Brien," Yefim calls out, taunting me with his thick eastern European accent.

Shit. Like all the trash talk before the fight wasn't enough.

"Did you hear me, you pussy?" he fires back when I don't answer. "Did you hear me, you goddamn coward?"

Coward? Fuck you. It's what I think, but not what I say, focusing instead on the streams of water that gather along my feet before they swirl into the drain.

It doesn't help. The rage that's building, the one I only manage to barely keep in? It stirs in my gut like a heavy pot filled with hate, sin, and all the curses my Ma would still beat my ass for saying.

"What're you doing?" Yefim asks.

His voice is closer, he's drawing near. It doesn't matter that I'm standing here naked. He wants to be next to me. I shudder, that feeling I keep buried drilling its way up.

"I know about you," Yefim says, not bothering to keep his voice low. "But everyone knows, don't they? Even if you don't want them to."

My body shakes a little more, but it's not from the cooling water. It's from his words and all that anger they trigger. *Don't do it. Don't go there.*

"You like to keep it a secret. Don't you, pussy?"

Yefim laughs when I keep my trap shut. He thinks I'm backing down, just like Easton did before his face met the mat. "He's crying," he calls out to Easton. "What? Not so tough now?"

That's where he's dead wrong. Every muscle I've conditioned serves a purpose—to take down those who fuck with me. And right now, Yefim is seriously fucking with me.

"You like to pretend that it's girls you like, don't you?" he says. "But that's not true, is it? Oh, no, that's not true at all . . ."

I raise my chin, knowing that someone's not leaving without bleeding, and I've bled enough tonight.

Yefim kicks at my calf. "What? Nothing to say? Can't speak without your boyfriend here?"

"Boyfriend?" Easton asks, laughing. "No fucking way."

"Yes. Way," Yefim insists. "Didn't you know this little pussy takes it up the ass—"

I punch him so hard, I feel his teeth crack against my knuckles. For someone with decades of boxing experience he never saw me coming. But I see Easton flying at me out of the corner of my eye. I toss him over my shoulder, slamming him hard onto the ceramic tile floor. Like in the octagon, I throw myself on top of him, my fists colliding against his skin.

Voices rush forward, telling me to stop. A woman screams, but I don't stop fighting off the bodies trying to grab me, breaking through the arms wrenching me back. I need to hit him—I need to feel my fists meeting his face—I need to feel *something*.

God damn it. I need to feel alive.

I don't want the pain.

I don't want the terror.

But once more, it's all I feel.

Feel Me

An O'Brien Family Novel

by Cecy Robson

CHAPTER 1

Melissa

I stare at the nameplate perched on my father's desk: *District Attorney Miles Fenske*. It proclaims his position, allowing those who read it a glimpse of what he's accomplished. Yet it's only a glimpse. It's not a true representation of all he is, or all he means to me. The nameplate is cheap, unlike the generous soul who stares back at me with the same loving expression he's held since the first moment I saw him.

What are you thinking, Melissa? He signs to me, moving his hands in beautifully fluid motions.

We're alone in his office. He doesn't need to sign to keep our conversation private. He could whisper, and I would still be able to read his lips. But he knows I'm more comfortable communicating with my hands, probably because American Sign Language is one of the many things we learned together. As a child I considered it our very own secret language, something he and I could share away from the hearing world.

That you're making a mistake, I sign back.

My comment earns me a smile, but I can see his concern, despite the crinkles around his eyes that deepen when he grins. "You're going to have to trust me," he says aloud.

I let out a breath. He knows I trust him. How could I not?

I was brought to the Lehigh Valley District Attorney's

office when I was about six years old, after my biological mother had attempted to sell me in exchange for drugs. My mother probably thought it was a brilliant plan. Being born with profound hearing loss, I couldn't speak, couldn't communicate, and couldn't understand. Which meant, I couldn't tell anyone what was about to take place.

My primal instincts ordered me to run, that I was in danger, so I did—thank God I did. I kicked and fought, dodging the hands trying to grab me, and scurrying out of my window.

To this day, I remember the way the cold metal grating of the fire escape felt against my bare feet, and the way my mouth struggled to form what I thought were words as I banged on my elderly neighbor's window. Miss Lena, the lady with too many cats and twice as many grandchildren, yanked me into her apartment when she saw me. She called the police, but by the time they arrived, my mother was gone. I never saw her again.

Not that I regret it.

I was placed in foster care, confused and frightened about what was happening and certain I'd eventually return "home". Instead, I was brought before the young Assistant D.A Miles Fenske. He was supposed to handle my case, dispose of it, and move on. He was never supposed to welcome me into his heart. Yet that's exactly what he did.

"Melissa," he says. His words aren't clear—not as clear as they can be, my hearing aids can only do so much, but I hear enough to sense the emotion in the way he speaks my name. "Why are you so sad?"

I raise my chin. "Declan O'Brien will never be the man you are. He's not the right D.A. for this position." I shake my head. "He belongs in the Trial Unit, Arson, Fugitive, anywhere else but where you've placed him."

"I know you don't like him . . ."

I raise my brows.

". . .and that your first encounter wasn't a positive one..."

"That's because he was an asshole," I mumble.

He chuckles. "I assure you he deeply regrets what he

said. But Declan is smart, quick, and kind."

I don't agree. Not completely. Is Declan intelligent? Brilliantly so, and absurdly astute in court. With short wavy blond hair and a dashing grin that lights his blue eyes, he's also gorgeous, and he knows it. But is he kind? I'm not so sure that he is. "He'll never be the man you are," I repeat.

"I'm not asking him to be. I simply want the best person for the job, someone who will help the victims who need him most."

"That's what you claim. But he doesn't have experience handling delicate cases where offenders often inflict irreparable trauma."

"No, but as the head of Victim Services, you do," he offers with a knowing gleam.

My nails dig into the wooden armrests. "If you're trying to hook us up, I'm going to be seriously mad at you."

The edges of his mouth curve. "I'm only asking you to help Declan as he transitions into his new role. This new assignment won't be easy on him."

"Because he doesn't want it. He wants to be the head of Homicide." I stand with my hands out, pleading. "Daddy, please reassign him. The Sexual Assault and Child Abuse Unit is not where someone who seeks glory belongs."

My voice trails as I catch a glimmer of his pain. "Daddy?"

At once, his face scrunches, flushing red only to grow alarmingly pale. I race around his desk, clutching his shoulders to keep him upright as he grips his side and beads of sweat gather along his receding hairline.

It's only because he lifts his bowed head and a healthier shade of pink returns to his cheeks that I'm not screaming for help and dialing 911. "Daddy?"

He offers me a weak smile and pats my arm. "I'm all right," he says, leaning back in his chair.

"No, you're not," I say, my eyes stinging. His light blue dress shirt clings with sweat along his arms and plump midsection. He's not well. My father is . . . *sick*. "What aren't you telling me?"

His hand slowly eases away from his side. For a moment his eyes search my face, as they've done a thousand times throughout my life. "The doctors discovered new tumors along my colon," he finally says. "They're planning to resection my bowel and dispose of the affected area with the hope of avoiding chemo this time around."

Very carefully, I straighten, despite that my heart has all but stopped beating. My father was diagnosed with colon cancer years ago and barely survived the aggressive treatment. If it's returned, now that he's older, and not as healthy . . .

"When were you going to tell me?" I ask, struggling to keep my voice clear as it shakes, my fear likely worsening my speech impediment.

He sighs. "Friday, over dinner."

To give me the weekend to absorb it, no doubt. "And your surgery? When is that?"

"A few weeks." He frowns as if debating what to say. "I'll be out of commission for a while. In my absence, Declan will lead the office as acting District Attorney." He looks at me then. "And I ask that you help him, regardless of your feelings toward him."

Declan

"This isn't where I fucking belong." I'm beyond pissed, and started typing my resignation letter at least six times today only to delete it. Yet for as much as I don't want to head the Sexual Assault and Child Abuse Unit, I'm not a quitter. "Fuck," I mumble, dragging my hand along my face. "*Fuck.*"

My brother Curran crosses his arms over his chest, not caring how it creases the shirt of his Philly PD uniform. But then Curran doesn't care about shit like that. "It's still a promotion, Deck," he says. "You got this D.A. spot straight out of law school and have made more of a name for yourself than most douche-bag attorneys ever will." He holds out a hand. "No offense to the douche-bag attorneys of the world."

"That's my point. After all I've accomplished, I should be the one leading the Homicide unit."

I shove away from my desk and pace. When Miles gave me these new digs, I thought it was just the start of all the good things coming my way. When he assigned me a county car and a personal secretary, it only reinforced that my hard work had paid off. I was on my way …until I wasn't.

"I spent months dismantling a mafia empire, Curran."

"I know," he says. "I was there."

"I brought down a major crime boss—and his second in command, and his third."

"Yup. Saw that, too," he agrees.

"I received international attention—the trial of the century, the media called it—and for what? To be shoved someplace I don't belong."

"Why don't you think you belong there?"

Out of all my five brothers, Curran is probably one of the biggest ball busters. But he's not messing with me now. He's being serious.

"Do you want to hear about babies and women being hurt? Day in and day out?" I ask. "These are the cases I'm going to be dealing with."

"Someone has to do it, Deck. It's the right thing."

"I'm not saying it isn't. I'm only saying I may not be the man for the job. This shit's disgusting, what these low-life assholes are capable of."

"Is this about Finnie?" He huffs when I straighten and don't answer. "Christ," he mutters.

As easy as that, my brother nails it on the head. For all he sometimes pisses me off, my brother isn't stupid. "Finnie didn't deserve what happened to him," I say, feeling my anger burn down to my gut.

"Of course he didn't," Curran snaps. "No one does. But as his brother, you owe it to him to put monsters like the guy who hurt him away."

I sit back in my chair and rub my jaw. "I don't know if I can."

Our youngest brother was sexually assaulted by a neighbor when he was ten. It screwed with his mind. What he doesn't realize is we've all suffered, too—not like he has—of course, not like he has. That doesn't mean we don't hurt for him or haven't spent sleepless nights worried about him.

Nothing bad was supposed to happen to Finnie. He was the baby. The one who counted on us. The one we were all supposed to keep safe.

With this new assignment—hearing stories like Finnie's on a regular basis?—God *damn* it. "I don't think I can do this," I say yet again.

"Deck, you have to, man."

A knock on the door interrupts us. I know who it is before I even ask. "Come in," I say, assuming my attorney pose because for now, I have to. For now, I'm a professional. Even though all the Philly boy in me wants to do is rage.

My boss, Miles Fenske walks in, followed by his daughter Melissa. Miles smiles warmly, nodding my way.

Mel? What can I say? She's the one person who's never been taken by my charm. Today's no different. Unlike the other females who work here, from interns to attorneys, she doesn't meet me with a grin, doesn't flash me a little leg, doesn't pretend to flirt. Brown hair, brown eyes, creamy skin, with a steel-hard exterior, she walks in with her hips swinging, her bright red dress hugging her hourglass figure, her full lips pressed into a firm line, and her unyielding stare meeting mine.

She doesn't like me. Not that I blame her. Too bad this is the one woman I can't seem to get out of my damn mind . . .

READ ON FOR AN EXCERPT FROM

Inseverable

A Carolina Beach Novel

by Cecy Robson

PROLOGUE

Callahan

Three days.

That's all I have left until this shit ends.

Three days shouldn't feel like forever, not compared to the eight years I've bled to the Army. Thing is, good men have been killed in less time. In as quick as a blink, a squeeze of a trigger, or a small breath right before a grenade blows is all the time it takes to shove someone right out of life and well into death.

That's what makes three days as long as it is. Three days is plenty of time to die.

My eyes tear when the wind picks up and shoots grime through the small hole of my lookout point. This blown out piece of cinderblock is only big enough to allow me a view of the street below, but not so small I don't get smacked in the face with more filth. The tarp flaps above me as I spit out another layer of the dirt-sand mix spackling my teeth. Christ Almighty, I need a swig of the water resting near my elbow. But my thirst, like everything else has to wait.

I have a job to do.

I adjust my hips against the cracked cement of my bed, bathroom, and home all rolled into one, thankful that the agonizing ache stretching over the lower half of my body has settled into a now familiar numbness.

Out of all the points I'd scouted, and all the accumulated years spent in this position, I should be used to it. And in a strange way, it should almost be home. Yet nothing ever has been home.

But in three days, maybe something finally will be . . .

I shove my thoughts away and breathe as my fellow Rangers stalk along the street. It's then I see them, a mother and daughter walking straight toward my team. Less than one city block separates them from the men counting on me to keep them alive.

The hell? How did they get past the other sniper unreported? Rogers is new on watch. But the quick paces these two are taking should have clued him in that something's up. I train my scope on their faces; their expressions are blank, unreadable. 'Cept that's not what keeps my attention.

The little girl can't be more than five. So why the fuck isn't her mother holding her hand? I lift my radio and bark a warning, dropping it beside me as I lock my scope dead center on the woman's head.

The radio crackles and Modreski chimes in, yelling at his team to hold their positions. He asks me what my plan is, knowing if something's caused the short-hairs on my neck to rise, he and the boys damn well need to listen. But I don't hear him, with a breath and a squeeze of the trigger, I leave a kid without a mother.

Just beneath the sleeve of her *abayah*—the dress completely covering her body—I see it, a detonator that would trigger the explosives likely strapped to her chest. A few Rangers I know—Simons and Boreman, rush forward. I start to mutter a curse, pissed at her for making me shoot her in front of her kid. But the curse lodges in my throat when I see the kid isn't looking at her mother lying next to her dead.

She's watching my advancing team as she lifts the detonator clasped tight in her hand.

Chapter One

Trinity

"Trin! You coming?" Hale calls.

Even over the steady hum of the ocean, his deep voice cuts through the small opening of our lifeguard station.

"I need five more seconds," I yell back, my thick southern accent drawing out each of my words.

"That's what you said nine minutes ago," he complains.

"But I didn't mean it last time," I holler back.

I grin because even though I can't see or hear him, I know he's chuckling, no matter how much he's trying to hold it in. I hurry and finish writing the schedule on the white board and cap the dry erase marker, before tossing it in the small cup holder to join the rest.

No sooner do I reach for my beach bag and throw the sandy thing over my shoulder than the office phone rings.

Most people would run away, ignoring it, after all by now it's seven thirty and way after closing. But I've always been one of those goody-goody responsible types—you know the ones the teachers assign as classroom monitor and who always turned in her library books a day early? What can I say, I'm all about a good time.

I lift the receiver before it finishes ringing. "Magenta Groves Beach Resort, lifeguard station seven, this is Trinity speaking. How may I help you?"

"Trin. Screw the whiteboard and get in the damn car!" Hale yells through the receiver. I whip around as his voice echoes behind me, as well as through the phone. He hops up the steps as he disconnects, laughing like that was the best prank ever.

"Why did you do that?" I ask.

"Because I knew you'd stop to answer the phone, even though the rest of us have been waiting on you."

I pretend to scowl, but don't quite manage. Me and scowling don't go hand and hand. Life's too short to wrap your mind around everything that's wrong with it. So I grin, because that's something I can do and do well.

"You think you're so smart. Don't you?" I ask, placing the phone back on the charger.

"You forgot good-looking," he says. "But I'll let it slide on account of I'm modest, too."

I laugh, but don't argue—at least about the good-looking part. We've only been back at Kiawah for a week, but already Hale's wavy blond hair has bleached significantly and his skin tone deepened to a light bronze. His steps are slow and purposeful as he crosses the small space separating us and stops in front of me.

"Let's go, Trin," he says, hauling me along. "You've done enough for the day."

I readjust my bag over my shoulder, and follow him out of the office, the usual bounce to my walk kicking in despite my heavy bag.

"Here. I'll take that," Hale offers, reaching for my bag.

I step just out of reach, knowing he has his own stuff to carry. "I've got it, big guy," I tell him.

"You sure?" he slams the door behind us. I stare out to the beach where a young couple is chasing after their little toddler as Hale fumbles with the lock.

"I'm sure," I reply, my attention staying on the young family. "Hey, Hale, you know how I always mind my own business."

"Nope," he says, leading me forward.

"Well, this time I can't," I continue, ignoring his comment. "For your own good, I have to tell you that this maybe your last chance to do something about Becca. The summer hasn't quite started, but it won't be long before it's gone."

"Yeah. I know," he mumbles.

"And?" I ask, turning back to him.

He tugs on my long ponytail. Unlike Becca, my best friend in the world, I'm neither tall, blonde nor leggy. My hair is as black as midnight in winter, and I'm just barely five feet three. And where her eyes are light and striking mine are a dull brown. But I do have something my bae doesn't have. Freckles. Y'all feel free to envy me at any time.

"Well?" I press. "You going to do something about that girl or aren't you?"

He shoves his key into the pocket of his long red lifeguard shorts and glides the sunglasses perched on top of his head back onto his face. "I guess we'll just have to wait and see," he tells me.

His smirk widens into that grin of his—the one capable of sizzling panties like coals over a fire. I shake my head. "Boy, between that smile of yours and that face it's a wonder Becca's not running to you rather than away."

He flings his arm around my shoulders as our feet dig through the sand. "Now, sugar, I'm sure I don't know what you mean," he says, keeping his grin in a way that tells me he's lying.

"Come on. You can have anyone you want. And if it's Becca, you need to act fast before those girls slapping each other just to lie their beach blankets near your post lead you astray and down a long dark path of sin, sex, and STDs."

"Is that so?" he asks.

"I'm just watching out for you," I say, stepping with him onto the gray weathered steps leading to the lot. "It's the kind of friend I am. You know, the kind who likes to pretend you're still a virgin and not the manwhore you've become."

He laughs hard enough to shake us both as we reach the edge of the pier. Ahead of us in the sandy lot, Sean, Mason, and Becca look up from where they've been waiting for us.

Mason's dark skin glistens with sweat, likely from having dragged all the heavy equipment we weren't using back into the shed. But he's got the muscle and the stocky build for it. Poor Sean has the endurance to swim a few miles and back, but his long-limbed body is better suited for reaching things the rest of us can't, and his personality is best for those who don't mind the occasional dip in the gutter and can appreciate his not-always brilliant remarks.

But of course it's Becca Hale hones in on.

I can't blame him. Becca is leaning against the Jeep, poised like Miss America and as alluring as Miss Universe.

"What the fuck's taking y'all so long?" she yells.

But that mouth of hers makes her all Becca, so does that smile that pulls Hale closer.

"You know how she gets," Hale hollers, hooking his thumb my way. "Had to get the floors waxed, the office dusted, and mend that sea gull's broken wing before setting it free."

"You did all that shit?" Sean asks, moving forward. "Man, and here I was thinking you were just working on the schedule."

Mason who tends to be the most serious among us just shakes his head and laughs, because that's what we all do around Sean.

Becca backs away toward the driver's side, keeping her grin as she points to our boys. "Alex Pettyfer, Nathan Owens, Channing Tatum, y'all got the back," she tells them. She grabs my bag and tosses it onto the floor of the passenger side. "You, get to ride with me, cutie."

I almost ask to switch with Alex Pettyfer, aka Hale. But I've known Becca long enough to know something's up. So I hop in the front, barely snapping my seatbelt in place before she shifts in gear and tears out of the lot.

We catch the road leading out of the resort. Mason tugs on my hair just like Hale had, just to say "hi". Like most men I meet, he thinks I'm cute. As in a kid sister or a BFF cute. Not cute as in, "hey how about you let me rip off your thong with my teeth?" You know what I mean? The kind of "cute" that really matters.

I've pretty much resolved myself to BFF status, even though I wish I could be more.

Hale, whether because of what I said, or because he realizes time is running out for him to make a move, leans in between the seats, his attention fixed on Becca. Unlike me, that's not sand filling out the cups in her swimsuit.

"Hey, Becks, how about we catch dinner Tuesday after work? Maybe even a movie?"

Becca's wild hair—highlighted in alternating shades of blonde and blonder—slaps around her gorgeous features as she grins. "I don't know. The boss may not like me dating a co-worker." She looks at me then. "Isn't that right, Boss?"

I crack up. All my lifeguards can do whatever they want during their time off. But these four in particular? These four that have been my friends since before any of us learned to read, swim, or cuss. I know they're a good bunch. I know they have my back. For all we joke, the minute their toes dig into that smooth white sand, it's on.

I perch my legs up and over the dash and cross my arms behind my head. "As your fearless leader, I hereby let that be your call, ma'am."

Okay. Maybe I'm not so fearless. And "leader" is a pretty loose title considering all I do is run a few drills each day and make sure everyone has a shift.

"I'll think about it," is all Becca tells him.

Hale is a good guy. Good enough to slink back and give her space. Like all my male besties, he's had a crush on Becca since he hit puberty and his male parts saluted her in celebration. Capable of stirring erections with a single glance was Becca's super power. Mine is the ability to make people snort drinks through their noses at my jokes. I adjust my head beneath my hand after another glance at my beautiful friend. We all have our gifts, and if mine includes making others smile, I can't complain.

Her grin widens as she takes the road that leads to Your Mother's Coconuts, better known to the locals as "Your Mother's". Once off the resort we're no longer lifeguards expected to abide by the rules. We're just fresh college grads ready to run amuck, do some skinny-dipping, and partake in all the fun our young selves demand.

In less than a minute, Becca is screeching to a halt at the far end of the half-filled lot. It is a quarter to eight on a Friday and our work week is done. With a hoot and a few hollers, our buddies jump out the back, rousing the other lifeguards who beat us here to do the same.

"Where the hell have y'all been?" the new girl calls out. "I'm thirsty."

Sean holds his hands out. "Then what're you newbies waiting for? Order up the first round."

"Us?" she asks, looking at her friend. "*We* have to pay?"

"Damn straight, yeah," Sean says like it's obvious. "Everyone knows virgins always buy the first round. Ain't that right, boys?"

The rest of my team, even those loitering on the outside deck, start chanting "virgins, virgins, virgins," pumping their fists in the air.

"Aw, hell," her friend says. "Come on. Let's go get our cherries popped."

They walk in, but we don't follow. Becca's made no move to slip out so I know she means to talk. I smile softly. "What's up?"

She looks to the ocean, where the waves sweep in to bathe the sand with all its salty heaven. But I doubt she really sees it, even though like me, Kiawah is a part of her. She crinkles her nose and then takes my hand. "Last summer," she says.

"Yeah, last one," I answer quietly, knowing how she feels because I'm feeling it, too. I squeeze her hand, my tone mirroring all the emotions fluttering inside me. "Time to grow up, right?"

"I wish we didn't have to," she mumbles, keeping her stare on the sea as if trying to gather some strength from it. "You still serious about applying to the Peace Corps?"

I was hoping we didn't have to have this conversation any time soon, but I've kept things from her long enough. "I applied over winter break, Becks."

Her mouth slowly falls open. "I told you to wait—to not do something drastic just because of what those doucheheads did to you."

The "doucheheads" she's referring to are Hunter, my ex-boyfriend, and Blakeney, my ex-friend. They once held my heart, until I caught them in bed and they ripped it from my chest.

Her words chip away at me. Not because I'm not over Hunter, or Blakeney. I am. I'm just not over their betrayal. I could never hurt anyone I claimed to love or called a friend. But they didn't feel the same.

I try to smile, knowing Becca needs my reassurance. But I can't quite manage this time. "You know I've always talked about going and serving. Ever since I was little."

"So you're telling me, if he'd stayed faithful and been a real man instead of a little bitch—if you'd agreed to marry him like he kept talking about—that you still would have signed up to join the Corps? Come on, Trin. Finding him fucking Blakeney was like a pen being slapped in your hand, forcing you to sign on that dotted line."

"No, it wasn't," I insist.

I don't want tonight to be about the bad things of the past. Not with the five of us together after too many months apart. But here we are, focusing on things I've tried hard to forget. "Becks, as much as I thought I loved Hunter, and as much as I believed that he wanted to marry me, I realize now we never would have worked out. I'm going into the Peace Corps, exactly like I've always planned. But knowing who he is— who he *really* is—he wouldn't have waited for me, and he sure as anything wouldn't have joined up just to be with me."

Even through her sunglasses, I can tell Becca's eyes are narrowing. "He's still a douche head, and so is she."

"I won't argue with you about that," I tell her. My head falls against the seat rest. Do you want to know something about Becca? She's sweeter than maple syrup and about as kind as people get. Until you hurt someone she loves. I'm among the lucky few she loves. But it's because she loves me, that she reacts the way she does.

She pushes her sunglasses up to her head, pegging me with enough disappointment to make me ache. "When do you leave?" she asks.

"September. But I won't know my placement for another few weeks." I answer so softly, I'm not sure if she hears, but her tensing posture assures me she does. "Daddy used his connections at the UN and arranged it so I'd have time to take my boards and have one last summer here with all of you."

"So from Princeton to the Peace Corps. From rich kid, to just another volunteer. "She sighs in that way she does when she's trying not to cry. "Nice," she says, not that she means it.

My attention falls to our hands and to how hard she's holding me. "It's the right thing to do, Becks," I tell her.

"Helping people *is* the right thing to do. Signing up for twenty-five months with no way out, that's above and beyond." She shakes her head. "Hunter and Blakeney are assholes for what they did to you."

They are. But she needs to know that's not why I applied. "Becks, it's time to grow up and move forward, and to do the things we've always planned."

"What if I don't want to?" Her voice splinters and tears glisten her eyes. "What if none of us do? I don't want life to go on without the five of us together—you, me, Sean, Mason, and Hale—especially you, Trin."

Like me, she wishes she could stop time, and that somehow things could be different. But somethings can't be helped, and this is one of them.

Her parents and mine had offered to send us backpacking across Europe, but we chose to come back here. Back home to spend one last summer doing what we loved, and to pretend to be forever young, forever free of life's demands, forever friends. As I look to my pseudo sister, I swallow hard and hope that the latter stays true.

Tears trickle down her cheeks, causing my eyes to sting. But Becks doesn't need me crying with her. Right now, she needs my strength, and maybe a little of my humor.

"*Trin, Becks*!" Sean hollers from the deck. "What the hell? We've got shots waiting and horny women who can't wait to have a piece of me."

"Sorry!" I yell, hopping out of the jeep. "Becca dared me to spell my name across her belly with my tongue and I couldn't refuse."

Instead of taking it for the joke it is, Sean freezes. "No, shit," he says.

Becca doubles over, practically falling out of the driver's side seat. I hurry around to steady her and lead her forward. Sean continues to stare at us, his eyes clouded with whatever dirty thoughts are swimming through his mind as we stumble into Your Mother's.

My laughter fades as I look to where the rustic blue double doors open up to the rear deck. But I'm not staring at Hale as he points to his raised shot glass filled to the rim, or at Mason who's smiling politely at the women admiring his muscles. And my, I barely notice Sean shooting past us.

I'm too busy gaping at the smoking hot bartender with the Army Ranger tat inked to an arm as thick as my thigh.

Holy Baby Jesus in a manger sleeping on a bed of hay.

"Hmm," Becca says in a purr. She leans in close to whisper in my ear. "Who do we have here?"

Brown strands of wavy hair spill around his strong features and startling light eyes, and a thin beard lines a jaw I could probably pound horseshoes on. If I knew anything about horseshoes. Or horses. Or, pardon me, what was my name again?

Not to be rude, or inappropriate—I do have morals, after all—but that tight blue shirt stretching across his broad chest is one pec flex shy of ripping in half. Or me ripping it in half when I straddle him.

"You want to straddle him?" Becca asks, a delighted gleam fixing on her face.

I look at her, realizing I spoke out loud. "No?"

She busts out laughing. This time, she's the one dragging me forward. "Come on, Trin. Time to have fun."

We stroll toward the hot guy. Or as I call him, 'my future baby daddy' because for the first time in too long I'm looking—we're talking full-out gawking—at a man. He has my attention and whether he means to or not he's not letting go.

I smile his way, not because of what he looks like, but because I can't seem to help myself. I think maybe Becca smiles at him, too. But "sex in a tight T-shirt" isn't impressed by her charm, and he sure isn't captivated by mine. He scowls—as in *scowls*—which of course earns him a wink from me.

Hey, sticks and stones, or whatever, I'm going to get this guy to smile. Even if it's clear he doesn't want to smile at me.

Photo by Kate Gledhill of Kate Gledhill Photography

CECY ROBSON is a new adult and contemporary author of the Shattered Past series, the O'Brien Family novels and Carolina Beach novels, as well as the award-winning author of the Weird Girls urban fantasy romance series. A 2016 double nominated RITA® finalist for Once Pure and Once Kissed, Cecy is a recovering Jersey girl living in the South who enjoys carbs way too much, and exercise way too little. Gifted and cursed with an overactive imagination, you can typically find her on her laptop silencing the yappy characters in her head by telling their stories.

www.cecyrobson.com

Facebook.com/Cecy.Robson.Author

instagram.com/cecyrobsonauthor

twitter.com/cecyrobson

www.goodreads.com/CecyRobsonAuthor

9 780997 194777